About the Author

Robert Fraterrigo grew up in the Bronx, NY, during the 1970s and '80s. Sports and street games were an important part of his childhood. So were comic books and baseball cards. Robert wrote creatively during his high school and college years. He graduated from the Bronx High School of Science and received an engineering degree from the City College of New York. Choosing a career within the federal government put an end to his writing dreams. Twenty-four years later, Robert retired and began to reignite his joy of writing during the COVID lockdown. *Divided Freedom* is his first book.

Divided Freedom

Robert Fraterrigo

Divided Freedom

Olympia Publishers
London

www.olympiapublishers.com
OLYMPIA PAPERBACK EDITION

Copyright © Robert Fraterrigo 2024

The right of Robert Fraterrigo to be identified as author of
this work has been asserted in accordance with sections 77 and 78 of
the Copyright, Designs and Patents Act 1988.

All Rights Reserved

No reproduction, copy or transmission of this publication
may be made without written permission.
No paragraph of this publication may be reproduced,
copied or transmitted save with the written permission of the publisher,
or in accordance with the provisions
of the Copyright Act 1956 (as amended).

Any person who commits any unauthorized act in relation to
this publication may be liable to criminal
prosecution and civil claims for damage.

A CIP catalogue record for this title is
available from the British Library.

ISBN: 978-1-80439-671-1

This is a work of fiction.
Names, characters, places and incidents originate from the writer's
imagination. Any resemblance to actual persons, living or dead, is
purely coincidental.

First Published in 2024

Olympia Publishers
Tallis House
2 Tallis Street
London
EC4Y 0AB

Printed in Great Britain

Dedication

I dedicate this book to my wife, my love, my friend, Cyndi.

Acknowledgements

Thank you to my wife, Cyndi, and my sons, Nick and Vinny. The three of you gave me all of the ideas and motivation I needed to write. I would also like to thank Donna for being my coach and cheerleader as I began to write my first novel.

Chapter 1

"I can't fucking believe it," was all that repeated in his head. Sonny Rizzo had gone down this road many times before. He was supposed to be on a beach with an umbrella drink in his hand, thinking about what he wanted for dinner. Instead, he was driving to work, doing something he never wanted to do again.

Sonny is a retired federal agent from the old government. He had a stellar career filled with exciting cases. He was promoted and was a supervisor for five years, up to his retirement. Then history took a turn and changed everything forever.

His plan was twenty-five years as an agent, then done, retire. Full pension. Live life as it was supposed to be lived. Work if you want and live where you want, but do it out of love and passion rather than necessity. Grow old with his wife, see the world. Wait for the grandkids to come. Show them the world. But then America elected "him" as President, with a four-year gap between administrations. In his first term, he lit the fire. In his second term, he undid the good work accomplished by the democrats during the four-year gap. He started his fire again, but now he poured the gas on the fire too. It only took him five years in total to destroy the United States of America.

Historians and professors said how quick and easy it would be to see our society crumble. The signs came through gas shortages, natural disasters and terrorist attacks. But who really thought it would happen so quickly? So here they are, ten years since "he" was first elected, and the country is divided with no signs of ever coming together again.

On one side, you have the United Socialist Territories (UST), where Sonny lives, which was founded by the democrats. It is the area from New England, down the East Coast to North Carolina, California, and Puerto Rico. It can be described as the Wild West with sanctuaries. Governed by a committee called the Council, no one person has more power than another. There are lots of freedoms and equality. Medical care is free, but most of the good doctors left and went to the other side to get rich. There are no rich people in the UST. You can choose to work, or not to work, and still have food on the table and a roof over your head. Every salary is the same. The only perks you can get are called FCs (First Choice). FCs are earned mostly by going above and beyond your duties. When eating meals, you can use an FC to choose your food before anyone else. At the doctor's office or hospital, you can use an FC to jump the line and be seen first. Although, frowned upon, you can also sell and trade FCs.

In the UST, drugs are legal and very available. Most of the hardcore users live in specific areas by choice, but you still get "clean" areas that have problems. The people are first in the UST. Everyone must be fed, have clothes, and a roof over their head. Nothing moves forward unless those criteria are met. It's a good way to live, but not an easy way.

The other side is called the Conservative Nationalist Union (CNU), started by "his" republicans. It is a Christian nation, largely made up of Caucasians, with very few groups of minorities. No one from the LGBTQ community is allowed in the CNU. They believe homosexuality is morally wrong and it is not tolerated. The CNU is run by a dictator, but no one likes that title. So, the position is still called president. "His" fascination with walls is still very strong. He built them around North

Carolina, up through Virginia, Maryland and Pennsylvania. California is also surrounded by a wall, completely isolated from the rest of the UST. The president finally got his wish and built a wall across the southern border with Mexico too, as well as the northern border with Canada. The CNU and Russia are close allies. Russia was there from the very beginning of our separation. There was no hiding the collusion.

Sonny works for the Office of Public Conflict Resolution Specialists (PCRS). He's a cop without the appropriate gear. No patches or badges. The only visible identifier is the clothing. Not uniforms, just red, white and blue caps. The Council believed they should keep the colors of the USA. Also, no visible weapons to carry. Those are locked in the car. God forbid they frighten someone by having a handgun visible on their waist. But everyone is allowed to carry a concealed weapon in the UST. How is that fair and just? Added to that insult is the title. They are not called Agent nor Officer. They are Handlers. You know, a really respectable title.

The Council felt law enforcement had such a bad reputation that the title of agencies and employees should be changed to be more friendly. Also, there are no supervisors in the division. They are all equals. Handlers who arrive on the scene of an "incident" confer with each other and determine the best course of action. However, this only applies to non-violent situations. Violent situations have the tendency to create shit shows.

Sonny's physical office, officially called a Hub, is geographically located right smack in the middle of town to make it as fair as possible with regard to response times: *In this PC nation, everything must first be fair and equal.* It makes Sonny wonder why he's *here* and not *there*. Thankfully, or unfortunately, that thought never lasts long. As bad as it is in the

UST, he couldn't live in the CNU.

As a Handler, he is forced to live near the edge of the Hub's area of responsibility, or territory. This way, when Handlers are not working and are at home, they can more quickly respond to an emergency near the edge of the territory, than a handler who was working near the Hub. *It's fair.* That being said, Sonny's Hub is in the worst area possible. The Council felt his twenty-five years as an agent made him a better fit for the shitty areas. Isn't that great? Not only is he forced out of retirement to work again (his pension disappeared along with the federal government), but he also has to work in law enforcement again— get shit pay, just like everyone else, and work in a shithole. He could stay home and do nothing, but he still believes in earning a living. Sonny only has himself to blame for picking this profession again, but he had his reasons. The biggest was that he felt he should be as close as possible to the Council, so he could continue to receive information that was not available to the public. It's better to be in the know. This town, the Hub, has the highest violence rates in the UST. Guns, drugs, prostitution, and gambling are just some of the highlights. This is the part of the UST that most resembles the Wild West. Sonny can't believe it only took ten years to get there.

Other than his hat, the only visible piece of equipment Sonny has is his body camera. It's always on to protect the public. Every sneeze, every fart... It's all captured. Thankfully, they are allowed to put them on standby during bathroom breaks. Sometimes Handlers keep them on during bathroom breaks after big meals. At least some of them still have a sense of humor.

The body camera makes it very difficult to work in this high crime area. The reality of working there is knowing when to look away. That's almost impossible when you're filming as you work. Sonny can't walk five-feet without seeing a crime, so he has to let most of the small ones go. He also has to let most of the big ones go too.

Everyone's information is available to the public. No transparencies. Everyone Sonny "handles" becomes a potential threat to his family. The deterrent is life in prison for threatening, or violence against, a Handler and/or his family. The Council believes it works because violence against Handlers has all but disappeared. That's because they pick and choose their arrests, I mean "detentions." They are also forced to make alliances with many undesirables, just for their own protection.

So how do they look the other way while the cameras are recording? Fight hi-tech with hi-tech that works. The Council believed it was better to switch from recording devices on the cameras to streaming it live. They wanted the ability to intervene in real time, rather than seeing something on the news that could have been properly handled. Since this tech is relatively new, it is very unreliable. It regularly malfunctions several times a day. However, the Council still felt this was a better choice. The Handlers in high crime areas carry devices called jammers that can disrupt the feeds. Since the feeds are on a ten second delay, the handlers have plenty of time to hit the switch when they see something they would like to forget. No one will say who created these devices, and no one cares. It helps them do their jobs.

Sonny was in his car, heading to his office... I mean Hub. As he got closer to the center of town, the terrain became less suburban, and more urban. More traffic lights, more stores, apartment buildings, and more people. Garbage and drug addicts are prevalent. It is amazing how quickly the government was able to transform most of the territories to conform to the Hub model. For most areas, the Hub, located at the center of a territory, was more like a city or town center. As you got further away from the Hub, it became more residential. Erecting these Hub models created a great number of infrastructure jobs, and by doing so, kept the masses very happy knowing they had work. The big cities were a different animal.

Sonny's day starts with a review of his prior days' work by members of the Council. The review is also graded as to how it was handled. This is where he can earn FCs or have them taken away. If the Council believes Sonny acted improperly, or if he could have more efficiently handled a situation or detention, he is given pointers on what he could have done better. It's rare that an FC would be taken away, but it does happen. To get fired, you basically have to deliberately do or say something that was not PC, or commit an act of unprovoked violence. You can take all of the drugs you want, as long as you are clean for twenty-four hours prior to starting work. Even then, if you come to work having taken drugs less than twenty-four hours ago, you are sent to a detox center for twenty-four hours. It's treated as an illness. Forget about being a responsible person and doing what you're supposed to do. This lack of responsibility bothers Sonny.

Once his review is complete, as usual, Sonny is sick to his stomach because of the grading process. Sonny quickly gathers his things and heads out.

Everyone in the Hub knows who he is, so it's in his best interest to know who they are. His feeling has always been to be visible and approachable. Although, most people in this downtown area are scum, Sonny can't let them know that. Kill them with kindness is what he does. A smile will always take you far.

He parked his car in front of gazebo in the park. His pack of familiar druggies are always there to watch it. All it takes is a box of coffee and a dozen donuts. Sure, it was money out of his pocket, but it was well worth it, and he made up for it in other ways.

Sonny hardly ever walked down Park Place. It was appropriately named as it was the *place* where the druggies *parked* themselves. Buy, sell, use. It was all done down there. And it was all legal now. He walked down Collins Street instead, where gambling and prostitution are king and queen. The ladies knew him by now and were always friendly; teasing him and offering their services for free, but they knew he just liked to window shop and never buy. Most of the prostitutes were women, although there had been a growing population of men. No one judged on Collins Street, well, at least not to your face. People who came to feed their pleasures were taken to a room where they privately asked for whatever they wanted, performed by whomever they wanted. This was where you found most of the out of towners, people from other Hubs. As discrete as it was, you didn't want to run into your neighbor at one of these places.

As for the gambling, it was usually all business without problems. Since salaries were predetermined and capped, the UST made most of its money from gambling. They would make more if it wasn't for the skimming off of the top. The people who ran these mini casinos were always taking money for themselves. Sonny didn't know how they did it, and he didn't want to find out either. This was one of those times you turned and looked the other way. Too much money involved, which was dangerous.

After passing the ladies, he headed into Johnny's place, the most popular casino on the strip. Technically, it was called Collins Casino 8 (have to be fair to all of the casinos), but everyone knew it as Johnny's. Johnny was all smiles. Why not? He had the best spot in the area. He knew, that Sonny knew, he was up to something illegal. But he wasn't sure if Sonny knew exactly what he was up to, so he kept him happy. Sonny walked in, and was quickly greeted and provided with an escort to the slots area. He was seated and offered food. Johnny joined him as soon as he could. All smiles, all laughs. He asked Sonny how his family was doing and offered him a job. Johnny knew where Sonny stood regarding a job at his place, but always made sure the offer was on the table. He never took Sonny's money for the meal. Sonny's solution was to put the money back into the casino by playing the slots. Two or three times a month, he hit it big. Did Johnny have a hand in that, or was he just lucky? Sonny couldn't prove it one way or another, but he was no fool. But he was OK with it. Someone had to win, so why not him? Today was not one of those lucky days.

Sonny headed back out into the street. Average crowd on the street, especially for such a nice day, weather wise. He walked about a block when he just so happened to look into a window of a smoke shop. That was when he saw his first crime of the day – a junkie swiping a whole box of chewing gum. Quickly, he reached in his pocket for his jammer and clicked it on, to scramble the body camera video. He waited for the shoplifter to exit the store. As Sonny approached him, the smell coming from his body overtook him. Somehow, he remained focused.

Sonny grabbed him by his arm and said, "It's in your best interest to put the box back."

Sonny had seen this guy before, so he knew not to mess with him. He complied. Disaster averted.

Now you may wonder why Sonny was not concerned about being picked up by a merchant's camera, or a camera on the street. Well, that's because there aren't any. They are illegal because they are a violation of privacy. I'm sure the big picture of the UST is getting a little clearer now.

Chapter 2

Sonny's wife, Maggie, worked for a sub-committee of the Council called the Cultivators. They were responsible for evaluating policy for its "fairness to the public." That statement disgusted Sonny. An example of a proposed policy they would deliberate on is national holidays. As it stood, New Years was the only remaining holiday. Christmas is a Christian celebration, so it was not fair to the other religions that didn't have days off for their holidays. Presidents Day is for a government that no longer existed. The same went for Veterans and Memorial Day. Columbus Day and Martin Luther King's birthday had always been argued. Ultimately, they were taken away because it was believed they served only specific groups. Remember, if someone was offended by something, it was looked into.

Sonny made sure he didn't have to deal with the chewing gum caper by turning off his camera, too small of an incident, but he did need for *something* to happen. He had to prove he was doing his job. Crime was everywhere, so he couldn't pick and choose. Arguments in public were the best. At most, some profanity and a few swings at each other was enough to gain the attention of the people on the street. No one wanted a commotion near their place of business, so the de-escalation of the incident was generally handled before Sonny arrived. Sonny was made aware of these incidents quite quickly. The other good part of this was that the parties involved in the incident stayed on the scene and fully cooperated. They wanted to tell their story, and not get into bad graces with store "owners" for starting trouble.

It was around twenty minutes after Sonny dealt with the shoplifter that he was alerted to an incident near the gazebo at the park. When he arrived on the scene, he visually assessed the situation. One party was an unknown man, who was clearly bleeding from his head. Nothing life threatening, just enough to give the towel on his head a red streak down the middle. The other party was Tracks. One of the guardians of Sonny's transportation. He looked to be fine. *This* was Sonny's case of the day!

Coffee and a box of doughnuts paid off big time when it came to Tracks. His life story was sadly too familiar. He lost his son to the war in the Middle East. His wife blamed him and left. She went to the CNU when the country divided. Drugs became legal, and that's all she wrote. He was a good guy at heart and had always been truthful for as long as Sonny had known him. His family came from a long line of military and law enforcement careers, so he had a soft spot for Sonny.

Sonny made sure his camera was on, and spoke with Tracks. It seemed the other party was quite interested in Sonny's car. Tracks saw the guy circling around it a few times and told him to get lost. He yelled for Tracks to mind his own business. Tracks said the car was his business. A few more words and insults later, the guy wound up to take a swing at Tracks, who ducked the punch and swiftly responded with a punch of his own. The guy fell to the ground and hit his head on the concrete. End of story. Since this interview was being recorded, Tracks was smart enough not to mention anything about the coffee and doughnuts. As far as the powers that be were concerned, he was just a good citizen. Now Sonny spoke with the other party, Joey Bones. Bones said this morning someone took his hat right off of his head while walking down the street. When he turned around, no one was there. Sonny asked him if the wind could have blown it off. He said no, someone took it. Bones said he was walking near the park when he passed the car, which he didn't know was Sonny's, and saw his hat sticking out from under the seat. They both approached the car, and Sonny asked him to show him what he was talking about. Bones said you could no longer see it because when Tracks hit him, he fell on the car, bounced, then hit the ground. The hat must have gone under the seat when he bounced off of it.

Bones was smart enough to know they would not be able to go into the car, because the severity of the crime did not warrant a search. But he didn't know Sonny had the keys. As Sonny was writing some notes, he pretended to run out of ink. He asked Bones if he had a pen. He smirked and said no.

Sonny said, "Oh, I forgot. I have an extra pen in the car."

The look of fear on Bones' face was priceless.

Sonny unlocked the car, retrieved a pen, and looked under both seats. "No hats here."

Within a heartbeat, Bones urinated on himself. That was when Sonny quickly hit the button, scrambled the camera, and laughed his ass off. The crowd enjoyed the laugh too. When Sonny called in a personal history check for Bones, it seemed he might be in a little trouble. He was no stranger to the Handlers. Quite a few run-ins with the law; too many "small" incidents. He might have a short stay in a rehab facility coming.

Sonny called in for Bones' transportation to the holding facility. When the wagon showed up, they quickly put a garbage bag over his lower body, detained him (can't say cuff any more), and off they went. The beauty of the body camera was that you didn't have to write a report. It was done for you by a civilian who viewed the recording. You just sign off on it for accuracy. This kept Sonny out on the streets where he was needed.

Sonny thanked Tracks for his service, and let him know he earned a bacon, egg and cheese bagel for the rest of the week. He thanked Sonny, but said that he didn't eat pork. Tracks began to tell a story of a pig, Gummy, he had when he was a kid, and that his dad had him take care of it. He took Gummy everywhere. For years, Gummy and him were inseparable. Then one day, when he came home from school, he washed up for dinner. He didn't see Gummy around, but that was normal. His dad was promoted to an executive position in the sheriff's office, so they had a celebratory feast. His grandparents, aunts, uncles and cousins were there too. When dinner started, his dad gave a small speech and thanked everyone for their support. Off they went. Salad, fresh bread, soup, and finally the main course. You guessed it, ham. After a few minutes, everyone praised his mom for the ham. They all swore it was the best they ever had. Sweet and tender. Tracks said he finally realized what was going. He cleared his throat to get the attention of the room.

Tracks stood up and said, "Don't thank my mom for the ham. It was all me. Five years of sticking marshmallows up Gummy's ass paid off."

Sonny almost pissed his pants. And there was Tracks, still with a straight face. Sonny swore he missed his calling. Finally, Tracks showed him a grin and thanked him for the bacon, egg and cheese bagels, and actually had the balls to ask for extra bacon. Sonny said that after a story like that, he deserved it.

With his day done, Sonny went back to the Hub to wash up and change clothes. On the ride home, he spent every day thinking about the big picture. Was this it? What's next? Seek residence on an island? Another country? Try and make changes here? How? Had everything changed so much that he couldn't go back or make things better? Did other people feel the same? Where were they? How could he reach them? His head hurt. Too many questions. Too many people to worry about. Sonny felt he and Maggie had some decisions to make.

Did you ever drive home, and once you arrived, not remember the drive itself? Usually, it was because of different thoughts racing through your head. That was the same thing for Sonny, but it was also because he didn't want to see the transition of areas. Where he lived, you would never know our country divided. Rural America at its best. Trees, parks, schools, playgrounds, you name it. One big thing was missing. No more big box stores. Only mom and pop shops. "They" felt a personal touch was much better, so no more chain stores. That was actually a good thing. If chain stores were allowed, who would own them? You couldn't accrue wealth, so why would you go through the headaches of owning several stores knowing your salary would be the same. That meant they would have been government run. No thanks.

Sonny got home before Maggie, so he checked the mail, and did a quick check around the property. You never knew who Sonny might have pissed off. He didn't want unexpected company. All clear outside and he heard the big mouth dog, so he knew all was clear inside too.

The mail was now the best way to send and receive all communications. Although, the internet was still up and running, the CNU, with hard ties to Russia, had always been accused of hacking their systems, so no one trusted the internet to conduct business. Everything else was still there, like games, recipes and porn, just no transactions. All monetary transactions were done through the mail. But it wasn't like Sonny needed to look at the bills. His rent was always the same. The same as everyone in the UST. They were just lucky enough to be able to keep their old house because they were government employees. If not, they would have had to enter a lottery for housing rentals. That's right, rentals. No one was allowed to own property. Gas, electric, cable, cell phones... all the same price. So why keep sending bills? Why not just deduct the money from the paychecks?

"They" decided by deducting the money directly from people's accounts, it was taking away a freedom, which was the right to be made aware for what they were being charged. Was that a right? It also would have taken away jobs from people that create the bills, collect the money, and deliver the mail. *Have to be fair and equal!*

The slow cooker was on, so dinner was going to be ready in thirty minutes. Sonny checked the guide on the TV to see what was on. Maybe the boys were playing today. Their boys, Gavin and Andrew, were both professional athletes when the US divided. They had no choice but to live in the CNU. No sports in the UST. There was too much work to do for the community to play games. All stadiums and arenas were converted into housing and shelters. Although, they spoke with them once a week (a CNU-UST agreement), Maggie and Sonny only saw them once a year, during their vacation time abroad. Everyone in the UST was allowed four weeks of vacation a year, but only one week was allowed to be outside of the country. This way, if an emergency was to arise at your job, you could be recalled to work rather quickly. The government said this was a temporary rule that would be changed once the UST was in a comfortable place. Who were they kidding? It would never happen.

The boys lived comfortable lives. Morality was huge over there, so it was in your best interest to get married and settle down. That was, unless you were a powerful person with many friends on top. Some things don't change. There were still the same classes of people, and the rich were still pulling away from the middle and lower classes, with regards to wealth of course. For the rich, it was one great big party that the middle and lower classes had to work. The best way to describe the CNU was that it was still very similar to the way things used to be in the US, but now the middle and lower classes had no voice at all. The middle and lower classes believed everything the president said about socialism and lack of freedom in the UST, so they were content believing they made the right choice to be in the CNU.

Both boys were married with one child each. Gavin had a boy; Andrew had a girl. Sonny couldn't believe they were missing out on their early lives. They always talked about the end game, which would be when they both retired. They could easily relocate to outside of the CNU. Although, the CNU closed its borders, they had excellent treaties with many countries because of their wealth. The UST spent most of its money on itself, so it wasn't an attractive trading partner. Their goal was to relocate to the islands in Caribbean. The boys had plenty of money and could build enough housing for all of them, and their wives' families too. But that was a good five years away, at best. Sonny could no longer wait that long. Something needed to be done. Besides, there was no guarantee Maggie and Sonny would be allowed to live somewhere with them all. The motto there was "The UST for You and Me," but it should be "You and You" because the needs of the greater good far outweighed personal needs. Not many people were granted permission to relocate, and with both of them working in the government, Sonny felt their chances were really low.

The knucklehead, their dog Razor, was going bananas and

barking his head off, so Sonny guessed Maggie was home. Two rings of the doorbell, and in she came. If there were no rings and the door opened, that meant trouble. Dinner was done, so Sonny already set the table. He saw Maggie was upset. He let her wash up and gather herself before he engaged her. Sonny was greeted with a really strong hug, the kind that knocked the wind out of you. This must be pretty bad.

Maggie said a new policy was drafted today regarding healthcare. The system was so fragile and small that it couldn't handle the current load. The doctors that remained were always threatening to leave. They wanted to help, but they couldn't in that current state. Therefore, anyone over the age of seventy who was ill, and had a recovery rate lower than sixty-five percent would be sent to an alternative hospital, which would be worked by natural healers, only using natural remedies. Basically, you're sent there to die. This would supposedly reduce the workload faced by the remaining physicians. Wow! Now they were going to send people to their death.

Something's got to give. They were there to try and help the masses. As problematic as the UST was, it always put people first. Freedom is always good. This could be a great place. But they are both in their late '50s. They didn't see their children or grandchildren much. They were missing out on the joys of life. It was a tough ten years for them. Nothing changed in the UST. They were not making the difference they hoped to make in the UST. They were just working jobs. Sonny kept thinking they needed to get out now. They couldn't delay any more. They needed to come up with an exit plan before the UST completely fell apart.

For the remainder of the dinner, they eat in silence. Sonny tried to come to grips with what he had just learned. Maggie already absorbed it and was reacting the way a normal human being should—with disgust and anger. Sonny asked if she wanted more wine. She just threw her empty glass at the wall.

"That's it!" she screamed. "I can't do this anymore."

Sonny was initially stunned, but then felt relieved.

"Funny you should say that, because that's exactly how I feel" was his response.

They needed a plan. Sonny was sure they had the know-how and means to come up with one. It was just that it had to be fool proof. It was a one-shot deal and their lives depended on it. They had to come up with a list of people they could trust. There was no way they could do something like this alone. Maybe there were others already planning an escape. They would also need help from the other side, the CNU. If they did make it safely out of the UST, they had to make sure the CNU would not just send them back. They probably needed help from the boys. Sonny was sure their money could help. All of sudden, his stomach dropped. Sonny realized they were actually planning a move from the UST to the CNU. They were at the point where they would rather live in a place where their beliefs didn't exist, just to be with their family. At this point, Sonny was OK with it. They gave it a try in the UST, but it didn't seem as anything had changed, nor would it.

Trustworthy people... where does Sonny begin. He felt he had to start with the doctors. They are the ones who had the most work and were threatening to leave. Thank God, he still kept in touch with "Double D," Dr. Don Walker. Double D was a childhood friend who had always been there for Sonny, and he had known him for over forty years. Sonny knew his whole family. It had been about two or three years since they were contact, but that never stopped them from being buddies before.

Sonny decided to reach out and set up a lunch or dinner.

Maggie would take a close look at the Cultivators. She said a few of them were acting a little irritated. It may be nothing, but it was worth looking into. If not, her only other possibility would be to ask her friend, Becky, who was the assistant for the members of the Council. Becky would definitely know about many different things that could help, but Maggie wasn't really close to her. It would be a risk.

They continued to throw ideas at each other for about fifteen minutes, while they ate dinner. Just talking about leaving had a settling effect on them. Maggie seemed to settle down and Sonny didn't feel as anxious or angry any more. Adding some more wine to the conversation helped too. When they were done, they looked at each other and nodded their heads in agreement. They were going to pursue this.

They were now feeling better and switched their focus to the boys. It was April, so there was always a chance both boys were playing at the same time. But not tonight. Andrew's team was traveling; they played tomorrow. They were heading to the NBA playoffs. They had a real shot at winning it all this year.

Gavin *was* playing tonight. He was pitching for Miami tonight. They had an hour until his first pitch. They cleaned the kitchen and placed the leftovers away in the fridge. They put on some sweats and cuddled in front of the TV with a giant frozen margarita. Just as they got really comfortable, here came Razor to join the party. He didn't know he was too big to be a lap dog, so now it was three on the sofa. Sonny couldn't wait for the margarita to kick in.

As usual, Maggie could barely stay awake for the game. She actually made it through four innings; an improvement from her usual one and done. Gavin looked great and on his game. Seven innings, one earned run, three hits, and fourteen strikeouts. Hall of Fame numbers. Sonny was so happy for his boys. They had great lives, great families, and good heads on their shoulders. Their root beliefs were still intact. They had respect for all people. Sonny knew the boys missed them, and they missed the boys. Their choice to stay in the CNU may not have been easy, but it was the right choice.

They fell asleep on the sofa, and Razor made sure they paid for it. He was up at first light, acting like a toddler. Running, jumping, and barking for attention. The sun began to shine in their eyes, so Sonny got up and closed the curtain. Now awake, he had no choice but to engage Razor. He acted as if he hadn't seen Sonny for years. Emotionally needy and demanding attention. He was too much. Sonny fed him, gave him some water, and sat on the porch. Not a cloud in the sky. A slight chill in the air, but not cold. The trees were starting to bud. The birds were chirping their spring mating calls. So peaceful.

If the world only knew what they were up to. Their lives were about to drastically change. For the better? Sonny hoped so. This whole thing could go south in a hurry. He didn't like having their fate in the hands of others, but they had no choice. They couldn't do this alone. Over and over, he kept playing options out in his head. It just wouldn't work without help. Physically getting out of there and into the CNU wasn't the hard part. Creating a plan where they could stay where they landed was the hard part.

Sonny waited to the last possible minute to wake Maggie. Sonny wished he could have left her sleeping, but she had work to do as well. It was Friday, so weekend mode kicked in. It took a little more time to get into the mood because of what they were facing, but good music had a way of making things better. Music and dancing filled the house on Fridays. It was always extra special as the weather got warmer. That was when the morning dance party tended to flow outside of the house. They played some old school R&B from the '90s. It was a good mix. "This is How We Do It," "I'll Do U," "I Got Five On It," and "Return of the Mack" had them remembering the early days of their marriage, where things were extremely easy, when compared to today's issues. All they wanted was to go back to those days. The days when the boys were young and most of their difficult decisions were about who was picking up who and what was for dinner. Sonny knew you couldn't turn back the clock, but hoped to get some of that back. They had to try.

A hug and a kiss followed by a long stare into each other's eyes. Again, silence. They knew what they had to do and what the circumstances were, so no words could express that feeling. The dancing was over. Just like that, it didn't feel like Friday any more. It was still clear and sunny, but the silence took them away from that. It was like Monday again. Cloudy and cold. Starting all over, not knowing what the next five days would bring. Not knowing how the Council would react to the recent events regarding the sick and elderly. Not knowing if this was the day someone would be waiting for him at his house, ready for redemption of a detention he made. Sonny was tired of not knowing and not having the power to make a difference. He wished this day was the Friday of their old lives, bringing change in the weekend ahead. The Friday that brought their families together again, living peacefully with no worries. The Friday that would have their leaders wake up from a nightmare and restore what was once a great place. It wasn't perfect, but it was better than this.

Chapter 3

Maggie was off to work with a tough day ahead of her. Listening to everyone and looking at body language for signs of despair was not easy. Although, reading people was one of her strong points, this had to be done on a larger scale than ever before. This also took time. You had to consider people having domestic and/or financial issues, and you couldn't confuse them with a bigger picture of disgust with our society. She really had to get to know everyone a little more.

Sonny's job, reaching out to Double D, shouldn't be nearly as difficult. He was his buddy. They had lots of history together. Sonny could trust him. He decided to give him a call and leave a message. Just a simple 'hello, it's been a while, give me a call.'

As Sonny took the drive toward the Hub to work, he should had felt relieved knowing they were working on getting out of there, but he didn't. The drive made him angry. Sonny became furious over all of the wasted time trying to make the UST work. Seeing the terrain change from rural to urban brought back feelings of the way it was before the division. Although, changes in areas were always visible, it just wasn't the same. These changes were forced, and extreme. It was a beautiful suburban neighborhood one block away from an urban nightmare. Parks and trees on one street, garbage and druggies on the next. How could this place stand for equality when it clearly wasn't? The luck of the draw could have you in the suburbs or downtown. There had to be lots of unrest within the population. Where were they? Why didn't they have a voice? How could Sonny find them?

He called Double D on the ride in. If by some chance he picked up, Sonny was sure he would make him feel better. He was the funniest person Sonny knew. However, it was as suspected... right to voice mail. Hopefully he'll call back tonight when he's home.

Sonny became anxious, and really gripped the wheel hard. All of these thoughts and emotions were too much. He had to pull over. Luckily, he was on the good side of the Hub. He pulled into a parking lot of a mini mall and start balling!

"Why am I crying? Why do I feel this way? What's with the emotions? Anger and happiness at the same time? What's going to happen if they find out about what we're trying to do? What if they catch Maggie? What will they do to her? What if the boys get in trouble for asking about getting us over there? Will they lose everything? This is too much. I need to take one step at a time. I know this, so why these thoughts? Is it age? Have I reached my breaking point? I need a quick relief. I need a drink."

When Sonny got to the Hub, he quickly logged in and somehow quickly got through his review. He didn't remember going through it. It took an hour, but Sonny felt like he just sat down when they said he was done.

He just wanted to get out of there and over to Johnny's to relax. Sonny ran downstairs, grabbed the doughnuts and coffee, and headed out. He parked the car at the gazebo, handed out the goodies, and headed over to Johnny's. He was quickly seated, and ordered a Long Island Iced Tea. Johnny was at the table before Sonny had his first drink. Johnny knew something was up because Sonny never ordered anything strong. Sonny would go as far as a light beer or a sweet umbrella drink. Boy, would

Johnny and his crew give him shit for that. Johnny didn't say a word. He looked at Sonny, but really didn't look at him. He was either waiting for an opening to say something, or waiting for Sonny to say something. After about ten minutes of silence, Johnny asked if Sonny wanted a refill.

"Yes," Sonny said, before he finished the question.

Now Johnny had a true look of concern on his face. "Let's get outta here. It's too bright in this place."

They quickly walked through the casino and out of the back door. Feeling slightly buzzed, but not vulnerable, Sonny started to think about why Johnny was taking him outside. Sonny believed if Johnny gave him another drink or two, he would have been able to hold something over his head, like video of a drunken officer on duty. But Johnny didn't take advantage of that. Was he looking to get something bigger on Sonny? Or was he just being nice? Sonny needed to proceed cautiously.

A large SUV-type Range Rover pulled up.

"Is the car clean?" he asked the driver.

"Yes," he said, giving Johnny the keys.

He got into the driver's seat. Sonny road shotgun

Sonny asked Johnny where they were going. He said to just relax. Sonny knew he shouldn't have, but he closed his eyes. For some reason, he felt safe. He knew Johnny long enough, but not close enough to be so relaxed for their first car ride together.

When he opened his eyes, Johnny said, "We're here."

They were at his house. It was in the woods. Sonny was not certain of the location. The place was huge. A brick mansion with a two-car garage. They walked around the side of the house to an oasis. His backyard looked like a million dollar resort. They pulled up a couple of chairs next to the pool.

Johnny said the pool was heated and Sonny could go in if he

wanted to swim. Sonny declined. Now, Johnny was a little more talkative.

"Dude, what the fuck?" he asked.

"You always order those fruity little teenage girl drinks. Long Island Iced Tea? You must be in some deep shit. Next thing you know, you would have asked me for drugs and a girl. That's not you. What's going on?"

"Lots on my mind," he told him. "I really miss my boys and grandkids. That's all."

Johnny replied, "I'm not buying that," as he moved his chair closer to Sonny.

"Coming in and ordering drinks while on duty is a life changer in the wrong direction. If you don't want to tell me what's wrong, that's fine. But don't lie to me. Just give me that much respect."

Now Sonny was confused. Johnny never spoke to him this way.

"What's your angle? Why are you doing this? Why did you take me here? Are you holding this against me? Do I now owe you a favor or you'll report me," he asked.

Then it hit him – "Oh Shit, my body camera! I'm done."

Johnny smiled and said, "Relax. I took care of that. I take care of that every time you come into my place. Just in case something does break bad, I don't want you recording anything."

"What? What do you mean you took care of it and you take care of it every time I walked in?"

"I have one of those gadgets," Johnny said.

"The ones that kill your video feed. But mine is a little different. It's a universal model," as Johnny chuckled.

"Are you kidding me? That's a serious offense. Why would you risk that? And why are you telling me? I can bring you in."

Johnny took a deep breath and said, "Let me tell you a little story. Back in 'fifty-eight, a young woman in Little Italy went into labor. It was during a huge snowstorm. Luckily, the police station was only five blocks away from us. But in these conditions, it might as well have been five miles. A neighbor went into the storm toward the police station as soon as he heard the young lady begin to scream. She was in bad shape and losing blood and going in and out of consciousness. The neighbor got to the police station in ten minutes. He started screaming at the desk officer. But the officer said he couldn't do anything. All of the cars and trucks were snowed in. The neighbor kept screaming and yelling that the lady desperately needed help and would die if they didn't get any help."

"Hearing all the noise, an officer walked down the steps and approached the guy. He explained the woman needed help and was only five blocks away. The officer said to wait right there for him, then ran to the back and out of sight. After few minutes, the neighbor began to worry, but then the officer appeared. He had a stack of equipment piled up on a backboard. You know, the board they strap people into that have back injuries."

"Help me pull this stuff to the young lady's apartment," he said. "The neighbor had created a small pathway from the walk to the station. With the wind in their faces, they marched five blocks, slipping and sliding the whole way. It took twenty minutes to get to the building. The neighbors gathered to bring up the equipment. The police officer ran up the stairs, thank God she lived on the second floor, and assessed the situation. She'd never make it to the hospital. The woman's pulse was extremely low, and she lost a lot of blood. She was also completely open and ready to deliver that baby. The officer knew he needed the help of the young mother to get the baby out. He cleared the room except for the young lady's mother. Her husband was stuck somewhere in the storm. The officer told the young lady that he has been in that situation before and he knew no matter how hard it was, he needed her to push. So, to make a long story short, the baby was born, the mother was saved, and they lived happily ever after."

Confused, Sonny said, "So, I'm in a snowstorm and need help? Please."

Johnny quickly snapped, "Stop and listen. My mom told me this story for as long as I can remember. She never wanted me to forget how I came into this world, and that was with the help of Officer Rizzo. Yes, your dad. That's why I look out for you and make sure you don't get into any trouble."

Sonny had such a look on his face. Johnny must have known he didn't believe him. "No way. That's bullshit," he replied.

"No, it isn't. During the transitional times, I pulled some strings for you to stay in this area. I helped Maggie get her position too."

Now Sonny started to get angry. "Don't bring my wife into this. How do you even know her name? Are you spying on me?"

Johnny waved his hand and said, "Just slow down and think. There were a few things that had to go in your favor for you to get your job and stay in the same house. You have a stellar record, but they don't want any old timers walking the streets. That's a young man's game. Think about it. You would have gotten a spot on a board somewhere and would have had to move. Think."

This was just too much to take in. The alcohol took the edge off, but it was still too much. Sonny had to get out of there. What if something happened on the streets and he wasn't around? How would he explain his disappearance?

"I don't know," Sonny said as he shook his head in disbelief.

36

He asked Johnny to take him back. Johnny said he could stay as long as he wanted, that the town was safe, and he made sure of it. Sonny really didn't want to know exactly what he meant by that. He just wanted to go.

Sonny was awake for the ride back, so he knew exactly where Johnny's house was. Good spot for it. Out of sight, in the woods, down a dirt path. Wouldn't be easy to find in the dark. They got back to Johnny's place and entered through the back door. Johnny stopped Sonny.

"Are we cool?" Johnny asked, as he didn't want Sonny to walk away with bad feelings.

Sonny said it was just a lot to take in all at once. He was honest. He told Johnny he felt violated that he knew so much about him and his family. He didn't like the fact that Johnny deceived him for years. Johnny said he understood, but it was all for good. No bad intentions. Sonny thanked him and told him he had to go. With a chuckle, Johnny asked Sonny if he still wanted that second Long Island Iced Tea. Sonny said he hoped he would never drink one again. Sonny walked out of the front door, hit the streets, and turned his camera back on.

Only two hours had passed on Sonny's little adventure. He had plenty of time to find something to work. He walked past the girls and got his usual cat calls. They never got old. He walked down to the gazebo and ran into Tracks.

He immediately asked Sonny, "What's wrong?" Really? Was Sonny that easy to read?

Sonny kept the lie going and told him he just really missed his family in the CNU. Sonny knew that of all people, Tracks would understand how he felt.

Tracks went on to tell Sonny how hard it had been for him since he lost his son. Sonny knew this story, but he never interrupted him when he told it again. Sonny would rather Tracks use that as therapy than a needle in his arm.

Tracks continued on about how his wife blamed him for their son's death in the war. He said he had no fight in him and began to blame himself after taking his wife's verbal abuse. He turned to drugs and his wife left him. When the country split, his wife quickly went to the CNU. He thought about her often and didn't know where or how she was doing.

Sonny asked him if he ever tried to look for her and reach out to her. He said she was better off without him.

Sonny really felt for the guy and wanted to help him turn his life around. Sonny started with an offer to buy him lunch, but the telling of the story took him down. He looked terrible. The look of anguish overtook his body.

"Thanks for the offer," he said. "But I have to go and take care of that thing."

That thing was time for his "medication." As Sonny walked toward the deli, a call came out on the radio. More pushing and shoving on Collins Street. Looked like Sonny wouldn't have to look for work to do.

Sonny arrived at the scene, and things had already calmed down. Both parties were apologetic for the incident, which was an argument over who was the better "date" at Johnny's. Sonny took their statements and their information and that was it. Once again, he made a BIG difference there in the UST.

Sonny looked at the time. Yes! The work day was over. It was time to go. He ran to the car, headed over to the Hub for a quick stop, and then home. When he started driving, he noticed his phone didn't sync with the car. He checked to see if the power was off. Strange. He never shut it down. Maybe Johnny's universal device shut everything down. He would have to ask him, about many things. How much did he have his claws in Sonny's life? With their exit plan, Sonny felt they couldn't move forward without knowing if Johnny would find out.

Sonny powered on his phone and saw that he had a message. Double D. He played it:

"Glad you called me. It's been too long since we last spoke. Do you want to meet up on Sunday, at a lake by my house for some fishing and drinking?"

Just as he knew. Double D was his boy!

Sonny called him back, and again, it went to his voice mail. "I accept your invitation and I will be at the lake by ten a.m. on Sunday."

Sonny felt a little better. Just hearing Double D's voice brought him some comfort. As he pulled up to the house, he saw that Maggie beat him home. He hoped she had a better day than he had. He rang the doorbell two times, and the door opened.

She answered the door and Sonny saw she was sad. He walked into the house and just held her. It wasn't a full out cry, runny nose and all. It was just a sad cry. After a minute or so, they start walking to the kitchen.

He asked, "What happened?"

She said nothing specific happened, and it was just a bad day with the usual nonsense going on at the meetings. As she began to tell Sonny she thought she would feel better knowing they were planning an escape, he chuckled. He got a quick shot to the gut, which he felt he deserved, and quickly explained himself.

"I'm sorry. I feel the same way. I thought I would feel better knowing we were planning to leave." Sonny had a few things he needed to tell her about. He suggested they eat first, thinking it may be hard to eat after his stories.

Chapter 4

Food had to be made, and Maggie remembered to defrost the steaks. Sonny got the grill going as she seasoned the meat. He boiled some water for the fresh corn. Twenty-five minutes later, they were ready to eat.

Razor knew something good was on the grill. He was circling the food as it was cooking. It did smell good. It had been a while since they had some good steaks. Due to some UST-CNU treaty, the CNU had already met the annual quota for meat shipments seven months into the year. A new agreement had to be reached before any more meat could be sent into the UST. The UST did buy some meat internationally, but it wasn't enough to make up for the meat coming from the CNU.

With a bunch of daylight left, they ate outside. It was still early spring, so there weren't many bugs out yet. The weather was perfect. A little cloudy, but blue still filled up the majority of the sky.

The one thing Sonny never thought the CNU would do was come to some agreement over global warming. It wasn't until major storms were annually destroying places where the higher ups owned property or spent time on vacation. Sea levels continued to rise at alarming rates. Even with a separated government, things still worked the same. Always reactive, never proactive.

The President quickly got his buddies (Russia and China) on board to correct this problem. All it took was three years of significantly reducing carbon emissions and the ice caps stopped melting, average temperatures dropped, the holes in the ozone began to shrink, sea levels stopped rising and showed signs of going lower, and the fish population began to boom. The scientists were once again surprised by how quickly the earth healed itself. Sonny felt that since now they knew the Earth was going to survive and they had a place to live, they had to make it a better place overall.

Dinner was perfect. He couldn't believe how much meat they were able to put away. Razor did help, but only with the fatty pieces. Not that he complained. The best was watching Razor eat corn on the cob. Back in the day, a video of this dog would have made $10k on that video show.

Sonny cleared the table and ran into the house to start making frozen margaritas. If they couldn't be at the beach, they wanted to feel like they were there. Plus, a little alcohol would help them get through their conversation. They grabbed the drinks and sat on the swing. Sonny lets Maggie go first.

She said most of her day was spent in committee, discussing the big problem of doctors leaving the UST. This month, the UST lost nine doctors. It would help if they knew how they were getting out, so they worked on plans on how to determine their means of escape.

Great! Now there were more eyes on how people were getting out of the UST. You would think the UST would allow people to come and go as they please. You know, the whole equality thing. But that wasn't the case. The CNU had walls to keep people out, but the UST had the walls to keep people from leaving. What a mess this was starting to be. Now Sonny wasn't sure if they could get out of there.

Maggie wrapped up quickly, just adding that Becky seemed

a little "off" during all of these discussions. It looked as if she was really concerned when they began zeroing in on how to find out the way the doctors were leaving. Maggie said her initial feeling about Becky, being a good source to speak with about getting out, was true. Of course, more time was needed to better confirm this notion, but Maggie felt she could begin to strike up some conversations with Becky, laying some ground work for getting pertinent information.

Now it was Sonny's turn. He decided not to burden Maggie with his day. He just told her he heard from Double D and that they were going to hang out on Sunday.

The alcohol gave Sonny a good buzz, but not like the drink he had earlier in the day. It was just enough to keep a smile on his face. Sonny felt Maggie felt the same way because she finally looked a little relaxed. They sat on the swing, watching the sun go down, and then Razor joined in the fun, jumping on their laps, laying down across their legs. What a pest. The world's largest lap dog, coming in at 100 pounds. They get a laugh out of it and continue gazing into the night sky. They needed to enjoy this moment of peace. The road ahead was going to be rough and they didn't know how many more opportunities they would have like this.

Chapter 5

Saturday morning. It was raining pretty steady. Supposed to get some wicked weather in the afternoon. Today they had their phone calls with the boys. It was going to be hard to speak with them, knowing what they were working on, and not being able to say anything about it over the phone. Their annual vacation wasn't for five months.

They decided to have a quick breakfast, then head over to the market for some fresh fruit and vegetables. On the ride back, Maggie had an idea. She said Becky always had her nails done, using different styles and colors. She said she could call Becky and ask her where she got them done because they were going out tonight.

Sonny said, "We are?"

Maggie said she could make it look like she forgot to ask her during the week and she really wanted her nails to look good. Who was Sonny to get in the middle of women and their nails? It sounded good to him.

Maggie quickly scrolled through her phone. "I'm looking for a place for us to go to and trying to find a good place to go to and get a dress."

Sonny said to himself, "Really? Do I have to dress up for this too? And how much is this going to cost me?"

Maggie's training kicked in as she called Becky when they got to the house. She made sure she sounded worried she wouldn't be able to get her nails done in time. Becky was surprised that Maggie called, but quickly got into "girlfriend mode" when Maggie mentioned nails. Becky's sister, Joan, did her nails. She worked part-time at a nail salon and did work on the side to get an unaccounted salary. Becky insisted that Maggie go to her house and Joan would come over.

Great. Step one in a process that would require more steps than a sky scraper. Now Sonny had to worry about clothes. Like he really needed that.

Maggie took off for Becky's house. She lived in what used to be called Howard Beach. She was lucky to be able to keep her house when she decided to work for the government. It's right by the water and a decent area. Lots of mob guys used to live in that area.

As Maggie drove up to Becky's house, she noticed all of the homes on the block looked the same. Nice, but not over the top nice. The only difference between the houses were the colors. As she pulled into the driveway, Maggie was greeted by Becky.

Becky said she was really happy to hear from Maggie, and it was great to see her outside of work. Becky brought Maggie into the house and introduced her to Joan. As Joan gave Maggie a hug, she quickly grabbed her hands and looked at her nails.

"These nails are in great shape," she noted.

"I can do something really nice with these." Becky said she would give Maggie a tour of the house after she finished.

She headed into the kitchen to prepare drinks and snacks. Joan took Maggie downstairs to the basement, where a full salon was located. A huge mirror with three salon chairs, sinks, dryers, brushes, hair product, foot massagers, nail dryers and polish, you name it.

Maggie wondered why she hadn't reached out to Becky sooner. Joan started off with a hand massage. It wasn't long before Joan started talking.

Joan said she heard Maggie was an agent back in the old days. She wanted to know what Maggie did, where she worked, and if she missed it.

Maggie played it down, not giving her too much information, but just enough to keep her talking. Maggie told her she worked for the US Secret Service during the Clinton administration, and after a few years, she transferred to the FBI.

Joan was really into what Maggie was saying. She said Becky never told her she worked for the Clintons.

Maggie said Becky never knew, because she didn't tell her.

Joan quickly changed course of the conversation and started asking questions about her and Becky. Her overall mood seemed to shift from friendly and excited, to concerned. Joan wanted to know why Maggie never told Becky about the Clintons if they worked together for a few years, and now here she was at her house. Maggie quickly responded that some people were intimidated with her past and what she did, so she usually didn't share details of her experience.

Maggie added that she loved the US but wasn't hundred percent into the political scene and didn't "play the games" needed to move up and be "in the know" with the government. Maggie was trying to paint a picture of her doing a job and going home. That's it. No extra flag carrying or rallies. Just a normal person with a job.

Joan seemed to loosen up again after Maggie explained her stance.

"I guess those positions could be a little intimidating. I never knew any agents, so I guess I would be worried about speaking freely in front of you. I get it," said Joan.

Maggie felt relieved and wanted Joan to keep talking.

Joan showed Maggie some photos of her nail work and asked if she liked any of them.

Maggie looked through them, trying to find one that would take the longest to do. "This one right here. Same colors too," said Maggie.

"You've got good taste," Joan smiled.

Becky entered the salon area with drinks and small bites to eat.

Joan told Becky she knew more about Maggie than she did.

Becky gave her a look like "What?"

Joan informed Becky that Maggie was in the Secret Service and worked for Bill Clinton.

Becky let out a big laugh. "He was hot!"

They all started laughing. Becky asked if Bill ever hit on her.

Maggie said no, but Bill was definitely an ass man, because he always had a smile on his face when she turned around to walk away from him. Another burst of laughter. This was exactly what Maggie wanted. More drinks and more stories.

Joan looked at the time and asked Maggie to turn back around because her nails were going to take a while to do.

From work, it jumped to fashion, then food, and finally family.

Becky knew Maggie was married, but nothing else. Now Becky understood why.

Maggie continued on about the boys and their families. This was perfect. Maggie was leading them down the road she wanted them to go down. Maggie carried on about how little they saw them and how much they missed them.

"I just wish there was some way we could all be together. Is that too much to ask for?"

Becky and Joan shot each other a look and quickly changed

the subject.

Now it was about pets. Maggie could go on for hours about Razor, so time went fast.

When Joan finished, Maggie loved her nails and couldn't wait to be invited back for a full day salon experience. It was hard, but she stayed focused.

Becky asked Maggie to come upstairs so she could give her a quick tour of the house before she left.

The first floor had the living room, kitchen, formal dining room, a full bathroom, and a guest room. Really nice furniture and décor. Again, nothing over the top. Just really nice. Upstairs were three bedrooms and two full bathrooms. The main suite was the nicest room in the house. Nice view from a huge window too. The bathroom had a double sink, a tub for two, and shower that could probably fit a whole family. All done in marble and glass.

Becky wished Maggie could stay longer, but knew she had to go.

Becky and Joan invited her to spend a day together.

Maggie got herself "in" with Becky and Joan, just as Sonny thought she would. Maggie got into her car and off she went. Mission accomplished.

Sonny was tempted to get something to wear on consignment. Only Maggie would never go for it. That would be the conversation of the evening. So off he went to Formal Wear #42, a.k.a. Tony's Dresses and Suits. Sonny knew he could get in and out of there quickly without using up all of his money. The only problem was he didn't know what Maggie was wearing.

Sonny played it safe and got a dark suit, light-colored shirt, and a few ties. Can't go wrong... right? Tony took care of him. He said Sonny could bring back the ties he didn't use. Sonny liked Tony. He always reminded him of Joe Pesci in Lethal

Weapon. Leo Getz... whatever you need, Leo gets.

Back home, Maggie shot Sonny a text and let him know she was on her way from Becky's. She would have plenty of time for the phone calls on the ride. Sonny had some free time. What to do with forty-five minutes.

Razor threw himself at Sonny's feet, probably knowing Sonny had time to waste. The only problem was it was pouring outside. Sonny moved furniture around and set up a soccer game. Razor would fetch the ball as long as Sonny kept kicking it. He always did his job, and continuously put a smile on Sonny's face and warmed his heart. Razor was the best. There was no time to talk when Maggie got home. She grabbed a quick snack and they called the boys.

It was good to speak with them individually, but it was way more fun to talk all together as a family. The boys still go back and forth with insults.

Andrew usually starts with "Baseball players aren't real athletes. You don't even have to run."

Then "Basketball players are dumb. And you wish you could throw as hard as I do."

Followed by "Baseball players play with a stick and a glove. How old are you?"

Volleyed with "I only work one time every five days, not four times a week."

It never got old.

They turned on the monitor and just as usual, the boys were already connected, waiting for them to join in. They knew their mother too well, always fashionably late to the party. They all looked fantastic. What beautiful looking people. These families are model quality. Tall, in shape, and wearing the right clothes.

Sonny yelled out, "Your mother raised you right. It looks

like you're ready for a photo shoot."

He hardly finished his statement when Andrew replied, "Stop lying to Gavin. We all know he was last in line for good looks." It began.

Gavin fired back. "I've got GQ next week. How's that Teeny Bop deal working out for you?"

Damn! Sonny missed them so much. He was holding back tears. He was dying inside. Damn that fucking asshole! He destroyed endless amounts of families when he split the nation.

Sonny gathered himself and they began to talk about the babies and how great they were doing.

Maggie and Sonny commented on their careers and how their season was going.

They quickly jump to planning their next time together.

They knew their father's stance. White sand, blue water and palm trees. He didn't care where, as long as it met his criteria.

They came up with a few places, including some with houses where they could all fit in and stay on the beach. That sounded perfect. Sonny knew they had to wait five months for this to happen. He didn't want to wait. He wished it could happen sooner. He wished they could tell the boys what they were planning. All in good time.

An hour call goes so fast. The ritual after was Maggie went into the bedroom, because she might have left the iron on and Sonny headed outside because he might have left the car running. After a really good cry, Maggie and Sonny both met up in the kitchen and give each other a quick hug. They didn't want to focus on the call. They just wanted to move forward. Sonny saw that Maggie was busting at the seams, dying to tell him how her day went. They were short for time. They had to go out and be seen to help facilitate their story. Sonny asked for the abridged version.

Maggie said, "I'm in," and smiled.

"That's it?" Sonny asked. "I can only imagine how the full story goes."

They both chuckled. It may not seem like a lot, but it was always a good thing to get in a quick laugh, no matter how quick. As they dressed, Sonny looked over at Maggie and warmth overwhelmed his soul. They had been together so long, and had been through so much, but Sonny still adored her and saw her as he did over thirty years ago.

She catches Sonny looking at her. "What?"

He replied, "Nothing. I just love you."

"Prove it," she tells him.

Just as Sonny began to grab and pull her in, Razor came flying out of nowhere and got between them. How did he do it? He always knew when someone was about to get affection and demanded he got some too. What a mood killer! They laughed, wrestled with Razor a bit, and finished getting dressed.

They went to Restaurant #11, otherwise known as Russo's. It was a popular place. FCs alone wouldn't save you much time on the line because everyone used them there. They got to the maître d', and Sonny gave him their name.

Scanning through the screen, he scrolled it a little and without using FCs, said, "Please follow me."

He grabbed a couple of menus and walked them down to a table next to the window, overlooking the river.

What was going on here? Sonny wondered if he should dare ask and risk ruining their dinner? They thanked the maître d' and Maggie shot Sonny a look and shrugged her shoulders. Sonny nodded his head affirmatively. Whatever that was, they deserved it.

While they didn't go to Russo's frequently, they always ordered the same: Maggie picked the red wine; they follow that with a house salad, baked clams, and antipasti. The main course was chicken parmigiana and penne ala vodka. Boring choices, but why mess with perfection? Desert was tiramisu and a slice of chocolate cake. Maggie asked for a cup of espresso.

They hadn't eaten like that in a long time.

It's like they knew what was coming, storing up for a long, hard winter ahead of them. As if they needed to survive on mostly water, so they needed to make sure they had some fat to burn in order to survive. Interesting feeling.

The rain stopped and the sky cleared. What a beautiful night. A full moon was reflecting on the river. It couldn't have painted a better picture.

When they got home, they changed into comfortable clothes, grabbed a bottle of wine, a couple of glasses, and headed outside to sit under the moon. Sonny looked into Maggie's eyes and smiled.

She swore she wasn't drunk, as she poured herself a glass of wine. Then she laughed and said she felt a good buzz and wanted to keep it steady.

Sonny said he didn't have a problem with that, even if she did want to go full wino on him.

She began to tell him how it went with Becky. It had been a few years, but she still had that gift of getting people to open up. After interviewing and interrogating people for over twenty years, you'd think she'd lose a step or two. But not Maggie. She was all over this and it was clear the first meet couldn't have gone better. Day one of their master plan was in motion and off to a good start. Now it was Sonny's turn with Double D.

51

Chapter 6

Sonny got up early and grabbed breakfast on the street. Maggie was still fast asleep. He went to Breakfast/Coffee #3, or Bagel Heaven as it was still known. Jack and Kerry were lucky enough to keep the place after the great divide. They had the best breakfast sandwiches around. Sonny didn't think Double D got around as much as he used to, so this would likely be a welcome treat. Sonny stuck to the basics: two pieces of bacon, egg and cheese sandwiches on toasted everything bagels, with a little ketchup and sprinkled with salt and pepper. Perfection! Sonny always lied to Double D and assured him it was turkey bacon and low-fat cheese. He always said he couldn't believe it was a slightly healthy sandwich. Sonny believed Double D always knew what he did, but he felt better knowing he shared this heart attack on a bun with Sonny. All that was left was their home made green iced tea. Sonny didn't know if they still got their own leaves to make the tea. He never bothered asking.

It was a quick ride to the course, so the bagels were still hot. Sonny took a sip of the iced tea. Oh yeah, still as good as ever. Sonny wasn't there three minutes before Double D showed up. He couldn't believe Double D still had his 1973 Camaro. Sonny heard him coming before he saw him. It still looked like it just came off of the showroom.

Sonny screamed out, "Double D in da house!"

Classic Double D got out of the car, all in leather. He hadn't changed a bit.

He sang his response, "My little B cup."

He jumped in the air and threw his arms up over his head. He began running at Sonny, full speed, screaming like a demon.

As he approached, Sonny screamed out, "I don't know if I'm still worthy enough to hug you."

Just as Sonny let out his last word, he got hit by Double D like he was still playing linebacker. That embrace was a long time coming.

Then the insults began. Double D grabbed Sonny's arm and said, "I guess you're not eating enough. What's the deal with these girlie arms?"

Sonny quickly responded, "But wait. Does Eddie Murphy know you borrowed his clothes?"

They laughed until tears come out of their eyes. They hugged again and Sonny whispered in his ear, "I've missed you so much."

Double D took the opportunity to ask Sonny, "Do you miss me enough to kiss me? It doesn't have to be lips and tongue."

Sonny planted the biggest, wettest kiss on his cheek.

"You slobbering fool!" he screamed.

"I've got a surprise for you in the car."

"I know what it is."

"And I'll name my next child after you."

As expected, Sonny pulled out his breakfast sandwich and he didn't know whether he should eat or drink the iced tea first.

"I haven't had this in ages," he said, opting for a bite of the bagel with the straw in his mouth, in an attempt to get them both down at the same time.

"You're an ass!" Sonny chuckled, watching him do this.

"And that's just the way you love me."

They grabbed the fishing rods from their cars and walked

over to the boat on the lake.

Walking toward the lake, Double D asked Sonny about Maggie. "Good" he told him. They filled each other in with how their families were doing.

Double D was carrying on about how well Sonny's boys were doing.

"I can't believe I was there for the birth of both of your kids, just to watch them on TV and see how monstrous they have become."

"How are your kids doing?" Sonny asked, as they approached the boat.

Double D said his son Paul had two kids, a boy and a girl, and was doing well at the power plant. He said his daughter Chrissy was fantastic. She helped run four shelters and was really making a difference on the front lines. He said his wife Sara was as sweet and gorgeous as ever.

Sonny updated Double D about their vacation plans with the boys and how they couldn't wait. Sonny said the boys hadn't changed, and they were still his goofy boys.

"And what about my girl?" he asked.

"Maggie is great. Work gets to her at times, but she's a rock. She still looks like she did when we married."

Double D laughed. "I always knew she had good genes."

They get to the boat and start loading up.

Sonny took a shot at Double D. "Why such a small boat? rental?"

He quickly responded, "Your mother is a small boat."

They cracked up. "Why did we wait so long to do this? What happened?"

"Look, I was busy, you were busy. We all have our health, and our kids are fine. Let's not focus on the last two years. Let's move on from here and make sure it doesn't happen again."

"Agreed."

They got out onto the lake and started fishing. Double D said the lake was private and the people who ran it always made sure the fish population was kept at a good number.

That meant they were in for a good day of fishing. Sure enough, not even two beers in, they started catching fish.

"This is perfect." Sonny hollered. "I could easily pull the plug at work and call it a career. I could become a professional leisure time fisherman."

Double D replied, "Don't tempt me."

An hour passed. They caught more fish than they drank beer. It was a first. But you couldn't drink while you're talking and too much time had passed to not catch up.

Just as Sonny suspected, Double D hadn't changed a bit. The kind of guy who walked into a room, took over, and stayed in control until he gave it up. He had a story for everything. He had been there and done that. He had truly lived a good life. The big plus was that he still got to see his children and their families on a regular basis.

"You know D," Sonny began cautiously. "Maggie and I have been talking and we really miss our boys. I know you know a lot of things about a lot of things. We don't want to wait any more. We are missing out on so much, and for what? What can we—"

Double D cut Sonny off, "Hold on right there. Are you seriously asking me this?"

"Yes. We can't afford to wait for the government to allow us to leave the UST and be with our family. I just don't see that happening anytime soon.

I know you understand how we feel. You know it's killing us to be away from them. I know you can tell us how to get out of here."

His reaction, "I wish you hadn't told me that. They are coming down on us at work for people leaving the UST. It's considered the biggest threat to our way of life."

"What are you getting at?" Sonny asked. "You can't help us?" Sonny stared at him. "Or worse, you won't help us."

"It's not that I can't or won't help you. I have to report you," as Double D slammed his fishing rod onto the deck. Sonny was startled and stunned. "Just knowing your plan implicates me. And knowing you, you won't stop until you succeed. That leaves me no choice. I can lose everything."

Sonny dropped his rod. "Are you fucking kidding me? *You*, a company man? You finally drank the Kool aid? Did a few years away from me really corrupt your mind?"

"They bugged my house. Hell, for all I know they bugged my boat too! They know we spoke and met up. It's been years. If you leave the UST, it won't be hard for them to put everything together. They also know that I know lots of things and people. I'm sorry dude, but this is the way it has to be."

"Bullshit! Our dream can't end here. You won't say anything. We've been through too much together."

"I wish it was bullshit, but it's not. I may not need to say something. They could have already heard you."

Double D began to sob and turned his back on Sonny. "I'm sorry. So sorry."

Sonny angrily got up and screamed as he charged Double D. Double D quickly turned around. Sonny grabbed him and began to throw him on the deck.

"Wait," he said out of breath. "Wait!" And then began laughing. "I'm fucking with you, Sonny! Now let me go…"

"What? I know you didn't just say you were fucking with

me."

Sonny got Double D into a choke hold and a sense of relief came over him, but not after escalating back to anger. To think he'd play a joke with such a serious subject, but then Sonny thought back to their buddy Tim, after Double D did his father's surgery. With a straight face, Double D came out of the operating room and told Tim that his dad didn't make it, while his father was waiting for him in recovery.

Sonny still had Double D in a strong hold. Sonny pulled his fishing knife from his waste and waved it in front of Double D's eyes. Sonny dropped it behind him, so Double D didn't see it was on the deck, put his thumb to Double D's back, pretending he was holding the knife to him.

"Now you have put me in a position I didn't want to be in," he warned. "I can't take the chance they don't have any recordings. I'm so sorry."

Sonny kissed the back of his head. "I love you, D. But this is about family."

"You asshole!" he said. "You don't think I know the difference between a knife and a thumb? What? Are you going to tickle me?"

"You fuck!" Sonny released him with a swift, sharp kick in his ass. "You really haven't changed at all. If anything, you've gotten worse."

Double D laughed. "I owe you a lot more after that ordeal!" He fell back onto the deck turning beet red, shouting, "That was priceless! I should have recorded the whole thing."

His laughter led to coughing, then grabbing his chest. "I think I'm having a heart attack," he bellowed. "My nitro pills are in my bag. Get them to me quickly."

Sonny initially thought he was fucking with him again. Only

Double D could pull off a heart attack after a prank like that. But he looked like he was in agony. He kept saying he couldn't breathe. Sonny ran to his bag, pulled out his bottle of nitro pills. He ran over to Double D and he said he needed at least two of the pills. Sonny opened the bottle and out comes M&Ms.

"I got you again! You're even easier than you used to be!" Double D quickly jumped off of the deck and ran to the front of the boat.

Now Sonny was ready to kill him. He was furious and amazed. Double D got him two times and really quick too.

Double D, laughing as he said, "I wanted to wait until you had a few drinks in you before I pulled that off, just to get you off of your guard. It looks like it would have worked without them."

Sonny couldn't believe what he just did, and this was serious matter, consuming Maggie and himself over time. Double D knew Sonny was going to get him back in a way he couldn't even imagine.

Double D apologized, in his own way, by handing Sonny another beer.

He said he knew how important this was, but it was the perfect opening for his plan. He would definitely help, but it wouldn't be easy. The easy part was physically getting there. The impossible part was getting to stay there. Doctors were the easiest to get over there without issues. The CNU always welcomed more doctors, especially good ones. You couldn't change your identity and say you were a doctor. The process for background checks was becoming more difficult to circumvent by the day. Double D had to check for loopholes. This one would need lots of finesse when it came to the law. It had to be something that hadn't been done yet and something no one saw coming. Of course, you could always set up a hearing and state your case. But the chance of winning a hearing was practically zero.

Sonny swore that Maggie was going to kick his ass after he told her what he did.

Double D said just to give him a heads up when she was coming for him, so he could load up on beer and not feel a thing.

"I deserve an ass whipping; I just don't want to feel it," laughed Double D.

They cut the fishing trip short. Sonny got what he needed. They could count on him.

It was a good day. Sonny just wanted to get home to enjoy it with Maggie.

Chapter 7

"I'm on my way home," Sonny said from the car.

"Oh…"

She sounded worried. Sonny quickly reassured her without saying too much by phone. "Great morning and we caught a lot of fish. I'll be home soon."

Sonny pulled in just before two p.m. Maggie was outside playing with Razor. They met him at the car. You could tell she was anxious. Embarrassed by the pranks, Sonny got right to gist, explaining everything Double D told him.

"We're going to be OK," he said. "Double D is going to help us."

The smile that came over her face was priceless. It looked like it hurt. The worry seemed to drain from her body.

While Sonny was out, Maggie prepared a "good outcome" weekend by planning a surprise BBQ. The grill was fired up, with a bunch of seafood ready to go. Lobster, shrimp and salmon. Sonny felt she planned for him not to catch anything. He put his catch into the freezer.

She also filled the pool up with water. It was nowhere near swimming weather. It was somewhere around 65 degrees, but who cared? Sunny without a cloud in the sky was good enough to swim. As soon as Sonny opened the gate to the backyard, Razor zoomed by him and jumped in. Sonny laughed and swore he thought Razor was a fish in a past life.

Maggie asked if Sonny was ready to eat, but he interrupted

her halfway and said to throw the food onto the grill. He ran into the house, put on a bathing suit, and pumped some music into the yard. Maggie started to make drinks in the blender. Sonny finished making them and brought them outside as she watched the seafood on the grill. They held up their glasses and toasted to family.

"I can't wait to do this, with a yard full of our family."

Maggie looked at him. "I don't care where it happens as long as it happens."

As they ate, drank and swam, Sonny began to think of how the week was going to go. How would he react when he saw Johnny? How was Johnny going to react when he saw him? When was he going to hear from Double D? Could he quickly come up with a plan, or was it going to take a while to develop? What about Maggie? How would Becky react? Would she want to be friends with Maggie? Sonny believed the panic that was setting in was all over his face because Maggie looked at him, told him to relax, and forced a drink down his throat. She said she knew what was worrying him, but they had to take it one day at a time. This was a marathon, not a sprint.

As the sun began to set, they cleaned up the yard, and put the food away. Razor was fast asleep on a chair, snoring like he was cutting wood. They walked in the house and locked up. As Maggie was taking a shower, Sonny ran downstairs and whipped up her favorite dessert, fudge brownies. He knew with her sense of smell, it wouldn't be long until she figured out what he was up to.

As soon as she stepped out of the shower, she screamed, "Brownies!"

After Sonny showered, he headed to the kitchen and three-quarters of the brownies were gone. "Seriously?"

Maggie had crumbs all over her face and they both cracked up. Maggie grabbed the rest of the brownies and tried to stuff them all in her mouth. He moved toward her, only to be ambushed by Razor. By the time he got through him, the entire batch of brownies was gone. Maggie ran to the sofa and sat down, then had the nerve to ask Sonny for a glass of milk.

He chuckled, realizing he lost that round, but the fight wasn't over. He opened the fridge and found another plate full of brownies. Did Sonny have a piece of paper stuck on his back that said SUCKER?

Maggie cracked up. "Sorry! I couldn't resist."

Sonny clearly had a target on his back today. He laughed, bringing her the milk, and they lounged on the sofa, watching TV until they couldn't keep their eyes open any more.

In the middle of the night, Razor jumped off of the bed and barked like crazy. Maggie and Sonny jumped up, noticing the floodlights around the property were on. Someone was outside of the house.

No audible alarms went off, so they weren't close yet. Sonny ran to the closet, quickly opened the safe and tossed Maggie a rifle, a backpack full of ammo, and a handgun. Sonny grabbed his rifle and backpack, and they headed to the bedroom windows to assess the situation. Was this finally it? Did someone finally come seeking redemption?

Sonny looked in the driveway and saw a 1973 Camaro with someone waving out of the driver's side window.

He sighed. "It's Double D."

Maggie lowered her weapon. "Why didn't he call?"

"No idea," Sonny replied.

Sonny went downstairs to open the front door. Razor went charging outside to the car. He must have still remembered

Double D because he cried like a baby for him to get out of the car. Razor jumped on him like a rabbit. Double D greeted Razor with equal affection.

As he approached the door, perhaps sensing Sonny's anger, he quickly said, "I'll explain everything in the house."

Double D said he wasn't lying when he told Sonny about how the government was cracking down on people leaving the UST. He said he couldn't call him with information, and that he would try not to call him at all.

Maggie came walking down the stairs wearing a robe.

"There's my sweetheart," he yelled.

She opened her arms to hug him, and when Double D did the same, she threw a right cross to his chest. He fell to the floor, gasping for air.

"You're lucky that wasn't to your face."

"I deserved it, but thanks for not doing it anyway." Then they hugged for real. "I missed you so much. Sorry for not being around the last few years."

"I missed you too," taking a seat on the couch. "We'll never let time pass like this again."

Double D said he did some research and felt he had an idea. He said it would require lots of work, but was confident it had a chance. He loved them and didn't want them to be unhappy any longer than necessary. The CNU was always looking for investigators. Not your run of the mill, wet behind the ears newbie, but seasoned investigators that knew how to handle certain situations. There were a few things to consider with this escape plan. They would be working for the staff of the president of the CNU. It was no secret the president had thousands of bones in his closet, and they would like to keep it that way. They could be sent anywhere in the world with only a moment's notice.

However, over time, as they gained a reputation, only the investigations of the highest matter would be brought to them. They would get less and less work, and just be on the payroll.

Now one of the biggest problems was where Maggie and Sonny lived. These investigators were always hired from within the CNU. They would not be trusted since they chose to live in the UST.

The plan would be that Maggie and/or Sonny dig up dirt, on their own, while living in the UST, and get it over the wall to the president's staff at the CNU. This could be derogatory information on the president of the CNU, information about projects and matters of the UST, or anything else that would benefit the CNU. They would have to build up trust and eventually ask for asylum. They would have to walk a fine line, which would be extremely dangerous. They didn't want to get caught as spies for the CNU and be sent to Puerto Rico.

While part of the UST, Puerto Rico weakened after hurricane Maria in 2017, and with a lack of support for re-building the island, the quality of life deteriorated. By the time the US split, Puerto Rico was becoming a hotbed for criminal activity. Russia attempted to take it when the US split, so a harsh negotiation took place between the UST and Russia, mediated by the CNU. Ultimately, the UST kept Puerto Rico, but had to agree to the export of coconuts and sugar at a considerably low cost. Without the means of supporting itself, and the UST unable to help, the UST began moving people off of the island and onto the mainland. This led to overcrowding of some cities, but at least the people could eat, work, and have a roof over their heads. Many people refused to leave and stayed behind. The majority of those who stayed were criminals. They wanted no part of the UST system.

It was decided by the UST to build super prisons using the people that stayed behind. This would pump some much needed money into the island, and solve the problems on the mainland. The prisons in the UST were falling apart and no one wanted to live near one. The goal of the courts was to keep as many people as possible out of jail, so money went into rehab centers instead of the prisons. By building prisons in Puerto Rico, the prisons on the mainland could be knocked down and new housing could be built in its place. With prisoners far from the mainland, and out of sight, the thought was that no one would complain about the number of people in the prisons any more. Built along the north and east shores of the island, non-violent prisoners worked the sugar fields and coconut processing plants. The inner island and areas south and west were mostly unmanaged and left as is. The people that lived there "Did what they had to do" to survive and were not part of the recognized society in Puerto Rico.

Since the south and west parts of the island were left alone, Russia easily got its way back onto the island and began to spend money. Small cities surrounded by casinos started to spring up in a few areas of the south shore. A small airstrip was upgraded to a small international airport, which brought in the high rollers from Europe. Along with the casinos came drugs and prostitution. All of these vices were not illegal in the UST, so the only issue was that foreign money was being used to sustain these operations, and no money went back to the UST. Knowing this would be a problem, these island operations thought it would be best to send money back to the UST. In doing this, the island was all but assured the UST would not get involved with any of the operations.

After the prisoners finished their sentences, they were not allowed to return to the UST. The CNU wouldn't want any part of them either, so they remained on the island, looking for work around the prison areas, or they went to the other side of the island in search of a better life.

Sonny said it sounded like a long term deal, unless they could uncover a major piece of intel. This was something they could start to work on and build up, as they tried other means of getting over there. Maggie agreed. Double D said this idea wasn't perfect, but it was just the first thing he came up with in a short amount of time. He promised he would come up with other plans. They let Double D know they were working on other plans as well. He cautioned them not to trust anyone unless they were certain they would not turn them in.

He said goodnight to Maggie, and Sonny walked him to his car. Sonny asked him if he was worried about being followed or tracked. Double D drove his Camaro a lot because they couldn't put a tracker on it without him knowing. It was so low tech that a quick sweep of the car uncovered anything that shouldn't be there. He promised he wouldn't come to the house like that again, and that he would come up with a better plan on how to reach out to Sonny.

He jumped in his car and off he went. Sonny looked at the time and saw they only had a couple of hours until they had to get up for work. That was just awesome.

Chapter 8

SONNY'S MONDAY

Monday morning, back to the grind. Sonny got up, showered, ate, fed Razor, let him out, wished Maggie a good day, and off he went. His drive in was consumed with his thoughts of Johnny. He decided to go right to Johnny's place to see him. Sonny decided he wouldn't say a word and wait to see what Johnny had to say. If he had nothing to say, Sonny wouldn't have anything to say. Then Sonny would do what he had to do and look into Johnny and his business a little more.

Sonny rushed through his reviews and headed to Johnny's. Johnny was sitting at a table facing the door like he was waiting for Sonny to come in.

"There's my boy," he said happily. "Come on in and sit down. I've been waiting for you."

"I'm not your boy, Johnny," Sonny said, walking over to the table. "Show me some respect."

Johnny said he was sorry and asked Sonny to join him, after addressing him as Mr. Handler, sir.

Sonny sat with him and Johnny offered him a drink. Sonny said, "You know I can't drink."

Johnny laughed. "Just messing with you." Sonny sighed.

Johnny said he knew all that information he gave last week was a lot to take in. Sonny looked around his place and noticed how empty it was. No gamblers, no girls, no customers. Sonny asked him if everything was OK. Johnny said he wanted no distractions before they spoke, so he made sure no one was around. This wasn't a bad thing, that he had done nothing illegal, and he would never compromise his job. Johnny said to think of him as his guardian angel and he could ask him for anything.

Johnny was acting as if he knew Sonny was trying to leave the UST and needed help.

"Nah," Sonny thought to himself and felt he was just being paranoid.

The only outsider who knew was Double D, and he wouldn't be caught dead around there. Actually, Sonny did wish he could ask Johnny for help. He was the kind of guy who can "get it done." But he didn't know him. Johnny said he could trust him, but that's what an untrustworthy person would say. Johnny had never hurt Sonny, but he couldn't trust him. But what would be his angle to turn Sonny in? He had everything he needed, and no one bothered him or came down on his place. Sonny had to keep working on that. Whether Johnny was on Sonny's side or not, Sonny had to keep Johnny believing that he was. Why make things hard by letting Johnny know Sonny didn't trust him? Sonny needed it to be business as usual. Sonny thought he might push this issue a little and ask him to do him a small favor. Like get him hard to get seats at a concert. Or reservations at a restaurant by the water for a romantic dinner with Maggie. He thought that could open the door a little with him.

Sonny began to ask Johnny about his mother and father.

Johnny said his mother and father were forever grateful for that wonderful human being, Officer Rizzo. They lived their lives sharing and giving to those in need. He never met Sonny's father because he was very young when his father was transferred to another precinct. His mother and father always made him promise to look out for anyone in Sonny's father's family, and to always be there if they needed anything. Johnny said this was all that he does for him.

Look out and make sure all is good with Sonny and his family. Sonny asked him how he knew Maggie's name.

He laughed and said they had famous kids, and their information was readily available.

Sonny apologized and said he should have known that.

From there, the conversation was casual, not forced. They continued to speak for some time, and Sonny decided to ask him for a dinner reservation—Seafood #2, located on the south shore of Long Island.

Johnny knew the place well and loved it. Before Sonny could ask him, Johnny offered to get reservations.

Sonny didn't want him to go out of his way to do that for him. Johnny said it would only take a phone call, and to discuss it with Maggie and give him a date and time.

Sonny thanked him and told him he just needed some time to digest this whole situation with him.

Johnny understood and he hoped they could build a good relationship outside of that environment.

The rest of the work day was a blur. Sonny was in cruise control as he defused altercations and called in for a repair of a street light. He could see this was going to be a problem. Now that plans were starting to be worked on, that's all he wanted to do. He didn't want to be at work anymore. It was only the first day and he already felt that way. He had to remain focused. He needed his job to support any plans they might come up with. He needed Johnny. He needed his connections. He needed the inside knowledge of the government. Maybe Maggie was working to get closer to Becky. Maybe Becky was working to get closer to Maggie. They had a few things in play, but Sonny wasn't satisfied with them. He felt they needed another plan, something he could get really excited about. Something with little risk and high reward. But was he dreaming? Would a plan like that exist? If it did, wouldn't other people be using it? Sonny was getting way ahead of himself. He needed to go one step at a time. He needed to work on what he had, Double D's plan. He needed to get some good information on anything the CNU might think was important. Funny, because he could get information from either side of the street, legal or illegal. He could get information through work, about upcoming events, treaties, policies, or something similar. He could also get street level information, like a heads up on a smuggling run to or from the CNU, or plans of an attack. Sonny was actually in a great position to gather information that might be useful. But where and with whom did he start? Tracks might be the guy. The big problem with him is his drug habit. Sonny would hate to rely on someone who could be easily bought with a bag of narcotics. But he wouldn't have to tell him his master plan. He could tell Tracks he wanted to move up his position in the government, so he had to get some bigger cases. Sonny believed that would work.

It wasn't hard to find Tracks at the end of the work day. He was always within a direct line of sight to Sonny's car. Sonny asked him how his day was. He said it didn't rain, so it was a good day. Sonny took a seat next to him at the park. He struck up a conversation about Tracks' life. Tracks always loved to talk about his family and the good old days before the split. He went on for over a half hour. Then suddenly, he stopped talking. He always stopped talking about his family as he got closer to the events starting in 2015. Sonny never asked him why he stopped at that point, but if he was going to have Tracks work with him, Sonny needed to know more about him, and he needed to see him in another light. As a kind person with authority.

So, Sonny pressed him about 2015 and why he always stopped the story right there.

Tracks got upset and began to curse at Sonny, and said he had no business asking personal questions like that.

Sonny explained that they had known each other for a few years now, and he wanted to know more about him, because he wanted to help him. Tracks said no one could help him but himself, and he wasn't ready for that.

They went back and forth a little, and finally Sonny apologized for prying into his business.

Tracks said it wasn't necessary, that he knew he wanted to help him. He said although it had been over a decade, it still hurt him to think about all that he lost. He promised Sonny he would know the whole story in time, but just not right now.

Sonny informed Tracks on how much he missed his family and that he felt the only way for them to be together more was for him to rise up in the government. Then Sonny laid out his plan to get better cases and how that would help him get promoted and move up. Tracks said he would always help someone out who was trying to get their family back together again.

Tracks whispered, "My ears are your ears."

He said he might have something for Sonny and would let him know the details tomorrow.

The kind of intel Tracks would be able to get for Sonny would likely be small scale, street level intel. It's a start, and like Sonny always said, the biggest cases always start with the smallest of crimes. Twenty years ago, he arrested a guy using a stolen credit card to buy a vacuum cleaner. That led to another guy who was in charge of a group of guys, and so on. When it was all said and done, it turned out to be one of the biggest credit card cases in NY.

Now Sonny couldn't wait to get home and speak with Maggie. He was dying to know how she made out. Again, he knew it was a slow process, but he felt like a kid again. Anxious and full of ideas, questions, and comments. He couldn't wait to tell her how he made out too. Wow. It was just like the old days. Get home after work and compare notes. They made their careers that way. Who else could go home after work and get fresh eyes on an investigation? Being together made them superior agents.

MAGGIE'S MONDAY

Maggie left the house and headed off to work. She had a sense of calmness come over her, feeling better knowing what they were doing. She was focused, but relaxed. She had a job to do and was ready for it. She had a strong feeling Becky would initiate everything.

She went into Bakery #14 before she headed into her office. Bakery #14 was famous for its muffins and coffee. She wanted to bring a little something to Becky as a small thank you. Two espressos and two banana muffins, a perfect breakfast. She arrived at the office and stopped by Becky's desk. She wasn't there, but Maggie left the coffee and muffin on her desk. This was a test. She wanted to see if Becky would think it was her who left them. Becky having Maggie on her mind would be a good sign. Maggie went into her office and got to work. Within fifteen minutes, there was a knock on her door. She looked up to find Becky standing there.

"Thanks for the breakfast," she said.

Maggie said you're welcome but asked her how she knew it was her. Becky said she knew the type of person Maggie was and that no one else in the office ever brought in breakfast from Bakery #14. They both laughed and Becky asked if she could join Maggie in her office so they could have breakfast together.

Maggie said "Of course."

Becky pulled up a chair and asked how the dinner went on Saturday. Maggie said the food and the ambiance were fantastic. Luckily, Maggie liked to take pictures, so she showed them all to Becky.

Becky said, "You guys look great together. What a handsome man, tell me about him."

Maggie gave herself an invisible pat on the back. This was exactly where she wanted to be with the relationship with Becky. She had to be sure not to push it too much, but still be excited with her new friend. Maggie gave Becky the scoop, all about Sonny's experience before the split and what he was doing now. Maggie did not want to lie about anything because Becky could easily verify what she told her. Maggie thanked her again for helping her out at the last minute and commented on how beautiful her house was, and to thank Joan for her too. Maggie went on about how she enjoyed hanging out with Becky and Joan. Becky looked at the time and said she had to get to work. She asked Maggie to join her for lunch. Maggie said she was going to eat in today because she had a lot of work to catch up on before Thursday's big meeting. Maggie said she was available tomorrow for lunch, and Becky thought that sounded be great. Becky added that she would ask Joan if she could meet up with them for lunch. Maggie thought that would be fun and was looking forward to seeing Joan again soon. Becky got up and left Maggie's office.

Maggie was not lying about catching up on her work. Thursday's meeting was about what to do about the growing number of missing persons. For the last two months, the number of people who "disappeared" tripled from the same time period last year. These cases were looked into and very rarely was anyone found again. No links had been made between the missing people.

This was a problem the Cultivators had to make policy on, once they determined what was happening. A group of investigators, called Landscapers, were at the disposal of the Cultivators. They were called Landscapers because it was a "safe" name, and because they developed cases and information from around the whole land of the UST. The Landscapers were supposed to be an elite unit, but Maggie and Sonny knew the people who put the teams together, and to say it lightly, they didn't have any respect for them. Most of the time, when Maggie used them and they didn't find anything useful, she gathered all of their notes, puts it all together, and found what she needed on her own. As usual, they had not come up with anything dealing with the disappearances. This did take a little pressure off of her, but she was a go-getter and didn't like to come up empty.

As Maggie had her head down at her desk, working to get things together, she heard footsteps come into her office. She looked up and it was Becky, with bags of food. Becky said she felt bad that Maggie was working so hard, so she bought her lunch, just in case she forgot to look up at the time. Sure enough, it was one-thirty p.m., and she hadn't even thought about lunch yet.

"Thanks so much. That was so thoughtful of you," said Maggie.

Becky just smiled and opened the bags and put some of the most delicious smelling food on her desk. It was way too much food for two people. Salad, pasta, grilled chicken and garlic bread.

Becky said, "Now let me leave you alone so you can eat and work."

Maggie gasped and said there was no way she could eat all of the food.

Becky replied, "Bring it home so you and your husband can enjoy it again later."

Maggie asked Becky to swing by again in about forty minutes to make sure she didn't fall into a food coma. Becky laughed and said she would send a search party. Maggie now knew she was in for sure. Not where she needed to be, but she knew she was going to get there in time. Now she wanted to come up with a theme to discuss during tomorrow's lunch. Small chitchat that didn't have anything to do with the master plan. Just something to lay down some more ground work. She ate some of the food, finished her work, and headed home.

Little did they know, Maggie and Sonny were involved in a race home. They were both excited to let each other know of the day's accomplishments. Sonny believed Maggie made it home thirty seconds before he did, because he saw her car in the distance as she turned down their street. She was flying! Not that Sonny was crawling along. As he pulled up behind her, he got out of the car and laughed.

She asked Sonny what was so funny, and he said he was trying to get home first so he would be in a better position to tell her how his day was. She cracked up because she was doing the same thing. He said he knew because of her smoking tires. With all of this commotion going on outside of the house, they heard Razor barking like crazy, so they rushed to open the door. He came dashing out of the house and practically tackled Maggie.

They headed inside and went through their normal routine of

changing clothes and washing up for dinner. The sky was gray, and it was supposed to rain, so Sonny thought grilling for dinner was out of the question. He didn't want to go out for dinner, since he knew they had a lot to talk about. He guessed it was time to open up the menu drawer. What would be their pleasure tonight? He asked Maggie if she had any preference for a type of food for dinner. She said it was Sonny's choice, so he had some thinking to do. He was thinking fresh and light, so maybe nice green salads topped with fish would do the trick. He ran it by Maggie and she was good with it, so Sonny called in for two salads, one with salmon, one with shrimp. Twenty-five to thirty-five minutes for a pick up or one hour fifteen minutes to one hour thirty minutes for delivery. Sonny did not want to wait an hour and a half for salad, so he had to head out again.

He yelled upstairs to Maggie to let her know he was heading out to get dinner. Razor was all over the place, so Sonny took him along for the ride. Healthy Foods #29 was only ten minutes from the house, so Razor was only getting a short trip. Sonny picked up the food and headed home. On the way back, he noticed a new tower being built about a half a mile from his house. It didn't look like the normal cell or WIFI towers that were going up. This was different. Sonny felt he should keep an eye on it.

They got home and Maggie opened the door and said she didn't know if she was more anxious to tell Sonny about her day, or if she was hungrier for dinner. She snatched the bag of food from Sonny's hands and ran into the kitchen. She said she would get some plates together and that she wanted to eat outside before the rain started. Sonny went into the yard and set up a table. As he went back into the house, he passed Maggie, grabbed some wine, then sat down for dinner. Maggie gobbled down a few bites and said she couldn't wait any longer, she had to tell Sonny about her day. Sonny just kept eating while he listened.

She spoke about the bakery stop, her morning, her plans, and her lunch. She did not want to speak about actual work. Sonny knew exactly how she felt. She said she was planning on talking about hair and nails during her lunch tomorrow with Becky, and that she hoped Joan would be there too. Maggie was confident she would find out if the girls had pertinent information related to their escape. Her hope was to get different avenues of escape from their current options. If they couldn't, she would determine if they could support their current plans. Sonny asked Maggie if she thought Becky was just fascinated with their lives and what they had done, or if she thought she was really trying to be her friend. Maggie didn't know for sure, but she felt strongly Becky was trying to be her friend. Maggie knew she was in a good place with Becky, but she still had work to do. Sonny wasn't worried about it. Maggie was fully capable of handling this situation. She did it hundreds of times before.

Now it was Sonny's turn. He told Maggie about how it went with Johnny and how Tracks said he would give him intel on anything big that was going down.

Maggie chuckled and said, "That's it?"

Here it goes again. Someone just messing with Sonny.

So, Sonny said, "Yes. That's it. I didn't want to push it too much. Plus, my stomach was upset so I was on the bowl for most of the day."

They both spit out whatever was in their mouths. They had a good laugh. They were heading in the right direction. Slowly, but cautiously. They knew it would take some time.

The skies suddenly opened up and they were getting drenched. They quickly grabbed the stuff off of the table and ran inside. They were exhausted. They had long stressful days. They were a little bit older from their working days back in the early 2000s. If they were still in their thirties, they would be ready to party. But now in their 50s, it was bed time. They put the food away, took care of the dishes, and headed to bed.

The next morning was pretty much a repeat of Monday for Sonny. Get up, shower, eat, feed Razor, let him out, wish Maggie a good day, and off he went. He had no plans for the day. He just wanted to sit back and wait for things to come to him. Then, "Shit!" He forgot to ask Maggie for a date for them to go for seafood. Sonny decided to call her later around lunch time and see how her mood was while she was with Becky. Sonny figured he would just stay away from Johnny's for the morning and look to see if Tracks had anything for him.

For the first time in years, Maggie was excited to go to work. She had her plan all set and armed with an array of nail colors and styles.

She arrived early, curious to see if Becky would pass by and say good morning. After logging into her system, she engaged the workload. She caught up a good amount yesterday, so it wouldn't be too bad for the rest of the week. Not even five minutes went by, and guess who strolled by to say good morning?

"Good morning," Becky said, with a big smile on her face.

She said Joan would be joining them for lunch. Maggie returned the good morning and said she couldn't wait to go to lunch because she had lots of ideas to share about her nails. Maggie asked where they were going, and Becky didn't know. Joan was planning a surprise for them, and that she always went big.

Sonny got into the office, took care of his duties, and headed out to the street. As he was parking his car, Tracks approached

Sonny as he got out of his car.

Tracks had a little something for Sonny, but not until midday. He said to meet him by the park around twelve noon. Sonny gave him the OK and said he would see him later. And there went Sonny, again. Walking the streets, another day closer to death. This was going to be a tough day. At least the rain stopped, and the streets were full of people. At least he could talk his way through the day. He called Maggie and asked her about scheduling their dinner. Sonny wanted to wait longer to call, but he didn't know what Tracks had for him and he didn't want to forget. Besides, Sonny would run into Johnny soon and he wanted to have an answer for him.

Maggie informed Sonny about how her morning went so far. Not bad. Seemed like Becky wanted to be friends. Sonny asked her about the dinner. She was available all week, but thought it would be better to schedule the dinner for Friday or Saturday night, so Johnny could work his magic on tough days for reservations. Sonny agreed and said he would ask him for Saturday evening, so they can have time to prepare, rather than rush and do it on a work night.

It wasn't even fifteen minutes after the call when Sonny saw Johnny. He was a few streets away from his place, walking toward the lunch spots. He saw Sonny and waved for him to go to come over. Sonny gave him a wave back and headed over.

Johnny went in to give him a hug, and Sonny quickly pulled away and advised him that wasn't a good idea. He pulled back and said sorry. Sonny said it was fine that they were seen being friendly and sociable on the street, but he didn't want to give anyone any ideas that it was more than that. All Sonny needed was for someone to report him and say he was playing favorites. Sonny's job allowed him to spend time getting to know the people in the area, which included meals.

Sonny asked Johnny where he was going for lunch and if he wanted company. Johnny hadn't made up his mind yet about lunch, but he wanted Sonny to join him. Sonny said he was in the mood for street hot dogs. It had been a while since he last had some and that it was time he did. The food carts were around the park, so it was a perfect spot. Sonny could meet up with Tracks once he finished with Johnny. They grabbed two hot dogs each, with the works, and had a seat by the park. Sonny said this was part of his duties and he paid for lunch.

Johnny laughed and said, "About time you picked up a tab."

Sonny laughed back. He said he spoke with Maggie and they would like to have dinner on Saturday evening at six p.m., if he could arrange it.

"Consider it done," was his response.

Johnny said they were going to love that place because they had the freshest seafood around. They had an appetizer that they couldn't pass on. He wouldn't tell Sonny what it was. He would make sure they got it. Sonny asked him not to do any more special favors, that the reservation was enough.

"What? I can't order something for you ahead of time? I'm not going to shakedown your waiter."

Sonny laughed. Sonny said he was right, but to make sure the waiter didn't get hurt. Johnny felt better doing something for him that he knew about, rather than something behind the scenes. Sonny asked him exactly what kind of things he had done for him. Johnny said that was a conversation for another time. He was afraid Sonny wouldn't be able to handle that kind of information.

Sonny said, "After saying that, now you have to tell me something."

Johnny laughed and agreed he owed him at least one story of his generosity.

Sonny already knew of a couple of things he did for him.

"You did mention something about getting me this position, which also allowed me to keep my house."

Johnny shook his head affirmatively.

"Without getting into names and positions, just let me say that it cost me quite a few favors to make that happen. Your spot was slotted for some big shot's nephew. I really had to take care of them so they could walk away from this."

Sonny asked Johnny what the favors were because he felt obligated to repay him somehow. Johnny wouldn't tell him. Sonny knew why he did it, and that should be enough. Besides, Sonny should be thanking his father, not him.

Sonny looked up to the sky and said, "Thank you, Dad."

He looked at Johnny and asked him if they were all square now. Johnny laughed and said they would always be squared away. They finished their hot dogs, and Sonny stayed on the bench for another fifteen minutes, giving Johnny time to get back before he moved on. He went back to the food cart and got a drink. As he turned to go back to the bench, Tracks was sitting there waiting for him.

Sonny asked Tracks, "Were you waiting in the bushes for Johnny to leave?"

He said, "As a matter of fact, I was."

Sonny laughed, Tracks didn't. What a piece of work! Sonny asked Tracks what he had for him. Tracks said this was a big deal and hoped it could help him out. Tracks said he heard that a guy in Collins Casino 9, the one 2 blocks from Johnny's place, was trying to payoff Johnny's girls so they could go and work for him. This was not exactly the case of the century, nor was it something

81

that could help Sonny reach his goal. It was good intel he could give Johnny, which helped Sonny get in closer to him. Sonny thought about explaining to Tracks a little bit better on what he was looking for, but he didn't. It was better that Tracks gave him some information, rather than no information. Maybe one day, Tracks would get lucky and have something really good for him. Time would tell. Sonny asked Tracks if he had any more details, and he said he didn't. Tracks seemed really nervous. He said he had to go, and just like that, he went back through the bushes and disappeared. Sonny thought he would have to be really careful with Tracks. This might be too much for him to handle.

On his way home, Sonny passed by the construction site of the tower to see if he could get any more information on it. Construction had already stopped for the day. There were no identifiable markings or signs anywhere on the site. Whatever this was, it was being kept a secret. Sonny decided he would run a few checks in the morning when he got to work.

Maggie was already home. She asked how Sonny's day went. He said they were set for dinner on Saturday night. He spoke with her about the information Tracks gave him and how he was concerned. She agreed the information was still useful, to get in good with Johnny. She also agreed Sonny should just let Tracks give him whatever he had, rather than give him boundaries. She was actually a little curious as to how Johnny would react to that information. Sonny asked Maggie about her day. It was successful, but not something he would like to hear about, because it was all girly stuff. Joan made lunch for her and Becky and brought it to the office for them to eat together.

"It was as if God was Italian and made the lunch in heaven. The best food I have ever had."

Sonny said if it was that good, she had to set them up for a couple's night. Maggie was in control for the rest of the lunch. She brought up styles of hair and nails from her high school days and said she believed the styles were coming back. Joan and Becky agreed. The rapport stage was going smoothly. Sonny thanked her for saving him from the details. They ate dinner, cleaned up and went to bed.

Wednesday and Thursday were pretty normal days. Nothing in particular came up. Maggie continued to build relationships with the ladies, and work was uneventful. Tracks didn't have any new information. Sonny didn't see Johnny, but that's not strange. He disappeared for a few days, and sometimes even a week, from time to time.

On Friday morning, while making his rounds at work, Sonny saw Johnny in front of his place. Johnny gave him a wave and Sonny returned it. Sonny quickly decided to give Johnny a taste of the information Tracks gave him about his girls. Sonny was going to be very vague. He crossed the street and went up to Johnny. They exchanged a hardy handshake.

Johnny asked if Sonny was ready for a great dinner tomorrow. Sonny said they were really looking forward to it. As they were speaking, Sonny kept moving his eyes toward his audio/video recorder on his chest, in hopes Johnny understood to jam it. As Sonny suspected, he caught on fast. He asked Sonny to step inside his place because he wanted to show him some ideas he had for upgrading the main floor. As soon as they got inside, Johnny said they were safe to talk. Sonny asked him if his girls were happy and if he had any recent problems with them. Johnny said everything seemed fine and asked why. Sonny suggested he should speak with his girls to make sure they were happy and that no one was trying to lure them away. Again, Johnny caught on right away and said he had a feeling some girls might be a little unhappy and he would look into it. He thanked Sonny for the "advice," and said he was happy with this exchange, and he hoped it would continue.

Sonny said, "Now that I know how much you did for me, it was the least I could do for you."

Sonny left his place, finished his work day, and went home. As usual, Maggie was home and getting dinner ready. Sonny talked about how it went with Johnny and he was confident this was opening new doors to their relationship. Maggie said her friendship with Becky was going exactly to plan. She figured she needed a couple of months more to be able to vaguely address leaving the UST. The reality of this being a long process became a little more clear. Hopefully Double D would have another plan for them.

It was Saturday morning, and their big seafood venture was only hours away. Maggie got up early and went to Becky's house to get ready for the dinner. When Maggie told Becky about the dinner when they were at work, Becky insisted that Maggie should hang out at her house with Joan to get ready. This was exactly what Maggie wanted. The goal was to be asked into a situation, rather than ask to get into one. This was a major step, so of course Maggie was happy to accept the invitation. It didn't hurt that Becky and Joan were really nice people with great ideas on hair, make up and nails. This was an undercover's dream come true. Sonny just lounged around, played with Razor and watched some sports shows, waiting for them to talk about his boys.

Maggie got home around 3 p.m., so they weren't rushed to leave the house. Maggie looked great. Sonny said she should have been friends with Becky years ago. She laughed and threw a hair brush at Sonny. Maggie said the day went great. Becky and

Joan were really nice and were the kind of people that would do anything for the people they cared about. She was confident that when the time came, they would help if they knew how.

Sonny laughed and said, "That's great! In the meantime, you will continue to grow as a diva."

Again, Maggie pulled another brush out of her bag and threw it at Sonny. They both got a laugh out of it.

Sonny checked the traffic and it was light. It would take about an hour to get to Seafood #2, so they left the house around four forty-five p.m. They hadn't been to Long Island for a few years, so they were curious as to how it had developed.

Chapter 9

As they went over the bridge, the parts of Queens they could see looked unchanged. But that wasn't the case with all of the neighborhoods now. It wasn't until you begin to look closely that you noticed the differences. Onto the Cross Island Parkway, then down to the Southern State Parkway. Again, all looked the same. You never hear much about Long Island on TV, but as usual, you still couldn't trust the media.

On the Southern State, closer to the shore, some of the old exits were closed to the public. These areas were like the gated communities you would see in Florida. But how could that be? Everyone was supposed to live together, amongst all of the people, not separated. Interesting. That was something else Sonny had to add to his list of things to check into. Depending on what that was, it was possible it could make big news. It could turn out to be a bargaining chip of some kind.

They arrived at the restaurant. It was a beautiful place. Right on the water. As they pulled up to the valet, they were greeted by name and whisked off into the restaurant. They wouldn't even accept a tip. Johnny must have given them their license plate number. They were taken through the restaurant and brought to an outside table, right on the water. The smell of the ocean was amazing. Since it was still spring time, and still a little cool out, they had one of those big propane heaters in their vicinity. The temperature was perfect. Maggie took off her sweater. From that moment on, the drinks and food did not stop coming to the table.

They started Maggie and Sonny off with a nice bottle of cabernet sauvignon. Sonny usually didn't drink wine, but this was really good. Then it was garlic bread, fried calamari, cold antipasto, clams oreganata, and lobster bisque. They asked the waiter why they were bringing this all out, and that it was way too much food. They said not to worry. All was taken care of. That Johnny!

They finished most of the food and asked the servers to wrap up the rest because they couldn't possibly eat anything else. Sonny asked for the check, and the maître d laughed.

He said, "You aren't nearly done here. We have so much more planned," and laughed.

Maggie and Sonny faced each other with confused looks on their face. Before they could say anything, the maître d asked them to relax and enjoy the view, and they would take care of everything else.

They shrugged their shoulders and said, "Fine. Why fight it?"

They cleared the table and Maggie and Sonny sat there, drinking their endless glasses of wine, enjoying the ocean. They began talking about how this was what they wanted. Some place by the ocean, living life with their family. Not a worry in the world. They must have been talking for a half hour. No one from the staff came over except to refill their glasses. They weren't being forced out. It was as if they were on their own island. After another fifteen minutes, the maître d came over and asked them to follow him. He said not to ask him where they were going and to just enjoy it. He brought Maggie and Sonny over to a stretch limousine. They were a little worried at first, but went along with it. Johnny wanted to take care of them, so let's see what that meant. They were so stuffed from dinner that they were almost falling asleep. They just snuggled up and enjoyed the ride. They were in the car for about twenty minutes when they pulled up to some sort of club or music hall. The doors opened up and they were once again greeted by name. They opened the velvet ropes and entered the club. They were brought right up to the front row. Sonny felt like they were in Goodfellas during the scene at the Copa. A few hundred people were seated in the hall, and they all looked at Maggie and Sonny as they were seated.

Sonny thought to himself, "I guess they wondered who the famous people were that had front row seats. We still really don't know what's going on. We have no idea who's coming out to perform."

Neither Maggie nor Sonny was able to see anything that would give it away on their way in. After about ten minutes, the curtain opened up. The stage was set up with acoustic instruments. Being in the front row, they were able to see the band before they went out onto the stage. Holy shit! It was Green Day, in a small, cozy hall, with an acoustic set. Johnny really went all out on this one. An hour and twenty minutes of pure bliss. Their music sounded so good. It translated well to being unplugged. They spoke to the crowd in between songs and gave insight onto how they felt when they wrote the song and played it during the corresponding time period. Somewhere in the middle of their set, Billie Joe pointed at Maggie and Sonny and said, "This one goes out to Sonny and Maggie."

Johnny did say, "You would get a kick out of it. Enjoy." Johnny had Green Day dedicate "Minority" to them. In his head, Sonny repeated the lyrics – was he trying to be funny? Was he trying to send Sonny a message? Or was he just telling Sonny how he felt? This just ruined his evening. Sonny wouldn't be OK until he knew what Johnny meant. They ended their set with "American Idiot." How appropriate. They left the stage and

Maggie and Sonny were quickly greeted and brought backstage to meet the band. What a great bunch of guys. They took their time to speak with them and took as many pictures as they wanted. Sonny could have never imagined how that night would have gone. But Sonny was still upset and wouldn't feel better until he knew what Johnny meant with the song choice.

Maggie and Sonny spent a good twenty minutes with the band before they started to feel bad for keeping them from their night. The guys laughed and said their night wasn't over. They said Maggie and Sonny would join them in the VIP section of the club upstairs. Now they were hanging with Green Day? Incredible. They left the band and were brought over to a bar, since the club wasn't going to open up for another half hour.

They were at the bar for about five minutes when Sonny heard someone say, "So this is the gorgeous young lady you keep to yourself."

It was Johnny. Sonny didn't know if he wanted to punch, hug him, or scream at him. Johnny must have seen that look on his face, so he introduced himself to Maggie. He said he was so happy to finally meet someone he had heard so much about. Maggie said she felt the same way. They thanked Johnny and said it was an unforgettable evening and that they owed him big time. Johnny said he knew Sonny knew how he felt about him, and this was the least he could do to show them a good time. He ordered a round of drinks and Sonny couldn't wait any longer. He had to ask him about the song choice. Johnny laughed and said it reminded him about Sonny and him. He was done with the moral majority and walked to his own beat. He didn't need authority. As for Sonny, Johnny didn't necessarily think of him as the authority. From what he knew about Sonny, he was not black and white. Sonny lived in the grays, especially in recent times. Although he had a slight alcohol buzz, Sonny was able to make sense of what Johnny said. Maggie looked at Sonny and shook her head in the affirmative. It looked like the more and more he dealt with Johnny, Sonny got the sense Johnny was truly on his side and somehow knew Sonny was not happy. Johnny excused himself and headed to the bathroom.

Maggie and Sonny had a quick discussion. Maggie was very pleased about what had gone on and then some. She said she believed Johnny was sincere with Sonny and that he was someone they might be able to trust. Sonny agreed and now they had to plan how they would get him involved. Sonny had to go to the restroom as well, so he left Maggie at the bar. On his way to the restroom, he bumped into Johnny and asked him to take care of Maggie until he got back. Johnny said with what he knew about her, she could take care of all of them. They laughed and Sonny continued to the restroom. When he got back to the bar, Johnny had Maggie in tears, laughing hysterically. Sonny asked what was so funny. Maggie said Johnny told her a story about how one of his girls was afraid to use the restroom in his place because she thought the other girls were dirty, so he had to get her a porta-potty. Then when he did, she thought it was disgusting, so she started using the regular restroom. Johnny didn't know this until the girl quit, but the other girls put laxatives in her drinks and would smear chocolate all over the toilet seats so she would have to clean them before she used them. Johnny didn't realize how vicious his girls were.

Johnny took them to the VIP section of the club. The guys in the band were waiting for them. They waved at them, not wanting to disturb their "situations." However, Billie Joe got up, and sat next to them.

He said Johnny filled them in on their history and told him

all about their family. Billie Joe said they were big fans of their boys and would love to meet them. Unfortunately, because of their political views and song lyrics, they were banned from going to the CNU, like most of the entertainers were. That's when he began to get serious. He said he knew they were agents back before the big split. He wanted to know about their careers and how they felt about it on a personal level. This was a conversation that could go many ways and end up peaceful or in an all-out war. Green Day had always been very vocal about the government and never pulled any punches. Maggie and Sonny, treading very carefully, but with a buzz, began to discuss their careers. They told stories of their biggest cases, cases with undercovers and confidential informants, cases involving narcotics and small cases that had funny stories. They didn't notice at first, but as they told a few stories, the rest of the people with them in the VIP section began to focus on their every word. They had them in disbelief as to some of the crimes and people they investigated, and in tears of laughter regarding some of the dumb things people did during the acts of their crime.

The music was very loud, and Sonny began to get a headache from the combination of the noise, laughter and alcohol.

"Wow," he thought. "I'm getting old."

It was around midnight and Johnny asked if they were hungry again. Actually, Sonny was, and so was Maggie. He said that they could head back to the restaurant to get a midnight snack. The guys in Green Day said they were in too. They all left the club, jumped in their cars, and headed back to the restaurant. The place was empty of customers. The maître d welcomed them back and asked if they had a good time. Green Day entered the restaurant and his face lit up. He said he was a huge fan and his wife would never believe who was at the restaurant. They all went back to the table they ate at earlier in the evening. It was now set up with a big round table, enough for all of them to fit in and still be able to speak with each other.

Sonny made it a point to sit next to the guys in the band. It was his turn to ask the questions. He wanted to know why they were so political. He wanted to know if something specific happened to them or if they were just tired of the "system."

They began to explain it started after 9-1-1, when we were in the Iraq war for a few years, and it looked like it would never end. They were fed up with the government and the lies, so they decided to speak out the best way they could – through their music. They wanted the youth of the nation to ask questions of the government and not to just accept things the way they were. It seemed like it was working. That generation asked the right questions and continued to fight for what they thought was right. It wasn't until that idiot got into office and changed things. He brought out the worst in the nation and divided it like never before. They were not surprised that he caused a literal split of the U.S., but were hurt they couldn't help stop it. They hoped they could help unite the nation again, but failed. They tried to help at the beginning of the split, but neither side was interested in healing and re-joining the union.

More drinks, food and conversation. What a night. It must have been at least 3 a.m. As much as they wanted the night to continue, Maggie and Sonny gave each other the look that it was time to go. Sonny went over to Johnny, and asked him to please allow them to give him some money for the night. Johnny said their money was tainted and he wanted no part of it. Johnny asked if they had a good time. Sonny just smiled. Johnny was glad they enjoyed themselves and they had to make a habit of it. Maggie and Sonny were in no shape to drive, so the limo would take them home and Johnny would have Ronnie follow them in their car.

Ronnie worked with Johnny, almost as a partner. They grew up together, so Sonny knew Johnny trusted him and he didn't have to worry about anything. They said good bye to Green Day and got some huge hugs. They said they had a great time with them and would like to keep in touch. They exchanged numbers and off they were.

As soon as they got in the limo, Maggie let out a soft scream and said, "We just hung out with Green Day... and they liked us!"

Now they had a good story to tell the boys.

The ride home went quickly. They fell in and out of sleep. Ronnie heard Razor barking his head off and said he had planned to tuck them in, but he was not good with dogs. They couldn't thank him and the limo driver enough. They tried to give them some money, but they were not having it. They said it was all taken care of and they were glad they enjoyed themselves. They were sure they would be seeing Maggie and Sonny again soon enough.

While the sun in Sonny's face usually woke him up, he got up hours into the morning. Maggie was still snoring. Razor was on the bed, loving the extra sleep. Sonny tried to get up without waking Maggie, but she popped up and asked for the time. A lazy Sunday. It had been a long time. Sonny got up to take care of Razor and Maggie said she would take care of brunch. After a quick feeding and walk, Razor still seemed a little out of it. He probably hadn't slept that long in a while too. As Sonny walked into the kitchen, he didn't smell anything. He looked at the table and there was a bowl of fruit, a bowl of yogurt and two cups of coffee. Maggie said that after a night like they had, and at the age they were now, they needed to take it easy this morning. Sonny laughed and agreed. As they ate, they talked about the night they had and couldn't believe any of it. From the dinner, to the limos and of course, Green Day. Johnny proved himself to really be connected. They just worried that they didn't pay for anything. Neither of them believed this would be something Johnny would hold over their heads, but you never know. Plus, they might have to get a little dirty anyway to get what they wanted and leave the UST. They could just chalk that one up to building rapport. They talked about having Johnny, and his guys over the house for a BBQ. It might not be the best idea with regards to a public view of the event, but they ultimately decided they were allowed to have friends, so what was the harm?

Today was phone call day with the boys. They couldn't wait! They had so much to tell them. Sonny believed they would impress them. They lounged around all day, did some laundry and watched lots of TV.

It was time for the call. This call was a little different. No dressing up or shaving. Just Maggie and Sonny, kicking it back on a lazy Sunday.

They finally beat the boys to the call. They waited three minutes for them to connect. As they connected, all they heard was laughter.

"Look at you two," and "Have a rough night," were thrown at Maggie and Sonny.

After the laughter calmed down, Maggie said, "Yes, it was a good night."

They described the night chronologically and stopped at the point when they are at the concert. They added some drama to the story by slowing it down and describing the whole scene in detail. Then they hit them with the Green Day concert. They were already excited for Maggie and Sonny before they told them the good parts. They all screamed when they told the boys the band dedicated a song to them and invited them backstage. With the looks on their faces, Sonny knew they were impressed. They finished the story and both boys said they wished they were there. Sonny said the guys in the band were big fans of theirs and would love to meet them. That put smiles on their faces. When they were growing up, Maggie and Sonny made sure they knew all the great music that came before them, as well as the modern day hits. They listened to Motown and classic rock. As they got a little older, they were introduced to bands like Green Day. They knew all of the hits. Next, they went on to the good stuff. The grandkids. They were getting so big, so fast. That joy they just had quickly disappeared. Sonny was becoming overwhelmed with the feeling of hatred for their nations. He excused himself with a fake cough and let Maggie continue without him. He grabbed a glass of water and calmed himself down. He didn't want anyone to see him like that. After a couple of minutes, he rejoined the conversation. He blamed the cough on the dryness of his throat from all of that drinking. They all got a laugh out of that. The boys said they had their vacation all planned out. All Maggie and Sonny had to do was show up. The time was getting closer, but it wasn't close enough. With that, they ended the call and set up their next one for next weekend.

Maggie knew Sonny faked the cough and asked if he was OK. He explained how he felt and that they needed to get their plan going. Sonny knew they were just starting to work on it, but he didn't know if he could last too long. His feeling was they needed a plan in place by the time they went on their vacation. Maggie said they didn't have enough time to make that work, but said they should set it as a goal. The feeling was at least they had a date to focus on.

Chapter 10

It was Monday, so up and out they go. Neither of them had any plans today to further their goal of leaving. They just decided to play it by ear. Especially with a wasted Sunday like they had and needed. Sonny quickly went through his work routine and got out into the street. He parked his car and didn't see Tracks. Maybe he would pop out of the bushes.

As Sonny was walking in the street, he didn't see Johnny, so he went into his place and he saw Ronnie.

He gave Sonny a big smile and went over to him. "How are you feeling?" he asked.

"Just great," Sonny responded. Sonny thanked him for the help with the car the other night.

He said, "Anytime for you."

Sonny asked him where Johnny was, and he said he was out of town for a few days for business purposes. He asked Ronnie to let Johnny know, if he heard from him, that he passed by looking for him. Sonny left the spot and headed back to the street to work. As his day finished up, he realized he hadn't seen Tracks all day. He hoped he was OK. Tracks had disappeared from time to time, but it had been a while since it happened.

Sonny headed home and got ready for dinner. Maggie was home first, so the meal was almost done. He asked her if anything good happened with her friends at work today. She said it was a good day. It was more ground work, light chit chat about nothing specific. She believed Becky was all in and she felt bad that she was using her. She felt Becky was genuinely a nice person and they should have been friends years ago.

Sonny reminded Maggie that since their end game was to leave the UST, she would not be in contact with Becky anymore, so she should just focus on the mission. He added that since Becky was so nice, to try and enjoy the time with her. It might be tough in the end, but it would help her while on the journey. Maggie understood, but said it was still hard. It wasn't like doing undercover years ago, when it was with really bad people. Becky was nice and she didn't want to hurt her.

A few days later, Sonny saw Tracks.

"Where have you been?" Sonny asked him.

Tracks said he was on a mission and couldn't blow his cover. He said he couldn't give details, but he was close to providing Sonny with some good information he could use to help him rise up in the government. Sonny wasn't going to bet the house on this information. Sonny decided to let Tracks do his thing and see what he got. If he did actually get some good information, Sonny would have to have a serious conversation with him about how he could not mention his name to anyone. Tracks might be a mess, but Sonny didn't think he would knowingly give up his name. But when he was on one of his "trips," who knew what he could say.

Tracks said he heard about how some people in the government were cheating the FC program.

How in the world would Tracks know something like this? He would have to know someone who knew someone that spoke to someone else. Let's see what he came up with now. Even if he gave Sonny something with a little truth in it, maybe he could work it up like the old days. And just like the old days, any information was better than no information. Even Tracks could get lucky sometimes.

Tracks continued and said these government people were somehow diverting the FC rewards to bogus accounts, where they were sold or traded.

OK, there's the street connection. Maybe Tracks did have something good.

Sonny made it clear to Tracks that it was very important not to mention his name when he was getting this information.

Tracks said, "What do you think, I'm an idiot?"

He waved his hands in the air and said he thought Sonny knew him better than that. He said he might be a mess, but he would never hurt him, after all of the things Sonny had done for him. Sonny just had to make sure he knew. It was an old habit, and a good one, from Sonny's old days as an agent. The idea was you repeat your instructions over and over until it became second nature to the person you were dealing with. Tracks said he should have solid information for Sonny early next week. He also said not to worry if he went "missing" for a few days. He promised he was clean, and he sometimes had to have serious alone time with no distractions. Sonny asked him if there was anything he could do for him, and Tracks said to just be his friend. Sonny gave him a few dollars and let him know he was a good guy who just needed a run of good luck. He said it was too late for him, but that Sonny kept him going with stories of the old days and his family. Tracks then slipped back into the bushes and he was gone. Sonny was beat. He needed some rest. He believed he was feeling residual laziness from the weekend.

"Wow, that sucks," Sonny realized. "I am old."

He wrapped up at work, and headed home.

Friday came and went. Still no sign of Johnny. Sonny guessed he never noticed when he was away from his "shop" for short periods of time. Sonny was sure it was business related. Johnny was the type of guy who ate, slept and breathed work. He knew he had to stay on top of things.

When Sonny got to the house, he saw an unfamiliar car in the driveway, parked next to Maggie's car. Was it Double D switching up cars to keep "the man" off of his tracks? Sonny parked his car and headed through the house, all the way to the yard. There he saw Maggie and Johnny cracking up as they messed around with Razor.

Johnny quickly got up. "I hope I didn't cross any lines coming here unannounced."

Sonny quickly responded, "Absolutely not!"

Sonny went over and give him a big hug.

"What you did for us last weekend was special," he whispered in Johnny's ear as he hugged him.

Johnny said he figured Maggie and Sonny needed a good night out, something a little more than a dinner, so he put the whole thing together. He needed a good night out too, so everyone was happy. Maggie said they were just talking about last weekend. Johnny knew the guys in Green Day for years, back when he was a rebel in the good ole days of the USA. He snuck backstage at one of their concerts and only got caught when he asked the security guard for a cigarette when he made it to the stage.

"It was a celebratory smoke," Johnny laughed.

The security guard didn't think it was funny, so he threw Johnny to the floor.

Johnny said he screamed out, "You gotta fight, for your right, to paaaarty!," which was fine, but they were lines from a Beastie Boys song.

They all cracked up. Johnny said the band cracked up too.

The band asked the security guard to leave Johnny alone and let him go. They felt anyone who could pull off what he just did deserved some stage time. The rest was history. They became really good friends after that, but really became close after the divide.

Luckily, Maggie and Sonny still had some ribs in the fridge, so they quickly whipped up some food. No beer, but plenty of stuff to mix drinks. Johnny said he didn't want them to go through any trouble for him, he just wanted to come by and say hi. They said that was nonsense and they had to make dinner anyway. Johnny really liked Razor. He said he wished he had a dog like him. Razor didn't hold anything back. All of his tricks and antics were on the table. He was glued to Johnny's side. They asked Johnny about having a BBQ with all the people from last week. Johnny asked if they were sure about that because some of those people were really shady. They all laughed, and Sonny said the shadiest people they knew weren't even there. Johnny said he could arrange that and all he needed were some dates.

Maggie and Sonny looked at each other and it was like they read each other's mind. Sonny was thinking they didn't want to delay anything like this, with the potential of possibly meeting more people who might be able to help them get out of there.

Maggie just nodded her head. Sonny said any weekend for the next month would be fine, and that they preferred next weekend because maybe they could have multiple get togethers for the whole month. Johnny said he didn't think he could handle that much partying. They laughed and agreed, but Sonny added that it would be fun trying.

They had some good conversation about the way things were going in the UST, their boys, Johnny's family and business. Maggie got up to take care of some plates and clear some of the things in the kitchen. That was when Sonny asked Johnny about where he was this week. Johnny said that was something he wasn't sure Sonny wanted to know.

Sonny asked him if he killed anyone, and he laughed and said, "Not yet."

Sonny said, "If you didn't kill anyone, yet, what's the worry?"

Sonny heard it all before and he wasn't about to turn Johnny in considering all he had learned the past few weeks. Sonny was happy to know Johnny still had respect for him and his position to not just come out and tell him.

Johnny said, "OK, you asked."

Johnny asked Sonny about a few of the girls that worked for him. Specifically, he asked him when was the last time he saw Margie, Dawn, and Celia. Sonny had to think a minute, because he didn't remember the last time he saw them. He said it had been a while since he saw any of them. He then asked about Cherry, Babie, and Chloe.

"Wow, it's been ages since I've seen them, Sonny said.

Sonny just figured those girls just moved on, found better jobs, got hitched, or just left the business. Johnny said he had to start off like that so Sonny would believe his story. Johnny went to Puerto Rico from time to time to get new girls for his place. Most of the girls in that line of business were trapped and never get out. They either worked until they lost their looks and appeal, got bought by some rich guy, or were found dead somewhere because of an overdose or other unknown reason. Johnny went down there to give the girls a true path to a life. He "bought" the girls he felt had the best chance to succeed in the UST. He brought them back to his place, through normal UST channels since they were citizens, and provided them with a two year contract, so he could earn back the money he spent on them. They agreed to work for him for two years, with food, room and board, and then they were free and clear. Most of them continued their work as prostitutes so they could save more money. Some of them became waitresses, dancers, dealers, or even wanted to learn how to do the books. He left it up to them. Johnny had two years to help the girls get a skill so they could be productive in society and not rely on anyone.

Sonny tried to get a grasp on what type of person Johnny was. He couldn't just judge the book by its cover. He did own a brothel and gambling business, but it was more than that. Sonny always assumed he was shady, but what proof did he have beside the type of business he ran? There were no real rumors on the streets about anything specific that he did. Did he just like to keep that aura of mystery around his name to keep his street cred? Sonny believed he truly cared about people and he was trying to make this a better place to live in. Sonny didn't know how much he could verify what Johnny said, but he would try. If this was true, Sonny felt they could speed up their plans by including Johnny in them. It could be a big breakthrough.

"You're a true humanitarian. That is some good work you are doing with the girls. I'm glad you told me," Sonny said to Johnny.

Johnny continued, "I'm just trying to do something for the girls that I wished someone had done for my cousin."

Johnny said he didn't want anyone to know about this because he was afraid somehow someone might try to exploit what he was doing. He thanked Sonny for the information he gave him about someone trying to lure his girls away from his business.

Johnny asked his girls if it was true and they gave him all the answers he needed. He said one of his associates paid this guy a visit and convinced him it was in his best interest to find his own girls. He promised Sonny no permanent damage was done to him.

Maggie came back and Johnny got up to leave. Johnny promised next time he would call before he came over. Razor said his good byes and Johnny said to let him know if they ever bred him because he would love a dog like him. And just like that, Johnny was gone, leaving behind more hope than Maggie and Sonny had before he arrived.

The first thing Sonny did was tell Maggie about what Johnny did to get his girls and how he handled them. Maggie was impressed and agreed it might be time to include Johnny in their plan to leave. They discussed how they might be able to verify his story. Maggie said there were records of employees kept in the archives. Every business, especially brothels, had to list all of their employees, in case something happened, and someone needed to contact an old employee. She said she didn't have access to this database but believed she could get Becky to help her. She would come up with an excuse on why she needed that information. Once she had the full names of the girls, between the two of them, they should be able to find them.

Maggie and Sonny had a good Saturday. They got up early, and took a walk with Razor on the beach. They got back home, had lunch and headed to the mall. They did some shopping, had some dinner and finished up with a movie. Malls were different now, since there were no chain stores or restaurants. Every store had a number and a generic name. All equal. The movie theater was running 80's classics. Sure, they could watch the movies at home, but nothing was as good as going to the movies. It was still an escape. Buying overpriced fresh popcorn, candy and drinks, then sitting in a dirty theater with a floor that crunched. Of all of the things that had changed, movie theaters pretty much stayed the same. They compromised on a double feature. Sonny chose his favorite action movie, *Aliens,* and Maggie chose her favorite girly movie, *Legends of the Fall.* They played a game during the movies to keep each other from falling asleep. You couldn't hit the other person with anything harder than popcorn, and no sticky drinks, just water. The trick was to not get the other person too wet or dirty to wake up. At the end of the movies, the person who looks the cleanest lost. This also added the probability of cheating by pouring water on yourself. When someone was accused of cheating, it usually led to an all-out soaking, so it didn't happen too often. A funny thing happened this time. They both stayed awake. First time ever. Sonny guessed they were just too excited and just thought about things when they were bored, rather than fall asleep. After the movie, they called it a tie and celebrated with some ice cream before they went home, where they fell asleep.

Sunday was a lazy day. They stayed in bed as long as they could, watching some TV and just talking about how great it would be once they were back together with the boys. They could take the grandkids on nights their boys wanted to go out and they could wake up with them, enjoy the morning, make breakfast and just enjoy them.

Around noon on Sunday, Sonny got a call from Johnny. He said he spoke to his people and next weekend was fine for a BBQ. Sonny asked him who he asked, and he said Ronnie, the limo driver, and the maître d at the restaurant. Sonny thought that was great and asked if there was anyone else he wanted to bring. Sonny never asked if Johnny was married or if he had kids, but Sonny believed he knew what he was asking.

Johnny said, "Not this time. We'll talk about it."

Sonny proposed next Saturday at noon for the start of the BBQ. Johnny said that was fine and he was looking forward to it. He asked if they needed anything, or if there was anything people could bring. Sonny said no, and to let everyone know to just show up and be ready to have a good time.

They had a whole week to prep. They had plenty of time to get it together. The question now was whether or not to invite Becky, Joan and their families.

Maggie and Sonny discussed it and they really couldn't come up with a good reason for not inviting them. The worst case scenario was that their husbands had some bad business go down between them and Johnny. Sonny proposed they ask Johnny if he knew them. Maggie agreed. If nothing else, this would give Johnny another time where he saw they trusted him and valued his word.

Sonny called Johnny back and said Maggie wanted to invite a couple of friends and they wanted to make sure there were no problems with that. Johnny said it was their house and he respected any decision they made regarding the BBQ. Sonny thanked him, but said he had to give Johnny a heads up because of possible business related issues. When Sonny mentioned that Maggie's friends, Becky and Joan Russo, were married to Joe and Paulie Russo from Howard Beach, Johnny said he knew of the Russo family, but not personally. There were no problems inviting them. He actually looked forward to meeting them. Great. Sonny's only other thought was Double D. He would love to have him and his family there, but Sonny needed to be more comfortable with the group before he asked him, because of his position. Maggie agreed with Sonny and said this group alone was a big step. She was right.

Becky and Joan accepted the invitation, coaxing their

husbands by telling them they would be meeting some old school agents from the old government. Maggie and Sonny prepped all week. They had a few extra FCs, so Sonny made sure they got some good cuts of meat at the butcher shop.

On Friday, Sonny got a call from Double D. He was in the area and wanted to meet up. Sonny informed him he didn't get off of work until five p.m., but he needed to see Double D right away. Sonny bought sandwiches and drinks and went by the gazebo near his car.

Sonny zapped his camera a few minutes before they met. His intentions were to turn it back on at the end of their lunch, after they did all of their serious talking.

Double D was waiting for Sonny.

"You still suck," yelled Double D.

He's so loud. They gave each other a huge hug and sat down on the benches. Sonny looked around to see if he could find Tracks, but no luck. Double D snatched the bag from Sonny's hands and quickly dug into the sandwich. Feeling it was warm, his eyes lit up. He looked at Sonny and he smiled.

"Awesome," he screamed.

Eggplant parm with San Marzano tomato sauce and fresh mozzarella. A sandwich he couldn't order at work because he was a doctor and he needed to lead by example. That meant no fried foods. His wife didn't know how to make it, so he only got to enjoy it from time to time.

Double D said things were getting bad with the people on top in the UST. He heard many of the senior members on the Council were looking to step down and retire. He believed these senior members wanted to leave before things changed for the worse because they already knew they had lost their influence in the Council. These senior members feared the Council was quickly becoming very selfish when making decisions that affected the common good. The one example he cited was the proposed change in care for the terminally ill that Maggie spoke of weeks ago. Since these senior members were in the minority, the majority ruled against them and said the UST was still not stable enough for them to leave. This was exactly what Sonny was worried about. When it was time for him to retire, Sonny was afraid they would say the same thing, and not allow him to leave. As more and more time passed, the Council sounded more and more like the former president, who brought this all down by continuing to lie for his own benefit. Double D said it was starting to remind him of those days of the split. The Council was showing signs of taking care of themselves before they took care of the people. Then they lied about it. Most of the people blindly believed them, just like they did of the president. Double D believed another 'revolution" was coming and didn't doubt that it had already started. He believed this one would be violent, since most people had guns. How ironic. The party who established the UST was pro-gun control when it started. It quickly changed when they believed the CNU could be a threat, and they ultimately ruled they could not deny anyone from protecting themselves with firearms. The CNU was for everyone bearing arms, so now the whole damn continent was armed.

Double D said this was the type of information the CNU would want, and it might be enough for a one-shot deal to get them over to the other side. He also said this would be very dangerous to work and Sonny wouldn't have any protection if he got caught. It would probably mean a straight ticket to Puerto Rico. Double D said he could provide Maggie and Sonny with the names of the members on the Council who were trying to retire and that was it. He was sorry, but if he gave Sonny any more information, he would have to dig a little more and that wasn't possible at the present time, because of the Council's status. Sonny agreed and said he totally understood. Double D said to talk it over with Maggie and let him know. Sonny asked him about how he would be able to get this information over to the CNU. Double D said that would be another conversation that needed to happen. When it came to matters of "spying," he was limited and felt it was more Sonny's area. Sonny laughed and said he couldn't wait for that conversation. Sonny added that he would speak with Maggie in the evening and get back to him tomorrow. Sonny told him the plans about the BBQ, and Double D agreed it might be better that Maggie and Sonny got to know the group a little better before he showed up. Then he frowned and asked when he was getting an invite for a private BBQ at their house. Sonny said to name the day and it was done. Double D said he would speak with his family and get back to him. Sonny gave Double D the heads up that he was going to turn on his camera, and to keep the conversation light and about their families. Double D gave a nod and on it went. They talked about their families and their jobs, and ended with how great Sonny's boys were doing.

After they parted ways, Sonny crossed the street and was approached by Ronnie and he said, "If you have the time, Johnny wants to see you."

Johnny was seated at their favorite table with a plate of antipasti waiting for Sonny.

Sonny laughed and asked him if he was trying to get him fat. Johnny said no, he just liked giving his friends good food. Sonny sat down and Johnny immediately asked him how he knew that doctor and why was he speaking with him. Amazing. Little did Sonny know he was being watched in his own area. Then again, they were out in the open, but how did he know Double D was a doctor? Sonny said Double D was an old friend who wanted to meet for lunch, and asked Johnny how he knew he was a doctor. Johnny knew the identity of anyone who came into town with the help of his "extra eyes." Once they got the heads up that a new face was in town, they were identified by either license plate, facial recognition, or if the bought anything with a card. Sonny didn't know the places in this town were so connected to each other and shared information. Johnny said it wasn't everyone, but it was a majority of places. Between all of them, they had a great deal of connections to get information on people. Johnny was really starting to give Sonny a great deal of information about himself that was illegal. Did he trust Sonny that much, or did he have something over his head that he could use to keep him quiet?

Since the door was already open, Sonny just asked him. "Why is it that you all of a sudden trust me so much? I could bring you in and you would be facing many charges."

Johnny laughed and said Sonny forgot he had been keeping tabs on him for years, and Johnny knew Sonny a lot better than Sonny knew himself. All of the years building up a snapshot of his character, along with all of the recent events, had led him to believe he was a person of honor and did what he thought was right, rather than follow the law to the letter. He had seen and heard enough to know that he can now consider Sonny a friend. He knew Sonny wouldn't turn him in for the things he knew about because he felt this was doing the right thing.

Sonny understood where Johnny was coming from, but still thought he was taking a big risk by opening up so much. Was this an ongoing test? Did he want to be Sonny's friend so bad that he has just decided to go for it and potentially lose everything he had? Did he have an exit out of there if things went bad for him? Before Sonny thought any harder about it, he stopped and laughed to himself. Johnny was right about him. Nothing he let him know about was something he would consider extremely bad. He wouldn't turn him in for any of it. Johnny added that he was a good judge of character and was never wrong about a person. In another world, he believed they would be good friends, almost brothers. Sonny said Johnny was right, and he wouldn't turn him for anything he knew about him.

Johnny said, "You see? You answered your own question."

Sonny's attention turned back to Double D. He asked Johnny why he was concerned about him. Johnny wasn't concerned about him. He just wanted to know why he was in town to speak with Sonny. Sonny assured Johnny he had nothing to worry about, Double D was a family friend for years and he would get along with him well. Johnny asked if he was coming to the BBQ, and Sonny said he was invited, but couldn't make it because he already had other plans. Johnny couldn't wait for the BBQ. Sonny was excited too.

After Sonny spoke with Johnny, he called Maggie and asked her if they needed any last minute items for the BBQ. Maggie said it looked like they were in good shape, but to get a few more bags of ice, just in case. Sonny finished his day at work and picked up some ice. He also picked up some nice flowers for Maggie. She worked pretty hard getting this all together. The way Sonny pictured the house when he pulled up was Maggie would be on a ladder somewhere, doing some type of last minute touch up, or hanging something new. The last thing he thought was that he would find her sitting in the yard, having a drink, and listening to music. But that was the case. She really did it this time. She was totally ready a day before the event. Sonny tried to hide the flowers behind him, but Razor kept circling and gave it away. Maggie smiled and said she was going to ask Sonny to get flowers for her, but decided to wait and see if he would do it on his own.

"Yes! I'm getting lucky tonight!" Sonny screamed.

Maggie laughed and said, "You're pretty confident."

Maggie said she didn't want to make a mess, so she ordered some pizza for dinner. Sonny filled her in on the day's events with Johnny and Double D. Maggie was intrigued with the information provided by Double D. She agreed this was the type of information the CNU would love to have. If they ever had ideas about re-gaining control of the whole nation, this information would help them. Their goal would be to provide this information to the CNU without opening the door for a take-over. They would need to identify one of the disgruntled members of the Council and approach them. This was extremely dangerous because they did not know anyone on the Council. A cold approach could have them detained and labeled as traitors from the CNU or revolutionists. They would need to review the minutes from the Council's meetings and try and identify someone who might sound as if they were unhappy, and looking to go in a different direction than the Council. Then they would need an "inside" contact to hopefully make an introduction to this member of the Council. Maggie said she would casually ask Becky about the Council and see if she volunteered any information she could work with. Sonny would work on getting minutes of the meetings without raising any flags.

After all of this serious talk, Maggie had a good laugh about what happened with Johnny. She said Sonny was slipping because he didn't know about how people were identified going into his area. She laughed and said she might have to give him some remedial training on how to work investigations. Sonny just laughed back and said to make sure she didn't break her nails the next time she had one of her super-secret meetings at a salon. They toasted to success, finished their pizza, and went to bed discussing how they thought the BBQ would go with such a mix of people.

Sonny's phone rang at 6 a.m. It was Johnny. He laughed and said Sonny should have been up already. Sonny could tell he was excited for the BBQ. He had a good feeling about the day. Johnny knew Sonny said they didn't need anything or any help, but he couldn't help himself. He got a bartender for the day, and a DJ who needed to set up for some serious karaoke. He wanted to send these guys over by 10 a.m. but wanted Sonny's blessing first. A bartender was a great idea, and a DJ was too. Sonny said 10 a.m. was fine. Johnny would go with them as well, to help them out and provide anything else Sonny might need. Now Sonny began to think if this was over kill for a BBQ with less than twenty guests. He felt it probably was, but he was OK with that. Maggie and Sonny got up and started to get ready. Razor must have sensed something was going on, because he had lots of extra energy. It was a beautiful day. Not a cloud in the sky, with almost no wind at all. They had the heater on for the pool, just to take the edge off of the low water temperature. Sonny helped Maggie put out some balloons at the tables. Next was getting the liquor out to the bar by the pool and putting the beer on ice. All of the meat and fish was seasoned and marinating, so no need to pull that out until it was ready to cook.

At 10 a.m. there was a knock at the door. Razor did a bee line to the door. There was Johnny, the DJ (Tony), and the bartender (Pat). Of course, Johnny couldn't come empty handed, so he brought a bottle of eighteen-year-old Macallan single malt scotch.

"Are you kidding me?" Sonny said. "That's a serious drink. How did you know that we loved Macallan scotch?"

Maggie and Sonny took them to the back of the house and the bartender started to set up the bar the way he liked it. The DJ wanted to see how their house speakers were set up before he brought in any equipment. Sonny showed him where he could tap in with the system. He was very impressed with the sound setup.

He asked who did it for them, and Sonny said, "It was all me."

Now he was really impressed. He was only going to bring in two large main speakers and his DJ equipment. Johnny and the DJ went out to their truck and started setting up. By 11:30 a.m., they were all done. They took a moment to have a toast with the awesome scotch Johnny brought over. The DJ wanted to test the system, so he said to do the toast using the microphone.

Sonny grabbed the mic, raised his glass and said "Here's to a great day."

No sooner than when he lowered his glass, the DJ started playing "Hey Ya" by Outkast. The few of them that were there began to shout. Maggie and Johnny ran up to Sonny and grabbed their own mics. Then Sonny realized the DJ set up teleprompters for the words. That was awesome. That was serious karaoke. The only audience they had, Razor and the bartender, were screaming and barking. Sonny could only imagine how this would play out once they had some food and more drinks in them. It had the potential to be an all-time epic party. DAMN! Where are the boys? They needed to be there.

Sonny was getting angry. He wanted to scream and cry. Maggie just grabbed him and brought him into the house. She knew exactly what was happening. She told Sonny she knew he missed the boys and that they should be there. She felt the same way.

"Treat this like work," she said.

Sonny began to relax a little and gave her a soft kiss on the lips.

"I love you and we will get back together with them. Sooner rather than later. We need this to help us get there," Sonny mumbled through his tears.

Maggie said the guests were about to arrive and to take as much time as he needed to gather himself, then go outside. He counted to one hundred and went out after her.

Johnny went up to Sonny and asked if he was OK. Sonny gave him "the back story," and Johnny said he looked like he was in serious pain. Sonny said it was because of all of the years being on his feet at work, carrying equipment. Johnny advised Sonny to make sure he chased the pain meds with the scotch, and he would feel like a new person. Sonny laughed and said he was way ahead of him, as he sipped some more scotch.

As soon as the clock struck 12, the doorbell rang.

Ronnie, the maître d, Tommy, and the limo driver, Steve were at the door. Sonny saw another car pulling up as they went into the back. It had to be Becky. Four of them approached the door.

Sonny said, "You must be the Russo's."

They laughed, and in unison, with a NY Italian accent answered, "How did you know?"

It was easy for Sonny to pick out who Becky and Joan were. Joe and Paulie, he wasn't so sure. Sonny knew plenty of Italian Fat Joe's in his life. Paulie was usually a scrawny little guy. One of these guys was about 175 pounds. The other guy was a good

325.

Sonny took a shot and said to the big guy, "You must be Joe."

He laughed and said, "Wow, how did you know? Did this (he pointed to his stomach) give it away? You must have grown up in an Italian neighborhood." They all had a good laugh.

As Sonny brought them through the house, Becky asked where Maggie was. He said she was talking with the DJ.

Paulie laughed and said, "You guys hired a DJ? Classy party. I'm so under dressed."

They were all dressed nicely, in shorts and shoes.

Sonny said, "Classy? I guess Maggie didn't tell you about the DJ. And actually, you're probably over dressed for his taste." The shots began.

Sonny took them to the back and pointed to where Maggie was, near the pool. Maggie looked up and screamed like a high school girl, greeting her friends she hadn't seen since the last day of school in the spring. Becky and Joan screamed back.

Maggie called them over and said, "Let me introduce you, guys."

After hearing the screams, Johnny ran over and wanted to know what he missed. Sonny said he missed the ladies turning back into teenagers. They laughed. Sonny introduced Johnny to the Russo family. Johnny asked Joe and Paulie to follow him over to the bar so they could leave the ladies alone to talk. Steve was really interested in the music and setup, so he was by the DJ booth, talking with Tony. Ronnie and Tommy met the rest of them at the bar.

Pat said, "It didn't take you guys long to rush the bar."

Sonny sarcastically answered, "And it won't be the last time."

Paulie looked at Joe and said, "We forgot to bring in the bottles. I'll go get them."

Joe shook his head and threw the car keys at Paulie. Sonny said it was fine, they had plenty to drink. Joe said it was some really good stuff and that he insisted they drink it today.

Sonny said, "Fine. You don't have to twist my arm to make me drink. I think I'm safe to say that goes for everyone else as well."

Johnny said, "You know this group."

They started by drinking beer. It was nice out, they didn't eat yet, so they kept it basic for the moment. Paulie came back with two bottles of red wine and a bottle of sambuca. Sonny gave the bottles to the bartender. Sonny looked at Joe and Paulie with a disgusted look.

Joe asks, "What's wrong? Not good enough for you?"

Sonny said, "What? No cannolis?"

Johnny spit out his beer and cracked up.

Paulie said in a sarcastic tone, "Sorry. Today my grandparents were stepping on grapes to make the wine, so I couldn't stop them so they could make the cannoli cream."

They all let out a simultaneous laugh that was so loud and obnoxious, the group on the other side of the pool yelled at them to keep it down. Sonny grabbed a few beers and brought them over to the other group. He was still laughing as he passed out the beer. Maggie asked what that was all about. Sonny said it was just boys being boys, and they were having a great time. He whispered to Maggie that they should get some of the food out. She grimaced and said she was talking so much, she forgot. They excused themselves and headed to the kitchen.

They already set up the trays and burners, so all they had to do was transfer the food outside. They took two trays out and

Johnny grabbed Ronnie, and they both went inside to grab the others. In all, there were five trays of food. This was the stuff on the lighter side, since it was lunchtime. Maggie and Sonny held the other stuff, the steaks, shrimp and lobster, for dinner.

Everything was great. The music was '80s and '90s classics. After a few rounds of beer, Pat said he would start mixing up the frozen drinks, and wanted to know if they wanted margaritas, pina coladas, daiquiris, or anything else. With almost a unanimous vote, it was margaritas. Pat said he would make regular and strawberry.

Joe and Paulie looked at each other and Joe said, "What? No men drinks?"

Johnny said he spoke with Pat and the understanding was that they wanted cosmos.

Paulie shouted. "Vaffanculo!"

Joe cracked up and said, "You guys found Paulie's kryptonite. He's really sensitive when it comes to drinking."

Paulie said, "Real men don't need mixed drinks. Just give it to me straight."

Joe said rather quickly, "OK. You have small hips and walk funny." Paulie took a swing and punched Joe in the arm. They were uncontrollably laughing.

With that, Paulie tells Pat, "Shots of tequila, all around."

Now it was getting real. Tony and Steve, seeing the party was starting to liven up, said they were ready for some karaoke. Joe pushed everyone out of the way and rushed to the microphone.

"I have to start the party off right. You know, with Sinatra," said Joe.

Sonny quickly grabbed his video camera and set it up to record all of the singing. This was going to be some good stuff.

Joe leaned into to Tony and whispered something in his ear. Joe got into position and waited for the music to start.

He saw the teleprompters and said, "So, this IS a classy party."

As the music started, Joe snapped his fingers in tune. "Fly me to the moon, let me play among the stars..." Wow. He sounded great. Everyone was on their feet, cheering him on.

Becky leaned into Maggie and said, "That's how I knew he was the one for me. He had it all, but once I heard him sing, I knew."

Maggie smiled and gave Becky a hug. As Joe finished up, they all egged him on to sing another song. He said he couldn't, that it was bad luck to open up with back to back Sinatra songs. He promised to sing more later, but not now.

Next was Johnny. Sonny was really curious as to what song he would sing. He always had dance, rock and pop playing at his place. As soon as Sonny heard the first few bars of that mellow Caribbean beat, he knew what it was. Johnny went there. Bob Marley.

"Don't worry, about a thing, cause every little thing is gonna be all right..."

Now he had everyone singing along. "Rise up this morning, smile with the rising sun, three little birds, pitch by my doorstep, singing sweet songs, of melodies pure and true..."

Johnny stayed up for an encore and sang the Cake version of "I Will Survive." The ladies let out a scream.

It was tequila time. They made their way to the bar. Sonny asked Pat to give everyone a regular sized shot. They did have to eat. Sonny guessed everyone was feeling great because no one questioned him, and they just took the shot glass. Sonny raised his shot glass and thanked everyone for coming and ended with,

"Here's to good times with good people. Salud!"

Of course, Maggie had to add her famous toast, "Cheers big ears."

It did go down smooth. It was like the best tequila they ever had.

After the shots, Maggie and Sonny went into the kitchen to get the steaks and fish. As they walked toward the grill, Tommy came over and said he would take care of the grilling. Maggie and Sonny said he was their guest and they wanted him to relax and enjoy himself. Tommy said that was nonsense. If they enjoyed the food at his place, it was because of him. He started in the kitchen and trained most of the people that worked there now. He really wanted to do this for Maggie and Sonny and said it really wouldn't take long anyway, and it would be worth it. They agreed to let him grill, but only if Sonny helped him. He said the only help he needed was to make sure his drinks kept coming. Maggie went back into the kitchen to start the side dishes and Tommy and Sonny started grilling. Tommy complemented them on the prep. Everything looked properly seasoned, and it was all at the right temperature. He wasn't going to ask anyone how they wanted their steaks, because only people who don't eat rib eye ordered them well done. It was a crime to see no pink or red in a steak, so everyone was getting a medium steak, and if they didn't like it, he was sure there were some other people who could help out. Sonny said not to look any further than him.

Tommy said, "Sorry, but I thought Joe would be the guy."

They laughed and agreed.

As the day was growing short, the frozen drinks were finished. They went back to drinking beer. Maggie got everyone seated and ready to be served. They had two tables set up, so it was perfect. She went back into the house to get the sides. Just like Tommy said, everything was cooking fast. They started to pull the food off of the grill as it was finished. Tommy said he could handle it by himself and asked Sonny to ask everyone what they wanted, and they could start serving. Sonny went to the tables and started getting orders. Johnny popped up from his seat and said he would take care of the other table. Team work at its best. After everyone was served, Tommy split the remaining food in two and placed a plate at each table. There were a couple of extra steaks and lobster tails. The shrimp were all gone. Bon Appetit! Sonny was happy to see they finally got Pat, Tony and Steve to sit down and eat.

The wine the Russo's brought was fantastic. It paired perfectly. Tommy asked about it and said he would like to add it to his restaurant.

Paulie, again in a NY-Italian accent said, "We'll talk about it afta. You know, afta we eat."

Good food with good people. Sonny couldn't imagine how long it would continue, after eating all of the good food. Considering the age of the group, Sonny gave it a couple of more hours. The good thing was they were prepared for the short and the long game. They had enough food and drink for a few days.

Sonny sat in between Maggie and Johnny. Johnny got Sonny's ear early on, and Maggie didn't want to interrupt, so she left them alone.

Johnny asked about how their boys were doing and when they would see them again. It was like he knew what they were planning to do. Sonny started off easy and said they wished they could retire now and move out of there and be with the boys. Their plan was to wait until the boys retired, in about fifteen years, then ask to re-locate to somewhere they can all live, like somewhere in the Caribbean. They were worried because they were not guaranteed the UST would grant them permission to re-locate, and besides, they didn't want to wait fifteen years. He could see Johnny was taking all of it in. Sonny knew Johnny felt bad for him.

Johnny exhaled and said, "Let me find out some things. There might be other avenues for you to take. Give me a few days."

There it was. They were in. Just knowing what he knew about Johnny was enough for him to get excited. Sonny knew he would come up with something good. He knew people who knew people. Sonny took a chance and went for it, and asked Johnny about his family situation.

"What about you? Wife? Kids?" he asked.

Johnny said not many people knew, and he wanted it that way, about his family. He said he knew Sonny wouldn't say anything, so he was comfortable telling him about them. He had a wife and a young son, and for obvious reasons, he kept them out of the spotlight. He wanted to have Maggie and Sonny over his house for lunch, nothing like what was going on today. He said Ronnie and Steve were the only people there that knew about his wife and son. He asked Sonny what he thought he was doing when he wasn't around. He was usually spending time with his family. Johnny said he would like to talk more about them, but there were too many people around. Sonny agreed, and they moved on.

As dinner was wrapping up, Tommy started to bus the tables. Sonny got up and asked him to stop, that his masterful grilling was more than enough. Everyone stood up and cheered for Tommy.

"Great meal," "When can I hire you for my party," and "The sweetest lobster and most tender steak I ever ate," were just a few of the statements made by the guests.

Sonny spoke about having dessert with Maggie, and they agreed it would be better to have it later in the evening. Sonny let everyone know their plan, and they agreed. Most of them said they were stuffed and needed time to digest.

As they cleared the tables, Tony put on some classic soul music from the '60s. They sang along as they cleaned up, and then moved on to dance. It was the perfect speed. No one would have been able to move any faster without throwing up. As Sonny was dancing with Maggie, he saw Johnny speaking with Joe and Paulie. He wished he could have been a fly on the wall next to that conversation.

Sonny thanked everyone for coming. He said, "You are all good people. Well, all except for Paulie."

There's always a target in every group. How it became Paulie, no one will ever know. Paulie jumped up out of his chair and ran after Sonny. Sonny ran around the pool and Paulie followed. They were all laughing so hard. It was like a cartoon watching them run around the pool. Razor saw them running and decided to join in. He ran behind Paulie and barked as he kept pace with him. Paulie never knew he was being chased. Sonny felt a sharp pain, grabbed his leg, and stopped running. Paulie caught up to him, and as soon as he was in striking range, Sonny jumped into the pool. Paulie was dressed too nice to get wet, so he just shook his head and laughed. Sonny swam to the other side of the pool, got out, ran toward Paulie and went in for a hug.

Paulie said, "Get away from me. You'll get me all wet." Sonny just held his arms open, and Paulie said, "Ah, what the hell," and went in for the hug.

Tony ramped up the music. It was all dancing from there on. Since there were only three women at the party, they got to dance

122

with all of the guys. The drinking and dancing went on for about an hour. Tony saw they were all slowing down, so he cut the music and gave them a break.

Sonny looked at Maggie and she shook her head and said, "How about coffee and dessert?"

Joe said, "You don't have to ask me twice."

Pat turned on the espresso machine and Sonny went inside with Maggie to get the pastries and cake.

Paulie saw them carry out the plates and said, "All right. So, you do have cannolis."

As they were eating and drinking, Sonny felt the energy of the group just fizzle away. He got the feeling people were going to start to leave. Sonny looked at the time and it was already midnight. Tony came over and asked if they wanted more music or if they were done. At first, no one wanted to say they had enough. After a few silent awkward seconds, everyone began to look at each other and laugh.

All at once, they all said, "We're done."

Tony said he would start packing up and Steve went to help out.

They laughed and Sonny thanked Johnny for everything. He said he had a blast and couldn't wait until the next party, where Chris Rock was going to open for the DJ. Sonny looked at Johnny and asked if he knew Chris too.

Johnny laughed and said, "You never know."

Before Sonny knew it, everything was put away and people were heading out. The Russo's thanked Maggie and Sonny for the time of their lives.

Joe said, "I never knew people could still throw a BBQ like this," and went in for a hug.

Paulie thanked Sonny and said next time, he was going to

come back hard, now that he knew everyone. Becky and Joan came in for a group hug. They said they were happy to finally meet Sonny. They said they had a beautiful house and couldn't wait to get together again. As the rest of the guys left, Sonny thanked Pat, Tommy and Tony for all that they did. They all said it was no problem and thanked him for a spectacular BBQ. As Johnny left, Sonny gave him a huge hug.

Johnny said, "For you, nothing is too much."

Johnny said he knew how Sonny felt and would get back to him about what they spoke about. What a day. Words couldn't describe it. It was just that Sonny didn't think they could still have so much fun. It was good while it lasted. Just a quick blow off of steam. Damn that bastard! He ruined this great nation of ours. It didn't have to be.

Maggie's eyes were practically rolling back in her head. Even Razor seemed beat. Off to bed.

Chapter 11

Sonny slowly opened an eye and it was daylight. No pounding headache. He opened the other eye and checked the situation. Maggie was snoring, and so was Razor. He took a quick look at the time. It was 9:15 a.m. Not bad considering he had no idea what time it was when he went to bed. He felt good. He tried and get out of bed without waking Maggie or Razor. Razor immediately popped up. Maggie kept on cutting wood. He decided to let her sleep a little while longer. Sonny led Razor down to the kitchen. It was clean. He looked out back, and the same thing. It was all clean. They all did a great job. He was not particularly hungry, so he decided to make some toast and have it with some fruit. He put the coffee on and took care of Razor. It was a warm and sunny morning and he wanted to eat outside. Sonny decided to ask Maggie if she wanted to join him. He tried to wake her peacefully, but Razor wasn't having any of that. He ran into the room and jumped on the bed. Maggie sat up quickly and, in a panic, asked what time it was. Sonny laughed and said it was almost 10 a.m., and that everything was OK. He asked if she wanted to have breakfast outside and she said yes, but to give her a minute to wake up and put something on. He left the room, grabbed the breakfast from the kitchen, and went outside. Maggie came outside ten minutes later, in a thick robe. Sonny laughed and she said she was cold. For the next ten minutes, they laughed and told stories from the day before, a BBQ for the ages. Sonny suddenly remembered the camera was still on. He got up to turn

125

it off, and noticed it was already shutdown. He asked Maggie if she did it, and she didn't remember, but she might have turned it off when everyone left. It looked like it recorded a little over nine hours, so it should be OK. That stuff was priceless, so he hoped it all came out.

Sonny let Maggie know he brought Johnny into the loop on what they wanted to do. He gave her his reasons why he felt it was time and he let her know exactly how he told him. She thought it was a small risk, but it was still a risk to tell him. She would be surprised if Johnny used this information against them, and felt Johnny really cared about them. There was no reason to panic now, it was already done, so they had no choice but to wait and see what he could find out.

They really took it easy that day. They felt good, no alcohol regrets, no headaches, just an overall calmness. They lounged around the pool, had a light lunch, took Razor on a long walk and thought about dinner. Sonny ran out to the store to pick up fresh veggies to go along with their leftover surf and turf. Their phone call with the boys was on Tuesday, so they kind of prepared for that. Sonny took a look at the video and made some quick cuts so they could give the boys a taste of how it went. Maggie took some notes so they wouldn't have to waste their whole call on the party. As the sun went down, they spoke about how good they felt going into the new week. They were excited to have Johnny on board. They felt like they made really good progress last week. They kept their end game in focus and really enjoyed themselves. They were thankful for that, as they needed a break.

Monday afternoon, Sonny got a text from Double D. He wanted to have a couple's dinner that night, if it worked for them. Sonny called Maggie and she said it was fine and to ask them if they wanted to have dinner at their house instead of going out.

They still had food they didn't make for the BBQ on Saturday. Sonny called Double D and said they were good for dinner, and that they would like to have them over rather than go out. Double D was waiting for that invite and of course, he'd rather go over than go out. They agreed on 7 p.m. Double D said he would bring dessert.

Sonny wrapped up the day around three p.m. On his way home, he picked up some fresh bread. He made it home by 4:15 p.m, and Maggie was getting ready. The house was clean and tidy, so by the time they prepped the food, it was only 5:30 p.m, so he sent Double D a text and let him know they could come over a little early if they wanted to. He said they would be at the house in about a half hour.

Razor alerted them that he heard a car pulling up in the driveway. Sonny went to the front of the house and saw Double D pulling in. He screamed to Maggie that they were there, and she said she would turn on the grill. Double D and Sara got out of the car. She ran over to Sonny with her arms wide open, jumping into his arms.

"It has been way too long. I've missed you so much."

Sonny said she was right, and he missed her too. Sonny went over to give Double D a hug and he passed him a pastry box, with a big number seven on it.

Sonny said, "No way. 7's famous red velvet cupcakes?"

Double D laughed and said, "Of course."

Double D said something smelled really good. Sonny said it was nothing but the best for friends. Ribeye and lobster tails. Double D knew the time was right for a great meal at their house. When Sara saw Maggie on the grill, she screamed. Maggie smiled and screamed back. Sonny took over the grill and Maggie gave Sara a huge hug.

Sara said, "I missed you, you sexy bitch. You look like you haven't aged at all. What is your secret?"

Maggie responded, "A balance of good food, good wine, and great company."

Double D went in for a hug with Maggie and said, "You weren't lying. She looks the same as the day you married her. Too bad you look like her perverted uncle."

Sonny ran over to him and gave him a good punch in the chest.

Sonny said, "Remember, you're still on thin ice with me. Watch what you say, or you'll end up in traction."

Sara said, "Oh, boy. I miss this like I miss my hemorrhoid. Can't you guys just behave for a little while? Can't I enjoy this reunion with a little peace?"

Maggie laughed and said to follow her inside for some drinks. Sara agreed, as long as it was just her and Maggie. Double D promised he wouldn't ruin their talk, and he was hoping it would lead to his fantasy of finding the ladies making out in the kitchen.

Maggie smirked and said, "How do you know it hasn't already happened and you missed it?"

Double D grabbed his heart and said, "Don't mess with me like that."

They were going to have another great night.

Sonny asked Double D to grab a couple of beers from the cooler by the bar. He cracked them open and they talked as Sonny continued to grill dinner. Double D said the place looked good, so the party couldn't have been too wild. Sonny laughed and said he had to see the video of the party when he put it together. Sonny talked about the people, the food, the drinks and the fun they had. Double D couldn't believe it. He was upset he missed it, was definitely going to be at the next party. He wanted to drink heavily, but was afraid to since he had to work the next morning. He promised he would come over on a Friday with his pajamas, so he wouldn't have to go home after drinking.

Double D laughed, then said, "Who am I kidding? I don't own pajamas. I'm commando baby!"

Sonny cracked up and responded, "This is not a clothing optional home like yours. I don't want to go blind, so no commando for you."

Double D asked how it was going on the escape plan. Sonny explained about how Maggie was working with her co-worker, and about Tracks and Johnny. He said to be very careful because things were really clamping down.

"There's a buzz going around the halls at work that a new virus has hit western Pennsylvania. It has not been made public yet, but it doesn't look good. According to our treaty with the CNU, we have to notify them when a new virus comes up and it gets to level two. It's almost there, and at that point, our borders will be shut down and almost no one will be allowed to move from the UST to the CNU. Thankfully, we learned from our mistakes ten years ago on how to handle an outbreak. At level two, we will be on complete lockdown and isolated from the rest of the world. This might actually create a new way for you to get out of the UST, we would have to wait and see. If you guys were doctors, it would have been easy."

Sonny apologized that they took "the easy way out" and became agents. Double D smiled.

Dinner was ready and they took the food to the table. The ladies must have been watching the men, because they came out as they were setting up the table. Sara said the food smelled amazing. Maggie said they had to set a date for the next dinner at their house. Sara agreed and said she would have a date for them by tomorrow. The food was amazing. Maybe it tasted a little better since they weren't so drunk as they were the day before. Double D filled Maggie in on the potential virus threat. She knew it was a matter of time before the next one hit. Sara tried to change the mood by bringing up the BBQ. She said Maggie told her all about it and she couldn't wait to see the video. Sonny said the video probably wouldn't do any justice to how it actually was, and they had to make it to the next one.

Sara said Double D filled her in on their plans to leave the UST. She promised to help in any way she could and felt bad that they were sad and missing their family. They all finished eating and drinking and cleaned up the table. Maggie and Sara brought the plates into the house and said they would bring out dessert. Sonny grabbed a couple of beers and went to sit poolside with Double D. Double D asked if Sonny found a contact from the other side. Sonny said that he hadn't started to look for anyone yet, but this virus might be a good opportunity to get in good with the CNU. The virus stage was moving quickly, but it wouldn't be a level two for at least another two weeks. Sonny felt giving the information to the CNU before they were officially notified by the UST would be a great start. It might even fast track them to getting over there, if they could follow it up with another important piece of info. Double D said he could give Sonny plenty of info on the new virus without being detected. Sonny said he made a good point and he would start to get a good contact. He asked Double D to get him all he could about the virus and to keep him updated as time went on. Double D didn't think it was a problem and he could get the information in a couple of days.

The ladies came out to the pool area with the red velvet

cupcakes. They were as good as ever. Moist and flavorful. Not too sweet. The only problem was it didn't go well with beer. Sonny asked Double D to help make some sangria and Sara quickly jumped in. Shewould love to help because she wanted Sonny's recipe. She remembered how good the sangria was and hoped to steal it from him someday. As Sonny mixed up the sangria, Sara explained how upset Double D was when he got home after Sonny told him they planned to leave the UST. Double D knew how much pain Maggie and Sonny were in and he would get them back with their boys no matter the cost. Sara saw the boys last week on TV with their families at a charity event. She said they looked great, and that was more of a reason for Maggie and Sonny to get back to them. Double D had been banging his head against the wall day and night, trying to find a way for them to leave. Sonny knew how good of a friend she and Double D were to them. Sonny gave her a hug and said hopefully the sangria recipe would work as a down payment. Since it was Monday, and everyone had work in the morning, Sara and Double D decided to leave and said next time it would be at their house. Maggie and Sonny thanked them for the virus news and for their company. They all promised to be closer and to stay safe while trying to get a good plan to get out of there. They got in their car and drove off. Another great evening with friends.

Sonny asked Maggie, "Is everyone trying to make it hard for us to leave?"

Maggie smiled and said, "It sure does feel like it."

As they were cleaning up, they discussed the virus angle of a plan and agreed it could help. Sonny would speak with Johnny in the morning and see if he knew someone that might help.

Chapter 12

Double D promised to provide Sonny with some information regarding the new virus before the end of the week and he had to see Johnny today about a possible CNU contact. When Sonny finally got through his morning and headed out to the streets, he parked his car, and there he was, sitting on the park bench. Tracks had clean, new clothes, and a haircut.

As he walked over toward Tracks, he got up and greeted Sonny with a salute and a smile.

Sonny went in for a hug and said, *"You look marvelous,"* using his best Billy Crystal voice.

Tracks laughed. Wait, Tracks laughed. Something great must be happening. He said thank you and asked Sonny to sit with him. Tracks said while he was digging around for information, he came across a new rehab program. He spoke to a few people about it and decided to give it a try. The reason he had been missing for a few days was because of the training he was getting. They didn't call them "meetings" anymore because they were being trained how to live again. They cleaned Tracks up, gave him new clothes and sent him out to look for work. He was able to stay in a room they provided for a few days as he looked for work. After a couple of days, he didn't find anything and was worried he wasn't out there helping Sonny, so he left. Sonny let him know not to worry about him and that he should take care of himself before he could take care of others. Sonny was proud of him and wanted him to go back. Sonny promised he would help him look for a job too. Tracks said he was in a good place because of Sonny. Sonny had always treated him with respect and listened to his stories with interest. If he did clean up, he would owe it all to Sonny, for always believing in him. For that, he had to help him, and he didn't want to take care of himself until he did help.

Sonny said, "You are doing this in the wrong order, and I want you to go back and look for work. I will ask around as you are working, because many people around here owe me something for letting certain things slide over the years."

Tracks knew he was serious, and wouldn't take no for an answer.

He said, "Ok, I'll go back. But I do have some good information for you."

Great. Sonny asked him what he had. Tracks said he had the names of the "higher ups" that were part of the FC scheme, and he knew how it all worked.

The proper way the FCs were distributed was through the Finance Council. The Finance Council would get information, monthly, from employers on their employees who earned FCs. The Council would next electronically send the FCs to the bank account belonging to the employer. The employer would then distribute the FCs to the appropriate employee(s).

Tracks said two members of the Finance Council, Jake Persaud and Tom Adams, were friends with a banker, Anthony Altucci. Anthony set up accounts at the bank for fake charities, who claimed to have small projects that needed to be completed. These "charities" worked with volunteers who got FCs for their time. The government didn't look too hard at these charities because they were helping the UST by volunteering their time and it didn't cost them anything to give out FCs. Anthony created

133

up to ten charities at a time, with dozens of employees for each charity. This always stayed under the radar because these charities only lasted a few months until the "project" was completed. Then Anthony created a new charity in its place. Persaud and Adams created the fake paperwork for the charities created by Altucci. They sent the FCs to the bank for each of these charities. Once they were in the account, Altucci had runners, mostly his family, sell the FCs on the street. The buyer had their name added as a volunteer for the charity, and that was it. They electronically got their FCs. The runners, Altucci, Persaud and Adams all got a cut of the proceeds.

Tracks said this had been going on for years. He said they kept the cash and used it to pay for different things like home improvements and restaurants. He said that's why many of the government employees lived in communities on the other side of the bridge (like Queens and Long Island). They built up their houses and put money into the community pool to help pay for all kinds of projects in the community. This way, all of the homes got built up and no one questioned anything. They all lived in beautiful homes and didn't care where the money came from. Since it was a closed community, no one else could go in and see what they had developed. Tracks said the UST may preach they were for equality for all, and they were great at helping the needy, but they were just like their counterparts in the CNU. Corrupt. The split exposed how similar the two sides really were when it came down to looking out for themselves.

This was proof. The UST was no different than the CNU. It only took an ex-drug addict a couple of weeks to get this information. Sonny wondered how many people actually knew about this.

Now how would this information benefit the CNU? Internal

corruption in the UST wouldn't have an impact on the CNU. If the CNU had plans on taking over some or all of the UST, this could help sway the people to move over. If nothing else, it would create unrest in the UST.

Sonny said, "This is huge! I never imagined you could get information like this in such a short time. I think you have just re-written the undercover rules and broke all kinds of records."

Tracks smiled, again, and said he was glad Sonny thought he did a great job, and he was happy to provide Sonny with information that could help him move up. Sonny was so proud of how he was improving his life and just wanted him back on track immediately. Sonny promised him he would have job opportunities for him by the end of the week. Tracks thanked Sonny and said he would go back to the office tomorrow and get back into the program. Sonny offered to have lunch with him once he finished up with some rounds, around 12:30 p.m., and he said not today. Tracks had to find out if he had any second interviews for a couple of jobs. He would be getting a cell phone soon, and promised he would be easy to find. As he walked away, Tracks said he would see Sonny on Friday. Sonny hoped Johnny was around. He was getting really excited. Things were in motion.

Sonny got to Johnny's street, and he was outside speaking with people walking by. Sonny anxiously crossed the street.

Johnny must have been reading Sonny's body language because he shrugged his shoulders and laughed. Johnny ended his conversation and Sonny followed him inside.

A man grabbed Sonny's arms.

"Where do you think you're going in such a hurry? I need to see ID."

Before he could get a word out, Sonny looked up and saw

that it was Ronnie. He put his head down and laughed.

Ronnie patted him on the back and said, "What? Can't take a joke?"

Ronnie walked in with Sonny and said he still couldn't believe how great the BBQ was and that he wanted Sonny to tell him how to setup a party like that. Sonny said it was easy to do, especially when you had the right people.

They walked over to a table where Johnny was waiting for them. Johnny asked Sonny to sit down because it looked like he had a lot on his mind. Johnny shot a look at Ronnie and Ronnie said he was going to speak to a few of the girls about "a thing," and he would come back when he was done.

Now that they were alone, Johnny asked Sonny how far along on the exit plan they were. He wanted to know who they spoke with and what they knew. Sonny was not going to hand up Double D, but Johnny knew he was a doctor. If Sonny let him know about the virus, he would know who he got it from. Plus, did Sonny really want to tell Johnny about the virus? The best way to keep a secret was not to tell anyone. But if he didn't tell Johnny about it, and he found out later that he knew about it and didn't tell him, it could create problems. Sonny kept thinking about this dilemma while he started to tell Johnny about the plan. Sonny explained how they wanted to get important information over to the CNU in hopes of gaining entrance into the CNU. He went on about how Maggie and him had the potential to obtain really useful information. He updated Johnny with the information he got from Tracks. When he finished telling him the scheme, Sonny paused for a moment. Johnny looked at him really hard and must have seen Sonny was dealing with an important decision.

Sonny took a drink of water, and Johnny said, "It's me. No

one else is around to hear anything. I told you, you can trust me. Our conversation here stays here. I would never tell anyone, nor would I move ahead with helping you without your blessing. Just tell me."

He was right. He hadn't given Sonny any signs of betrayal. But this wasn't about Sonny. This was about exposing Double D.

Sonny knew Johnny knows he spoke with Double D about the plan. Even if Sonny didn't tell Johnny anything else, and he was planning on betraying him, Johnny would just have to let "them" know to keep an eye out on Double D because he was helping Sonny. The more Sonny thought about it, the clearer it became. Double D was already exposed and telling Johnny what Double D was doing wouldn't change that.

With his mind already made up, Sonny began to tell Johnny about the virus.

"Before I tell you anything, I have to let you know a few things. This info must remain a secret. You cannot tell anyone else. You can make sure your family and friends are safe, but you can't tell them a thing about this. Of course, I am getting this info from someone else. The severity and nature of this information will put him at great risk. This comes from a person who is a lifelong friend and I will not allow anyone or anything to harm him or his family. Before I say anything, you must promise me, the promise of all promises, that in no way will you mention anything I am about to tell you. I'll understand if you can't make such a promise."

Johnny took a deep breath and said, "I will not pretend I know how you feel in your situation. I can't imagine how difficult it is for you to trust someone, almost blindly, with your family and your friend's family on the line. It is one thing for me to say you can trust me. It is another thing to show you that you can trust me. I am not a vicious person. I am not a person who runs his business with an iron fist. I want the people around me to be better than they are. I help new girls all of the time. I told you about that. Doesn't that let you into my heart a little bit? I have let you into my life more than anyone else. I do this out of respect for my parents, who respected your father. When I say I won't tell anyone else, I mean it. I'm a sponge, not an open faucet."

Sonny assured Johnny he trusted him and that he just needed to hear him defend his word, because of old habits he picked up as an agent. Yes and no answers were hard for Sonny to take at face value. He needed something to back those words up. He went for it and told Johnny about Double D and the virus, and how important it was to get someone from the CNU who could help out.

Johnny looked like his head was going to explode. He quickly signaled to the bartender that they needed drinks. He said to bring the whole bottle.

Johnny shook his head and said, "Another virus? It's only been ten years since the last one, and we know what a disaster that was. That idiot president was responsible for almost wiping out the whole senior citizen population. Twenty million dead. I can only imagine what he would do now if he found out. Probably nothing again."

The bartender brought over glasses and a bottle of scotch and went back to the bar.

Johnny poured the drinks and raised his glass and said, "Here's to survival."

They banged glasses and drank the scotch like a shot. Johnny poured another one and said they needed to drink this one slowly. Johnny had so many questions about the virus, like what it did, how it was spread, and how close were they to a cure. Sonny assured him Double D would provide him with more information by the end of the week. Sonny could only assure Johnny that Double D didn't feel like it was time to panic. He felt it was under control for now.

They drank in silence for the next couple of minutes. This seemed to ease Johnny a little bit. He said to please let him know what he found out from Double D as soon as possible. Sonny promised him he would. Then Johnny said something Sonny was hoping he would.

"I do have a guy from the CNU who could help you."

Sonny wanted to scream. He wanted to cry. He wanted to laugh. But what he did was grab Johnny in the biggest hug, which almost hindered his breathing. Sonny fought as much as he could, but a few tears ran down his face.

Johnny whispered in his ear, "There's still a lot of work to be done, but this is going to work."

Sonny released Johnny from the death hold, poured a couple of drinks, and toasted. "Here's to great friends, the kind you know you can count on."

Johnny said he grew up with a guy, Mike Reynolds, who worked for the government in the CNU. For obvious reasons, he didn't hang out with him on a regular basis, but he did meet up with him on business trips and spoke with him every few months. He said he was a guy from the old neighborhood and would do anything for him. He was an agent, but Johnny totally trusted him. Sonny said it sounded good and asked him when they could meet or speak with him. Johnny said he would call him and set up a "private call," where they would have to drive to Maryland and make point to point encrypted contact.

"It sounds more difficult and mysterious than it really is.

Trust me, we've done this before and there's no danger."

Sonny replied, "I get it. We need to be relatively close to him, so I assume he will be right over the border, within a quarter mile of us."

"Exactly. It sounds like you've done this kind of stuff before?" Johnny said with a sarcastic smirk on his face.

Sonny smiled and said, "Make it so."

Johnny nodded and urged Sonny to go and finish his day. He promised he would have an answer for Sonny before he went home. Sonny let Johnny know his schedule was completely open and he was ready to make the trip whenever he could set it up. Now Sonny needed to get back to work.

Sonny made sure he stayed within the vicinity of Johnny's place. A few hours later, Johnny was waving at him out front of his place. Sonny made sure his camera was offline for most of the day, so nothing would be captured. He walked into Johnny's place and he guided him out of the back door. They walked a few hundred feet, into the tree line, and stopped at a break in the woods.

Johnny smiled and said they were all set for tonight at 11 p.m. He said he wasn't going with Sonny because it would be easier if he traveled with a woman. Sonny said there was no way he would take Maggie with him and risk both of them getting caught. He said he wasn't thinking of Maggie. He had a young woman who worked with him before on "discrete and sensitive" operations. Her name was Luna and she had the perfect skillset for this "meet." She would not know Sonny's name, nor why they were taking the drive. Johnny asked Sonny if this was OK.

"As long as you trust her, I trust her" he said to Johnny.

What other choice did he have? He was completely in Johnny's hands.

Johnny looked Sonny in the eyes and said, "This will all be fine. I got you."

Johnny said to be ready at 6:30 p.m. and he would pick him up, alone, at his house. Then they would discuss everything in detail. It was almost the end of his day, so Sonny went back to his office, finished up what he needed to do and went home.

He called Maggie and she said she would probably make it home before he did. That meant they would have time to talk before Sonny left.

As he got closer to the house, Sonny saw the mystery tower had been completed. It had a small "house" that probably was the control room. The whole site was still boarded up, but it looked like it had power and was operational. He drove on and pulled up to the house.

Maggie was home. It was 5:15 p.m., so he didn't have time to waste. As he went into the house, he said hi to Razor and gave Maggie a kiss as he headed to the bedroom. Sonny was going to change into some dark clothes. Not all black, but just dark clothing that will be hard to see at night. He got dressed and went to the kitchen. He told Maggie he didn't have much time, but he had a lot to tell her. He explained everything that happened today while he was at work. The things Tracks told him, his situation, everything he told Johnny, and everything Johnny told him.

Maggie agreed that at this point, they were in Johnny's hands. She also felt that it wasn't such a bad thing. She still didn't have full confidence in him, but felt he wouldn't hurt them. She asked Sonny to be careful and remember what this was all about. To let their family be their strength and help them through these times. Sonny agreed and gave her a big hug and kiss.

Maggie said, "I guess you forgot we had a call today."

"SHIT!"

Sonny had never forgotten a call with the boys. It was at 6:15 p.m., so he would only have a little time to talk.

Sonny didn't have time to prepare the video or write some notes down about what he wanted to tell them. He asked Maggie to make sure she told them all about the party since he would have to cut his time short.

They made the call and saw the whole family. As always, they all looked like they walked off a magazine page. Sonny let them know his time was short because he had to take care of something. He asked them how they were doing and if anything new was coming up soon. It was all status quo for them, just waiting for the time they could all meet up. Sonny gave Maggie a good intro on how to follow up with the party stories. Sonny said they had a party for the ages. He said it involved food, drinks, karaoke, and dancing. Sonny said they had evidence and the video was coming soon. Razor started barking.

Johnny was outside.

Sonny said goodbye to them and whispered into Maggie's ear, "Please don't wait up for me. God knows what time I'll be back, 4 a.m., 5 a.m., or just in time to make you breakfast."

Maggie shed a tear and told Sonny to be careful. He wiped it from her face and said to be strong for the boys.

Chapter 13

As they were driving, Johnny filled Sonny in on some details. He said they were going to meet Luna at a gas station. She would refer to Sonny as Max, and she knew nothing about him. All she knew was that they had to get to Williamsport, Maryland to make a call. She was good at knowing her surroundings and how to handle situations on the fly. She defended herself well, knew how to conduct counter-surveillance and how to drive, really well. Johnny swore she could have been a getaway driver. Johnny gave Sonny a radio and said it was totally secure with the most modern protections. He got it from his buddy Mike, who gave it to him for situations like this.

When they arrived at the location, Sonny had to reach out to Mike at 11 p.m. by saying "Giancarlo sent me."

Luna had the coordinates for their contact, which was in a park by the Potomac River, and it should take about four hours to get there. Mike would be on the other side of the river, in West Virginia. Sonny and Luna would be driving in an old school van, from the late 1990s, that had no side windows. The license plate went back to a man who lived in PA. Luna had a copy of the registration. Johnny stressed that Sonny trust Luna and to listen to her when she had something to say. Johnny was glad Sonny had on dark clothing and a hat. He knew he didn't have to tell him about that. Sonny asked Johnny how much it was going to cost for Luna's help, and he said nothing. Johnny helped Luna through some tough times, and she refused to take money from

143

him when he asked for her help. Sonny said he would feel more comfortable knowing she was paid help, especially with the potential risk she was taking. Johnny said they might be able to take care of her in another way, after her job is done. That made Sonny feel a little better.

They got to the gas station and met Luna. She was in her late '20s, early '30s. A very attractive young woman. She was wearing a dark blouse and skirt. As Sonny and Johnny got out of the car and approached her, Johnny handed Sonny a driver's license, with his photo on it, in the name Max Romano, and a home address in PA. He gave one to Luna too, in the name of Maria Romano.

Johnny said "Max, meet your wife Maria," and laughed.

Luna shook Sonny's hand and said not to call her Luna, just Maria, this way there was no mix up later on.

Sonny agreed and said, "At least we have around four hours to get our backstory straight."

Johnny wished them good luck and said there shouldn't be any hiccups. Johnny drove off, and Luna and Sonny got into the van. Luna said she preferred to drive and asked if Sonny was OK with that. Sonny said he had no problem getting driven around.

The interior of the van didn't have any back seats. It just had a mattress, sheets and a few pillows. Perfect for long term surveillances.

They immediately began discussing their back story. Luna said she was a high school teacher at the Philadelphia School of Science. She taught algebra and had been their teaching for ten years. She was thirty-five years old and her birthday was March 17, so it would be easy to remember (St Patrick's Day). They were married for five years. They didn't have any kids yet, but were planning to start a family soon. Today was their fifth wedding anniversary, and they were celebrating it in the park, by the river, on a warm spring evening. She reached back behind her seat, pulled out a big bag, and handed it to Sonny. In it was a bottle of champagne and two flute glasses. She said they got married in FDR Park in Philadelphia and honeymooned, the following day, in the Riviera Maya at the Moon Palace, for seven days. They were both only children and Sonny's parents were dead. She didn't know her parents because they abandoned her when she was ten years old. All Sonny needed to do was come up with a job, then they could discuss their house, likes and dislikes. Sonny was impressed. She was very thorough. She knew this wasn't too risky of a thing they were doing, but she always liked to be prepared for the worst.

He said, "I get it. I would rather be over prepared than under prepared. Plus, we had a few hours to kill."

Sonny said he was a gym teacher and baseball coach at her school, for twenty years. That's where they met, ten years ago when she first got to the school. They began hanging out after a year. They began dating after two years because she was hung up about his age, being fifteen years older than her. That feeling went away after she saw how good Sonny was with the children at school. She never liked baseball, but began to enjoy watching Sonny coach the games. He proposed to her, on her birthday, by asking for her hand by using the baseball scoreboard. She thought it was cheesy and that's why he did it. She accepted and they were married three years later. They had a long engagement because that was around the time of the big split (USA) and they didn't know how things were going to work out in the UST when it was established.

Sonny asked Luna to make a stop so he could grab a drink. He ran into the store and bought a couple of beers. As they pulled off, Sonny opened the beers and gave one to Luna. He said 1 beer wouldn't kill her. She laughed and said it was exactly what she needed. They picked up their discussion with decorating the house, colors of their rooms, description of their backyard, and their cars. They then went on about their hobbies and favorite activities. They discussed their favorite foods, restaurants, and the things they liked and disliked about each other. She said she didn't like Sonny's ears, that they were too big for his head. He laughed and said he didn't like her fingers, that they were too small for her hands. She immediately shot a nasty look at Sonny and took her right hand down off of the steering wheel.

She said, "That was just plain mean."

Sonny laughed and said that was the safest thing he could say. He didn't see her whole body for that long before they started the trip. He wasn't going to comment on her face or hair. So, he thought fingers would have to do.

She looked at Sonny and said, "Really?" then had a good laugh too.

They were about an hour away from the park. It was only 9:30 p.m., so they were good for time. They took about fifteen minutes to themselves to go over all of the information. For the final forty-five minutes, they tested each other on their history. By the time they were near the park, they felt confident they knew it well.

Before exiting for the park, Luna told said the van had a built-in camera jammer, that worked for anything within 500 feet of the van. This way, the van could avoid being captured on video and traced back to their starting location. She said it also had a transmission jammer, but that had to be manually turned on. They would need it in case someone came up on them in the park. This way, they couldn't call for backup or help.

No one was at either entrance of the park, so they went in the secondary entrance and turned off the headlights once they entered the park. They drove about a quarter mile into the park and stopped right next to the Potomac River.

Luna said, "We're here."

She turned off the van and opened the side facing the water. She said to keep this door open while he made his call, and that she would be walking around the vicinity of the van just in case someone was around their location. She would be within ear's distance, so Sonny could just call out for her and she would come back. She wished him luck and left the van.

Sonny turned on the radio and asked if anyone was there.

A person responded, "Please get off of this line. This is a restricted line of the CNU."

Sonny said, "Giancarlo sent me."

The person on the other line said, "I was expecting you. Everything good?"

Sonny said everything was good and asked if he was fully aware of his intentions. He said he was, but said he wasn't sure if the outcome was going to be what Sonny wanted. Usually these things were to develop "friendlies" on the other side, to use for a constant flow of information. People had moved over to the CNU after giving intelligence, but it was only after a few years. The shortest amount of time he was aware of was four years. If the information was really important to the CNU, and with a certain circumstance, he might be able to move the timetable up to a few months. But it had to be really important information, not just a corrupt person or a plan to build closer to the western border. It had to be information like an assassination attempt or a military action against the CNU.

Mike wanted to know what Sonny had for him. Sonny began

by telling him about the information Tracks gave him. Mike felt it was good information, but not the kind that would thrust him over the wall. With information like this, the CNU would package it together with similar actions of corruption in the UST and start a new propaganda attack. The CNU was always trying to get the people in the UST to rise up against the government, in hopes of overthrowing the government and re-uniting the country again. The CNU would be in power and have no opposition from any other group. The CNU would grow without any checks or balances. It was what they wanted ten years ago, but there was too much going on and they knew it wouldn't happen. This way they waited ten years and totally crushed the government by turning its own people against it. He said his boss got the idea from Russia.

Sonny knew Track's information was good, but something that would only wet their lips. Sonny said the next piece of information was something really important. As he began to speak, Mike cut him off when he said the word virus. He said this was the kind of stuff he was looking for. He asked Sonny to continue. He said that's all that he knew, which wasn't much. Mike wanted to know when Sonny would have more information about the virus. Sonny was expecting more before the weeks end. Mike explained to Sonny about how it went down in the CNU after the split, regarding the virus. The president took a little heat for it because the masses thought he didn't react quickly enough and that he never seemed to care about all of the deaths. Fortunately for him, the large majority of the people that held him responsible left for the UST. It remained a dark day for his administration and he would greatly appreciate a chance to redeem himself, especially if he could also make the UST look bad at the same time. As Mike asked Sonny a few more questions he couldn't answer, Sonny heard someone running toward the car. Sonny said he heard something, and had to end the call. Mike would make arrangements for another call on Friday. Sonny reached over the dash and turned on the transmitter jammer. He looked out of the back window of the van and saw Luna running toward the van.

As she got to the van, she took off her top and started taking off her skirt. She told Sonny to hurry up and get undressed. He saw the look in her eyes and knew she wasn't kidding. He wondered why this was happening and quickly remembered Johnny told him to trust her. Sonny got undressed quickly.

He kept his underwear on, and Luna said, "Everything!"

OK, off with his briefs. Luna was topless and only had on a G-string. She said a guard was coming and to quickly get on his back, on top of the mattress. She kept the back door of the van open and mounted Sonny. She said to act like they were having sex. To make noise, grab her tits and slap her ass. She said she would take care of everything else. She quickly began grinding on him, like the best lap dance he ever had.

She was moaning and screaming "Oh yes!"

Sonny had to join in, so he started yelling, "You're so hot! Don't stop!"

She grabbed his hands, said to get to work and placed them on her tits. She was so hot. Sonny felt guilty as hell, but she made him feel like his life depended on their performance. It seemed like they were going at it for an eternity, when in reality it couldn't have been more than two minutes. Sonny felt they had to make enough noise for the unknown person to know what was going on.

Out of the corner of his eye, Sonny saw a man watching them, about 50 feet away from the van. He was wearing a park ranger hat. Sonny winked at Luna and motioned with his face to alert her someone was watching.

After another thirty seconds, they heard a voice say, "Now that's some serious fucking!"

Luna jumped off of Sonny, grabbed a blanket and let out a soft scream, as if she was startled.

Sonny said, "Hey what are you, some kind of pervert?"

He said, "I'm not a pervert. I just know good talent when I see it."

Sonny answered, "You better watch yourself. That's my wife you're talking about."

He said he didn't mean any disrespect, that they were just good at it. He shined a flashlight on them and asked for ID.

He must have seen the champagne because he asked if they were celebrating something. Sonny said it was their anniversary. Sonny said his ID was in the front of the van.

Sonny asked Luna "Hey Maria, where's yours?"

She said it was up front also. The ranger walked around the side of the van and opened the driver's door. He sat in the seat and asked where the IDs were. Sonny pointed to the compartment under the arm rest. He yelled back to Luna, telling her to get dressed. Sonny asked the ranger if they were in any trouble. He said probably not, as long as they didn't have any prior incidents. He said they would probably just have to have some counseling.

Before he could grab the IDs, Luna opened a compartment in the back of the van and removed what appeared to be a gun, went to the front of the van and fired a shot at the ranger. Sonny knew from the sound that it wasn't a real gun. Luna smiled and said it was a tranquilizer. The ranger went out within a second of getting hit with the dart in his neck. They took him out of the seat, and propped him by the water, under a tree.

As they started to fully get dressed, Luna said when they do a blood test on him, it would come back like he was drinking all night.

Sonny was worried about the ranger. Luckily, he knew a little bit about them. The park wasn't huge, and it wasn't in a dangerous area, so he would be working by himself. The radio jammer would have kept him from calling in his discovery. Luna said he would probably be unconscious for around six to eight hours. That meant either his next shift, or more likely a morning runner, would discover him by the tree. Since he was such a pervert, Sonny felt good knowing he would get into a little trouble. To top things off, even if they looked into the possibility of a van being there, they would find nothing on video.

Sonny thanked Luna for everything she did. She said Johnny referred to him as family, and when Johnny said his family needed help, it was the least she could do. Johnny helped her through some hard times in her life, and now she had her act together. She gladly helped Johnny whenever he asked. Sonny believed she was to Johnny as Johnny was to him.

It was a long ride back. Johnny was there waiting for them. They got out of the cars and Johnny asked Sonny how it went. He gave him the thumbs up. Luna said there was a slight hiccup and they had contact with a park ranger.

It was around 6 a.m. already. Sonny asked Johnny to make a stop for some breakfast. Sonny picked a bagel and a coffee for Maggie. They pulled up in front of the house. They planned to meet up later in the day, around 3 p.m., since Sonny was going to try and get a little sleep before going into work late.

Sonny began to think about why Luna and him had to go through such a charade of fake sex. He guessed a story of watching two people having wild sex would not arise any suspicion like a couple talking in a van. There would have been many more questions if they were just talking in a car. No eye contact with wild sex going on. That was some serious quick thinking on Luna's part. Johnny was right about her.

As Sonny walked into the house, he was greeted by Razor. He noticed the TV was on, so he deducted Maggie fell asleep on the sofa. Yup, there she was, snoring like a pro. She woke up as Razor was barking at him. She immediately smelled the coffee.

She softly said, "Is that for me?"

Sonny laughed and said of course it was for her. She got up and gave him a huge hug. She missed him and was worried about the meet. Sonny said everything went great and he would fill her in with details after her shower. She said OK, and that she was going into work late too, so they had plenty of time to talk. She finished her coffee and asked Sonny to put the bagel away until she got out of the shower. Sonny didn't eat his yet, so they could still enjoy breakfast together.

Sonny took Razor out for a quick walk while Maggie took a shower. He kept thinking about the ranger. He wondered if he did get a good look at them and if the drug was going to act like alcohol. It was assault on an officer, which was dealt with harshly, well harshly for the UST. He couldn't risk getting caught, especially on the first "meet". Like Johnny said, trust Luna.

He got back to the house and Maggie was getting dressed. Sonny warmed up her coffee and the bagels. He didn't know if it was guilt, but when she came into the kitchen, she looked stunning. She looked better than when they got married. He gave her a hug and a kiss and told her she looked great.

She made a face at him and said, "What are you guilty of something?"

He put his head down, and quickly raised it up.

He said, "Yeah, guilty of loving you."

She cracked up and asked if he was practicing his lines for when he went out with the boys. He said he had to practice them somewhere. This is what he would have to deal with, twenty-four hours a day, if he told her about what happened with Luna. This made him feel better that he decided not to tell her.

Before he gave her the details of the night, Sonny wanted to know how the call with the boys finished up. Maggie laughed and said she withheld most of the details. They kept prying for more information, but Maggie maintained her "sponge" stance. She wanted them to see the video when it was done, rather than spoil the fun.

With that out of the way, Sonny went over everything with Maggie, step by step. When he got up to the part with Luna running back to the van, he just said she hid at the front of the van and shot the ranger with a tranquilizer as he approached the door. Then he continued with the real story of what happened.

Maggie was concerned about whether or not the ranger got a good look at either of them, or the fact that it was an assault on a ranger. They stayed silent for a couple of minutes. Maggie said it was out of their hands and hoped for the best. Sonny agreed. He let Maggie know he was meeting Johnny in the afternoon and he should be hearing from Double D any day now. Maggie asked if he thought she should step up her talks with Becky, because she felt like Sonny was doing all of the work.

Sonny said "Come one. This is not a contest. This is for us."

Maggie agreed, but still felt she had to get a hand in this process. They both felt Becky was an ally and wouldn't hurt them, but they had been lucky with who they had been trusting. Sonny felt this luck would run out, and why do that now? Maggie said she could just throw something out there, innocently, like "I wish I could retire now and be with my boys. I wish there was a way to speed up the clock." Sonny was fine with that. Maggie gave him a kiss and went off to work.

It was only 8 a.m. Sonny put on the TV and tried to fall asleep. He could get up at 11 a.m. and still make it into work by noon. He saw Gavin got a little roughed up last night. Four earned runs in six innings was a little high for him. No problem though, because the season was still young and there was plenty of ball to be played. Andrew didn't play last night. It was Round two of the playoffs for him. He had been looking really sharp. He smelled the championship and couldn't wait to take a bite out of it. Razor fell out quickly. He must have been up all night with Maggie.

Suddenly, Sonny heard the alarm on his phone. It was 11 a.m. He decided to take a shower to wake himself up. So, he took a shower, got dressed and took Razor for another quick walk.

He looked at Sonny as to say "I'm sleeping here. Leave me alone."

They literally walked around the house and Razor pulled Sonny to bring him back in.

Sonny made it in before noon. He did his morning ritual and headed out to the streets. No sign of Tracks, which made him feel good. He didn't want to rush over to Johnny's, so he enjoyed the sunny day and took a stroll. About fifteen minutes into his walk, he received a message from the Council. He was asked to report back to the Hub and be in a position to receive a call at 1:30 p.m. He scrambled back to his car and headed for the Hub. He wondered what this was about. Nothing crazy had been going on around there lately. No influx of undesirables, no violence, nothing much going on. Maybe he had his recorder off more than it was on, and they wanted to come in and check out the system. He guessed he would find out soon enough.

He pulled into the lot and ran upstairs. He had just enough time to make a bathroom stop before the call. He finished up and went into the conference room and waited for the call. The video call came in and it was Glen Adams, the brother of Tom Adams from the Finance Council. Sonny never met him before, but he seemed to be upset. After their formal greetings, Glen jumped right into the issue.

Glen said they had an issue with a ranger at the Maryland border last night. Sonny's stomach dropped. His ears began to ring. His legs began to twitch. He could have easily passed out. But somehow, he kept it together. Sonny had to pay attention to what he was saying. Glen continued. A ranger, Dave Edwards, approached a van in a park where a couple was having sex. He attempted to ID the individuals when he was shot in the neck with a tranquilizer gun. They were able to get him to give partial descriptions and rough sketches were made of the suspects. Glen said the reason he was contacting Sonny was because they picked up a transmission made from a secure radio. He said they cannot record or listen to the conversations because of the coding, but they captured the radio identifiers. Glen said the radio was in contact with someone on the other side of the river, West Virginia. Since this was a case of assault on a ranger and possible treason, Glen said this investigation took priority over everything else. Then Glen got down to the reason why he called Sonny. He said when they cross checked the radios used, they found one of the radios was turned on and used in Sonny's area of responsibility about a week ago. Glen said to expect to hear from the park ranger this afternoon. He and a partner would be meeting Sonny tomorrow to start the investigation.

"SHIT!"

Sonny needed some time to think this through. He quickly got his thoughts together and said he got into work late today because he was feeling under the weather, and he wasn't sure if he was going to make it to work tomorrow. Glen said to work it out with the ranger when he called him. Glen hoped Sonny would feel better soon and they would be speaking again soon. What the fuck was Sonny going to do? He couldn't call Maggie and talk about it on the phone. He couldn't call anyone. He had to head over to Johnny's before this ranger called.

He walked into Johnny's and he saw him at one of the card tables. Johnny saw the look on Sonny's face and quickly took him out the back door.

Johnny asked, "What the fuck is the matter? You look terrible."

Sonny took a deep breath and told him about the call he just received. Johnny took it all in and paused for a minute. He said he didn't know they could track the radios, that this is something new they could do. They had to evaluate what they knew so far. They couldn't listen to the call, good. The ranger didn't get a good look at Sonny or Luna, good. Sketches were made, good and/or bad. They didn't know where they picked up the radio usage in the area, bad. They were coming tomorrow, bad. Sonny could call out sick tomorrow without any suspicion, good. Luna didn't go around there, so she probably wouldn't get identified, even with a good sketch, good. On the other hand, Sonny was screwed. They agreed Sonny should be out sick tomorrow and probably the next day, regardless of how the call went with the ranger. Sonny said he would have the ranger send over the sketches he had, this way they could assess the potential of either Luna or Sonny getting identified. Sonny could also have him send over the coordinates they had for the radio activity.

Johnny tried to calm Sonny down by saying, "We will get through this. Shit happens all of the time and we work through it. Let's see what the ranger has and knows, and we will deal with it."

Sonny shook his head in agreement, but he guessed he wasn't truly convincing. Johnny pulled him back inside and said they were having a drink or two, no matter what he thought. Sonny couldn't argue with him on that.

They sat down and had a few drinks. Johnny asked Sonny how it went with Maggie this morning.

He said, "That's one thing you don't have to worry about. I didn't tell her the "Maria" story."

Johnny quickly raised his glass and said, "Amen!"

Johnny said he wouldn't alert Luna until he felt she needed to know, but he would contact Mike to fill him in on what happened and to set up the next call. Sonny asked Johnny about how he contacted Mike and why they couldn't just use that to speak with him. Johnny said he was a registered confidential informant with the CNU. This allowed him to contact Mike, even when he was unavailable. He used a HAM radio to reach him. Of course, Mike wasn't on that radio 24/7, but his office was. He just lets them know he needed to reach Mike and they gave him a time when Mike was on the radio. The good thing about the HAM radio was that you had sixty seconds before the UST could hear and locate you. That's why it was only for a quick contact and why they had to get close to use the secure radios for anything more. Johnny said now that they knew they could track down the secure radios, they needed to know how long it took for the UST to figure out a communication was being made and where its locations were. This could be a game changer and they might need to find new ways to communicate.

They finished their drinks and headed back to work. Sonny asked Johnny to go by his house at around midnight. Sonny figured the ranger wouldn't call too late, so he should have more information before midnight. Johnny said that was fine and he would see him tonight.

Sonny finished up his shift in a daze. He vaguely remembered speaking with a few people and even might have broken up a few disagreements. He hoped he did well, or his reviews would be hell. He called Maggie on his way home and asked how she made out with Becky. She said not bad, and they would talk when they get home. Sonny said he would get home first and asked what she wanted for dinner. She said she felt like take out, so he volunteered to make the pickup. Sonny stopped at restaurant #5, which was Japanese food. He got enough sushi to feed a small army. For some reason he was starving. He got home, set the table and waited for Maggie. She was only five minutes out, so he just kept Razor busy until she got home.

Maggie got home, washed up and they sat down for dinner. She seemed pretty hungry too. They were quickly chowing down on the sushi. They came up for air and laughed. Maggie said she only had a small lunch and she hadn't had sushi in a while. Sonny said he was just hungry, and asked her about how it went with Becky.

When she mentioned she wished there was a way to be with the boys now, Becky nodded her head and said, "There are always ways to get what you want. We'll talk."

Sonny asked Maggie what she thought that meant. Maggie didn't know, but it sounded good. She said Becky made plans for them to meet up at her house over the weekend. At least Maggie had some good news. Maggie asked Sonny what happened today.

He looked at her and said they had problems. She stopped eating and asked him to elaborate. He let her know everything Glen told him, except for the part with Luna.

She shook her head, "What now? What are we going to do?"

Sonny grabbed her hand and went over what he discussed with Johnny. She took it all in and asked when he thought this ranger was going to call. He shrugged his shoulders and said he didn't know, but probably soon. Sonny let her know Johnny was coming over around midnight.

They finished dinner and Maggie said she was going to make a pitcher of sangria, to go with the dessert she bought, a few slices of Brazilian brigadeiro cake. The perfect combination for an alcohol and chocolate induced coma. Probably something Sonny would need to get him through the rest of the night. He turned on the TV and put on one of those backyard makeover shows. He heard Maggie moving around, getting the liquor out of the cabinet. Then the phone rang. It was a number Sonny didn't know, so it had to be his ranger friend, Dave Edwards, from the Chesapeake and Ohio Canal National Historical Park.

Before he answered the phone, he thought about disguising his voice, because he was supposed to be sick. He decided to go with a slight cough and sniffle every so often. Dave introduced himself and said he was happy Sonny was on the case, because he heard all about his experience as an investigator. Sonny asked him to run down the story for him. Dave said he saw a dark colored van enter the secondary entrance to the park, a little before 11 p.m. The park was closed, but he always got people trying to sneak in and party by the river. He parked his car by the lot near the entrance and walked down to the river to look for the van. He worked by himself, since the area was not rated for high crime and there weren't usually any problems. His normal course of action was to call in the van and let the office know he was going down to investigate. But he could not get a signal on his phone, so he made an entry in his log book and he left a voice recording on his phone. As he approached the van near the water, he said he heard the moaning and groaning of people having sex. He left his recorder on his phone on as he got closer to the van. He said the side and back doors were open and he shined his flashlight into the van from the back door. He identified himself and asked what was going on. It was a man and a woman, on a mattress, with champagne and glasses nearby. He asked if they were celebrating something and the man said it was their anniversary. The woman got off of the man and grabbed some sheets to cover up. He asked the gentleman to provide ID, at which time he walked over to the driver's door and the man moved up inside the van, toward the front. He opened the door and sat down in the driver's seat. He called out to the woman by name, Maria, and asked her where her ID was. She said it was upfront as well. The man said it was in the compartment under the armrest. He remembered opening the armrest, and that was it. The next thing he remembered, was waking up under a tree at around 6 a.m.

Sonny asked him if he was OK, and if he got a good luck at the couple. He said except for initially feeling a little woozy, he felt fine now, but he never saw either one of them standing up, so he couldn't provide heights. It was dark and they both knew how a flashlight in the face worked as far as being able to identify someone. He provided enough information for sketches to be made, but he wasn't confident they were all that accurate. Sonny asked if there were any details about the couple that stood out, that might help him identify them, like tattoos, scars, or an accent. Dave said he really didn't get a good look at the woman, only that she had huge breasts. He would be able to identify the man better than "Maria," but even then, he didn't know how good his memory would be. Sonny asked him to send over the sketches and maybe he would recognize one or both of them. He let Dave know he wasn't feeling well and that he would be out from work for the next two days. Dave noticed his coughing and sneezing and asked if he was OK. Sonny said it was probably just a head cold, but that he started feeling worse when he got home. Dave said he would wait until Monday to meet up with him because he wanted to work with the best on this, because he was assaulted and made to look like a fool. He took it very seriously, as it tarnished his reputation. Sonny knew he had to play this one carefully. Dave would send the sketches over shortly and he would call Sonny on Sunday evening to see how he was feeling and to set up a meet time for Monday. Before they finished the call, Sonny asked him if he knew the coordinates for where and when the radio was used. Dave would send that information along with the sketches, and hoped Sonny felt better soon, as he was looking forward to working with him.

Within a minute of hanging up on the call, Sonny received the sketches. Luna's sketch wasn't even close. She had nothing to worry about. He would have been better off giving a description of her chest. The sketch of Sonny was better, but still way off. You know how those sketches were, pretty generic. But when the person was identified, you always say, "Yeah, I can see the resemblance now." Sonny still had to come up with some kind of plan.

Maggie heard Sonny was off of the phone and came back into the living room.

She asked, "So, are you going to keep me waiting all night to tell me how it went?"

He showed her the sketches. She asked if Luna's sketch was accurate. He smiled and said it was way off. He showed her the other sketch.

She said, "Hmm. Pretty simple. Not too close, but it could be you. We have to come up with something."

Maggie quickly punched Sonny in the arm and said, "Stupid. You're going to be off for four days and you already have some stubble. Time to bring back your beard."

He laughed and said, "That's perfect!"

Once or twice a year, the beard made an appearance, usually in the fall or winter. That should be enough to throw him off. Maggie asked him about the radio. Sonny received the coordinates, with the dates and times, but he needed to run them. He said he would have it done in a couple of minutes. Maggie grabbed the sangria and cake from the fridge, and brought it to the living room, where they enjoyed some TV, booze and cake. He ran the coordinates and the radio was turned on four times in the street, a few feet down from Johnny's place. The good news was it wasn't inside Johnny's place, but it was a little too close for comfort. He had to check his video he recorded while working against the dates of the radio activations. Hopefully Johnny's jammers were strong enough to reach outside his place.

The sangria was perfect. She had nailed Sonny's recipe. The cake was out of this world. It had been a while since he had it, so he ate it slowly. Plus, the cake was so dense, eating it too quickly would pound his stomach and send him to the bathroom. As the hours ticked, Razor and Maggie started snoring. It was almost midnight, so Sonny carried Maggie up to bed.

She woke up midway through the trip to the bedroom and said, "Are you doing what I think you're doing?"

He laughed and said to enjoy the ride. She laughed because

she didn't think he was still able to bring in the groceries, let alone pick her up and bring her to bed. She apologized for not being able to stay awake when Johnny came over. Sonny assured her that was fine, that he had it under control. He tucked her in and gave her a kiss. She grabbed him before he could leave and hugged him like there was no tomorrow. She asked Sonny to promise her that everything was going to be fine and they would be together with the boys soon. He promised her he would take care of everything and they would be with them sooner than she thought. Razor jumped into the bed, Sonny left them in the room, and closed the door behind him.

He waited outside, in front of the house, for Johnny to arrive. It was a little cool, but it felt good. In about ten minutes, Johnny pulled up to the house. He parked the car, got out and looked around for Razor.

"Where is he?" he asked.

Sonny laughed and said he was probably snoring in bed with Maggie. Johnny loved Razor and reminded Sonny to let him know if they ever bred him. He asked Johnny if he wanted to go into the house, the yard, or if he wanted to speak there in front of the house. Johnny felt the front of the house was just fine.

They went over the conversation Sonny had with the ranger. He showed him the sketches and gave him the details where the radio got hits. Johnny seemed a little relieved. He agreed Luna should be in the clear. He felt Sonny's sketch wouldn't get him identified, but worried that it was slightly accurate, in a very general way. Sonny let him know what Maggie suggested, and he laughed.

He said, "Leave it up to the women when it comes to appearances. They know best."

He agreed that with a beard, it would be hard for the ranger to recognize Sonny, especially if he wasn't confident about what he saw. When they discussed the radio, Sonny asked Johnny how far his jammers worked on the street. If someone was recording and walked past his place, it would be off for about 500 feet. He said the problem would be if someone was recording and approached from the other side. They would record the front of the car, and then eventually lose signal because they would be within 500 feet of his place. Ronnie usually parked his car around the front. Johnny always told him to park in the back, but Ronnie never listened. Maybe in this case, it was a good thing he didn't listen. Sonny said he would review his video and let him know what he had. Johnny spoke with Mike, and he actually felt this incident with the ranger was a good thing. Mike said if Sonny got him some really good information on the virus, he might be able to accelerate things, because he might be identified for assaulting the ranger. Interesting. Sonny never thought of that. He could control the ranger and make it look like he was getting close to identifying him. Sonny couldn't wait to tell Maggie. He asked Johnny to set up a meet for Friday, and he would get in touch with Double D tomorrow and hopefully, he would have some good information for him. Johnny agreed and said Mike was a little worried about how the UST was catching up with technology. Mike asked Johnny to get Sonny's schedule and if possible, Mike might schedule an in person meet. Johnny said Mike would give him the details when he called him. Sonny thought that worked out fine because he was going to be out of work on Friday. Johnny would reach out to Mike in the morning and get back to Sonny as soon as he spoke with him. Sonny would be home all day, so he could just go straight over after he spoke with Mike. Johnny said that would work out just fine, and he would bring dinner.

"I would usually say no to that, just as a reflex. But if you say you're bring dinner over, I know it will be outstanding. Thank you and I can't wait."

Johnny laughed and said, "I guess you think you know me already. I was bringing hot dogs, but now you put on the pressure."

Sonny locked up the house and went to bed. The conversation wasn't too long, so he felt Maggie might have never really gone back to sleep. Sure enough, she was sitting up at the edge of the bed when Sonny went into the bedroom.

"So, go ahead. What did he say?"

Sonny smiled and said Johnny also felt a little relief to some potentially really bad news.

When Sonny filled Maggie in on what Mike said, she replied, "I never thought of that. That's great news!"

Sonny laughed, "I said the same thing to Johnny."

They hugged, even a little tighter than before. He repeated to Maggie, "Like I said, everything is going to be fine. This is going to happen soon."

Maggie smiled, "I love you and I know you will make this happen."

Sonny got into bed and they comforted each other to sleep.

The next morning, Maggie got up singing, so Sonny knew she slept well. He asked her to keep it down a little because "some of us" hadn't slept as well as she did. She threw some clothes at him and said he wouldn't have a hard time going back to sleep when she had to go to work. Sonny got out of bed and scrambled toward her. She screamed and ran into the bathroom. She tried to lock the door, but he was already there. He pinched her ass and tickled her stomach. She was laughing and screaming, and Razor came flying into the bathroom to join in. Sonny couldn't remember the last time they acted that way in the morning. They had some good days recently, knowing what they were trying to do and making some progress, but nothing to this degree. This was pure fun and happiness. It was the beginning of another day of promise, but this time they had a map. This time it was real. Sonny didn't want to let Maggie go, but they had things to do. At least for a few moments, they were able to enjoy each other. Sonny was looking forward to when this was commonplace again. Maggie kissed him good bye and said she would try and get home early for dinner.

Chapter 14

Sonny tried to stay awake, but he must have been really tired. He passed out on the sofa, with the TV on. Razor hopped up next to him and started snoring too. He had a dream of when the boys were younger, when the moron first became president. The boys must have been twelve and fourteen years old. It was summer day. It was early morning and the boys came running into the bedroom and jumped into his bed. They were excited because they were heading to the Caribbean for vacation. It turned into an all out battle royale, with knees and elbows flying around. They didn't have a care in the world. They were all at peace. Maggie was laughing so hard, with pure joy in her face. Sonny finally pinned Gavin, who was already bigger than he was, and he tapped out. Maggie was having a hard time with Andrew because of his scrappiness.

Sonny let go of Gavin to try and help her, and Gavin yelled "Respawn," and jumped right back in.

Sonny got hit in the head, probably by someone's knee, and it knocked him into another place. He was standing in front of a huge wall.

He could hear his boys yelling, on the other side, "Please come over. We miss you. Please dad. Make it happen. Come over soon."

The wall had no doors or edges. It was smooth. No way to climb it. Plus, it was too tall. Sonny couldn't see how far up it went. Visions of the president signing the separation order began to pop up on the wall.

He said, "From this will be the birth of two great nations, working side by side, regardless of their differences."

Sonny began screaming, "No! Don't do it!" and started pounding on the wall.

The wall opened up and two agents came out and started chasing him. He ran along the wall, as fast as he could, but they eventually caught up to him. They threw him on the ground and one of them hit him in the head with a baton. Sonny woke up and quickly jumped up off of the sofa, scaring the shit out of poor Razor. It was almost noon. He had things to do.

He called Double D. Surprisingly, he answered. After the usual greetings, Sonny asked him about dinner.

"I know you mentioned you wanted to do dinner at your house this week. Are we still on?"

Double D replied, "I have a few things going on today, so we should be good for tomorrow night, if that works for you and Maggie. We have lots to catch up on."

Great. It sounded like he and Double D were on the same page. Sonny said Maggie was clear the rest of the week, so tomorrow worked out just fine.

Double D said to come over any time after 6 p.m., and jokingly said, "Do you need my address?"

Sonny laughed, "I'll give you a dress!"

After the call, Sonny made a quick lunch for himself. As he was making the sandwich, he thought about how he could speak with Johnny without any issues, just in case someone was listening in. He had an idea, so he called Johnny from his work phone. He called his place and asked to speak with him.

Johnny got on the phone and Sonny said, "Hi, Johnny. It's your friendly neighborhood handler."

Johnny quickly asked how he was feeling, since he didn't see him around today. Sonny said he felt OK, but not good enough to go to work. Johnny asked how he could help.

Sonny said, "The last time I was at your place, probably Tuesday, I left my sunglasses on your office table. Did you happen to find them because I would like to get them from you tonight, since I will be doing some sun therapy in my yard tomorrow."

Johnny said, "You know, I did find them. I didn't know who they belonged to, but I figured someone would be coming around asking for them soon. How can I get them to you?"

Sonny said he could meet him at gas station forty-two, which was a quarter mile away from his house. Johnny said that was not a problem and he could meet him there at 8 p.m. Perfect. If anyone was listening in, they would have nothing on them. Why so paranoid all of a sudden? The whole radio intercept thing had him worried. Never the less, he would be meeting with Johnny tonight and Double D tomorrow night.

Sonny figured he should give Maggie a heads up, so he called her and said they had dinner plans tomorrow with Double D at his house. She said that was fine and she would whip up a good dessert to bring over. He asked her how things were going, and she said great. All was good. She would be home early, so maybe they could go out for dinner, nothing fancy. Sonny asked her if the diner would work and she said that was fine. Diner 15 was famous for their burgers and hot dogs. Their shakes were out of this world too. It was an old style 1950s soda shop. It was good, cheap, and quick. Sonny worked out for an hour, showered, and took Razor our for a long walk. It was almost 3 p.m., so Maggie would be home soon. Coming home early to her means around 4 p.m. He had just enough time to finish his walk and get some quiet TV time to catch up on at least one show. He had to shake off that dream.

When Maggie got home, she rushed through the door and said she was going to take a quick shower and change her clothes. Sonny said that was fine and let her know the only thing pressing for time was meeting with Johnny at 8 p.m. Maggie was done in about a half hour, so they had plenty of time. They decided to head to the diner a little early and take a walk around the park, which was across the street. They parked the car and walked through the park. During the car ride there, Sonny tried to keep the conversation light, not mentioning anything about their plans. He just wanted a break from all of that for a little while. During their walk, Maggie asked what was wrong. Of course, she knew something was bothering him. They were together for almost thirty years. Sonny knew she would keep asking all night, so he decided to just tell her about the dream. He explained it to her in detail and let her know how much it bothered him. Maggie believed all dreams were signs of things to come. She said all of it, the boys crying out, the wall and the agents, were just a culmination of everything they were trying to do up to now. They knew the boys wanted to be with them, there was a wall, literally, that prevented them from going to them, the agents connected to the incident with the ranger, and the president was the cause of it all. Now that she laid it all out in front of Sonny, it made sense. He was so glad he didn't hold out on telling her. They sat down by the lake, in silence for a good fifteen minutes, just enjoying the time. It would have been longer if Sonny's stomach hadn't started to make noise.

Maggie said, "Had a light lunch today I guess."

Sonny laughed and said, "Yes, I wasn't too hungry today."

They walked back to the diner and were quickly seated. They

both ordered burgers and shakes. Maggie got fries and Sonny got onion rings. As always, the food was great. They finished up and headed home.

It started to rain when they went into the diner. It slowed down on the way home. By the time they got home, it stopped. When they got out of the car, it smelled like summer time. The wet grass smell, after it gets watered on a sunny day. Sonny asked Maggie if she wanted to take Razor for a walk and enjoy some more peaceful time together. Of course, she wanted to. All she had to do was change into some sneakers. Sonny grabbed Razor while Maggie changed her shoes and they met at the front door. Sonny still had a good half hour before he met with Johnny. They walked a little less than a mile, round trip. All they spoke about was about when the boys were young. Sonny guessed that when he gave her the details of his dream, it must have brought up some old memories. They remembered their vacations and their weekend trips, which were mostly based on the sport at the moment. They went all over the country for baseball and basketball. They usually had a two-week window in the summer, where they had no tournaments. Those were some quickly planned trips that were packed with fun. They usually dragged their favorite cousin, Sam, with them wherever they went. Sam was three years older than Gavin, but he loved to travel with them because he had two older sisters. Sam was like our third son. Our boys looked up to him, and he was a great role model. Sonny was so happy Sam was with their boys and remained an important part in their lives. He was the agent for both of them. He was highly respected and always got requests from other athletes to represent them. But Sam was happy with just two clients. He made plenty of money and had lots of free time to spend with his family. Although Maggie and Sonny were not with their children,

Sonny slept well at night knowing Sam was there. Maggie said she asked the boys to have Sam be on the next call. Sonny was happy she did that. They hadn't seen him for about a year.

They got back to the house, and no sooner than they walked in, Sonny had to leave to meet up with Johnny. He grabbed his keys and got into the car, and a car pulled up to the house. Johnny knew how to read between the lines.

"Great, you saved me a trip," Sonny yelled at Johnny.

Johnny said he knew the drill, a gas station near his house. He said that's all he needed to hear.

Sonny asked him where his glasses were, and he said, "Glasses? We don't need no stinkin' glasses."

Sonny said he lost all respect for him because he said that. They laughed and went inside.

Sonny totally forgot that Johnny said he was bringing over dinner. Whatever was in the bag smelled awfully good. Sonny knew he could force a little more food down. He didn't think Maggie could. He asked Johnny what he brought, and he said it was his wife's famous lasagna, and they were in for a treat. Luckily, Maggie was still in the bedroom. Sonny said she wasn't feeling well, and she probably wouldn't come out, and most probably wouldn't eat. Sonny asked Johnny to bring the food into the kitchen while he checked on Maggie.

Sonny went into the bedroom and said, "I totally forgot that Johnny was bringing dinner. I gave you an out by telling him you didn't feel good. So, I'm thinking you can hang out here for a little bit, then come out to say hi."

Maggie said that was fine but asked what Sonny was going to do.

"I'm taking one for the team!"

Maggie cracked up and Sonny hushed her to keep it down.

"That just means more sit-ups for me tomorrow."

Sonny left Maggie in the bedroom and went out to the kitchen. Johnny already had the table set.

"Why did you do that? This is my house and you're my guest. Please, you're making me feel bad."

Johnny said he didn't mean to upset Sonny, he just wanted to help out. He asked if Maggie was OK, and Sonny said she would try and come out shortly.

Johnny wasn't kidding about the lasagna. Sonny praised him for marrying such a good cook.

"It's amazing you're not four–hundred pounds."

Johnny laughed and said he was worried that would be his future. Razor was circling the table, but he wasn't getting any of that.

Maggie came out before they finished and said, "That smell got me up."

Johnny said there was plenty if she wanted some, but Maggie said her stomach was still upset. She said she was looking forward to having some tomorrow for lunch. Maggie said good night and took Razor to the bedroom with her.

Sonny let Johnny know he spoke with Double D and he would have more information on the virus for him tomorrow night at dinner.

Johnny said, "Great. I'll confirm with Mike that you will talk on Friday night."

Sonny said it would have to be late again because he was getting the information at dinner, and he didn't know where Mike wanted to meet. Johnny said he would come right over to the house tomorrow once he spoke with Mike. He usually heard back from Mike around noon. Sonny suggested he call him around noon tomorrow and thanked him for giving him back his glasses.

If he heard from Mike, they would meet at his place at one p.m.

"All you have to say is you're sorry that you have to cut me off, but you have something to take care of. If not, just go along with the conversation and we'll hang up mutually."

Johnny said, "That's great, but what if I hear from him after 1 p.m.?"

Sonny said, "The earliest I could get away is around 7:30 p.m. Let's say we meet up at your place at 9 p.m., ready to go."

Johnny occasionally mentioned an apartment he had. Sonny just didn't know where it was.

Johnny looked at him and said, "You need the address, don't you?"

Sonny smiled and said he shouldn't worry because he didn't dig around to find out where it was.

"Yes, please give me the address."

Johnny smiled.

"You're on a good run right now. All we have to do is take care of the ranger business, and all is good."

Sonny said, "I hope it's a personal meet. I don't want any more worries about radios."

Johnny laughed and said, "Mike will be on top of that, just like Luna was."

Johnny got up quickly and ran for the door. Sonny chased him out of the house.

He stood in front of his car door, and said, "Sorry, I couldn't resist."

Sonny said he was lucky his bedroom was on the other side of the house.

Again, he said, "Sorry. It was just too easy," and laughed.

Sonny said he would get back at him, someday, somehow. They said goodnight and Johnny left. Sonny went back into the house and put away the lasagna. Maggie screamed out to bring her some water. He poured her a glass and went to the bedroom. She asked how it went, and Sonny told her the plan. She felt good about this, not like last time. She guessed it was because she had "first meet" jitters. When you're an agent, and you have a case where someone was going to cooperate and wear a wire, the first time they meet with your target is very nerve racking. You play it over and over in your head, and you try and think of all possible outcomes of the meet. Then it happens and it's over without a hitch. On the second meet, and most meets after that, you feel less anxious and calm down a little bit.

They laughed and said, "Old habits" and went to sleep.

Maggie was nice to Sonny this morning. She let him sleep. He opened his eyes, she was gone, Razor was still in the bed, snoring, and it was 10 a.m. He hadn't slept like that in ages. He guessed everything caught up to him and he needed a re-boot. Sonny still had a couple of hours before he had to call Johnny, so he just lounged around and played lazy. These days didn't happen often, so he wanted to enjoy a couple of hours of daytime peace. He made a light breakfast and ate outside by the pool. It was a little brisk out, but the sun was out with barely a cloud in the sky. The air was filled with the smell of Maggie's flowers growing in her garden. The smell of re-birth. It's funny how well the environment corrected itself. Sonny decided to jump into the pool and do some laps for his workout. It was heated to about 85 degrees, so he would only get cold when he got out of the water. He swam for about twenty minutes, got out of the pool and ran into the house. Razor, who was watching him do laps, almost tackled him on his way into the house. He was so lucky he didn't get Sonny. They would have had a serious wrestling match and he would have lost his biscuit privileges.

It was noon, so Sonny grabbed his phone and called Johnny. Johnny picked up the phone and sounded very professional. He knew it was Sonny.

"It's Sonny. Thank you for returning my glasses."

Johnny said he was glad to get them back to their rightful owner, and then cut Sonny off because he was taking care of something. That was the cue. They were on for 1 p.m. at his place. Sonny hurried up, took a shower, and got dressed. He grabbed a snack and a water from the cabinet and off he went. He was across the street from the building and waited for Johnny to arrive. There wasn't a lot of foot traffic on this street. It was pretty quiet. Sonny guessed that was why Johnny picked this location. It was easy to see if you were being followed. Within five minutes of Sonny parking on the street, Johnny showed up. He got out of his car, looked right at Sonny and went inside. Sonny waited a couple of minutes, then got out and went inside.

Sonny didn't know how Johnny did it, but when he went into the apartment, there was a huge table of food waiting there to be eaten. Cold cuts, fresh bread, salads, olives, spreads, it was all there.

Sonny laughed and said, "Johnny, you're just like my mother, always with the food. I must have put on ten pounds since we started meeting up."

Johnny laughed and said he promised to lighten up the meals from now on. They made some sandwiches and Johnny asked about Maggie, and if she was feeling better this morning.

Sonny said, "She was good enough to go to work. She only takes days off when she needs a mental recovery. She always goes to work when she's sick."

Johnny said that sounded like his wife, when she was still working. Johnny then began to talk about the meet.

He said, "Mike will meet you tonight in Philadelphia, at the Wyndham Philadelphia Historic District Hotel at midnight. That gives you plenty of time to get there. He will be in room 821 and waiting for you to reach out to him once you arrive. Make a reservation using the license I gave you and pay in cash. Don't use a credit card for incidentals. Leave them $500 cash for that. When you are ready to leave the house, call this number (Johnny handed Sonny a piece of paper) and I'll answer like you called a restaurant. You reply that you were sorry, it was a wrong number. Then give me ten minutes to meet you at the same gas station, and I'll give you a car to take. I will also give you a burner phone in case of an emergency."

Sonny liked this plan so much better than the original meet. Johnny said Mike was familiar with that hotel and the area. He felt it was a safe location for a meet like this. People were always coming and going, so no one would notice either of them. Fine. That's settled. Sonny asked Johnny if anything was new on the streets, specifically, any new faces. Johnny said nothing new or strange was going on. Sonny's sub, Will, was doing what he always did, stay out of people's way and goes home without a scratch. Sonny made an extra sandwich to take home with him.

Johnny laughed and said, "Good stuff, huh?"

It was the bread. It's always the bread that makes a good sandwich. Sonny rolled his eyes, packed the sandwich and headed for the door. Johnny wished him luck and said to let him know how it went. Sonny asked him if it could wait until Monday, or if he wanted to swing by Saturday afternoon. Johnny said Monday was fine. He wanted to give them a little more recovery time from the party.

"How old do you think I am?" Sonny asked Johnny.

He smiled and said, "Old enough with that gray beard. You

177

might want to do something about that."

Sonny gave him the finger and left.

When Sonny got home, he was surprised to see Maggie was there. He walked into the house and called out her name. She came to the door and said she had "spring fever" and needed to leave work. They laughed. Sonny asked her about Becky. She said they were going to meet tomorrow at Becky's house for a day of fun. Sonny mentioned he had to leave around 9:30 p.m. for Philly, where he was going to meet up with Mike, which gave them plenty of time to have some fun with Double D at his house. Maggie was happy about that and went to the kitchen to finish making desert.

Maggie finished making her world famous chocolate chip cookies and they were ready to go. Traffic was light, so they got to Double D's house quickly, arriving right at 6 p.m. They hadn't been to the house for a while. It looked really good. New siding, freshly paved driveway, and colorful flowers around the front yard. Sonny felt he had to give Double D some shit about that. They pulled into the driveway, and Double D came out to greet them.

Sonny got out of the car, held his arms opened wide and yelled, "I have to give Sara a big kiss. She finally domesticated you."

Sonny heard Sara scream from inside the house "Damn right! It only took me twenty years," and she made her way outside.

They all said "Group hug" as they ran to each other.

Sonny really missed them. They were great people. They couldn't get the time back, but Sonny wanted to make the best of what they had left.

Maggie handed Sara the box of cookies, and Sara said,

"Yummy. These are still warm."

They went inside and Sonny noticed they didn't have a dog. He asked why and Double D said it was getting too hard when they died. He made a promise with Sara never to go through that again. So as much as it pained him not to have a dog, it wasn't as bad as saying goodbye. Sonny understood. He didn't ever want to think about how old Razor was getting. As far as he was concerned, he was his forever dog.

Maggie went with Sara into the kitchen to help her get dinner onto the table. Sonny went with Double D and grabbed some beer and wine for the table. They made pasta with alfredo sauce, eggplant rollatini, clams oreganata and garlic bread. It smelled good. Double D said grace before they ate. It had been a long time since they did that. It made Maggie happy. They went through the bread and clams really fast. They were all hungry. Maggie asked Sara about Paul and Chrissy. Sara said they wanted to come over and have dinner with them, but they felt the four of them should re-connect on their own before they cut in. Maggie felt that was nonsense, she saw them grow up and would have loved to see them. Sara said Chrissy loved her job. Sara always knew Chrissy would grow up to be a person who helped others. They were very proud of her. All Paul cared about was his family. He used to go to work and be all into it. After the birth of his kids, all he wanted to do was spend time with them all. He always took four vacations a year. Every minute he could, he was with them. They always vacationed together at least once a year, depending on everyone's schedule.

Double D waited for a lull in the conversation, then said it was time to get down to business. Double D put a binder together for them. It detailed the virus and everything they knew about it so far. It definitely was going to be a problem. It spread fast and easy. The good thing was it knocked you on your ass for a week, but it wasn't deadly. Only in very rare cases, less than .01 percent, did they see anyone die. There was no vaccine, but they did have a treatment, which made the symptoms less severe. The people on top who were making the call on this had been keeping it quiet for a few months. If all of this information got to the CNU and the rest of the world, the UST would be in a world of trouble. They had done a great job at keeping it quiet because the patients just think it was the flu. It was slowly making its way east.

Sonny said he had a meet at midnight in Philadelphia and asked Double D if he should be concerned about getting the virus. Double D said he should be fine. The locations of the cases were mostly in very rural areas. The people there didn't travel to the cities often.

That made Sonny feel better, but of course, Double D had to add a little more and said, "Besides, even if you got it, no one would know because you're already a lazy ass who complains too much."

He got a good laugh from the rest of the table. Sonny said the first thing he was going to do after his trip was to head to his house, hide in the bushes and wait for him to come out. Then he would jump on him, cough in his mouth and lick his face.

Double D said, "Stop it, you're turning me on."

Again, big laughs from the table. Sonny couldn't win with this guy.

"You're gonna pay for this," was Sonny's reply, as he waved his hands at him in anger.

They finished up with dinner and Sara brought out the cookies. Maggie and Sonny forgot to bring ice cream, but luckily, they had some. Double D went to his bedroom and got the binder. It contained lots of information on the virus. Sonny asked Double

D if this was in any way going to trace back to him, because he didn't want his name coming out as tied to something illegal. Double D said he lucked out because he picked this up from the printer. Someone printed it all out earlier in the day, and it was left on the printer for hours. He grabbed it from the printer when he left for the day. He didn't print it out, so it wouldn't come back to him. Double D briefly explained all of the recent finds and updates on the virus. It was mostly medical and scientific findings. The biggest issue was still not informing the CNU. This evidence just proved how long they knew about it and what they were doing about it.

Double D brought out the dominos and asked if they had time for a game. It was only 8 p.m., but the domino games lasted for hours.

Sonny suggested they play some poker instead, and of course, Double D jumped on that and said, "Poke-her? You keep what you do in your own house to yourself."

He got a punch for that. Sara must have heard Sonny, so she brought out the cards. Double D said he would go and grab some more wine from his cellar and Maggie said she would join him to make sure he picks the right bottle. Sara and Sonny had a small conversation about the plan. She was one hundred percent in their corner and she hoped everything went smoothly. Her and Double D would do anything to help them. Sonny knew that he could count on them. They hugged and Sara said all Double D did when he got home was discuss options for them to leave. Sonny loved that guy. A heart of gold beat in his chest.

Maggie and Double D came back with a great bottle of wine. Double D said Maggie knew a lot about wine and even had a keener eye to spot bottles that he had hiding in the cellar. They all sat down, had some wine and played some poker. It was just like old times. Hanging with people that knew how to have fun and when to turn it off. God, Sonny missed them.

The wine was flowing, the laughs were plentiful, and the game was out of control. The ladies, as usual, came up with a way to cheat the guys. It always took them a few hands to realize it, but the guys figured it out. Then accusations were made, lots of denials go flying around the table, then after all excuses were ruled out, the room was just filled with laughter. It was getting late, and Sonny had to head to Philly. Sonny said he would reach out to Double D tomorrow, after he got back. Double D said he would be home all day, so to just call him and tell him he was coming over. Sara would be out all day, so it would just be the two of them. Perfect. Maggie was going to be out with Becky, so at least Sonny had someone to hang out with.

Maggie and Sonny headed home and Sonny let Maggie out of the car to go into the house. He called the number Johnny gave him and it went as planned. Sonny went into the house and grabbed the bag he made with a set of clothes and stuff he would need for the night. Sonny said he would head back home around 11 a.m., then stop by Double D's house. Maggie would call Sonny and let him know when she left to go to Becky's house, which should be around 10 a.m. Sonny turned off his phone because he didn't want it to get pinged around the Philly area. She said she understood.

They kissed and exchanged, "I love you" as they embraced.

Maggie said to be careful and get home safe. Sonny smiled and said he felt like he was heading off to college. She gave him a slight slap in the cheek and said she was being serious.

Sonny said, "I know," and grabbed her even harder.

He pet Razor as he left the house, and headed for the gas station.

Sonny got to the gas station and Johnny was already there waiting for him. He was in a late model sedan, black with four doors. Perfect "under the radar" car. He gave Sonny the burner phone and wished him luck.

Johnny paused and said, "Oh, I almost forgot," handed me a condom, then took it back and said, "Sorry, you won't need it for this trip."

Sonny's response was quick and harsh. "You piece of shit!"

Johnny was cracking up. He said, "It was way too easy. I couldn't help myself."

Sonny said, "You'll help yourself right to a black eye if you keep messing with me like that. You know that's a sensitive topic."

Johnny quickly responded, "Sensitive, or do you mean touchy?" as he quickly ran toward Sonny's car.

"You son of a bitch. I'll get you back," was all Sonny could say.

Why did everyone feel they had to mess with Sonny? As Johnny pulled away in Sonny's car, he said Sonny should call him when he was twenty minutes out from the gas station, so he could meet him, and they could switch the cars. Sonny nodded in agreement and he wished him luck.

Sonny felt so relieved this was a one on one meet. He felt so much better knowing who he was speaking with. As he had learned, body language meant so much when you're speaking with someone. He got so good over the years that the new agents used to refer to him as the human polygraph machine. He would know if Mike was holding something back, or if he was not being one hundred percent truthful with him. As good as Luna was controlling the situation, Sonny liked to control things. It was just his nature. Now that he had a burner, he called the hotel for a room. He knew he shouldn't have waited so long, and should have reserved a room earlier, but he didn't want to use any known phones. It was Friday, but he didn't think a hotel in Philly was a hotspot for weekend warriors in the spring. He called the front desk and luckily enough, they had a room. Thank God he got a room. He listened mostly to Green Day on the drive down. The drive went quick. It was a busy area, but not too busy. Mike made a good call on this spot.

Sonny parked the car in the lot and went into the lobby. It was almost midnight, but there were a lot of people at the bar area. He checked in and got his room. It was on the 7th floor, so not so far from Mike. He went into his room, relieved himself and washed up. It was time to meet up with Mike. Sonny grabbed the binder, went to his room and knocked on the door.

The person inside asked who it was, and Sonny said, "Giancarlo sent me."

It wasn't planned that way, but Sonny knew he would know it was him if he said that. Sure enough, he opened the door and let Sonny in.

He asked Sonny how the drive was and if he ran into any problems, like being followed. Sonny said everything was fine, and he complemented him on the choice of hotels. Mike went there frequently, and knew everyone kept to themselves. There was a revolving door of employees there too, so no one remembers him. They sat at a table and Sonny gave him the binder.

"Wow, this seems to be a lot of information," was his response as he looked through the pages.

Sonny repeated to him what Double D said about the virus. Mike stared at Sonny and said this was a really big deal. Mike looked and asked around at work, and found out this information on the virus, together with the fact that Sonny might be discovered, could fast track things and get him over quickly. Sonny had to fight back tears of joy.

The big break they needed came in the form of a cover up by the government. Things never change. Had the UST now taken on the worst traits of the CNU, and therefore becoming more like them? Was there a difference between the two sides anymore? Of course, there were still major differences, especially with equality and certain civil rights issues, but they operated in the same ways. Cover up things that could hurt you and always look out for themselves. This, together with the information Sonny received from Tracks, proved to him that the country only divided for the greater good of those on top. They made the decisions, and profited from them. The leaders on both sides lived better than the average person, and had more than the average person. At least the CNU didn't try and hide this fact. They believed in "the strong shall survive and rise to the top." The UST claimed they were "equality for all," but current events proved differently.

Mike asked if this binder would identify anyone who helped get the information. Sonny said it was printed out by someone other than the person who gave him the binder. That was enough detail to give him about the transaction. Mike would get right on this and get it to his superiors. Things from there on would move quickly. He suggested that Maggie and Sonny begin to get things in order and think about what they wanted to take with them when they moved to the CNU. They would have to travel light, so he advised they took only things that would fit in a backpack. He was sure they could give other things of importance to Johnny to hold onto and ultimately get back over to them. Mike asked Sonny to have Johnny reach out to him on Sunday at 2 p.m., so he could setup another meet with Sonny. His best guess was that they would meet up again on Wednesday, somewhere around this area. He wanted to give himself some time to get things moving on his side, and for Sonny to figure out how close the UST was to discovering who was involved with the incident with the ranger.

Mike said to try and get updated information on the virus. Before the CNU would confront the UST with their knowledge of the virus, they would like to have as much information as possible. They wanted to show the UST was far along in the stages of identifying and diagnosing the virus and they still hadn't exposed its existence to the CNU and the world. The CNU would probably try and discredit the UST as a nation, therefore strengthening the possibility of a takeover of the UST by the CNU. They would try and get backing from the rest of the world, and most of the population of the UST, through a propaganda campaign. The CNU would only do this without the need of force, or so they claim. At no time did Mike seem to be deceitful. Sonny said he would make sure Johnny reached out to him on Sunday. Mike thanked Sonny for the information and said this was going to work out in his favor. Sonny went back to his room. He was so anxious to speak with Maggie or Double D or Mike, but he couldn't call them. He couldn't call anyone. He didn't think he would be able to sleep without a drink. His only option was the mini bar for $10 shots of vodka and rum. Luckily, they had a small bottle of tequila. That should do the trick. He took two shots. The bottle held more than he thought. He put on the TV, and quickly fell asleep.

Sonny got up at around 10 a.m. Checkout was 11 a.m., so he took a shower, got dressed and got on the road. He felt so good. Last night was a complete success. No issues. A roadmap was laid out for their escape. He wanted to blast the music and roll down all of the windows. The only problem was the heavy rain. He settled for playing moderately loud house music with the A/C on. Not the same, but it worked. He was flying on the highway. He needed to slow down a little. He didn't want to get stopped in this car. When he was about a half hour out, Sonny called Johnny.

The conversation was Sonny saying, "Half" and Johnny grunting, "Got it."

He wondered if he woke Johnny up. Sonny got to the gas station and Johnny was there waiting for him.

Johnny asked, "How did it go?"

Sonny gave Johnny a play by play on everything he discussed with Mike.

Johnny smiled and said, "I hooked you up good, didn't I?" and gave Sonny a hug.

Johnny said he would make sure to call Mike on Sunday. He also asked Sonny what his plan was for dealing with the ranger. Sonny had to review video at the HUB to see if anything was captured at the times the radio was powered on. Johnny asked about what if the ranger recognized him.

Sonny rubbed his beard and said, "Maggie is going to make sure this is the right color. I have no worries."

Johnny laughed and said he liked his confidence and he felt the same way. Johnny didn't think they had to worry about the ranger. Sonny said he would go right to his place first thing on Monday when he got to work. They switched cars and drove off.

Sonny gave Double D a call to let him know he was heading his way. Double D said he had the drinks on ice waiting for him. Next, Sonny called Maggie. She picked up and quickly said she was with the ladies and asked how it went. Sonny knew that was code for keep it short and brief.

All he said was, "As good as we could have wanted it to."

Maggie said, "That's good news. I should be heading home right after dinner, around 8 p.m. I'll call you from the car. Love you."

"Love you too, be careful."

By the time Sonny got to Double Ds house, he was starving. He pulled into his driveway and knocked on the front door.

Double D yelled, "Come in. It's open."

Sonny walked in and Double D had full disco lights flashing around the house. Within seconds, the music got cranked up.

Double D was yelling, "Party time!" from the back of the house.

This guy was ridiculous. Never a dull moment. Sonny walked to the back of the house, toward the living room, and Double D charged at him, in a grass skirt, oversized glasses and a sombrero.

He handed Sonny a beer and sang, "Y'all want this party started right? Y'all want this party started quickly, right?"

Sonny couldn't stop laughing. Double D was wearing a Mexican hat, a Hawaiian skirt and giving Sonny an Irish beer. Only Double D could pull this off. They sat in front of the TV and Double D lowered the music and took off his glasses.

He asked, "Seriously now, how did it go?"

Sonny gave him all of the details.

He started smiling and said, "Is it me, or is this the exit plan happening soon?"

Sonny said he didn't want to get too optimistic, but it sounded great. Double D liked the fact that Mike didn't want to get anyone involved.

He said, "I know you wouldn't give me up, but it's good to hear Mike doesn't want to either."

Double D promised to get Sonny more information on the virus as soon as he could. Sonny explained to Double D how the communication worked with Mike, and that he would reach out to him when he had the next meet date with Mike, which should be Monday. Double D said new information on the virus came out every day, so he should at least have something for Sonny whenever the meet was going to happen.

With business out of the way, it was time to have fun. There was a good fight card on, so that took care of the night's entertainment, or so Sonny thought. They drank beer, they ate wings and they laughed. At around 5:30 p.m., Double D said they needed to get ready. For an instant, Sonny got worried. But he had such a good buzz going that the "worry" in him just flew out of the window.

Sonny said, "Okay, I'll bite. Ready for what?"

Double D said, "For the ladies. We're getting in-house massages."

"Great!" Sonny thought to himself. "Just make me feel more guilty."

Double D said, "Don't worry. They are legit. It will be the best massage you've ever had. Sara ordered one for me on my birthday. She stayed, watched and laughed her ass off. The ladies make it fun, but it's totally innocent. No rub and tug. I promise."

Sonny practically spit the beer out of his mouth. Double D fell over the sofa and landed on his face. As he hit the floor, he farted really loud. Sonny screamed so loud that it became silent because he didn't have any more air in his lungs. Sonny's stomach hurt. His face hurt. He couldn't remember the last time he laughed so hard. Double D was the best. Still a couple of college boys at heart. It looked like they would never change.

The doorbell rang as if they queued it up. It was two twenty-something year old blondes with dark tans and huge breasts. Just as Sonny had imagined.

They said, "Hey, we're looking for a couple of guys that want to have a good time. May we come in?"

Double D came dashing out of his bedroom and had a shit eating grin on his face.

He said, "Right this way, ladies. We will pull out the tables for you. We would like to have it done in the room next to the where the TV is. Enjoy some wings and beer while we get set."

Sonny went with Double D to the back room so they could grab the massage tables. Double D had nothing to say. All he did was raise and lower his eyebrows like a circus clown, while making *boing* noises. Classic Double D.

Sonny said, "Don't think for a second that I forgot what you said. You're going to get a whoopin'."

Double D said he didn't care what happened to him in the future. He was only thinking about now.

They set up the tables and the girls started stretching. Bending over in front of them, but making sure to turn around every five stretches so they could get front and back views. Sonny started thinking. Just a few hours ago, he was focused on a dangerous plan to have him and his wife commit acts of treason against the UST in order to be with the rest of their family in the CNU. How did he get here?? He blamed himself, but it was Double Ds fault. But even if he was lying about Sara getting him this service for his birthday, there was no way Double D would disrespect his family in his house. Sonny decided he would just enjoy the show and the massage, so he asked the girls to help stretch him out.

Double D screamed out, "Me too! Me too!"

Now all four of them were on the floor like they were playing a game of Twister. They got Sonny and Double D on their stomachs, mounted their backs, and rode them like horses. Double D got up on all fours and gave his girl a ride around the house.

She screamed out, "Go horsey, go!" as they left the room.

Sonny turned his head and said to the girl on his back, "If you're going to spend some time here with us, especially on my back, I think it would be nice to know your name."

She said, "Just call me Daisy, short for Daisy Dukes" as she got off of his back, turned around and shook her ass in his face.

Sonny asked Daisy if they could start the massage because his body was hurting.

She said, "Sure, no problem. What happened, not having fun, or did I wear you out already?"

He smiled and said, "No, really. My whole body hurts and I hear you ladies have the best hands."

Daisy asked Sonny to take off his shirt and get under the blanket on the table. She said it was up to him if he wanted to take off his shorts or to keep them on. She promised, either way, she would behave herself. He decided to remain in his underwear. That's the way he had couple massages with Maggie, so this way he wouldn't get in any trouble for that.

Daisy asked Sonny which area she should concentrate on, and he said to act as if he fell off a roof.

"Gotcha!" she said.

She started on his head, neck and shoulders. She was good. As Sonny started to relax, in came Double D, still giving his girl a ride. He said he was ready for his rubdown.

He asked Sonny how he was feeling, and he said, "All I ask of you is to be silent. Give me an hour of peace."

Double D laughed and said, "You know that can't ever

happen."

Sonny replied, "I know, but I had to ask."

Daisy said to her partner, "Juicy, you have a big mouth on your table."

Juicy said, "You're a bad boy. I'm going to make you pay for that."

Double D said, "Please, make me pay."

Sonny laughed and tried to get back to his peaceful place. Daisy worked her way down his back, to his waist area. He started feeling really good and relaxed. Sonny felt he might have to get them to go over his house for a tame couple's massage. Surprisingly, Sonny was able to stay in his relaxed zone, even though there was a lot of giggling and whispering going on at Double Ds table.

Sonny heard things like, "Where have you been all my life?" "I'd like to marry your hands," and "I'm like the anti M&M, I melt in your hands."

What a character.

Daisy finished up on Sonny's thighs and calves and said "All done. Just lie there for a few minutes and relax."

Sonny answered, "That was one of the best massages I ever had. I need your card."

She handed Sonny her business card. "Best Massage Therapy and More" was the name of the company. Sonny looked over at Double Ds table and Juicy was straddled on his back, rubbing his shoulder with her hands and rubbing her chest on his back as she motioned up and down, from his shoulder to his lower back.

Double D said, "Where did you get the massage balloons from? I didn't see you with them when you came in."

Juicy laughed and said, "You are a bad boy."

Sonny didn't want to get up off the table, but he had to get his wallet so he could tip Daisy. He went into Double Ds bedroom and grabbed his wallet. He gave Daisy $60.

She said, "Thank you so much. If you're going to call me, I have most weekdays free. Fridays and weekends are tough."

Sonny said that was fine because it would be a couple's massage as part of a day of fun with his wife, so a weekday worked. Juicy finished up with Double D and went to the bathroom with Daisy. Sonny asked Double D what he owed him.

He said, "Absolutely nothing. You can't put a price on what we just went through. War I tell you; it was war!"

He's a nut. The girls came back in and he tipped Juicy. They asked if they had a good time.

Sonny said, "You were great. I had a lot of fun. Thank you so much."

Double D added, "From the moment I saw the both of you, I knew greatness was flowing through your veins. You will be repeat guests in this house."

They gathered their things, and left.

Double D said he had a lot of space in a storage place he rented and if Maggie and Sonny needed to keep some of their stuff there, he said he could make it happen. Sonny thanked him, but he let him know he wanted to keep him out of this as much as possible. Once they left, Sonny was sure a search of their house will be done. If it was completely empty, they were going to seek out who had the stuff and why. Double D agreed but said he could take some small items and keep them safe. Sonny said they would talk when the time came.

Now that Sonny reconnected with Double D, it was going to be hard to leave him. The only good thing was he was in good standing with the UST because of his status as a doctor, so he could travel freely. They would be able to meet up a few times a year. Sonny couldn't wait to tell Maggie how everything went today. He was sure she was going to be really curious about the "party". Sonny let himself get setup again. He would not hear the end of it.

Sonny got home and took care of Razor. During their walk, Maggie called and said she was on her way. He said OK, and that he was walking Razor.

She replied, "Oh, you can still walk? Feeling good? Relaxed?" and snorted like a pig.

Sonny laughed and said, "Just you wait until you get home."

She laughed and said she would be home at around 8:15 p.m. Sonny had a few minutes to spare, so he planned a little something for her.

She pulled up to the house at 8:10 p.m. and quickly went into the house. She was greeted to the smell of incense and candles all around the house.

She laughed and said, "Where are you?"

She walked into the living room and there he was, in a satin robe and slippers, with a pipe in his mouth as he watched Gaia TV. She almost fell to the floor laughing.

She finally got some words out and said, "So it changed your life so much you're into yoga? And where did you get a pipe?"

Sonny started laughing and said he got the pipe from their costume locker in the basement. It was part of something one of them wore at one time. She ran to Sonny and gave him a huge hug. They started making out like teenagers, and one thing led to another. Before Sonny knew it, they were in the bedroom getting busy! Maggie smiled and said if she would have known he would react like this, she would send him out to party with Double D every day. They laughed, giggled, huffed, puffed, sweat, and moaned. It was the best five minutes they had in a long time. They were in good shape for their age, but this was a major workout. They stayed next to each other, holding hands, for another five minutes. In between their heavy panting and breathing, there were plenty of laughs.

"How old are you?" "Who are you?" and "What's your number?" were a few of the exchanges they had.

Sonny pulled Maggie over to him and they gave each other a soft, love felt kiss on the lips.

Maggie softly said, "I miss that guy," and jumped off of the bed, smiling.

Sonny asked, "What does that mean?"

She said all she meant was why was it she couldn't remember the last time they enjoyed each other like that. She missed it.

Maggie went to the door, where Razor had been scratching and barking for the last half hour, and let him in. Maggie went into the bathroom, and Razor jumped on the bed. Sonny chased him off and kicked him out of the room again.

Sonny joined Maggie in the bathroom for a shower. He asked her how it went with Becky and she said Becky told her she knew people who facilitated trips to the CNU, but she didn't know if that could help them out. Maggie pretended like it wasn't a big deal and asked if Becky could find out more information, because maybe all she needed was some time with the family to make her feel better. Becky said she would ask and let her know. Sonny thought that wasn't bad, but it didn't even come close to what he learned from Mike.

Sonny hugged her and said, "We need to have a bag ready in case we have to go quickly. He said we needed to travel light, so only to take a backpack with us."

They were wasting gallons of water and were beginning to look like prunes, so they got out of the shower and got dressed for bed.

Maggie said, "I guess we wouldn't need to bring clothes, towels, toiletries or things like that. I would just probably pack things that meant something to me. What would happen to everything else we left behind?"

Sonny said, "Between Johnny and Double D, we can have them take things we couldn't carry with us, and eventually get them over to us. Of course, that means no furniture, clothes, electronics, and other things that can be re-purchased."

Maggie said that was fine. Between her jewelry and a few small keepsakes, she could fill a backpack. Sonny reminded her that he digitized all of their photos and videos, and he would take about four hard drives with him along with a few other things. She felt good about that. They changed the bedsheets before they let Razor back in. He jumped back into the bed and crawled his way between the two of them. Sonny believed Maggie fell asleep first, but Razor was a very close second. It took Sonny a while to fall asleep. He was relaxed, but anxious. There were still many unknowns about how this would play out. He needed to know everything before he could run through it for potential problems.

Sonny woke up around 10 a.m. Maggie and Razor were both gone. He went into the kitchen and saw through the window that Maggie was in the yard with Razor. They were at the table and Maggie had coffee and food. He looked in the microwave and a plate of ham and eggs was waiting for him to heat up. He gave it thirty seconds, grabbed a glass of OJ and met Maggie outside.

He received a sarcastic "Good morning to you, sleepy. How are you feeling? You had a *big* day yesterday."

Sonny smiled and said, "What about you Miss Bendy, or

should it be Miss Flexy-pants?"

They both laughed and Maggie said, "I didn't think I could get my leg up that high anymore."

They laughed and giggled all through breakfast. Sonny felt the move was giving them new life too. Like a second wind. Sonny felt that knowing no matter how bad the circumstances were, they would be together as a family and feel invincible. Maggie wanted to know when Sonny was going to speak with Johnny about the call with Mike. Sonny said he would find out when he got back to work.

She said, "That's right. You already told me that. I forgot. I'm just excited and I don't want to wait until tomorrow."

Sonny reminded her he would be hearing from the ranger tonight about meeting up tomorrow, and he needed her skills to work on his beard.

She laughed and said, "How could I forget that? I think that will be the highlight of my weekend. Get it, highlight?"

Sonny gave her a really sarcastic, "I bet you can't wait."

She quickly got up and put her dishes away. She said to give her a minute and to meet her in the bathroom. This was going to be fun.

Sonny cleared the tables, wiped them down, put away the dishes, and headed for the bathroom. He opened the door and what did he see? Maggie painted a handle bar mustache on her face and had clippers, scissors, and combs laid out on the sink. She also had a big smile on her face.

She said, "You'll see. I'm going to make you look ten years younger."

He said, "I'm not settling for anything less than eleven years."

Maggie said to knock it off and to let her get to work. She

already had the "magic stuff" mixed and ready to go. Sonny had helped her hundreds of times with hiding her grays in between trips to the salon, so he knew what to expect. She used a small comb to get the "stuff" onto his beard. His mustache was still dark, so thankfully they didn't have to mess with that. It literally took about two minutes, and she was done. She kept staring at Sonny's hair, then looked at his eyes, then stared at his hair and looked at his face.

"Can I? It will look natural. I promise."

Sonny laughed and said, "If I don't like it, I'm going to shave my head, so go for it."

She mixed up some more dye and said this one only lasted for four or five washes, so he wouldn't have to shave his head if he didn't like it.

This took a little longer. She used brushes, combs, and lathered it in with her hands. After she was done, she said he had to wait twenty minutes, then he had to rinse everything off with water only. Sonny said he would just rinse off in the shower because it would be a lot easier. She said to make sure he wore shorts or something because he didn't want to get anything on his under regions. He asked why and she shot him a look.

Sonny said, "Forget it. I understand."

He sat there for twenty minutes, grabbed an old pair of shorts, and went into the shower to rinse off. When he was done, he wiped down the mirror and took a look. Wow! Not ten or eleven years younger, more like fifteen. He should have listened to her and done this years ago. It was natural looking, not too dark all at once. He thought as time went on, he could make it a little darker.

Maggie heard the shower go off and asked, "So, how is it? Do you like it? Come out already!"

"Ok, here I come."

Sonny opened the bathroom door and stepped out.

Maggie's jaw dropped and she screamed, "I knew it! I told you it would look natural. My God, you look great. I might have to wash it out or not let you out of the house."

Sonny laughed and said, "Of course, you wouldn't want me to look good when I left the house."

They both laughed and Maggie said, "Seriously, it looks great. Do you like it?"

Sonny said, "Yes. It looks natural."

Maggie looked at him and smiled and asked if he had something to say to her. He asked her what she could possibly mean. She said that he knew what to say.

He frowned and said, "Fine. I should have listened to you and done this years ago."

Maggie ran to Sonny and gave him a hug. She suggested they head out for the day, since it stopped raining and the sun came out. Sonny said that was fine and asked her where she wanted to go. She wanted to just drive south, near the shore line, and stop when they wanted to. That sounded like a good plan. They packed some food, got dressed and headed out to the road.

They put on some old summer music from the early '90s and drove down I-95. They sang and re-told old stories from when they first met and started dating. Most of the time, Maggie was running her fingers through Sonny's hair.

Every so often, he would get a "You look good, too good" or "I'm so talented. Look what I did for you."

Sonny didn't know how it was her moment, but he let her have it anyway. Every few minutes, a song would come on that reminded them of certain bars or clubs, and even vacations. They spoke about trips to Mexico and Puerto Rico, and places like

Rascals and Webster Hall. They may have met later in life, when they were around twenty-six years old, but they had a jam-packed history of good times together. They were not high school sweethearts. They didn't meet at camp. They met as young adults, just as they were "coming into their own." Sonny knew it was the perfect time. They dated different people, then met, so they knew what they were looking for in a partner. It all worked out great.

They drove a few hours and stopped at Dewey Beach in Delaware. Neither of them had been there before, so it was a good idea to stop there. It had a Jersey shore feel to it, but it was a nicer beach. It wasn't crowded, but there were people on the beach. Some of them had dogs and they felt guilty they didn't bring Razor. Then again, he would have been going nuts in the car. He's never been on a long ride before. They laid out the blanket and relaxed on the sand as they ate a lite "dunch." After they ate, they walked down to the water. They dipped their toes in and quickly took them out. It was freezing. It was a beautiful color blue, but freezing. Sonny missed the Caribbean. They walked up and down the beach for about forty-five minutes. They got back to their blanket, packed up, got in the car and headed home. Maggie immediately fell asleep. Sonny put on some soft music, but it wasn't enough to drown out the sound of Maggie's snoring. At one point, it got so loud and in a pattern that Sonny pulled over and recorded some video of her sleeping. The boys were going to love this. They got home and Sonny woke Maggie up after they pulled into the driveway.

She looked up and said, "We're home already?"

Sonny laughed and said, "You've been out for hours. Please wipe the drool off of you face before you get out."

She shook her head and wiped her face.

She said, "You probably recorded me because I was snoring."

Sonny laughed and said, "Of course I did."

They went into the house and took care of Razor. Maggie said she was wide awake now and she was a little hungry. Sonny reminded her they had leftover pizza in the freezer. She said that would be perfect. She heated the pizza up as Sonny walked Razor. When he got back, the pizza was ready, and she set up in front of the TV. They ate, watched a few shows, and spoke about the day. When they were done, they cleaned up and went to bed. It was a long day in the sun, and their first day in the sun since last summer, and it wiped them out. Surprisingly, Maggie fell asleep quickly. She must be catching up on her sleep. It had been very stressful the last few weeks. Razor was wide awake. He must have missed them all day. Sonny decided to take him for another quick walk. Sonny hoped a little more fresh air would make him sleepy. He thought about how tomorrow would play out. Funny, he never heard from the ranger. He was supposed to call. It was only 10 p.m., but Sonny figured he would call earlier. Sonny finished the walk and decided not to go to bed, just in case the ranger called. He put the TV back on and waited. At about 10:45 p.m., the phone rang. It was him.

Dave apologized for calling so late, because he had to make arrangements for traveling up there. Sonny said it was no problem, that he was a night bird. Dave asked if it was OK to meet up with Sonny tomorrow after 2 p.m. because he had some personal things to take care of and that was the earliest he could make it. Sonny had to review video, then speak with Johnny, so a late meet was fine.

Sonny said, "You know what, don't rush to get here at 2 p.m. Let's set a time, say 3 p.m., but it's not written in stone. Just give me a call when you're about an hour out, and I will make sure I am free by the time you get here."

Dave thanked him and said that took some pressure off of him.

He said, "You don't know what I've been going through all day, trying to make this work."

Sonny said he understood and that he had been there before. Dave said he was looking forward to meeting him and they hung up. He sounded like he was a good guy. Sonny hoped he didn't run into any problems with him. Sonny would hate to have him take another hit at work. Dave seemed like he felt bad enough now. Imagine if something else happened.

Sonny shut off the lights and headed for the bedroom. Maggie was still sleeping. Razor gently jumped into the bed and fell asleep. It was good to know that the fresh air helped him sleep. Sonny felt a little better. The conversation with Dave kept him up a little while, but then he fell asleep knowing he needed to be on his A game tomorrow, to make sure nothing crazy came up or happened. He couldn't wait to hear what Johnny had to say too.

Maggie and Sonny forgot to set the alarm. They got up late. Not monumentally late, but late enough to get them moving. Sonny got breakfast ready and took care of Razor, while Maggie showered and dressed. When she was done, they switched places. While Sonny was getting dressed, Maggie came in, kissed him and wished him luck, and left for work. Sonny finished getting dressed and headed to work. With luck, he would still get there on time. He called Maggie to see how she was making out on her ride into work. She said she would make it in time. They quickly spoke about how great the weekend was. Maggie would see if Becky had anything for her. Sonny would call her after he got a few reviews on his new look. She laughed and said they better be stellar remarks, or someone was going to pay for it.

Sonny made it on time. He headed to his desk and began to pull up the video that matched the times Dave gave him for the radio activations. There were five different dates, all during his hours of work. Scratch that, one time was after his work hours. Sonny would have to see who was on that day. This could be a problem. The way the system worked was if there was an incident, the Council pulled the video and had it reviewed by the next day, and a copy was maintained on the government's main server. If nothing happened, the video remained on the server of the Hub for at least ninety days. After the ninety days, it was transferred to the main server of the government, reviewed and archived. The four events that happened on Sonny's watch were still way under the ninety days.

Sonny pulled up the first one, and nothing was captured near Johnny's place at the time the radio was powered up. He pulled up the second one. He had video around Johnny's place at the time the radio was powered up. Luckily, he was going in the right direction for Johnny's zapper to do its job on his camera feed. No cars or license plates were captured. The third video was like the first. Nothing near Johnny's at the given times. The fourth video was a problem. The video was pulled for review and copied to the main server. It was the day Tracks and Bones had their run in at Sonny's car. Bones was making a stink that he was setup. This was a problem. His hearing was delayed because no one could find Tracks to testify. Once they located Tracks, he would be given a five business days' notice to appear. The issue was when the video was reviewed, it was reviewed in its entirety. When there was a video drop, the times were recorded and kept with the video as the hearing progressed. Sonny could easily wipe anything that showed up on the HUB copy of the video, but he did not have access to the main server. At the beginning of the hearing, when the evidence was introduced, a comparison would be made of the video, the HUB copy and the main server copy, to assure there was no tampering. Sonny could wipe something from the HUB copy, and he would have a minimum of a week before someone knew it was tampered with. He decided to review the video before he had a heart attack for nothing.

Sure enough, he had video in front of Johnny's place, two minutes before the radio was turned on. He could see Ronnie in the car, messing around with something. He also saw Johnny walk up to the passenger's window and have a conversation with Ronnie. The video captured the license plate too. Sonny had no choice but to erase this segment. Even though it wasn't for the exact time, this was still enough to interview Johnny. He didn't want his name to come up at all. Sonny would have to get in touch with Stacks and make sure he knew to lay low. Sonny needed to buy as much time as possible. He hoped Mike would give Johnny some good news today. Sonny erased the whole part of the video that captured the car, Ronnie and Johnny. It just looked like the camera had one of its normal issues and recorded nothing.

Now, for the fifth video, it was recorded by Will. Sonny could access his video, but he would know that he did. No problem with that, since he had a reason to look at it. Sonny just hoped he didn't capture anything. Sonny pulled it up and got nothing but snow. Nothing recorded. Thank God. Another problem avoided. It was getting late, so he headed out to make sure he had enough time to speak with Johnny before the ranger showed up.

Sonny got to Johnny's and he was waiting outside for him. They went inside and Johnny said everything was going well.

He paused a second and said, "Look at you young man!

Maggie did a great job on the coloring. It looks natural."

Sonny said, "Maggie will love the fact you thought it made me look young."

Johnny laughed.

Johnny said Mike wanted to meet with Sonny on Wednesday evening, somewhere around the last location. Mike thought four or five of these meets might do the trick and expedite the process of getting them over to the CNU. The other good thing Maggie and Sonny had going for them was their boys. They were fine examples of citizens in the CNU. Successful, good looking and clean. Sonny cut Johnny off and said they had a big problem. Sonny explained everything about how the video system worked and what he had to do. Sonny couldn't hold out long enough to get in four or five more meets. Johnny said he understood and felt they were pressed for time as well. Sonny added that Double D promised to get him more information as needed, which would probably be daily. Then Sonny's phone rang. It was Dave. Sonny took the call and Dave said he would be in the area in about forty-five minutes. Sonny said he would meet him at the HUB. Johnny forgot Sonny was meeting with the ranger today. Johnny would reach out to Mike again and let him know issues came up and they needed to move things up. He thought the meet on Wednesday should be kept, and Sonny agreed. Johnny would go by Sonny's house this evening, around 8 p.m., and he would let him know how his call went. Sonny went back toward the HUB.

Sonny took a quick look around for Tracks, and he couldn't find him. He got into the office and queued up all of the video. He grabbed a few drinks from the fridge and went back to the video to double check the times. As he was reviewing the videos, Dave came into the office and tapped Sonny on the shoulder. It was now time for the moment of truth. Would he recognize him? If so, what would he do? There was only one way to find out.

Chapter 15

Sonny turned around and said, "You made it in one piece. I'm impressed."

Dave chuckled and said it was easy to find. Sonny showed him he was reviewing the video and said he wasn't lucky enough to capture any video. Dave said he would like to see the video anyway, just for curiosity and so he can say he reviewed it. Sonny asked him to pull up a seat. Sonny didn't tell him what each video showed because he wanted him to be open on what he was about to see. Sonny started with Will's video, just to get it out of the way. Nothing but snow.

Dave said, "It looks like you guys have the same problems we do. Too bad the Council doesn't listen to us and switch to self-recording units with the ability to stream. It's always about the money."

Sonny replied, "Agreed. We always tell the higher ups to get units that record. They claim to have the money for them, then change their minds when it comes down to crunch time on the budget."

The next two Sonny pulled up were the ones that had no recordings near Johnny's place around the time of the radio power up. No issues there, and no comments from Dave. The next one he pulled up was the one where Sonny was around Johnny's place, but his zapper shut his camera down. Dave asked if he could control the video, because he was looking for specific things.

They switched chairs and Dave started reviewing the parts when it went to snow, and when it got back to normal recordings. Dave said he couldn't tell now, but the signal drops may have been caused by outside tampering. He went to a training last month and they showed him a few things to look out for to determine if a jammer was used. Great. He's a techie. Sonny asked him what needed to be done, who did it, and how long it would take. Dave needed copies of all of the videos they looked at so they could all go through the process. He had the software that analyzed the video, but it was very time consuming. The process would have to be done on the whole tours' recording and it took about two days to process the video, then another two days to analyze. He would start it on Monday and have results by Friday morning. Now Sonny had only a five-day window without being discovered. He needed to stay relaxed and get out of there as soon as possible. They had to get out of UST now.

What was he going to say about the last video, the one where Sonny tampered with it? Could he tell or could he only determine if a jammer was used? He loaded it up and started watching the last video, right before it dropped. He saw it was getting closer to the coordinates of the radio activation and Sonny could see him start to get anxious. When the signal dropped, he dropped his head for a couple of seconds, then raised it and stared right into Sonny's eyes. Did he recognize him? Did this trigger something in his memory? Was Sonny being paranoid?

After an awkward few seconds, Sonny said, "What? Do you see something? What's wrong?"

Dave said, "What's wrong is luck. If it wasn't for bad luck, I wouldn't have any at all."

Sonny asked him if it looked like a jammer was used and he said he didn't think so. He didn't see any of the markers that identified jammer use. It was getting late, so Sonny said he would start copying the videos for him and they could go out to the street. Dave said that was fine, so Sonny started the process and off they went.

They walked around the streets, starting around the gazebo. It was a little later in the day, so not too many people were walking around. They went into a few stores, including the doughnut shop.

Michelle was behind the counter, and when she saw Sonny walk in, she said, "I like the beard. All that gray made you look like an old man."

Sonny said, "Thanks. You always know how to make someone feel good."

She laughed and said, "No. That's not what I meant. You are too young to have all that gray hair. It fits you so much better with a darker color on your beard. Don't shave it."

Sonny said she made him feel a little better and he would think about it. She offered them coffee, but Sonny thought it was too late in the day for him. Dave said the same thing. Sonny showed Michelle the two sketches and asked her if she knew who they were. Michelle said they look like everyone else.

"That could be me, you, him, that guy over there, I don't know."

They thanked her for her help and went back on to the street. Dave asked if Sonny just grew the beard. Sonny said he did and that he usually only did it going into the winter, but he wasn't feeling good and he didn't feel like shaving.

Sonny added, "Besides, my wife always bothers me about coloring my hair. So, I let her color the beard as a test. It looked OK, so I figured the true test would be at work today. So far, it's all thumbs up."

Dave said he could see the hair coming out of his hat, and that it was a light brown. He asked if Sonny had gray hair too. Luckily, Maggie took it easy on his hair, so it was still pretty light.

Sonny took off his hat, ran his fingers through his hair and said, "It's not all gray yet."

Dave laughed and said, "At least you still have hair," as he removed his hat and showed Sonny his bald head.

Sonny laughed and said, "Yeah, but that's a good shaped head to have it bald."

Dave laughed and said that he was lucky he did. They walked around, going into and out of stores and shops, showing the sketches. The responses were all the same. They could be anyone. Sonny didn't know if they were being honest, or if they were keeping quiet, trying not to get anyone in trouble. They went into Butcher Shop #4, Leo's place. Leo was in, so they were going to get a mini show.

As they walked in, Leo gave his big welcome "HEY! It's the stranger. Long time no see. What, did you forget about me? Are you a big shot now? Can't come by and say hello?"

Sonny opened his arms and said, "Come here Leo. I got something for you right here," as Leo came in for the hug.

Sonny said in his ear, "Feel better now? I missed you. I'm sorry for not stopping by. I'd never be too big for you."

Leo said, "I know. I just love to bust your balls."

Sonny said, "I know Leo."

Leo asked who his friend was. Sonny said he was a ranger from Maryland working on a case. Dave and Leo said hello, and Dave showed him the sketches. Leo said he never saw a girl who looked like that in his life. As for the guy, he swore the guy had been in his store. Leo mumbled a few things, trying to jar his memory.

He said, "You know, the guy from the park. He has an annoying voice and always talks down to his friends."

Now Sonny was really confused. He looked and Dave had a smile on his face.

Leo continued on, "The guy, he was raised by his mother. Come on, you know who he is."

Dave laughed and said, "He probably knows who he is." Forget it. Now Sonny's head was spinning.

Just then Leo screamed, "Respect my authority... Cartman you jackass. The kid from South Park."

Leo and Dave were hysterically laughing.

Sonny shook his head and said, "OK Leo. You got me on that one. That was actually a good one. The kid from the park. You are too much."

Sonny looked at Dave and said, "I told you we were in for a show."

They all took it down a notch or so, and Leo said he didn't recognize the guy either.

Then he paused, looked at Sonny, and said, "If you shaved off that garbage on your face, it could be you," and started laughing all over again.

Dave looked at Sonny and said, "I think you're right, Leo," and he started laughing.

At least he didn't recognize Sonny. Or if he did, he was acting really cool about it. Sonny waved at Leo and said he had enough. He said to stop by early next week and he would have something special waiting for Sonny. Sonny thanked him, said goodbye and left.

Once outside, Dave said, "He is a character. I don't come across people like that in Maryland."

Sonny smiled and said, "No one should come across people like him."

As they got closer to Johnny's place, Dave said, "This is the area where the radios were powered up. I really want to walk slowly around here and take some photos."

Sonny encouraged him to do whatever he needed to do. He took photos of all the shops and stores on the block. As he passed people in the street, he stopped a few to show the sketches. No one wanted to say anything and pretty much just shook their heads "no" as they looked at the sketches. Ronnie was standing in front of Johnny's place. They stopped and said hello to him. Dave introduced himself and showed Ronnie the sketches. Ronnie said sorry, but he didn't recognize them. Dave asked him if he ever saw someone walking around with fancy hand radios, that would have had a small antenna and numbers on the front. Ronnie said he never saw anyone walking around with a radio. Since Johnny's was the closest business to the radio hits, Dave wanted to speak with the owner. Ronnie said he would go in and get Johnny. Johnny came out and they said hello. Sonny introduced Dave to him and went over what Dave was trying to accomplish. Basically, Sonny put on a good show. Johnny looked at the sketches and said he didn't recognize them. He asked if he could have copies of them to show some of his regular customers. Dave said not yet, but he could give copies to Johnny early next week. Dave asked Johnny if had ever seen the radios in question. Johnny also said he never saw anyone walking around with radios of any kind. Dave looked at Sonny and said he was done there, so they wished Johnny a good night and walked on.

Next, they went into News Stand #2, which was next door to Johnny's place. There was not a lot of foot traffic in this place. Honestly, Sonny believed it belonged to Johnny. It would be smart to "own" the place next to yours when some questionable things were going down. Sal ran things in the store. They went in, said hello and Sonny introduced him to Dave. Dave showed him the sketches and asked if he recognized them.

Sal hardly looked at them and said, "I don't know them."

Sal was very silent and let Dave do all of the talking. Dave explained how important it was that they find them.

All Sal said was, "I told you, never saw them before."

They left the shop and Dave said, "It looks like we're not getting any cooperation. I say we're done. Let's get back to the HUB so I can get my videos and get out of here."

They went back to the HUB and Sonny gave Dave the copies of the videos. Dave asked Sonny to send him the video he just recorded on the street after it finished processing on the HUB's server. That would take a few hours and Dave didn't want to stick around and wait. He just wanted to head home, since it wasn't too late. Sonny said he would send it to him first thing tomorrow, when he got into work. Dave thanked Sonny for his help and said it was a pleasure to work with him. Sonny thanked him for coming and wished him a safe trip home.

After Dave hit the road, Sonny washed up and headed home. When he walked to his car, Johnny was there waiting. He said it saved him from making a trip to the house. He didn't get a good feeling about Dave and was worried he would screw up all of the plans. Sonny explained what Dave said about the videos and how he could look into them to see if they were tampered with. Johnny believed that was a huge problem. He would be speaking with Mike early in the morning, and said Sonny should pass by his place as soon as he could.

Sonny ran through everything he did with Dave to see if he could find any more issues or reasons for concern. His biggest question was why did Dave record video as they went through the streets? He knew Sonny was recording. It was a responsibility of Sonny's while working. Did he want to compare their two videos to see when the signal dropped in and out? Would he notice that the signal dropped off around Johnny's place again, when compared to the video they were reviewing? Sonny had to wipe it and wipe his too. If he could show they both had major failures, it would only warrant a diagnostic test of the system. Dave would be able to run them to see if they were tampered with, but he would be running the others first, so these wouldn't be done until the cat was out of the bag anyway. Sonny would make sure he went in early and to take care of that. This was becoming really stressful. Less than twenty-four hours ago, he was feeling on top of the world. How quickly things changed.

Sonny got home and Maggie was waiting for him in the kitchen. She said she already ate, and she would heat up the food she made for him. She asked how it went with Dave. Sonny detailed how everything happened, chronologically. She was relieved he didn't recognize Sonny, but she was stunned to hear about the videos. They went back and forth with ideas on how they could handle the video situation, and they came up with nothing. They concluded if they didn't get Mike to help them out and get them across soon, they would get caught and charged with treason. Sonny said they shouldn't panic yet. They should wait and see what Mike had to say when he met him on Wednesday. Sonny's plan for tomorrow was to head into work and wipe the two videos, Dave's and his. Next, he would go see Johnny and find out what Mike said. Then he would reach out to Double D and let him know he would need more information for a Wednesday meet with Mike. Maggie didn't think her conversations with Becky would help them now, since they were

213

short for time. Sonny urged her to keep it going anyway, because you never know what could happen next. Maggie said she was stressed and needed to work it off. She was going to run on the treadmill for a while.

Sonny suggested drinks instead, and she said, "After the treadmill."

Sonny said he would make a batch of sangria and it would be ready and waiting for her. He made the sangria and put it on ice, since Maggie would probably be on the treadmill for a while.

Sonny sat down on the sofa and heard Maggie scream out for help. Razor flew toward the gym ahead of Sonny. Maggie was on the floor, covered by a bunch of dumbbells that fell off of the rack. She was screaming in pain. Sonny took the weights off of her and asked what happened. She said she stretched out before getting on the treadmill and got light headed. She stood up, stumbled into the rack, and tipped the weights over and she fell. She had a big bruise on her ribs and on her thigh. Sonny asked if she wanted to go to the hospital. Like a trooper, she said no, let's try ice and Advil first. He helped her up and she moaned in pain. He asked what hurt and she said her ribs hurt, not so much her thigh. Sonny got her into bed, got some ice for her ribs and thigh, and gave her some Advil. He asked Maggie how long she wanted to give this a try before they decided to take further action. She said to give it a couple of hours because the ice felt good and to give time for the meds to kick in. Sonny asked her if she hit her head, and she said no. She asked him to leave her in the bedroom to get some rest.

Sonny said, "I'll be in the living room. Please let me know if you need anything."

She said she was fine and just wanted to close her eyes. Sonny asked her again if she was sure she didn't hit her head. She said she didn't. Razor stayed in bed with her and Sonny went and watched a little TV. About fifteen minutes later, he checked on Maggie and she was sound asleep. He changed the ice packs without disturbing her too much. He left her and Razor in the bed and fell asleep on the sofa.

Sonny woke up the next morning and checked in on Maggie. She was still asleep, so he gave her a gentle tap to wake her up. She opened her eyes and let out a moan.

"My ribs are killing me."

Sonny asked her about her thigh, and she said it didn't hurt that much. He asked if she wanted to go to the hospital. She wanted to take a shower first, then decide. He helped her off of the bed and she got up slowly. She wanted to do most of the work, to help determine how bad it was. Her first steps were taken slowly, but she was able to support herself. She took a couple of steps and said her legs were fine. Sonny asked her if it hurt when she took a breath. She said it hurt a little.

They looked at each other and said, "Broken ribs."

She went into the shower and she asked for Sonny to make her coffee and scrambled eggs. He asked if she was OK to be left alone, and she said she fine. He got the coffee going and made the eggs. He went back into the bedroom and Maggie just finished her shower. Sonny said he would call out sick and take her to the hospital. Maggie shook her head no and said he had too many things to take care of. She wanted to go into work, and if it got bad, she would have Becky take her to the hospital. Sonny asked if she thought she was OK to drive. She was fine in the SUV because she didn't have to move around that much.

Sonny said, "The only way I'll let you even try this is only if I can tape your ribs."

Maggie said that was fine. Sonny got some athletic tape and

began to tape her ribs. She winced in pain, but got through it. Once they were done, she said it felt a lot better. She got dressed and Sonny took her out for a test drive.

"You have to prove to me that you can do this before I let you go."

They pulled out of the driveway and drove down the street for about a half mile. She turned around and pulled back into the driveway. She said she felt fine and she would be OK to drive to work. She didn't make any faces or cry out in pain, so Sonny felt safe she would be OK. They went back into the house, had breakfast and Sonny grabbed his bag to leave for work. She wished him luck and said she would call him and let him know how she was doing. Sonny made her promise to do so, and she did.

Sonny got to work and started working on wiping the videos. It shouldn't take long, so he would have time to send Dave his copy. If he looked at it, Sonny was sure he would want to see his. Sonny could take care of that by the end of the day. That would buy him some more time before Dave might become suspicious after seeing both videos failed. Would that even make a difference? Sonny didn't know, but it was better to have some cushion than not have any at all. He finished up and sent Dave his copy, took care of his normal office stuff and headed to see Johnny.

Sonny didn't waste any time. He went right to Johnny's place and walked right in. The place was empty. Johnny was waiting at a table. Sonny sat down and asked him what happened. He said Mike was very concerned about what was going on, and he wanted to keep Wednesday's meet and asked for Sonny to bring more information on the virus. Johnny said he would be joining Sonny at this meet since Mike needed him to help get things moving. Mike had a plan and could get it together quickly. Johnny said Mike got the OK for them to move to the CNU, but he needed a sample of the virus. That would be the only way Maggie and Sonny could move over this week. Without a sample, they couldn't prove this virus threat was real. As far as his supervisors knew, this could be a game the UST was playing with the CNU, to test and see how many leaks they had in the government. Sonny explained to Johnny that he didn't want Double D too involved, and this sounded like it might be difficult for him to get a sample. Sonny would try and meet Double D for lunch and find out if this was something he could do. After lunch, Sonny would go back to Johnny's and let him know what Double D said. Johnny would be around most of the day, but he had something to do after 3 p.m. Sonny said he would be back before then.

Sonny left Johnny's place and called Double D. He asked him to meet up for lunch. He said he could meet Sonny at the gazebo by 12:30 p.m. and he would be bringing lunch for the two of them. Sonny couldn't wait to see what he was bringing. Double D said Sonny would be presently surprised. After Sonny finished with Double D, he called Maggie to see how she was doing. She said she was in pain and Becky was going to bring her to the hospital. Sonny asked which hospital she was going to so he could meet her, but she said not to worry, she was in good hands. Besides, there was nothing Sonny could do. She knew he had a few important things to take care of, and a trip to the hospital would delay them. She promised to call Sonny once she left her office.

She asked how things were going, and he said, "Things could be better, things could be worse. We'll talk later about it."

Sonny walked around to at least make it look like he was

working. He couldn't concentrate, but at least he could walk. He hadn't heard from Dave, so maybe he didn't look at his video yet. Sonny had to assume that would be low on his to do list, but he didn't know how Dave thinks. Still no signs of Tracks, Sonny didn't know if that is good or bad. He was feeling really anxious. He should have had a drink at Johnny's before he left. Sonny didn't know if people were staring at him or if he was being paranoid. He felt like he had the shakes, but did he? His shoulders were getting tight. He needed to sit down and relax. He walked down the street to the end, where the tree line began. He walked into the woods and leaned up on a boulder. If anyone saw him go there, they would just probably think he was going to take a piss.

Sonny closed his eyes, took deep breaths, and thought about the beach. He convinced himself everything was going to work out and they would be with the boys on the beach. Grandkids running around, a warm breeze, aqua blue-green water that was so comfortable it didn't even feel wet. The white powdery sand, the sound of the waves crashing, seagulls diving into the water. Sonny got to that peaceful place. He started to relax. He didn't want to stay there too long, but he also didn't want to leave too quickly. He waited for about ten minutes to pass, then went back to work. Not too many people were around, so he didn't think anyone saw him. He decided to get some water, so he walked toward the gazebo, bought a bottle, and sat and waited for Double D to arrive.

About twenty-five minutes later, Double D showed up with a bag.

Sonny asked, "OK, what did you bring?"

Double D opened the bag and it was leftover wings from the other night.

"Really?" Sonny said.

Double D laughed and said he wanted Sonny to be thinking about what he was bringing instead of any bad thoughts.

Then Double D laughed and said, "Nah, I was just fucking with you."

Go figure. Sonny got right down to business and asked him how difficult it would be for him to get a sample of the virus.

Double D let out a deep sigh and said, "This is going to be difficult. Do you really need a sample?"

Sonny explained how everything went down with Dave and what they were facing if Mike didn't get a sample. Double D said he understood and would make it happen.

Sonny asked if this would jeopardize him in any way and he said "If I don't do it right, yeah, I'll get caught. But you know me, I will do it right. I'll make sure they never know."

Sonny begged Double D to please make sure he could do it right, or to just forget it.

Double D said, "I got this. I know what I have to do, I just need to figure out how to follow through with it. We have live samples in my office, from people, and we have potential areas of infection, where we tested the air and water. I just need to take a live virus sample and replace it with a water sample. I could just make it look like a clerical error and have one less live virus sample and one more water sample."

Sonny said it sounded easy enough, but he knew Double D was going to need a window of opportunity. Double D said not to worry. He would take care of it.

Sonny said, "I'd kiss you right now, but I don't need anyone starting rumors about me."

Double D smiled and replied, "There will be plenty of time for making out. All I need from you right now is for you to grab my ass when we hug."

He was the best. He always kept things lite, even in the face of danger. He would have been a great politician.

They finished lunch and had a few more laughs. Double D asked how Sonny liked the party, since they really hadn't spoken since it happened.

Sonny laughed and said, "It was great. I think Maggie felt even better that night."

Double D looked at him and put his hand up for a high five.

"My man! I knew it would work. Don't you know that's why Sara was OK with it? We had circus sex that night."

They laughed so hard that people started staring at them.

Double D said, "That's the aphrodisiac of our time."

Sonny just lost it. He had to stand up and walk away for a second, just to gather himself and to stop drawing attention. Double D had to leave, so he went in for a hug.

As Sonny hugged him, he slapped his ass and said, "You only earned a slap. The full squeeze is for later."

He replied, "You were always a tease."

Sonny said, "Thank you, brother. You mean so much to me. You really are the best."

Double D replied, "Only for you. I love you too, brother. We'll get this done. It will all work out in the end."

Double D said he would call Sonny tomorrow night to let him know when he was coming over. It would be just him. Sonny said they should at least have a few drinks and he said that was fine.

Sonny went right back to Johnny's. He didn't think Johnny got up from the table since he last saw him.

Johnny asked, "So? Are we good?"

Sonny said, "He said he can do it. It won't be easy, but he can get it done."

Johnny replied, "That's great news. We'll meet up with Mike at around 11 p.m. on Wednesday. I'll let him know you will have a sample, this way he could make arrangements to get you over. I'm part of that plan, so at least you can worry a little less. I got your back."

Sonny answered, "I know you have my back. I have told you before, I don't know how I could ever repay you. I know you said knowing your parents are looking down at you makes you feel better, but I wish I could do something for you directly."

Johnny smiled and said, "I hope you don't think you're getting rid of me. We'll see each other during vacation time. Remember, I get around and I'll make sure you have plenty of time to make this up to me."

Sonny went back out and finished his days' work. He saw he had two missed calls and a message from Maggie. It was strange he didn't hear the phone ring, but he was pretty occupied with other things. He listened to her message and she said she tried calling when she got into the car, but he didn't pick up. She was about to get her ribs wrapped. She had one broken rib. Her leg was fine, it was just a bruise. The doctor gave her some pain meds and asked her to stay home from work for a couple of days. Becky would take her to get the meds, then pick up her car and head home. Sonny sent her a text, letting her know he heard her message and that he would meet her at home. She responded she got the message and she was driving home. A few minutes later, Sonny broke up an argument and then he was done for the day. He headed back to the HUB, wrapped up his day and went home. Dave never called, so his guess was he didn't look at the video. That's good for Sonny. One less headache.

He got home and Maggie's car was in the driveway. He went into the house and Maggie was sitting in the living room, with her feet up.

She said, "It feels like I'm retired again. At least for the next few days."

Sonny smiled and asked how she felt. She said she felt great, especially after she took one of her pain meds. He filled her in on his day and she was worried about Double D getting caught.

She asked if there was anything they could do to help him.

Sonny said, "You know there's nothing we can do. Double D is sharp. He'll figure it out. All we can do is pray he gets through this safely."

Sonny asked her if Becky said anything else about "ways of getting out of here." She didn't. They were focused on her injuries and getting her to the hospital. Becky laughed when she told her how she got hurt.

Maggie said, "Becky said it's hard to stay in shape. Sometimes a bitch gets hurt."

Maggie cracked herself up. At least she wasn't feeling any pain. Sonny hoped she got better fast. Who knew what plan Mike had for them? Maybe her injury would get in the way.

Sonny asked Maggie if she got her runaway bag ready. She said she needed for him to go into the attic and grab her personal storage box. She needed to go through it. He asked her about what other things she wanted so he could work on getting them to Double D and Johnny. Since Sonny had all of the pictures and videos taken care of, she didn't have much. Most of their things could easily be replaced. All of the things she wanted could probably fit in the back of a big SUV. That's good news, because Sonny really didn't have anything he wanted to keep. A few things had sentimental value, but nothing was really big. He started filling up the spare bedroom with the things they wanted but couldn't take with them. Sonny would see if Double D could take some of it with him when he came over. Sonny went up into the attic and got Maggie her storage box. He said things could be moving quickly from here, so he needed her to go through things now, rather than later. As Sonny loaded the bedroom, Maggie asked him to get her another box from the attic. There weren't too many things up there, so he let her know he would just bring all of the boxes down and they could throw out what they didn't need or want. For the rest of the night, they both organized what they were taking with them, what they were leaving behind to be saved for them, and what they were leaving behind that could be replaced. Sonny filled up the bedroom quickly and Maggie was right. All of that stuff could fit in a large SUV. Maggie fell asleep on the sofa and he left her there, since she seemed comfortable. Besides, she was off for the next few days and she was on meds. Nothing would wake her anyway.

Sonny woke up for work and Maggie was still asleep on the sofa. He tried to keep Razor as quiet as he could, but he still managed to make enough noise to wake Maggie up. She said she felt a little groggy and sore. He made her a cup of coffee and some toast, so she could take her meds. She got up to use the bathroom and she said she was a little light headed. He helped her get to the bathroom and waited for her to finish up. By the time she washed up, she felt better and she was able to get around by herself. She went back to the living room and Sonny showered, got dressed and went to work. Before he left, he made Maggie promise she would call him mid-day to let him know how she was doing.

On his way to work, he got a call from Dave. He knew it would come, but he just didn't know when. Dave said he was running the copies of the videos for signs of compromise, and it would probably take about a month to complete. He said he looked at the video Sonny sent him yesterday, and it was completely blank. He asked Sonny to check his video feed and let him know how it looked. Sonny said he was heading into the office, and he would check his video first thing when he got there. Dave didn't sound annoyed or bothered. He sounded like he had a job to do. No real feeling. That worried Sonny. Sonny decided to try and loosen him up when he called him back.

Sonny got to the HUB and pulled his video.

He went through it and said out loud, "Piece of shit! No video at all. Is anyone else having problems with their video lately? I didn't record a thing on Monday."

He didn't get a response, but that was normal for this group. At least they heard what he said. He called Dave and said his was blank too. Sonny asked him if he had problems with his system as well. Dave said his wasn't too bad, but it had its moments. Since he worked in and around a park, his system didn't have too much interference. The problems he had were usually system wide problems, which were extremely rare. That was why he thought it was strange his system was down on the night of the incident. Sonny made up a lie to see what frame of mind he was in.

Sonny said, "Leo said we probably killed Kenny and called us bastards."

Dave chuckled and said, "I wish I had people like Leo around when I'm working. I don't have any regulars."

Sonny said, "I'll give you Leo. He's passed his expiration date."

Dave laughed and replied, "In that case, I don't want him."

Dave went on about how lucky Sonny was that he had busy streets occupied by lots of people. His post was boring and he was looking to move up. This incident in the park set him back a little, but he could change that by finding the suspects. Sonny said he would help him all he could, all he had to do was ask. Dave thanked him and said he would keep him in the loop. Sonny felt a little better knowing he actually spoke with him. He guessed the guy was just frustrated. Sonny knew the feeling. Poor guy. He hoped all this stuff didn't hurt him too much.

Sonny went over to Johnny's and spoke with him about their plans with Mike. Sonny said Double D would be paying him a visit late that evening, hopefully with a sample. Johnny said they could meet up around 10 p.m. He asked Sonny to be dropped off at another location near the house. Sonny let Johnny know what happened to Maggie and he felt concerned. He too said he hoped her injury wouldn't get in the way of their plans. He asked how she was and said he would call her later. Sonny said he would let him know when he spoke with her, this way he didn't wake her up. Johnny said they would be staying at another hotel in Philly, so it wouldn't be too bad of a ride. It was up to Sonny if they wanted to stay the night, or just turn around and come home. Sonny suggested they stay the night, just in case something came up. Johnny agreed and said that was fine. He would call the hotel and make reservations for the both of them. Sonny asked Johnny to give him a shot before he left.

He raised his eyebrows and said, "Feeling a little anxious?"

Sonny smiled and said, "A little drink won't kill me. Only a bunch of little drinks will."

Johnny poured the two of them a shot of tequila.

He toasted "I know the saying is it's five o'clock somewhere, but damn this is early. Here's to a safe and productive day for all."

They had their drinks and Sonny went back to work.

Maggie called Sonny around the middle of the day. She felt

fine and she just woke up from a nap. Sonny said Johnny asked about her and wanted to wish her well, and she should expect a call from him soon. Sonny relayed the evening's plans to her and she said she would be fine to drive. She asked Sonny to call her when he was heading home so he could pick up some dinner. Sonny reminded her Double D was coming over, so she should make sure she ordered extra food. Sonny walked toward the deli to pick up some lunch and called Johnny on the way. Sonny got his sandwich and ate outside by the gazebo. And there he was, in the flesh. Tracks!

He looked awesome.

He walked over to Sonny and said, "Hi."

Sonny smiled and gave him a hug. Sonny said, "You look great and I'm proud of you."

Tracks said he got a job and a place to live. He wanted to go by and see Sonny to give him his cell phone number. Sonny asked if he could buy him lunch and Tracks said he wanted to buy Sonny lunch, but saw Sonny already bought something. Tracks went and bought a sandwich of his own and joined Sonny while they ate. He said he was working at a consulting firm, doing surveys for places that needed money for maintenance and upgrades. He made lots of new friends and was in a happy place. Sonny was so proud of him. Tracks heard people were looking for him. Sonny said it was about the incident with Bones, that he was fighting his charges. Tracks said he would go to the municipal building and get his notice. Sonny asked him to delay that. He didn't feel he could tell Tracks the truth, but he had to tell him something. He came up with a story that he needed more time to look into a few more things about Bones. Sonny said he was afraid if he didn't have everything lined up, Bones might get the charges dropped and it would hurt his chances of moving up in the government. Sonny said the information Tracks gave him was very helpful. Tracks was glad it helped, and he didn't want to derail his chances of moving up. Tracks promised to lay low until Sonny let him know it was OK to pick up his notice. That was a big stress off of Sonny's plate. They finished lunch, had a few laughs and Tracks had to get back to work. Sonny hugged him goodbye and reminded Tracks of how proud of him he was, by cleaning up and getting a job. Tracks couldn't have gotten that far without him. He said Sonny continued to give him the will to go on, no matter the shape he was in, and he would never forget it.

Sonny finished up the afternoon by stopping a shoplifter and calming a "John" down for complaining he didn't get all he paid for. He passed Johnny's place before he wrapped up the day. Johnny was outside, and said he spoke with Maggie. He laughed and said if it was anyone else, he could suggest that maybe Sonny threw her around in a rage. But with Maggie, she would throw him around. Sonny thanked him for that humiliation, as the rest of the guys were laughing. Sonny nodded his head and Johnny nodded back. They were set for later that night.

Sonny went back to the HUB, finished his daily duties, and headed home. He called Maggie on the way and she said she felt like having pizza. She would order a couple of pies for Sonny to pick up. She asked him to pick up beer too because they were running out, and she knew how much Double D loved his beer. Sonny picked up the pizza and beer and continued home. As he passed the tower, he saw more lights on than normal. It looked like whatever they were doing, it was being ramped up quickly. Sony kept forgetting to look it up when he was at work.

When he got home, he put the beer on ice and kept the pizza warm in the oven. Maggie and Sonny held out as long as they could, waiting for Double D to call. After an hour, they gave up and started eating. About fifteen minutes after they started eating, Double D called and said he was on his way. Sonny asked if he was OK, and he said everything was great. He sounded excited, so things must have gone well. About twenty-five minutes later, Double D showed up, with a hard covered case in hand.

Double D gave Sonny the case and said, "Here it is. It's on dry ice, which will last for at least forty-eight hours, so it's good to go."

Sonny asked him how he did it, and he said the reason why he was late was because he waited for everyone to leave before he took the sample. Once they were all gone, it was easy to make the switch. No one saw him, so he was in the clear. There were a few more pages of notes in the case, but nothing could compare to the sample. Double D asked if they always felt a rush when they worked as agents in the old days, because he really liked it. Maggie and Sonny laughed and said on days of an operation, they always felt the rush. Double D said it made him feel more alive than he ever had. The fact he committed a crime for the greater good, knowing he could lose everything, caused a feeling he never had before.

He added, "It gave me a boner too."

Of course it did. They were dealing with a man who never grew up. And they loved him exactly the way he was. Double D said he would hang around for a few rounds of pizza and beer. Sonny said Maggie would be dropping him off to meet Johnny so they could head to Philly for their meet with Mike. He saw Maggie struggle to get up and asked what happened.

Maggie told the story and he laughed.

"A trip and fall in the gym? You're so coordinated."

Maggie gave him the finger as she cleaned up the mess and

said, "I'm coordinated enough to do this and stick my foot up your ass at the same time."

Double D cracked up and said, "I love you too sweetheart."

They all laughed, watched a basketball game, ate and drank. Maggie felt good on her meds, and the guys felt good on beer.

It was close to 9:30 p.m., and Maggie smiled and said to Double D, "Time to get your ass out of my house. Please let the door hit your ass on the way out."

Double D laughed and said, "I love your ass talk. It turns me on."

Maggie laughed and said she was amazed that he never changed, but she was happy he didn't. Sonny gave Johnny a pizza pie to take home and made him promise he would give it to Sara. Double D wished them luck.

Sonny hugged him, squeezed his ass and said, "I told you I would do this in private."

Double D laughed and said, "You're my hero."

Sonny reminded him this wasn't only to help him, but this would also help the rest of the world. Before he left, Sonny showed him the bedroom full of stuff they wanted him and Johnny to take care of for us. He said he could take some of it now and the rest in a couple of days. Sonny helped him load up his SUV. They were able to get about half of it into the car. Double D said he would drop this off at his storage place in the morning.

Sonny put together a small bag for the night and asked Maggie if she was sure she was OK to drive. She said she felt better and it wasn't a long drive anyway.

Before leaving the house, Maggie said, "Please don't forget to take the sample."

Sonny said, "I got it," as he showed her the container.

Their ticket to freedom from the UST was in the form of a vial in a hard case. Sonny would guard it with his life. They left the house and Maggie drove in another direction, away from their usual meeting place. Sonny asked her where the new meeting spot was, and she said it was near the parking lot for the strip mall where Pizza # 6 was. It only took a few minutes to get there. Johnny was waiting in his car. Sonny gave Maggie a kiss and she said to be safe and wished him luck. Sonny said it would go down like last time. His phone, which was already off, would be off until he got back to the area tomorrow morning. Sonny had to work, so he was planning to get home by 6:30 a.m. He gave her the name of the hotel they were staying at, along with his UC name, just in case of an emergency. She said she would be fine and for Sonny to stop worrying. He got into the car with Johnny, and off they went.

Johnny said, "It looks like you got the sample."

Sonny smiled and said, "Double D always comes through."

Johnny hoped they had time to celebrate because he really wanted to meet Double D. Sonny thought that would be great, and hoped it would happen too, but that was not something he was thinking about. He was focused on getting all of their ducks in a row and getting out of the UST. They spoke about how Maggie and Sonny would adjust to the CNU. Johnny brought up a good point that Sonny didn't even think about. The CNU "retained" the old government structure. It might be possible to start receiving their pensions again, or to get some sort of payout or credit for it. That would be awesome. Sonny knew the boys would take care of them anyway, but he would rather they earned their own money and took care of themselves. They arrived at the hotel. The Kimpton Hotel Monaco, literally a block away from the Liberty Bell.

They parked the car and checked into their rooms. They planned to meet up by the elevators on the third floor in ten minutes. Sonny went to his room, dropped off his things and quickly washed up. He had a view from his window of the park where the Liberty Bell was located. He snapped a few pics to immortalize the moment. He met Johnny by the elevators, case in hand. They went up to Mike's room on the 6th floor. Mike said he was short on time and had to leave as soon as possible, so they got right down to business.

He said, "The sample I assume?" as he pointed to the hard case.

Sonny nodded his head, gave it to him, and said there was some additional information in the case as well. Mike looked excited and believed this was their ticket out of the UST. He asked what was going on with the ranger investigation and anything else that might get in the way of the plan. Sonny filled him in on what was going on with the hearing regarding Bones and the issues with the ranger investigation. Mike didn't think things would escalate this quickly, but the fact that Sonny gave him a sample of the virus meant things could speed up. The higher ups in the CNU were waiting for the sample and promised to grant Sonny and Maggie asylum in the CNU if they produced one. Mike said he had to bring this directly to the lab for analysis before a deal could be finalized. That could take a few days. Luckily, Mike had a plan, and that's why he asked Johnny to join them.

Johnny was friends with a guy who ran a "good will" exchange between the CNU and UST. It involved having youth sports teams from the CNU and UST play each other at different locations. This Sunday, when security was at its lowest presence, a girls' volleyball team was traveling to the CNU for a series of games. The driver and chaperone were volunteers with the organization. Johnny arranged for Maggie and Sonny to get a full security clearance with new identities. His friend agreed to have them drive the girls to the CNU. They would have no problems getting through the checkpoint. Maggie and Sonny would just look like regular people who volunteered to help. Nothing would come back to Johnny since his buddy would have hired them directly. This sounded like a solid plan.

Sonny said, "I like this plan. How easy will it be to get the identities squared away, and will there be any issues with your friend or the families of the girls going to the CNU?"

Johnny said he was already working on the IDs and they should be done by Friday, along with all of the clearances. There shouldn't be any issues with the girls or their parents. This was not the first trip for the team. They knew they got different people to take them over. The only other adults with them in the bus would be the two coaches, who they would meet on Saturday, a day before the trip. As long as the IDs went through, this should be a smooth trip to the other side. Sonny really liked this plan. Maggie would be happy about it, and the fact that her injury would not hinder their move. No sneaking over the border into the woods and across a river.

Mike said he would call Johnny on Friday at 10 p.m. to make sure everything was still a go. He should have the lab results by then and the answer from the higher ups about granting asylum. Mike suggested they pack up, just in case they weren't already set to go. Sonny said they were ready to go and they already moved half of their stuff to a storage facility. Johnny said he could take the rest of it.

Johnny smiled and said, "It looks like we will be able to have a small sendoff. I'm glad."

Sonny smiled back and said, "It sure does look that way."

Mike had all that he needed and if they didn't have any more questions, he had to go. Sonny shrugged his shoulders and looked at Johnny. They had nothing else. Mike wished them luck and said he hoped the next time he saw Sonny would be on the CNU side of the bridge with Maggie.

They left Mike's room and Johnny asked Sonny to go back to his room so they could talk a little bit. When he opened his door, Sonny saw a cart full of beer on ice next to his bed.

Sonny laughed and said, "You were sure things were going to go well, weren't you?"

Johnny said, "Either way, we would have needed a drink."

They drank and went over the plan, trying to come up with possible problems. After an hour, Sonny said he needed some sleep because he had to go to work in the morning. Any more drinking and he would sleep through the alarm in the morning. Johnny volunteered to drive back so Sonny could get a little more rest before work. Johnny would head in to his place around noon.

Sonny went to his room and tried to get some sleep. The beer took him down a notch, but he was still a little hyped up from the great news. He couldn't wait to tell Maggie. Somehow, things fell into place and they got their wish. Hopefully, their good luck wouldn't hurt someone else. Sonny would never forgive himself if Johnny or Double D got caught helping out. That was a thought he would like to bury, but he couldn't. Right now, that was his biggest worry.

The alarm went off at 4:15 a.m. Sonny had just a little over three hours of sleep. He hoped Johnny felt better than he did. If not, he would have to drive back. Sonny decided to shower when he got home, so he got dressed and went to wake Johnny up. Sonny knocked on his door and Johnny was already up. When

Johnny opened the door, the smell of coffee hit Sonny in the face. He gave Sonny a cup, grabbed his stuff and they headed to the car. He also picked up some sandwiches. Sonny asked him where he went, so early in the morning, for coffee and breakfast sandwiches. Johnny asked him if he really wanted to know and laughed.

Sonny said, "You're right. Thank you for breakfast, wherever it came from."

Johnny said he felt good to drive, so Sonny shouldn't worry about taking a nap on the way home. Johnny would have Sonny back at the strip mall by 6:30 a.m. Sonny leaned the seat back and asked Johnny to wake him when they were a half hour away, so he could call Maggie and have her pick him up. Johnny said not to worry, he would make the call to Maggie. Before Sonny dozed off, Johnny asked if he was ready for this to happen.

"I've been dreaming about this happening. This is all that has been on my mind. Just knowing we'll be back with the boys in a few days has me feeling like I'm on top of the world. We have a good plan, and it's backed by good people. If I said I was feeling great, it would be an understatement."

Johnny smiled, "You can't imagine how happy I am for you and Maggie. You all deserve to be together. I am so glad I was able to help you get to this point. I just started to really get to know you, and I'll tell you, I'm going to miss seeing you five days a week."

Sonny grabbed his hand and said, "Thanks. I'm going to miss you too."

They got to the strip mall. Sonny asked Johnny if he called Maggie. Johnny said she would be there to get him in five minutes. Johnny laughed and said Sonny was snoring hard. Sonny said that's the way he got when he wasn't sleeping right.

Sonny felt good, wide awake, so he figured he would be fine for the rest of the day. Maggie pulled up and had a passenger in the car. Johnny and Sonny got out of the car and went over to Maggie. Razor was jumping all around the car, so Sonny let him out. Maggie said Razor knew she was going to pick him up and demanded to go with her. That's Razor. He knows what he wants, and he knows how to get it. Johnny was petting and rubbing Razor all over.

Johnny asked what they were going to do with Razor when they left on Sunday. And just like that, Sonny looked at Maggie and a tear came to his eye.

Maggie said, "Oh my God. I didn't think about that. How could I leave my baby behind?"

Sonny put his head down and started shaking it. Just then, it hit Sonny. He looked at Maggie and signaled her about Johnny. She shook her head in agreement.

Sonny said, "I know how much you like Razor. I think it would make both of us happy knowing you were taking care of him."

Johnny said, "Really? I would love to take care of Razor for you. I am honored that you even asked me. I could get him back over to you within a couple of months…" and Sonny cut him off and finished his sentence with, "I know, you got a guy."

They all laughed, although Sonny's laugh was through tears. He knew Johnny would take good care of Razor. He had no worries there. They said bye to Johnny.

Johnny said, "Knowing I'll have Razor for a while pays off all of your debt. I love that guy."

Razor said bye to Johnny and jumped back into the car.

Sonny asked Maggie how she was feeling. She was still taking the meds, but she was starting to feel a little better since she wasn't moving around too much. She asked how it went, and Sonny said "Sunday is the day."

She screamed with joy, which made Razor bark like crazy. Sonny explained the plan on how they were going to drive a volleyball team over the bridge, and into the CNU, where Mike would meet them. Her screams of joy quickly turned into a scream of pain. She laugh-cried and said she moved too quickly, and it hurt her ribs. Sonny promised he would ice her down before he went to work. She didn't know Sonny was going to work and asked him to stay home. Sonny thought about it and decided he should go into work and finish up the week. He didn't want anything to come up and blindside them during the weekend. Saturday was going to be a nice day, and they could spend it with Razor. Maggie said he was right, and he should make sure nothing comes up at work. Sonny asked her about her job and how she was going to say goodbye to Becky. Becky was off on Friday, and they already made plans to hang out. Perfect. Sonny said that Johnny wanted to have some kind of sendoff, and so did Double D. Sonny knew she was still in pain, and didn't know if she was up to hosting a small gathering at the house. She said Friday night would be perfect, but wanted to know what exactly a small gathering meant. Sonny said it would be Double D and Sara, Johnny and maybe his wife, if he could convince him. She agreed she could handle that as long as Sonny bought the food and drinks on the way home on Friday. Now that the dinner was set, Sonny could concentrate on other things.

They got home and Sonny ran into the shower, not to waste any time. Maggie went back into the bed with Razor. Sonny came out of the shower and saw Razor curled up in a little ball.

He said, "I bet that's how he slept all last night."

Maggie laughed and said, "Of course."

Sonny asked, "What are you going to do today?"

Maggie was going to spend the day spoiling Razor. That meant a day of bacon, doggy treats, sleeping in the bed, and eating pizza. What a life. Sonny figured he could give Razor to Johnny on Sunday, before they made the trip. He didn't say what time the trip was, but Sonny couldn't see it being too early. He would ask him later this afternoon. He gave Maggie and Razor a kiss and left for work.

Sonny got to the HUB and took care of business. He rushed through his routine so he could get out as soon as possible. It was a rainy day, so no too many people were out on the street. These were days where the brothels made their money. People covered up because of the rain and go into them undetected. Sonny made his rounds, stopping in on a few places to say hi and to keep dry. It was lunch time. He grabbed some pizza and took his time eating it. Pasquale, the guy who ran the pizzeria, was a good guy, and Sonny hadn't spoken with him at length for a while. He was a Brooklyn guy in the better days. He was one of the guys who got a bad luck of the draw at the time of the split and wound up getting moved out of his house and re-located to the suburbs. Sonny felt he got a good deal out of it, but of course, he was thrown out of the neighborhood. Sonny guessed he was right, and would probably be upset too. He said Sonny looked different. Sonny said his wife did a little touch up on his hair. He laughed and said his wife always tries to do the same to him, but he won't let her because he's "a man." Sonny felt that emasculated him in Pasquale's eyes. Oh well. He said it looked good on Sonny, but it wasn't good for him. Exactly. Sonny was less than a man. Pasquale spoke about his old neighborhood and how much it changed. He went every weekend, to see his family and friends. He tried to convince them to move up there because it was so much nicer, but they didn't want to leave.

"What are you gonna do?" was his favorite saying.

Sonny finished his pizza and waved goodbye. Pasquale wanted Sonny to swing by more often because he reminded him of better days. If he only knew about the better days ahead of him. Even so, Sonny knew he was going to miss the store owners. They were mostly good people who were thrusted into bad situations, like the rest of everyone else, and made the best of it.

It was a little after 2 p.m., so Sonny went to go see Johnny. He looked terrible, so Sonny didn't think he got any sleep. He was sipping on scotch and seemed really mellow. He poured Sonny a glass. Sonny asked if he was OK, and he said last night took a lot out of him.

"Those all-nighters are behind me now. I'm officially an old man," he laughed.

It wasn't until now that Sonny realized who Johnny reminded him of. There was a group of guys he hung out with when he was in high school. They were so much fun to hang out with, but they had a ruthless side to them. Cross them and you were done. Not killed, but severely beaten. People used to ask Sonny for safe passage through the neighborhood. Johnny reminded him of Sean, his closest friend. He was a lot like Sonny, smart, athletic looking and a sharp sense of what was going on. The biggest difference was his temper. If you crossed him, you paid for it quickly and harshly. Sonny saw him a couple of times before the split. He always wondered how he was. Johnny acted just like him. Sonny believed that was why he had grown so close to him so quickly. He rarely let his guard down this quickly. Sonny was lucky Johnny was the way he was. Too bad he didn't get to know him sooner.

Sonny asked Johnny about the plan for Saturday and

Sunday. He said he would arrange for Maggie and Sonny to meet with the coaches and his friend, Charlie, on Saturday evening. They would give Maggie and Sonny all of the details about the trip. The bus was scheduled to leave at 1:30 p.m. on Sunday. With a mandatory pitstop, this put them around the border at 4 p.m. That was the time of a tour shift for the guards on the bridge. The guards coming in were screw ups who didn't care about a thing. Maggie and Sonny would have no issues crossing when those guards were on. The reason they were cutting it so close was because the coaches want to get there as early as possible. 1:30 p.m. was the best Charlie could do. They would try and have it changed when they speak with them on Saturday. Sonny's story was they had a family matter to take care of which would have them unavailable until around 1 p.m. Johnny said to remember, Maggie and Sonny were volunteers and to not let the coaches make them feel bad.

Sonny said, "Maggie is in the zone. She will politely cut them to shreds without them even knowing it. We got this."

Johnny chuckled and said, "I know."

Sonny said it was a go for a party at the house tomorrow and asked if he was bringing his wife.

Johnny asked who was going, and Sonny replied, "Just Double D and his wife Sara."

Johnny thought for a second and said, "Normally, this would be an easy no. But this will be the last time my wife will get to meet you before you leave, and it's going to be a small gathering with good friends of yours. I will speak with her, but I'm sure she will want to go."

Sonny said, "That's great news. I can't wait to meet her. And her name is..."

Johnny smiled and said, "Angelina."

Sonny smiled and said, "Of course it would be Angelina. An Italian Goddess who fell from the heavens. Nothing but the best for you."

Johnny laughed and said, "Things work out for me."

They spoke for a little while longer and Sonny saw it was getting late.

Johnny said, "Tomorrow is a big day. If Mike gives me the thumbs up, you're out of here. If by some chance he calls me earlier than 10 p.m., I'll come looking for you on the street. If not, I'll come by your house after the call and pick up the stuff you want me to hold for you."

Sonny said, "That works for me."

Sonny went back to the HUB, saw he had no new messages and finished up his day. He got in the car to drive home and called Maggie. She said she was feeling a little better. She wanted to go to the beach with Razor, but the weather didn't cooperate. She just fed him all his favorites and let him sleep in the bed. Sonny said he was heading home. Maggie made dinner, so he was off the hook for picking something up. Sonny got home and was greeted by a yawning four-legged creature. Razor couldn't keep his eyes open. Maggie said the only time he got off of the bed was when he ate. Sonny washed up and they sat down for dinner. Maggie seemed to be walking better. She asked how things went, and Sonny filled her in with what Johnny said about the weekend. She thought the timing was good and she felt comfortable with the plan. She wrote down what Sonny needed to pick up for the dinner party and asked if Johnny's wife was coming.

Sonny said, "Angelina should be blessing us with her presence."

Maggie laughed and said, "Angelina? How fitting."

They cleaned up the kitchen and headed to the living room.

Andrew's playoff game was on. It was the first game of the finals. Sonny was starting to tear up just thinking about it. Maggie looked at him and asked what was wrong. Sonny just realized they would be there with Andrew when he won the championship. She smiled and didn't realize that either. This was a perfect time for their exit. Things were a little complicated for them in the UST, with the Bones and ranger incidents, so it was good time to leave them behind. Maggie didn't have anything crazy going on at her job, so it was easy for her to go too. Summer was coming, which meant trips to the beach with the grandkids. Andrew's season would be over soon, and Gavin's season was just starting. What a good time to leave.

They had some beer and popcorn. Sonny didn't know if that was going to mix well, but that's all they had. It was on. Andrew's team (Badgers) versus the Outlaws. As usual, Andrew had a slow first quarter. He was one for three from the floor. It didn't look like he was feeling any pressure. He looked focused. The second quarter was much better. He was six for nine, with four assists and a few rebounds. This was a well-rounded game for him. At the half, it was tied 51-51. Thankfully, Maggie and Sonny ran out of popcorn and beer, so their stomachs had a little settling time before bed. The third quarter started, and Andrew hit two quick jumpers. He finished the third quarter going four for seven. He had twenty-five points going into the fourth quarter, losing 75-72. This was a great game. Not too many mistakes. Maggie was in the zone. She said she felt like it was the good old days in AAU ball.

They came out in the fourth, making shot for shot. Andrew went two for four, when suddenly, he fell to the ground in pain. Sonny knew he was nursing a sore ankle. He had problems with his ankles since he was in middle school. Sonny hoped it wasn't anything crazy. They took him out and the trainer started working on him. The game kept going point for point. It was 98-94 with four minutes left. Sonny saw Andrew on the bike for a while, then he started jogging back and forth. He looked like he was OK. Sure enough, he went back into the game with three minutes thirty-nine seconds left. They moved the ball well. He looked like he was on solid ground. It was 101-99 with one minute left. Badgers ball. They ran the ball through Andrew, and with two seconds left on the shot clock, he hit a three pointer from the corner. Maggie and Sonny went crazy, the crowd went crazy, Razor went crazy. It was 102-101 with seconds left and they took a time out. Sonny saw Andrew get up from the bench, arguing with is coach. They just took him out of the game. I guess coach felt he wasn't one hundred percent and he wanted his best defense out there. Sonny got it, but didn't necessarily agree with it. Andrew hadn't shown anything to make the coach worry he couldn't take care of business defensively. Then Sonny thought about Bill Buckner. The coach wanted to do the right thing and keep him in the game to win the World Series while he was on the field. We all know how that ended. Besides, this was game one, not the last game of the series. Andrew needed to realize the team needed him healthy for the series, not just one game. Andrew sat, the time out was over, and the game continued. The defense was strong, and the Badgers forced a turnover with eighteen seconds left. They were quickly fouled, and went to the line. Andrew's teammate, Ollie, hit two for two, so they were up 104-101. The Badgers defended against the three pointer and let the Outlaws come up the court. No fouls and one of their guys hit a layup to make it 104-103 with nine seconds left. Again, Ollie was quickly fouled. Again, he hit two for two. 106-103 with eight seconds left. The Badgers defense let the Outlaws get to mid court, and with three seconds left, fouled them. They went two for two and coach called a time out. 106-105 with three seconds left. James, another of Andrew's teammates, inbounded the ball and with one second left, he was fouled. He hit one for two. The score was 107-105. The Outlaws inbounded the ball, took a half-court shot, and missed. Badgers win!

A perfect ending for the day. Maggie and Sonny were so excited. They waited to see all of the interviews. It started with Andrew and they quickly asked about his injury. He thanked Maggie and Sonny for giving him the tools he needed to be successful, and dedicated this game to them. Maggie and Sonny started crying. They raised their boys right. They were respectful and loving people. He went on to say his ankle was a little sore, but he was able to put pressure on his foot without a lot of pain. The swelling was minimal, and he figured he would be ready to go with the day off before the next game. That was a huge load off of Sonny's mind, and all of the minds of his team and fans. Maggie and Sonny were so excited and nowhere near ready for bed. Sonny found two more beers in the fridge outside, so they popped them open and toasted. They watched a little TV, and they both fell asleep on the sofa. Razor was nowhere to be found, so he probably fell asleep on the bed.

Chapter 16

Maggie woke Sonny up the next morning.

"This is probably your last day of work. Go in with a big smile, come home with a bigger one."

Sonny got up, showered and changed. Maggie made breakfast for all, including Razor. Lots of eggs and bacon. Sonny finished up and said he would leave work early so he could pick up everything she wanted for the dinner party. Becky was going to call Maggie at 9 a.m. and they were going to figure out where they were going to meet. Maggie would let Sonny know when she found out. She wished Sonny a good day and he went off to work.

Sonny got into the office early, so he viewed some of the video files that were being looked at. He saw the file for the Bones incident was pulled, along with the video. That would only happen if the hearing was scheduled. He called Tracks to find out if he was served his notice of appearance. Tracks said when he spoke to his sponsor, he advised Tracks to get served, since he already knew it was coming. The sponsor felt that delaying the acceptance of the notice was delaying justice from being served. Tracks thought about it and decided to pick up the notice. He knew Sonny would understand because he was cleaning himself up and he wanted to do the right thing. Sonny said he did the right thing and cut the conversation short. This wasn't good. If Tracks would have avoided the notice, and Sonny went over to the CNU, the charges against Bones would have been automatically dropped and the videos would not have been an issue. They would have remained sealed and no one would have ever seen the copy on the main server. Now that Tracks accepted his notice, the process began, and the comparison of the videos would begin. Sonny had to get his hands on the server copy or somehow destroy it. He had no access to the main server of the Council, but Maggie might know a way. He called her and went over what happened with Tracks. She asked if there was any other way to take care of this problem, and Sonny said there wasn't. The server copy needed to be erased or damaged. She said to give her a few minutes and she'll call back.

Sonny was in an all-out panic. There is no way he could leave this Sunday, knowing Johnny and Ronnie would get locked up for helping them get to the CNU. It was out of the question. Sonny had to finish up and get out into the street and see Johnny. He had no reviews to do, so he quickly left the HUB and went straight to Johnny's.

Johnny was in front, so when Sonny walked past him, he said, "We need to talk now."

He must have heard the urgency in Sonny's tone, so he followed him inside. Sonny spoke about the video and what needed to happen. This was the first time Sonny had ever seen Johnny worried. He could see Johnny was trying to make sense of it all and come up with a plan. He had nothing. Johnny called Ronnie over and got him involved in the conversation. Ronnie started shaking and needed to sit down. Ronnie and Johnny had it good in the UST, since it began. There were few rules in the beginning, and they knew how to work around them. As new laws were passed, they learned how to work around them too. They were never in danger of getting in trouble. This was the first time they were facing adversity. There was no way Sonny would let them down. Sonny said he was working on a plan and not to worry, that he would get back to them this afternoon.

Sonny was in full panic mode. He decided to call Double D and ask him if he could meet for lunch. Double D said he was kind of busy and asked if it could wait until dinner.

Sonny said, "I really need your opinion on something. It impacts dinner, so I would really appreciate your opinion."

Double D got the hint, because he said he could free up his schedule at 11:30 a.m., as long as that wasn't too early. Sonny said that was fine and he could meet him in the lobby of his building. Sonny ran back to the HUB and put in a deviation order, since he was still working, but out of his district, and went to meet with Double D. It wouldn't raise any red flags. People did that all the time.

Sonny got there right on time. As he was parking, Double D came out of the building. Sonny pulled out of the spot and asked him to get into the car. As soon as he got in, Double D asked him what was going on. Sonny filled him in about the video being pulled and how he needed access to the server to take care of it.

Double D shook his head violently and screamed, "Fuck!"

He seemed more upset than Sonny was. He said there was no way of getting in there without being identified. Someone was always manning the department at the main desk and you had to be signed in to get into that area. Getting remote access involved getting someone's user name and password. They could have done that if they had more time. Double D said to give him some time and he would come up with something. Sonny dropped him back off at his building and headed back to work. Sonny called Maggie and she said she didn't have anything yet.

Sonny got back to work and went back to Johnny's. He asked him if he thought Mike might be able to help out. Johnny said that was a good idea, and he would reach out to him immediately. Johnny would put the call in as an emergency, so Mike would get back to him quickly. Johnny went to make his call and Sonny went back out to work, trying to keep his mind occupied. Sonny walked around in a daze. He probably couldn't tell you what day it was. He just hoped nothing crazy happened that he had to respond to on the street.

About an hour later, he got a call from Johnny who said, "I've got something I want to get your opinion on. Please come by when you can."

Sonny said he would be right over.

Johnny was able to speak with Mike and he let him know what was happening. Mike couldn't help, but suggested they "use the streets" for help. He wanted Johnny to let him know how things worked out before Sunday, in case they had to call the whole thing off. Johnny said he made a few calls and was waiting to hear back on them. Johnny didn't know what else to do. Sonny said he met with Double D and that he was working on something, as well as Maggie. Sonny would get back out to work and let Johnny know when he heard back from someone.

It was getting late and Sonny was almost done with work. The phone rang, and it was Maggie. She asked if he could talk because she had something. Sonny said he was about to finish up and could call her on the phone when he was in the car. She said to let Johnny know she had a plan, and they would need his help. She wanted Johnny to be at the house when they spoke about the plan. Sonny said he would take care of that. Before he made it back to the HUB, Sonny went over to Johnny's and asked him to meet at the house in an hour. He asked if he should bring Ronnie with him, and Sonny said yes.

Sonny finished up at the HUB and went home. He called

Maggie and let her know he was on his way. She asked if Johnny was coming and Sonny said Johnny was coming with Ronnie. Sonny asked if he should have Double D come over too. She thought it was best to keep him completely out of this. Sonny passed the tower on the way home and he shook his head again. He forgot to look it up. Sonny felt he would never know what it was for. Double D called before he got home. Sonny said they were taking care of the problem and would let him know what happened.

Sonny got to the house and Johnny and Ronnie were already there. Maggie went over the plan with them, and it wasn't ideal. Sonny went into the house and sarcastically thanked Maggie for waiting for him to get home before discussing the plan. All she did was briefly describe what they had to do, not the details. She added that she was extremely pressured by Johnny to tell him the plan, so she gave him a little to calm him down. They all sat down and Maggie began to lay out the plan. She couldn't think of any way to get this done, so she had to take a chance. She weighed the risks, and basically had no choice.

Since she was meeting Becky anyway, she let Becky know they were leaving for the CNU. She didn't give her any specifics. Becky seemed really happy for her, but was saddened to know Maggie was leaving her. Becky asked if there was anything she could do to help.

Maggie said, "As matter of fact, there might be."

Maggie spared her the details and informed Becky she needed access to the main server of the Council. She didn't tell her why, just that she needed access. Becky called her husband Joe, and they met up with him. Becky let Maggie explain the situation to Joe. Joe kept giving Becky a look as Maggie was talking. Becky continued to nod her head affirmatively.

When Maggie finished, Joe said, "Hypothetically, if I can get you access to the server, how do I know it's for what you just told me about, or if it's some part of a corruption investigation?"

Becky got upset and said, "Joe! Don't disrespect my friend like that."

Joe said he was just asking because this was a "big thing," and he was worried. Maggie understood, and promised it was only to help her get out of the CNU. Joe appreciated what Maggie said, but he needed something to help him feel better about this. When Maggie said Johnny was a big part of the plan, Joe nodded his head and was silent for a few seconds. He asked if Johnny would be there when they accessed the server. Maggie said she could make that happen.

Joe shook his head again and said, "OK. We got a deal. This guy owes me a favor, so there's no charge for the service. Becky really likes you, so you get the family discount."

Joe gave Maggie the address of the guy who could get in. He said all they had to tell them was "Joe Russo sent us." The problem was it had to be done after midnight, and was in the "Lower Bowel." The Lower Bowel was a section in the South Bronx that was off limits to the government. It was basically a haven for drug addicts and criminals. The Council had so many issues with this area, it just turned its back on it and "let it be." It was an extremely dangerous area. Before Maggie and Sonny asked, Johnny said he was fine with going in there. He knew some people in there, so if they got into trouble, he had backup. Ronnie wanted to go too, so it would be three of them. Johnnie would get them down there, and he would supply the weapons. If anything happened down there, they needed untraceable weapons. If anyone saw Sonny's standard issue handgun, they would know he was a handler and that would be bad. Johnny said they could meet at his apartment at 11 p.m. and leave from there. Ronnie and Johnny left, and Maggie and Sonny started analyzing the plan. They didn't want any trace of any of this coming back to them, so they pulled out an old map to see where the location was. Sonny had family who lived down there before the split, so he was kind of familiar with it. It was just that it had been over twenty years since he was down there. There were a few quick exits out of there, but who knew what changed. He would have to leave it up to Johnny.

Maggie was really worried about this plan. She knew it was the only way to get it done, but she felt uncomfortable about the meet location. Sonny understood. It had been years since either of them had gone into a dangerous situation like this. But Sonny had two guys with him that worked the streets and were used to meets like this. That gave Maggie some comfort, but she was still worried. Sonny tried to ease her worries the best he could. He asked if she took her meds and she said she didn't. Good, that meant they could have a drink. Sonny got a good bottle of scotch from the cabinet and they had a few drinks. As they talked things out, Sonny saw a calmness come over Maggie. Not something that would knock her out, just a slight removal of one of her many edges. They stayed in the living room and cuddled until it was time for Sonny to go. Maggie made sure he had nothing on him that would reveal his real identity. Sonny only took a wallet with some cash and the ID that Johnny gave him. Maggie cried as she gave him a big hug.

She said, "Please be careful."

Sonny promised her they would get the job done and they would be with the boys for Sunday dinner.

They drove to Johnny's apartment and Maggie asked about it. Sonny said Johnny kept it because he slept there on nights he worked late and didn't want to go home and wake everyone up. She gave Sonny "that look" and smirked.

He shrugged his shoulders and said, "What do you want me to say? That's what he told me."

They arrived a little early, so Sonny waited in the car for Johnny and Ronnie to show up. Sonny said he knew Maggie was scared, but it would all be fine. He promised to come home breathing and in one piece. Johnny and Ronnie showed up, so Sonny gave Maggie a big hug. She began to tear up, so Sonny left the car before it got bad.

While they were in the apartment, Johnny gave Sonny a handgun and said it was clean and untraceable. He went over how the neighborhood was setup and said he and Ronnie had been down their hundreds of times. He let his people know they would be there, just in case things went bad. They would be close by. Johnny didn't know anything about the address they were going to. They went down to the cars and started the trip. Ronnie drove so Johnny could go over a few more things. Johnny liked deals where no money was exchanged, but it also made him nervous. He knew Russo was known as a man of his word, so that was a plus. Johnny would take the lead and would go into this place first. He asked Sonny how long it should take, once they were in the server, and Sonny said it shouldn't take more than a half hour. Johnny thought that was good because the longer they were there, the more rivals would get word they were there, and might decide to try something stupid. Johnny's boys would be on top of that, if anything happened. Johnny believed they were probably dealing with hired guys, not an independent organization. One of the big guns down there hired these guys and kept them for themselves, only contracting them out for the right price or for the right job. If Joe knew where to go, and said they owed him a favor, Johnny, Ronnie and Sonny all believed these guys were owned by the family.

The last thing Johnny said to Sonny was, "If anything, I mean ANYTHING goes bad, you leave and don't turn your back. I will give you the keys for the car. All that I ask is you scream, "A-Team" when you get outside. That will signal my guys to move in. Promise me."

Wow. Sonny thought about it and said, "There's no way I could leave you guys behind. We all get out of there together, or I'm staying with you."

Johnny was getting angry and replied, "There's no time to argue this point. Remember, I know the area and I know what could happen. Me and Ronnie have been in many tight spots down there. We know how to stay safe and get out in one piece. Promise me you will just go if the time came. I need my guys in the street and you would be the one to signal them. Promise me."

Sonny knew he wasn't going to make Johnny happy until he agreed to leave at the first sign of trouble.

"OK, I promise."

Johnny said Sonny should remember they are counting on him to alert the troops and not doing so would not be good.

Sonny said, "I know. Consider it done."

Once they got close, Sonny didn't recognize anything. Everything was newer than he remembered, but it was still dark and dirty. Herds of zombies roamed the streets. He didn't think any of them knew where they were. There were lots of fences with barbed wire and cars set up as barricades. This was a war zone. There were riots down there when the split happened, but he couldn't imagine that all of this was just left over from then. He couldn't believe people lived down there. He hoped there were no kids around.

They pulled up in front of the address, which was a private house, among a row of private houses. There was a small group of armed men standing in front of the house they needed to go into. Johnny said to remember what he said and follow his lead. When they got out of the car, they gained the full attention of the three armed men. Johnny walked up to them first, with Ronnie behind him, then Sonny. Johnny knew one of the guys.

Johnny said, "What's up Big Red? I haven't seen you in a minute."

Big Red leaned into Johnny and gave him a hug.

Big Red looked up and said, "Ronnie? You're here too? And who's that holding up the rear?"

Ronnie said hi to Big Red.

Johnny said, "That's my friend Max, who needed some help, so his friend Big Joe Russo hooked him up. And here we are."

Big Red said they were cleared to go in, except for Ronnie.

Ronnie looked nervous and Johnny asked Big Red, "What is this about? I thought we were cool?"

Big Red said, "We are cool. Ronnie isn't. He had some business with an associate of mine, and it didn't go too well."

Now Sonny started getting nervous. The only thing keeping him calm was knowing Johnny's friends were around there, watching them, because they were still street side. You could feel the tension start to rise. Johnny quickly asked Big Red to let Sonny in, so they could figure things out.

Big Red said, "I don't have a problem with Max. He's a friend of Big Joe and he's free to go inside to take care of his business."

Johnny looked at Sonny and said, "Go ahead, Max. We'll take care of this and we'll come in side in a minute."

And just like that, Sonny was on his own.

Sonny knocked on the door, and someone asked who it was.

Sonny said, "Big Joe Russo sent me."

The door opened and the guy said, "I was expecting you. Come on in."

He peeked outside and asked what all the ruckus was. Sonny said there was something that went down, and they had to clarify things.

The guy said, "I don't know where you're from, but around here, clarifications can get bloody."

Great. Just what Sonny needed to hear. The guy introduced himself as Possum. They walked into the house and it was one big room full of computers and electronics. There was one armed man in there, right next to the exit. There was only one person on the computer.

They went over to her and Possum said "I'd like you to meet Stargirl."

Sonny said hi, and Stargirl barely looked around at him and said "Hey."

Possum said, "I was informed you needed access to the main server of the Council."

Sonny said, "Yes, I do."

Stargirl asked Sonny to take a seat next to her. She wanted to know what part of the server she needed to access. Sonny said she needed to access court records, specifically, evidence. Both Possum and Stargirl looked at each other, then looked at Sonny.

Possum said, "We never ask why a person needs to do something, but a clean cut person like you? Access to evidence? You must be doing someone a big favor."

Sonny said, "Yeah, something like that."

Suddenly, they heard rapid gunfire outside. Possum and Stargirl dropped to the floor. The armed guy yelled at Sonny to do the same. It went on for a couple of minutes. The armed guy was looking at the surveillance cameras to see what was happening, but someone quickly took them out. Then it went silent. It seemed like they were on the floor for an eternity. Then someone knocked on the door. The armed guy situated himself next to the door and directed Possum to see who it was. Possum quietly got up and asked who it was. Sonny heard the voice, and knew it was Johnny.

He said, "I'm here with my friend Max, who is inside with you. I'd like to come in."

Possum looked at the armed guy, who nodded and motioned for Possum to let him in. As Possum unlocked the door, the armed guy pointed his rifle, chest high, at the door. He was going to take Johnny out. Sonny couldn't let that happen. Possum opened the door and Johnny stepped in. Before Johnny cleared the doorway, Sonny shot the armed guy four times in the chest.

Johnny immediately dropped to the floor and called out "Max!"

Sonny said, "I'm fine. I took out the only guard. He's behind the door. There are two more of them in here. Possum is by the door with you and Stargirl is with me. They are good. Not threats."

Johnny got up from the ground and helped Possum to his feet. Sonny asked Stargirl if she was OK, and she said she was fine. They all got up and went toward the computers. Sonny asked Johnny what happened and where Ronnie was.

Johnny said, "Later!"

Sonny got the hint. He asked Stargirl if they could get back to work. She said she didn't know if she should help. Sonny asked why and she said because they just shot up her protection.

Possum looked at her and said, "He was sent by Big Joe. We

have to help him. Whatever happens outside is not our business. We only care about the inside stuff."

Still a little shaken up, Stargirl said she still didn't know. She needed a minute to gather herself.

Sonny grabbed her hand and said, "I know this was a lot to take, kid. But I need to get this done tonight."

Stargirl looked at Sonny and said, "I'm used to hearing the shooting, but I never saw someone get killed right in front of me. I didn't like him, but I never saw anyone get shot."

Johnny was on edge and yelled, "Get your shit together quickly or we're going to have a problem."

Sonny yelled at him to, "Take it easy," and promised Stargirl everything was going to be fine.

Sonny asked if there was anything he could do to help her relax, and she asked him to move away from her and leave her alone. Sonny went toward Johnny and Possum went to Stargirl's side.

Sonny motioned to Johnny to give Stargirl a break, and said, "She's a young kid who went through something traumatic. She'll come around soon. Besides, none of these young kids today have too many feelings."

Johnny said they really didn't have time to waste.

He yelled at Possum, "What's going on? Is she ready? We need to get this going."

Johnny said if they didn't get on this soon, they would have to leave. Sonny said there was no way they were leaving without taking care of the video. Johnny said they could delay the move and find another way.

Sonny said, "We are here now. This is the way. We have to do it now."

As Sonny finished his last word, Johnny walked over to

Possum and put a gun to his head.

He yelled at Stargirl, "Is this motivation enough for you, or do you want to see your friend's brains splattered all around here?"

Possum began to cry and beg for his life.

Sonny yelled at Johnny to stop and he said, "If this is the only way to take care of the videos, then this is the only way it's going to happen."

Stargirl was crying and trembling.

Sonny changed his demeanor with her and said, "You better get into the server now, because I won't be able to stop my friend from blowing Possum's brains out."

Stargirl gathered enough strength to get up and log into the computer. Within a minute, she was in the server. Just then, one of Johnny's guys came in and said to hurry up, because they only had about ten or fifteen minutes before it became a situation. Stargirl got Sonny to the evidence section and he took over. He found the videos and began to erase both of them. They were going to know they were tampered with anyway, so deleting them was faster than modifying them. It took four minutes to delete the first one, which was the original copy, with no tampering. They waited another minute for the second video to start to erase and then left. Johnny let go of Possum and he ran to Stargirl.

Johnny said, "You know this was just business, right?" as they left the location and went to the cars.

Even if Stargirl was to stop it, they only had the version where Sonny deleted the scene around Johnny's. Sonny jumped into the car with Johnny and gave him the keys. He waved to his guys and they drove off.

Sonny asked, "Where's Ronnie? What happened to

Ronnie?"

Johnny said he got shot. When things went bad, Big Red made sure he shot Ronnie first. Johnny found out Ronnie ripped off one of the cousins of the big boss down there, on a deal with a meat truck. The big boss found out about it and put a "pull notice" out there for Ronnie.

Johnny said, "I'm not saying he deserved to get shot, but when you mess with a boss's family, bad things happen. And I understand that."

Ronnie was in bad shape, but he should pull through. They quickly got him to a trauma center.

Sonny couldn't believe what just happened. He killed a man. Ronnie got shot. Johnny just threatened to blow someone's brains out. All Sonny wanted was to get back together with his boys. Did it have to come down to this? People had to lose their lives for this to happen?

People might suffer from PTSD so Maggie and Sonny could be with their family again? This was a fucked up place. This division of the country had made things worse. The system wasn't perfect, but at least people were together, for good or bad. The country continued to evolve, trying to make things better for everyone. Then that jackass became president and totally divided the people. His backers stood by him through everything. All of his lies. All of his actions. And why? Because the other side wasn't any better. They thought the wealthy were evil people and they should pay for everything. Tax, tax, tax. Sure, the president tried to take care of his wealthy friends. It was up to his backers to set him straight. But for some reason, they didn't. Were they scared of him? They were afraid to be outside of the inner circle, on their own, to feel his wrath and ridicule. Somewhere along the way, the government forgot to make compromises. Instead, everyone backed their own parties, at any cost. They didn't need a division of the land. They needed to change the rules. There were so many things that could have changed.

Instead, they took the easy route and said, "We'll go over here and do our thing, you go over there and do your thing."

After the division, the top of the governments didn't change. The CNU mostly kept things the same. The rich became richer. This time they didn't have any opposition to call them out. In the UST, where it was supposed to be equality for all, turned out to be just the same as the CNU. During Sonny's last days there, he uncovered corruption of the FC system, a system that was set up to reward people for hard work and good deeds.

So now people had to die. In all of his career, Sonny never shot at, let alone kill, someone. He knew he had no choice because he would have killed Johnny. It makes it justifiable, but it didn't make him feel better. Sonny took a life. He ended the life of someone's child. He couldn't shake that feeling. He knew many people who got into shootouts. They either took the bull by the horns and worked it out, or they buried the feelings and paid for it later on. Sonny knew Johnny said nothing would come out of anything that happened there, but was it true? What about Ronnie? Sonny knew he did something that triggered the whole thing, but would he be OK? He went out there because of Sonny. He would be home right now, instead of the hospital, if he didn't go out and help. This was way too much to take. Maggie would be so upset. How would she take the whole thing? Would they be in trouble with Joe and the Russo family? Would Johnny be in trouble with them? Would Becky blow the lid on the plan because of what happened? Should Sonny go and speak with Joe in person? Should Sonny avoid him and just get out of there and not speak with him about anything?

What would happen if this new virus got out? How would the CNU react to the USTs non-compliance of the treaty by not informing them of the virus? How would the UST respond? Sonny was at the point of not caring, as long as his family was together. Would the UST try and get back at Sonny's family because they were traitors who gave information to the CNU? Could they get back at them? Did they have hit squads? Could they poison them?

"What am I doing?" Sonny thought. "I'm all over the place. We will get through this. This will not be for nothing. Ronnie will be fine. Johnny will be fine. Joe will understand. The virus will be contained. Maggie will remain calm. We will still go to the CNU. We will do the drive with the volleyball team and get across the bridge. We will be with our boys. Life will be good. It will all work out." Johnny saw that Sonny was coming apart at the seams.

He yelled at Sonny, "Suck it up."

Johnny said what happened wasn't a good thing, but they made it out and were going to be fine. They had complications, but they did what they set out to do. Johnny was a mess too. He tried to act like he was the tough guy in a movie, but Sonny saw through him. He was visibly upset. Johnny drove them back to his apartment. Johnny said to take a shower first and he would lay out some clean clothes for him. Sonny showered and tried to wash away all of the hurt. He scrubbed his skin so hard he thought he was going to bleed. He pounded the walls of the shower and broke down and cried. He fell to the bottom of the shower and held on to the side of the tub. He played the shooting over and over in his head. Each time, it stopped as the guy hit the floor after he shot him. Sonny believed Maggie would make him think clearer. He felt Maggie would understand what he did and

260

would be able to talk him down. He needed to go home.

Sonny got out of the shower and Johnny handed him a drink. He said Sonny should stay the night so they could talk it out before they went home. He should be hearing from his guys soon about how Ronnie was doing. Sonny wanted to go home because he thought Maggie would be able to help him. Johnny needed to speak with Sonny for a while to help him calm down. Sonny understood. Johnny went over what happened on the street, once Sonny went inside the house. One of the guys outside signaled to a guy on the roof and five other armed guys showed up. Big Red told Johnny what happened with Ronnie and the meat truck, and said Ronnie had to pay for his actions. Once Johnny heard that, he called out "A-Team," and his guys moved in. When Big Red saw them moving in, he shot Ronnie and all hell broke loose. In the end, two of ours and four of theirs got shot. The other guys got away and that's why they were pressed for time after the shooting stopped. Sonny laid out what happened inside with Possum, Stargirl and the guard. He knew what was going to happen and he prepared himself to shoot first, once Johnny started to come through the door. Johnny thanked Sonny for saving his life, and said he knew he could count on him when the shit hit the fan. It wasn't until then, that Sonny began to feel a little better. He saved Johnny's life. He made sure his friend was going home to his family. Sonny shot someone who was going to take that away from him.

Johnny's phone rang. It was one of his guys at the hospital. He said Ronnie lost a lot of blood, and was in the ICU, but he was going to pull through. Thank God! Johnny went over to Sonny and they had the most meaningful hug two friends could have. It was like they squeezed out all of the bad things they just went through. Sonny was safe. Johnny was safe. Ronnie was going to be OK. Sonny deleted the video. The biggest problem they had to face was Joe. Sonny hoped it wasn't going to be bad. Johnny felt better and said that Sonny could go home now. Sonny asked if he was sure, and that he could stay the night if he wanted him to.

Johnny said, "You saved my life. Me and my family will forever be in your debt. Your father is looking down on you right now and is very proud of his boy. Please go home to your wife. I will be fine."

Sonny called Maggie and asked her to pick him up at the gas station down the street from Johnny's apartment.

She asked how it went, and all Sonny said was, "Mission accomplished."

Before he left the apartment, Sonny asked Johnny to call him, no matter what time it was, when he heard about Ronnie. Johnny said he would. Sonny asked what time he would be heading home, and he said around 6 a.m., because he wanted to be home when his family woke up. Sonny wanted to meet him for lunch and to discuss a few things before they met with his friend and the coaches. Johnny could meet Sonny back at the apartment around 3 p.m. The meet with Charlie and the coaches was set for 7 p.m. so they had plenty of time to talk.

Sonny asked Maggie to pick him up at the gas station so he could take a little walk and clear his thoughts, and put everything into perspective. He was alive. He promised her he would get the job done and come home. He did. Was everything else irrelevant? No, but "mission accomplished" was the right thing to say. Sonny killed a man. Nothing would change that. He had to accept it. Johnny was still breathing because he killed that man. Sonny didn't even know his name. He wouldn't ever know his name. Was he irrelevant? Just a side character in his story of escaping the UST. Did or would his parents know that their child was dead? Would anyone care? Would he be properly buried? Would he have a service? So much guilt. It wasn't from saving Johnny's life. It was from putting him and Ronnie in danger for his cause. They wouldn't even have had to worry about being seen on video if it wasn't for Sonny. There would have been no radio transmissions to worry about. Who was this person Sonny had become? Lying to Maggie and not telling her about his "sex capades" with Luna. Killing a man and assist in threatening the life of another? He had changed. He had to change. He was in a fight for his family. Did it justify the things he had done? He didn't know. He probably would never know. He just needed to accept it and move on. Make his peace. Live his life. Love his family. That would be enough to get him through this. It had to be.

Sonny got to the gas station, and Maggie was there waiting for him. She had a huge smile on her face. That was all about to change. They hugged and got into the car. She immediately knew something was wrong.

"What happened? Is everyone OK?"

Sonny's eyes teared up, and Maggie grabbed him. Sonny burst out into a full cry.

Maggie began to cry. "Are you OK? Tell me what's wrong. Please, tell me what's wrong."

Sonny motioned for Maggie to just drive home. Sonny needed to get off of the street. Maggie drove home, with tears in her eyes. If she only knew what the tears were for.

When they got home and walked into the house, Maggie realized Sonny wasn't wearing clothes that he owned.

They went to the bedroom and Maggie said, "Ok, you need to tell me right now. What happened?"

Sonny went over the whole story, step by step, as he lived it. When Sonny got to the part where he had to shoot the guard, she just hugged him and cut him off.

She cried "I know what happened next. I'm so sorry. You saved your friend. Remember, you saved your friend."

They cried a little more, then Sonny continued. When he got to the part about Johnny putting a gun to Possum's head, Maggie looked emotionless. Sonny finished the story, and she asked what the latest news on Ronnie was. Sonny said he was going to live, and Johnny would call with any new news. Maggie said Johnny did what he had to do. She was glad he was there. She knew Sonny wouldn't be able to do something like that.

Sonny replied, "It's one thing to threaten someone. But it's another thing to mean it."

Maggie said there was no way Johnny would have shot that kid.

Sonny said, "You had to be there. I have never seen Johnny this crazy. He was going to shoot that kid."

They went back and forth on this, then decided to just leave it alone. Their conclusion was Johnny didn't shoot Possum, and they left it at that. They cuddled in bed, and Maggie caressed Sonny's hair as he was falling asleep.

At around 7:30 a.m., Sonny got a call from Johnny. He said Ronnie was taken out of ICU and he was awake. He would have a short hospital stay, but he was going to be fine. They were still on for lunch, and he thanked Sonny again for saving his life.

Johnny asked, "You OK?"

Sonny replied, "Yeah. You too?"

"I'm alive."

Maggie and Sonny stayed in bed for a while and started talking about Joe. They figured they would have heard from him or Becky by now if they knew what happened last night. The real question was should they get in front of it and reach out to them first, or should they do nothing and leave it behind them when they leave on Sunday? The right thing to do would be to call Joe. But are they passed doing the right thing? Were they in the "looking out for ourselves" part of this journey? What would they do once Joe found out? It wasn't their fault. Technically, it was Ronnie's fault. Should they throw him under the bus? Are they now ruthless?

They decided to call Becky, feel her out, then reach out to Joe. The plan was to distance themselves from Ronnie. They had nothing to do with his business. Everything happened in self-defense. Possum and Stargirl weren't hurt. But Johnny threatened to kill Possum. Again, that wasn't Sonny. But he did it for Maggie and Sonny. They wouldn't know how they felt about it until they spoke with Becky and Joe. Since it was still morning, and Maggie and Sonny had a lot of daytime left before the meet in the evening, they decided to make the call now.

Maggie called Becky. She sounded like she was in a good mood. They chatted for a while, all in good spirits, and finally, Becky asked how everything went last night.

Maggie thanked her for her help and said, "We got it done."

Becky was happy to hear that, so at least she didn't seem to know anything about how things went down. Maggie asked if Joe was around, because Sonny wanted to personally thank him. She said he got called away early this morning and she hadn't heard from him. Maggie asked Becky to relay Sonny's message and to ask him to call him when he had the chance. Joe definitely knew what happened. He was probably discussing his options for retaliation. This was bad. Sonny had to let Johnny know what was going on. Sonny still had a few hours before they met up.

Sonny gave him a call. Johnny was at the hospital with Ronnie, so he asked Sonny to keep the call short. Sonny got Johnny up to date on what was going on with Becky and Joe. Johnny said they could talk about it later when they met. He wasn't too concerned, so Sonny played off of his emotions and relaxed a little. Sonny updated Maggie on the call, that Johnny didn't seem worried, and that calmed her down a notch as well.

Maggie and Sonny planned on spoiling Razor for the day, so they stuck with that plan. It was a beautiful sunny day, so they showered, got dressed, and took Razor for a ride down to the beach. Just knowing they were going to the beach made Sonny feel better. The sun, the sand, the water. It was therapeutic. Hopefully it would be able to take his mind off of what happened last night. Even just a little bit. The window was open for Razor to enjoy. Boy did that dog love to be in the car. He made friends at every stoplight. Before they got to the beach, Maggie stopped at the deli and got a half pound of cooked bacon. Razor was going to be spoiled big time.

The beach was crowded. Lots of people walking around with their kids. Not too many dogs out. Maggie and Sonny played frisbee and catch with a ball, and Razor was in heaven. Every few minutes, they stopped for a water and bacon break. Sonny didn't remember ever seeing his tail wag so fast. If he only knew what was coming. They walked down to the water and sat down at the edge. They made sure only their feet got wet because the water was freezing. But Razor didn't care. He was running into waves and jumping back onto the beach. He didn't have a care in the world.

Sonny's phone rang. It was Joe.

He answered the call and said, "What's up Joe?"

He replied, "You know what's up. We need to talk. I'll meet

you in a half hour by the benches next to the old City Hall."

Sonny said he was out, and needed to go home and drop off Maggie and the dog, so he needed forty-five minutes. Joe said not to bother going home. He was bringing Becky, so they could all meet there in a half hour. Sonny agreed and they packed up a headed for City Hall. Maggie asked how he sounded, and Sonny said he didn't get a good read. The good thing was that Becky was going and they were meeting in a very high traffic area. Joe wasn't looking for trouble. He wanted to talk. Maggie and Sonny spoke about how it could go down, but there were too many variables. They just needed to stick with "it had nothing to do with us" for as long as they could.

They arrived a few minutes early and decided to wait in the car until Becky and Joe showed up. They looked around and did their counter surveillance. Everything looked OK. No strange characters, no red flags. They saw Joe and Becky pull up, so they got out of the car and left Razor behind, with the windows cracked open. They were in view of the car, and they didn't think it would be too long. They all met at the benches and exchanged hugs and kisses.

They sat down and Joe looked at Sonny and said, "Before anything, I wanted to let you know that I know it had nothing to do with you."

That lifted a huge weight off of Sonny's shoulders. It was a good start, but Sonny knew they weren't finished.

Joe continued, "With that being said, some bad stuff happened, and it needs to be fixed. I lost a few guys and I know Johnny lost a few guys. Big Red told me you were fine, and you were inside when everything went down. My issue is this: how much did Johnny know? I know he had to defend his guy Ronnie, but did he know about the bad deal before you got there?"

Sonny said that when he spoke with Johnny, he said he didn't know about Ronnie's bad deal. Johnny understood why Ronnie got shot. He didn't like it, but he understood.

Joe said, "I'm not calling you a liar or anything, but I need to hear that from Johnny and Ronnie."

Joe went on about how he respected Maggie and Sonny for all the things they did for the old government, how he enjoyed hanging out with them, and how much of a friend Maggie became for Becky. He was a softy at heart and things like this mattered to him. As for Johnny, he said he knew he had a good reputation for being a stand-up guy that always did the right thing. They shared many business associates and they all had nothing but good things to say about him. Joe said that was the only reason he was sitting there with them, discussing things. Things would have gone down a little differently if he didn't have such a good reputation.

Sonny promised to speak with Johnny and was sure he would want to clear the air with him. Joe didn't know about Ronnie, so Sonny said he was still in the hospital, but it looked good for him. Joe said there was one more thing he wanted to talk about. He asked if Stargirl was able to get what Sonny wanted done in time. Sonny was very surprised on how quickly she got into the main server.

Joe said, "That's my girl."

Stargirl liked that guy Possum and they were both very upset with the way they were treated. Joe didn't think they needed to have a gun pointed at their head to get things done. He understood they were pressed for time, but he didn't appreciate how it was handled. Sonny asked Joe how they could make it right. Joe said that for some reason, Stargirl had never been able to break into all of the HUBs. She could do each one individually, but it took too long and the HUBs changed their security protocols more often than the Council did. Stargirl would need access to a computer in Sonny's HUB, so she could connect it to her server and gain backdoor access to the whole system. That would make them even. Sonny would have to bring Stargirl into the HUB and give her computer access. She could pass as his niece. If anyone asked why Sonny brought her in on a day off and let her get on his computer, he could just say he needed her to arrange his work computer the same way she arranged his home computer. It could work. They would find out what happened, but hopefully, that would be after Sunday. A small risk, but it had to be done. Sonny agreed with Joe to have Stargirl gain access to his computer. Sonny said they had to make it happen tonight around 9 p.m. Joe didn't think that would be a problem and he would call at 7 p.m. to finalize everything. They said their goodbyes, and Maggie and Becky had a long and big hug. They said they were going to miss each other, but that they could meet again soon.

Maggie and Sonny got in the car and Maggie said, "That didn't go too bad. Do you think Johnny will meet with him?"

Sonny was confident Johnny would meet with him. Johnny didn't seem like the type to let things drag on. He would want to settle things as soon as he could. Then Maggie asked how Sonny was going to get Stargirl into the HUB. Sonny laid out his plan and she asked if he knew how quickly it would trigger alarms in the system, which would lead them to his account being compromised. But Sonny didn't know exactly what she was going to do. If she just needed to set things up and could wait until Monday to access the whole system, they were clear and free. If it immediately triggered something, they were in trouble.

It was almost 3 p.m., so Sonny called Johnny and said he was going to be a little late. Maggie and Sonny hurried home and

Maggie said she would get things ready for dinner while Sonny was with Johnny. She asked if Sonny was OK, and if he was ready for the next couple of days.

Sonny said, "Knowing about the next couple of days is the only thing that's keeping me focused. I see us together with the boys. That's my dream that is becoming a reality. I'm ready. I can't tell you what will happen if I crash when this is all done, but at least I will be with my whole family."

Sonny pulled up to the house and let Maggie and Razor out. Maggie said to make sure Johnny was OK, and to reach out to her if he needed help.

Sonny got to Johnny's apartment. He asked Johnny how Ronnie was. Johnny said he was able to speak and open his eyes. He pulled through. Thank God.

But Johnny added, "But now he has to face me."

Sonny raised his eyebrows and Johnny said Ronnie put them in a bad spot. If he would have told Johnny, he would have stayed behind, and none of this would have happened. Sonny said he wanted to go over a few things.

"I met with Joe."

Johnny asked how he was.

Sonny continued, "Of course he was upset, but he understood I had nothing to do with it. He doesn't know if you knew about it and let things escalate."

Johnny angrily said, "What does he think? I go around looking for trouble. Didn't you tell him I didn't know anything?"

Sonny replied, "I told him you didn't know, but he wants to hear it from you. From your mouth to his ears."

Johnny was upset. "That fat fuck. I hate those Queens guys. They think we're still in the '50s and '60s. I'll call him. I'll take care of it. You don't think he holds me responsible, do you?"

Sonny said the conversation was calm and no tempers were heated up. He felt Joe was there to clear things up, not to start trouble. Johnny trusted Sonny's instincts. Then Sonny informed him about Possum and Stargirl, and what he had to do.

"Those young punks. I had plenty of guns pointed at my head by the time I was their age. Where did they think they were? Disneyworld? They commit crimes for money, in an area that goes unchecked."

They agreed today's youth were doomed. Johnny asked how Sonny was going to get that done. Sonny gave him the plan. Johnny asked how risky he thought it was.

"50-50 at best."

Sonny just didn't know enough yet. Johnny asked if he needed help with Stargirl. Sonny suggested he stand down and go home. He did enough and needed to unwind a little.

Sonny wanted to go over how the meet with Charlie and the coaches was going to go. Johnny said it was just that. A meet and greet. They would probably ask a bunch of background questions, like training in first aid. Johnny handed Sonny an ID for Maggie. He looked at it and laughed. It was under the same name, Maria, and the address Luna used. Johnny said the name was known at that address, so he used it over and over. He said their applications had them both retired, having worked for the old government as agents. He said they would know how to handle it. It was just his friend and a couple of "soccer moms," but for volleyball. He asked Sonny to call him once they were done, then he would call Charlie to get a feel on how the coaches liked Maggie and Sonny. He also gave Sonny a phone. He said to use it since no one could trace it, just in case they caught on to Sonny before they left.

Sonny said, "Good idea. Thanks."

Johnny also tossed him a set of keys. He said to use this car to drive to Charlie's house tomorrow. They wouldn't be back to get it, so why park their own car there? Johnny asked what they were going to do with their cars. Sonny said they couldn't do anything with them. Johnny could have them if he wanted them, but Sonny was sure the VINs would be on a watch list.

Johnny said, "Thanks, I'll take them. Don't worry about any list. I got it."

Of course, he did. He said he would take the rest of the stuff Maggie and Sonny wanted him to hold on to when he picked up Razor.

Sonny asked if he was ready for Razor. He said his family might even be more excited than he was. He showed them a picture of Razor and they couldn't wait to meet him. Sonny said he could take Razor tomorrow morning. They just wanted to have one more night with him, since they didn't know how long it would be until they saw him again. Johnny could pick him up at 11 a.m. Johnny wished Sonny luck and reminded him to call him when they were done.

On the way home, Sonny picked up Maggie's favorite dessert, chocolate fudge brownies from Bakery 12. A dozen was called the "Perfect 12." This would probably be the last time she would have them. When he got to the bakery, he had to wait ten minutes for a fresh batch to come out of the oven. When he got home and opened the door, Razor was too interested in the box Sonny was carrying. He kept poking his nose at it. Maggie, who had the nose of a blood hound, got a whiff of them two rooms away.

She said, "Perfect 12!"

What a sense of smell. Dinner was ready. They sat down to eat, and she asked how Johnny was doing. Sonny said Johnny was OK with speaking with Joe, and not to worry about it.

Maggie asked, "OK, but what about Johnny? Is he OK?"

"Johnny is OK. He was upset with Ronnie and he was going to set him straight, but he cares about him. Johnny and his family are so excited about having Razor for a while. Johnny also offered to help with Stargirl."

Maggie said, "OK. I guess he's OK."

Sonny said not to worry. Johnny would come over tomorrow morning to pick Razor up and she could see for herself. They finished dinner, cleaned up and took a short breather before meeting up with Charlie.

The meet was about thirty minutes from the house, so they left a little early. They imagined their first holiday together with the whole family, the Fourth of July. They could have it at Gavin's house this year, then have Christmas at Andrew's house. Of course, they would need to get their own place. That was where they would have Thanksgiving. Maggie said she could see it now, the décor, the kids running around, the smells coming from the kitchen, their boys going back and forth with their banter. It would be like the way their house was fifteen years ago. They were so close.

They got to Charlie's house and parked in front. Charlie came out to greet them. He asked how the ride was and he hoped they found his house easily. He brought them in and introduced them to his husband, Larry. They had a nice sized house. Maggie was impressed. They had a large dog, one of those mixes that didn't shed. His name was Tank. Tank must have smelled Razor because he was all over Maggie and Sonny. There were two women sitting in the living room. Charlie introduced Helen and Tanya, the volleyball coaches. They all sat down and Charlie explained why and how his organization started. He spoke about it for around fifteen minutes. It sounded like it was a good thing. When he was done, he let Tanya speak for a while about how they got into volleyball and why they thought this trip was so important. She spoke for about fifteen minutes too. When Tanya finished, she asked about Maggie and Sonny. Sonny looked at Maggie and she wanted him to take care of their story.

Sonny said, "We have been married for thirty years, and we met on the job, in the old government, at work. We have two boys and we liked traveling for sports with them, so this volunteer work seemed like a good fit."

Sonny was done in seven minutes. He painted a broad picture, and hoped it wasn't too broad. Charlie said he knew Maggie and Sonny were trained in CPR and first aid, and everything they would need for an emergency was in the bus. Charlie highlighted the fact that Maggie and Sonny were both former law enforcement officers, and that made all of them feel a little better. Helen asked if they could push the drive up to 11 a.m., so the girls could get settled in at the hotel before their first game at 7 p.m. Sonny smiled and said he knew they wanted to get their earlier, but Maggie and him had something they had to take care of in the morning. 1:30 p.m. was the earliest they could commit to, but they might possible be ready by 1 p.m.

Helen thanked them, but then looked at Charlie and said, "You knew we wanted to get there early. Can't you still call the other drivers?"

Charlie looked uncomfortable and said, "Helen, I told you they couldn't commit to the whole trip and that was why we had to change drivers."

Helen was a pain in the ass. You could just tell.

Helen said, "Ok, Charlie, I get it."

She said she would really appreciate it if Maggie and Sonny

could get there as early as possible. Sonny said they would do their best. She said all of the girls would be there by 11a.m, ready to go. The bus would be in front of Charlie's house, so they could leave the car at his house.

Sonny put his phone on vibrate when they went into the house. Joe called him eight times. Shit! He better call him back fast. Sonny called him and apologized for not picking up. Joe said if he didn't know anything about him, he would have sworn Sonny was avoiding him. Sonny said they had to finalize a few things before they left for the CNU. Joe said OK and that he, and Stargirl, would meet up at 10:30 p.m., at the location of Sonny's choice. Sonny said to meet him at a parking lot of a supermarket close to the HUB. He could wait there while Sonny took care of business with Stargirl.

Joe said, "OK. See you later."

Maggie was driving home while Sonny spoke with Joe.

She asked, "What did he say? How did he sound?" once Sonny got off of the phone.

Sonny relayed the conversation to her, and she asked how he thought Stargirl was going to react, being alone with him in the car. Again, something Sonny didn't think of. Sonny figured she would be OK with it, since Joe was allowing it to happen. Maybe the thought of her getting into the whole system means so much to her, she would forget about what happened. They would find out soon enough.

They got home and had a few minutes to spare. Sonny washed up and back out he went. Maggie said to be careful and to call her if anything happened. Sonny got in the car, and called Johnny, to let him know how things went. Charlie had already called him. Charlie felt it went well, and the ladies were happy with Maggie and Sonny. Charlie said to pass along his apology for Helen, that she was just a pain in the ass. Sonny called it. Johnny put in a call to Joe and they were meeting tomorrow afternoon. Sonny asked him if he was worried about it, and Johnny was not. He had a good talk with Joe, and they were just going to iron out some details over some cocktails. Johnny asked Sonny to be careful and not to trust Stargirl, that he should make sure he watched her every move. Johnny wouldn't put it passed her to alert someone on purpose, once she gained access. Sonny still knew his way around these systems, so he would know what to look out for. Sonny promised to call Johnny once they were done.

Sonny got to the meet spot and Joe was already there. Stargirl got into the car with Sonny, and Joe went around to his side to speak with him. He said he spoke with Johnny and they were working things out, trying to come to an amicable agreement. Stargirl was excited to learn she would finally get into the whole system at once.

Sonny looked over at her and said, "I'm really sorry we put you through all of that. I hope somehow you could forgive me. And your friend Possum too."

She said, in an annoying teenage voice, "Whatever. It's all cool. Possum went through something like that many times. I never did, but it's cool. As long as I get access, I'm cool."

Joe said, "Now that everyone's cool, let's get this thing done already."

Sonny said they would go into the HUB with no problem and should be able to get into the system within minutes. Sonny didn't know exactly what Stargirl was going to do, so he couldn't give Joe a time for its completion. She would explain it to Sonny on the way. Joe said he wouldn't get nervous until they went longer than a half hour. Sonny gave Joe the number to the phone

Johnny gave him and said to call if he got worried.

Once Sonny pulled away, he said, "I am truly sorry. I feel so horrible knowing I put you and Possum through that."

She said, "Whatever. I told you it was cool. Just get me into the server."

Sonny asked her what exactly she was going to do. She was going to set a timer on a virus to go off on Monday morning, when the office had lots of activity going on. She asked if 10 a.m. was a good time. Sonny said yes. Once it activated, it would map the HUBs server, which would also show how the other HUBs got into the Council's server. It should alert security that a breach occurred, but it would be too late at that point. She needed the mapping. New passwords were easy for her to get through.

They got to the HUB and Sonny asked her if she was ready.

She said, "Whatever."

They parked without a problem. They went upstairs and right to Sonny's desk. Sonny saw a couple of the guys and he saw they were confused as to why he was there with a young girl. Sonny decided to be proactive. He got into the system and handed the reigns to Stargirl."

He said, "Now do your magic and make it speak to me like you did with my home computer."

She looked at Sonny and rolled her eyes. Sonny intercepted the few handlers that were headed toward his desk. Sonny said his niece set up his computer at home and it worked better and was organized in a way that made sense. He wanted the same thing for his work computer, so he brought her to the HUB to work her magic. They seemed satisfied and walked away. Sonny knew he promised Johnny he wouldn't leave Stargirl alone at his computer, but he had no choice. He got back to his desk and watched her finish up. She planted a trojan on the main drive of the server and set it to go off on Monday at 10 a.m. Sonny logged off, and they left. When they got to the car, Sonny asked her if she had any problems. Stargirl laughed was angry at herself because the system was so old and easy to hack. It was so old, she forgot the ways to crack it. It could have been done at her place in five minutes if she had known how vulnerable it really was.

They made it back to Joe in twenty-five minutes. Joe laughed and said he wasn't worried one bit. He asked how everything went. Stargirl said it was easy and done. Joe was happy.

Sonny said, "In the last few weeks, I've done things I had never thought I would do. I did it all for family."

Joe smiled and said, "You never know your true self until your family is on the line. The things we do for our families are without regret. They come first."

Sonny shook his hand and said, "Agreed."

Sonny said bye to Stargirl, and she actually wished him luck in whatever he was doing. Joe and Sonny laughed. Joe wished Sonny luck and said he was there for him, if he ever needed him.

On the way back, Sonny called Maggie and said everything went well, without a hitch. He called Johnny and said the same thing. Johnny said to make sure he got a good night's sleep because he needed to be sharp tomorrow. Johnny was going to reach out to Mike and let him know everything was a go for tomorrow, and he would see Sonny in the morning. Sonny's last call was to Double D. He was totally in the dark from before the whole incident in the Bronx. Sonny wasn't going to tell him about that over the phone. He just said he was heading home and they were all a go for tomorrow. Sonny asked for him and Sara to come over tomorrow morning for breakfast.

He said, "Absolutely."

Sonny asked him to come over at 9 a.m. He said he would bring over some warm rolls.

Sonny got home and Maggie was waiting at the door for him. They hugged and said they couldn't believe it was happening. All the shit they went through paid off. All that was left was for them was to drive a bus full of girls over a bridge. They would be leaving some good friends behind, but knew they would see them all again. They went over everything, trying to think of anything they missed that might implicate any of their friends for helping out. They came up with nothing. Sonny felt they covered all of their bases. All that was left was to get a good night's sleep and to give Razor as much room on the bed as he wanted.

The alarm went off at 7 a.m. Amazingly, Razor was curled up in a ball, and didn't move much all night. Sonny actually slept. Maggie opened her eyes and asked where Razor was. Sonny laughed and pointed to him. She smiled and said he let her sleep too. By now, Razor was fully awake and jumping all over the bed. Sonny went to go feed Razor, while Maggie showered and got dressed. He asked her what they should make, and she said some eggs, bacon, and waffles sounded good. Yes, it did. Sonny ran Razor outside for a quick walk. It was another nice day. Only a few clouds in the sky. He finished up the walk and Maggie was already in the kitchen getting things ready. Sonny asked her if she needed his help and she said to just go and get ready, she would get things started. He showered and got dressed. Sonny got the coffee brewing, then mixed the batter for the waffles. Maggie worked on the eggs and bacon. Then the bell rang, and Double D and Sara were there. Sonny ran to the door and let them in. He hugged Sara and Double D. Sara pointed to the bag she was holding and smiled. Sonny touched it and the bread was still warm.

Sara went into the kitchen to see Maggie. Double D smiled and said, "This is it buddy. Are you excited?"

Sonny said, "I'm exhausted."

Double D wanted to hear how everything went down. Sonny promised to tell him after breakfast, because he wanted to enjoy the time with him and Sara.

They sat down to eat, and everyone was full of smiles. Maggie and Sara spoke about what Maggie was going to wear, because chances were that they would be on TV at some point. Maggie said she already had something picked out and she would show her after breakfast. Double D was excited that Sonny was going to go to Andrew's playoff games and see Gavin pitch down the stretch of the season. Sonny said he should come visit during playoff time, so they could go to the games together. Double D said the problem with that is he had to schedule a trip to the CNU two months in advance. Sonny didn't think there was a problem with that because even if the boys lost during one of the playoff rounds, Double D would still be there to hang with them.

"I'm going to miss you, buddy."

Double D said, "Don't start getting mushy with me. We still have some more time together."

They told stories of the old days, from when before they had kids. There was one vacation they all took to the Bahamas. The ladies dared the guys to do things the whole week, and like idiots, they did them. They drank, danced, snorkeled, fell asleep on the beach, got chased by security, and mooned the people on the beach. They did so much and had such a great time. When the kids were born, they all took a big trip to Disney World. The kids had a blast, but Sonny believed the adults had more fun. They always managed to have a great time, without getting hurt.

Breakfast was done and Sonny asked the ladies to go and

relax because the guys would clean up. They ran into the bedroom and didn't look back.

As they cleaned up, Sonny gave Double D the whole story of how they got to the server, the shootout, everything. He was amazed. He wished he was there to help. Sonny was glad Double D wasn't there because then he would have had to worry about him.

Double D then clarified himself, "When I say I wish I was there to help, I didn't mean during the shootout. You know I am allergic to bullets. I would have curled up into the fetal position and cried until the shots were over. I never understood how anyone could deal with being in a shootout."

Sonny put his head down and continued to clean up.

Double D said, "Dude. I'm sorry. I didn't mean to bring you down. Are you OK? Let's talk it out. You know you did what you had to do."

Sonny informed Double D that he felt he would never fully be over what happened, but he was using his family as his main focus to get him through the pain and guilt.

"I did it for them. For us to be together. I'm using that strength."

Double D said that was a good start, but he made Sonny promise to get help and speak with a professional about it when things settled a little. This was an important time when you deal with a traumatic incident like this. The closer to the event, the better. Sonny promised him he would get help.

Razor started up again and ran toward the door. Johnny must be there. Sonny opened the door and saw Johnny and who he assumed to be his family. Johnny gave him a hug and introduced Sonny to his two boys, Frankie, eleven years old, and Gino, thirteen. They looked just like him. Then he introduced his wife,

Angelina. Just as Sonny thought. A beautiful young woman who could be a princess of some island in the Mediterranean. Sonny gave her a hug and invited them all in. Razor and the boys immediately hit it off. They were wrestling and running around as soon as they went out to the yard.

Sonny whispered to Johnny, "What a pleasant surprise."

Johnny said he thought about it and figured of all of the people he knew, Maggie and Sonny were the most grounded, and Angelina had to meet them before they left. Double D and Johnny finally met and had time to talk. Angelina got cornered by Maggie and Sara, and they started to hit it off. Sonny was going to miss this. Somewhere along the way, they lost themselves and became isolated. Sure, they went out with friends from time to time, but they forgot how to have fun and enjoy life. The division of the country hit them in more ways than he had thought. Sonny believed they got so caught up in trying to make the UST a better place from the start, that they forgot to slow down and take a break once in a while. They were leaving these good people behind and it would never be the same. Sonny promised himself to make new friends and enjoy the rest of their lives together.

Time was flying by and Double D and Sara decided to leave. They did a group hug and started to cry. No one said anything. They just enjoyed the moment together. Sara and Maggie couldn't speak.

Double D said, "Good luck and Godspeed. See you on the other side," and they both walked out of the door.

Angelina and Maggie hugged and cried together. Looking at them, you would have thought they were childhood buddies. Johnny asked if Sonny was going to be OK.

Fighting through tears, Sonny said, "Actually, I'm great. I've known him for most of my life. He will remain in my life.

He has done so much for me. I'll always keep him in my heart and as part of my family."

Johnny said he wished he got to know Double D more because he seemed like a great person.

Sonny said, "You can know him more. Do me a favor and become friends with him. It would mean the world to me, knowing the two of you were together as friends. You can watch over him for me. Promise me you'll become friends."

Johnny smiled and said, "I would like that. Of course, I will do this for you. I just wish we had more time together."

Sonny smiled and said, "I'm sure you'll find a way for us to be together."

Johnny yelled out for his boys and said it was time for them to leave. Maggie and Angelina said goodbye and wished they had met sooner. Sonny grabbed Razor's bowls, toys and food. He instructed Johnny's boys on when and how to feed him. They had to make sure he was walked at least three times a day, and that he loved going in the car for rides. They promised to take good care of him. Sonny said goodbye to Angelina, and she took the boys to the car. Maggie bent down and hugged Razor.

As she began to cry, she said, "You better take care of those boys. You're going to have a good time and we'll see you soon."

She got up and said bye to Johnny, then quickly ran into the house crying. Sonny gave Razor a big hug too. He was sad they weren't going to see him for a while, but knowing he was in good hands with Johnny made him feel better. Sonny wasn't too sad. He was happy he was going to be hanging with the boys and treated it as he was having a vacation.

Johnny asked Sonny to give him a copy of his keys so he could come back up pick up the stuff. Johnny said he didn't have room in the car, since he brought the whole family. Sonny was glad he brought them.

"You have a beautiful family. I know why you keep them away. Don't ever feel bad for protecting them."

Johnny said, "Thank you."

Mike was already working on getting the dog and the rest of their things over to the CNU. Johnny didn't think it would be long before they were reunited with Razor. Sonny hugged Johnny and thanked him for everything. There was no way they could have gotten to this point without him. Johnny said Mike would be waiting on the other side of the bridge. He would take them as soon as they crossed and provide the team with another driver.

As Johnny walked with Razor to the car, he said, "Love you, brother. Be careful because I won't be there to watch over you."

Sonny smiled and said, "Love you too brother. Somehow, I know you'll still be watching me."

Johnny got into the car and drove off.

Sonny went into the house and found Maggie crying on the bed.

She said even though she wanted to leave the UST and be with the family, she was still going to miss this place.

Sonny said, "I know. I feel the same way. This was a good house and we had many memories here."

Maggie got up and they walked around the house.

She pointed to an area in the hallway and said, "That's where Gavin took his first steps." Then she pointed to an area in Andrew's room and said, "That's where Andrew said his first words."

They walked into the family room and Sonny pointed to the sofa.

He said, "And that's where we made Gavin and Andrew."

Maggie screamed with laughter and punched him in the arm.

She asked, "Why aren't we taking that with us?"

Sonny laughed, "Because I don't want any more kids."

Maggie smiled and said, "This was a great house, but it's just a house. Our home will be wherever we are with our family."

Sonny smiled and said she was right. They grabbed their bags and walked through the house one more time. Maggie and Sonny locked up, threw a big kiss at the house and drove off.

Chapter 16

Maggie and Sonny were silent on the drive to Charlie's house. The thirty minute drive felt like it was hours long. They got there at around 1:10 p.m., so earlier than they planned, but not nearly enough for dear Helen. The bus was in front of the house. Charlie guided them into his driveway. As they pulled in, Maggie and Sonny were greeted by dozens of cheers. Charlie said the bags were already loaded. All that needed to get done was get everyone on the bus and go.

Sonny looked at Maggie and she said, "Let's get going."

Tanya and Helen said hello and thanked Maggie and Sonny for coming a little early.

"Every minute counts," said Helen.

Tanya handed Maggie a small bag which had everyone's ID in it. She said once they got to the bridge, Maggie would get out and hand the IDs to the guard. They would run everyone's ID, then board the bus and verify the IDs belonged to people on the bus. Tanya said it didn't take long, especially because they had children on the bus.

Everyone got on the bus, and they pulled away. Maggie and Sonny started on their last drive through the UST. The girls sang songs during most of the ride. Tanya and Helen sat and spoke with each other. Maggie sat behind Sonny and was extremely quiet. At first, Sonny thought she fell asleep. He took a quick look behind him and she smiled. She had headphones on, and she was reading a book. As they drove through the UST, Sonny began to think of how good this place could have been. With the right people in charge, they could have taken care of all the bad things that were in the old government. Instead, they put up a front and continued with the corruption.

Sonny saw the bridge up ahead, and motioned to Maggie. She got up and he pointed to the bridge.

"We're here," Sonny said.

She went back to her seat and went through the bag again for accuracy. Not many people cross over to the CNU, so they drove right up to the gate. Sonny opened his window and said hello to the guard. Sonny informed him that Maggie had the IDs and asked where she should go. He said to open the door, and someone would guide her to the right place. Sonny wished Maggie luck and she got off of the bus. She was brought into the barracks, which were just off to the right of the gate.

A few minutes went by, and Helen said, "What's the delay? It shouldn't take this long."

Sonny said, "Relax. If everything was in order with the IDs, we should be out of here soon."

Sonny saw a car drive over from the CNU side and pull up in front of the barracks.

Mike and another person got out of the car and went inside. What the fuck? They were supposed to meet him on the other side. Technically, they were still in the UST. They needed to be on the other side for this to work. Maybe he was there to clear something up, a normal thing that they just got caught up in.

A few more minutes went by, then Maggie was escorted into Mike's car and they drove off toward the CNU.

At the same time, four armed guards approached the bus and directed Sonny to get off the bus. The girls started screaming when they saw them point their weapons at Sonny.

287

What the fuck just happened? Why was Maggie taken to the CNU without him? Who fucking crossed them? Sonny got himself together the best he could, for the sake of the girls. He stepped off of the bus and was cuffed on the spot.

As they brought him into the barracks, Dave stepped out from behind a wall and said, "Hi, Sonny. I hope you're having a nice day so far."

Sonny was brought into an interrogation room. He had been in one a thousand times, but never from the other side. Someone came in and gave him some water. Sonny must have been in there for a half hour. Good tactic. Someone entered the room to interview him, apologized for taking so long, and left. Sonny was given this time to reflect on what he just did and basically fall apart so he would admit to it all. Not Sonny. He was focused now. Maggie got through. She was with the boys. That's what was important. Sonny knew he could take care of himself without giving anyone up. After about forty-five minutes, Dave walked in with a stack of papers and a laptop. How predictable. He shuffled some papers for a few minutes and went back out to "grab something he forgot to bring in." This guy was textbook. Sonny was supposed to be scared because he had a pile of papers and a computer, and he went out to get some more. No creativity here. Just by the book. Sonny knew he would run circles around him.

Another ten minutes went by before Dave came back. He began to read off some charges. Treason, illegal access to a government computer, illegally obtaining national security information, assaulting an officer... Sounded like someone tried to screw Sonny over good, but he needed to see a pile of evidence before he got worried. Dave didn't mention anything that could be related to the virus, so at least that was one less thing to worry about. Dave asked what Sonny thought about the charges.

He said, "Sounds like a great story. I hope you tell it to me using finger puppets."

Dave smiled and said, "Finger puppets, hand puppets, I don't care. I have plenty of evidence to put you down and clear my name. All I need are the names of all of the players."

Sonny laughed and replied, "Players are part of a game. This isn't a game. Didn't you read that part of your textbook? Or are you one of those people who learn on the fly? If so, you should just keep flying out of here and stop wasting our time. Don't you know who you're speaking with? I was mastering this stuff while you were still split in half between your dad's ball sack and your mom's ovaries."

Dave wasn't smiling any more. Sonny thought Dave believed he would actually break him. Dave wanted to know if Sonny was asking for a lawyer. He laughed and said he didn't need one, he just wasn't going to talk.

Sonny asked, "Can we get out of here now?"

Dave said, "Fine, we can wrap this up and get out of here, but first I want to show you a couple of pictures."

He pulled out two pictures from his stack of papers. It was pictures of Maggie's bruises, taken in the hospital. They must have questioned her about domestic abuse. When she denied it, they opened a case to look into it further.

Sonny laughed really hard. "That's it? A couple of pictures of bruises she got at home when she fell?"

Dave said, "That's your story. Let's see what she has to say about it."

Sonny replied, "I know what she would say. Your problem is getting her to cooperate from the CNU. I guess that's already a charge you lose."

Dave said, "Don't worry about it. I have plenty of more charges you need to address."

Dave left the room. After about another forty-five minutes, a couple of officers came in and brought Sonny to a transport vehicle and took him to a detention center.

Since Sonny was a handler, he was put into isolation from the rest of the "guests." There weren't many detention centers left. The Council tried to expedite the few cases that went through there and either release the person and place them into some kind of rehab program, or send them on to Puerto Rico. There was only one judge, so things moved a little slow. Sonny could be in the detention center for a couple of months before anything was decided. At first, he thought that would be a good thing because he would be able to contact Johnny and Double D to help clear his name. Then Sonny realized that would put targets on them. The Council would be looking out to see who would visit, and quickly put them under investigation. Sonny didn't want anyone to go and see him. He had to figure out how to clear his name and keep everyone away. He had nothing but time now, so he knew he would come up with something.

Sonny was in lockup for two days. He was really lonely. He didn't speak with anyone. Not even the guy who brought him food said a word. Sonny tried to engage him, and he just ignored him. Sonny kept thinking about Maggie and how she got away. He was so glad she was with the boys. That was what he had to remain focused on in order to get out of there. Without notice, two guards went to Sonny's cell and said to face the wall and place his hands on it. They opened the cell and cuffed Sonny. He asked where they were going, and again, silence. They brought him to a room, cuffed him to a table, and left. About ten minutes later, a man dressed in a business suit was escorted into the room.

He asked the guard to uncuff Sonny. Once uncuffed, the guard left the two of them in the room. The man pointed to his lips, signaling Sonny to keep quiet.

When the guard locked the door behind him and a loud buzzing noise went off, the man said, "Now we can talk. I'm your lawyer. My name is Eric Choi. You can speak freely with me. I don't have to tell you about attorney/client confidentiality."

He looked familiar and Sonny asked him if he ever was an AUSA in the old days. He said he was, and he worked for the Southern District of New York in the late '90s and early 2000s. Sonny knew he recognized him. They began trading names with each other and they knew all of the same people. He worked in the public corruption unit, and Sonny mostly worked with the fraud and computer crimes units. Now they both knew they were dealing with intelligent people who knew the system.

When the country split, the UST kept the legal system intact, rather than try to come up with a system during the transition. Over the years, they made some changes, but it still worked very similar to the old way. The rules of evidence and witnesses were almost unchanged. The biggest change was with sentencing. The judge presiding over the case had final say and it was based on his opinion, not any sentencing report or letters of support. If you gave the judge a bad impression during trial, you probably didn't get a favorable sentence.

Eric said he didn't get a chance to look at the evidence they had against Sonny. Eric asked Sonny to tell him everything about what he thought the charges were based on. Sonny figured the best way was to tell him the whole story, from the beginning. Sonny didn't use the real names, locations, or positions of anyone he mentioned. He started with his history as an agent in the old government and the choices they had to make when the country divided. Sonny continued with their new lives in the UST and how they began to feel, being away from their family. Sonny got up to the point when he reached out to Double D, and Eric cut him off. He said they only had another ten minutes, so they could finish up the next day. For the last ten minutes, Eric spoke about the part of the story he already knew. He said Sonny would definitely have the sympathy of the court for what he went through, which was a good start. Eric needed to know how they got the charges before he could expand on his opinion. He gave Sonny his card and said he would be back at 2 p.m. tomorrow.

Sonny went back to his cell and stared at the walls all night. It was now daylight. With no one to speak with and no way of telling the time, Sonny understood how a person could go mad. He was feeling it after only three days. It made him wonder if he would be better off in general population. The guards just brought Sonny his second meal of the day, so it must be getting close to 2 p.m. He sat and wondered what was going on with Maggie. He had to ask Eric to find out what was going on with her.

The guards took Sonny out of the cell and put him in the same room as the day before. Within a couple of minutes, Eric entered the room. He went over what they already spoke about. Sonny asked him if he knew what happened to Maggie, or where she was. All Eric knew was she was in the CNU, and she wasn't being detained. As a potential witness against Sonny, Eirc would have to interview her. He didn't want to go too far, so he said they should stick to the plan and finish the story.

Sonny picked up his story where he met with Double D. He went on with Johnny, how Maggie worked her way in with Becky, their nights out, the BBQ, the whole story, without using real names. Sonny got into the plan to leave the UST, including what happened with the ranger, and stopped short of telling Eric about the virus and the shootout. Eric saw that Sonny stopped the story abruptly and asked what was wrong. Sonny said the rest of the story would help to easily identify a person or two, and would implicate him in other crimes that were not known at the time.

Sonny said, "No offense, but how do I know you won't leak this information to someone and then it magically comes up at trial? These charges against me are ugly and a true patriot of the UST might tell someone about what I have done."

Eric said it was an ethical situation and he never had them questioned. Of all the years he was a prosecutor, he never cut corners or took shady deals. It was his job to defend Sonny, not to hang him. Sonny thought about who his friends were in the Southern District of NY. The ones he knew and dealt with were stand up people who he trusted. He had to assume they would associate with similar people. Besides, he didn't have much of a choice. Sonny just wanted to make it clear where he stood and how he felt. Sonny continued on with the story of the virus.

Eric's eyes opened up wide and he stopped Sonny.

He said, "Are you telling me the UST is keeping quiet on a potential issue with a virus? Did they not learn from past events?"

Sonny assured him he had evidence and he provided a sample to the CNU. Sonny didn't think Eric knew about how the government worked in the UST. Sonny thought Eric might have believed the whole BS story of equality for all. He wrote a whole bunch of things down, then he asked Sonny to continue.

Sonny finished up with the virus part of the story. Next, he got into what happened with the videos and why he needed access to the Council's main server.

Before Sonny went into the story of the shootout, he said, "This next part is incriminating. I swear, I hope I can trust you."

Eric tried his best to reassure him, but nothing would satisfy Sonny. He just had to go for it. Sonny asked Eric not to stop him, to allow him to tell the whole story before Eric asked any questions, and he agreed. As Sonny went through the series of events, Eric continued to write plenty of notes.

Sonny was sure Eric's first question would be, "What the fuck were you thinking?"

Sonny finished the story and he wrote a few more notes down.

Eric said his job was not to bring in more crimes. It was to defend Sonny against what he was being charged with.

He said, "It's easy to figure out where most of the charges fit when compared to your story. You didn't mention anything related to domestic abuse, kidnapping, prostitution, and international sex trafficking of minors."

Sonny said, "Because none of that is true. Just hearing my story and knowing why I went through all of that, does it sound like something I would do? I know you don't know me at all, but with my record and desire to get my family back together, does that make sense?"

Eric said it didn't, but they still had to address it. Sonny said the only thing he might be able to tell him about was the domestic abuse. Sonny went through the day Maggie got hurt in the gym at home. Eric agreed with Sonny in his thinking of Maggie denying abuse and then a case was opened.

Eric said the rest of the charges, kidnapping, prostitution and sex trafficking, had to be related to the girls on the bus. Sonny assured him they were a real volleyball team and he couldn't think of why or how such charges were against him. Someone had to be setting him up. There was no other way it could have happened. Eric said he was going to meet with the prosecutor in a couple of days, and he was going to go over the evidence they had. He would come and see Sonny sometime early next week. Sonny asked him to find out more about Maggie, that he was worried about her and needed to know she was safe.

The next five days were really long for Sonny. The weather cleared up a little, so he was allowed some outside time. It felt good to get outside. The fresh air was good for his mind and body. Every time he went outside, guys would yell and curse at him from the windows. Maybe being alone was a good thing. Sonny was clueless as to what was going on outside of those walls, but he knew no one could contact him. He just wished someone would come, anyone, so he could have a conversation.

It was five days since his last visit with Eric, so he should expect him today. Sure enough, a little after lunch, Sonny met with him. He didn't look too enthusiastic today. He put his hands on top of the stack of papers, sighed, and began to speak.

"We have a long uphill battle on this."

He interrupted Sonny before he could get a word out.

He said, "Let me go over what you are facing, then we can discuss a plan."

Sonny agreed, and Eric continued. He said, just as they discussed, the treason, computer and information charges were easy to identify within Sonny's story. The other charges weren't mentioned in the story, but there was evidence against him for them. They were correct in the assumption for the domestic abuse charges.

Although, Maggie did not say Sonny abused her, she did not dispute the charges, and there was a witness on her behalf.

Sonny's thought to himself, "Huh? Are you kidding me? What does that mean? She didn't dispute the charges? And who the fuck would say I abused her? Who is setting me up and why?

This doesn't make any sense."

Eric saw Sonny was getting heated and he said, "Let me finish before you speak."

In support of the abuse charges was video of Sonny having sex in a van with an underage prostitute. How the fuck could they get video from the van? How could they assume she was underage? Sonny needed to find Luna to clear that up. Eric said there are also photos of Sonny in compromising positions with another prostitute.

"What? Photos with me and a prostitute? No way. This isn't true. They have to be doctored photos."

Eric finished up with the trafficking, prostitution and kidnapping charges. It all related to the girls on the bus. A search of the phone they took from Sonny uncovered phone calls made to a known sex trafficker in the CNU, who was questioned and said he was waiting for Sonny to bring him the girls from the UST.

"No fucking way. That was the phone Johnny gave me. There's no way he would have done that to me. No fucking way."

Eric gave Sonny a few minutes to digest what he just said. He saw the anger and frustration in Sonny, and looked a little worried, like Sonny was about to go off on him. Sonny started slamming his fists into the table.

"Who the fuck could be setting me up? How did Dave get all into this? He's technically capable of tampering with everything and setting me up. But how could I clear my name without the help of Maggie, Double D and Johnny? I need to speak with them. I need to speak with Dave, one on one, to clear the air with him. It was going to be bad enough trying to mount a defense for treason, but all this other stuff does me in. I need to think. I need time to think this through."

But Sonny didn't have a lot of time. Eric had a week to file a counter argument against the charges and how could he do that without Sonny's witnesses.

Eric said there was another way to go at this. Sonny might not like it, but it was a way of buying some time to go against the trafficking, kidnapping and prostitution charges. Since they all knew Sonny was guilty of the treason, computer and information charges, he could plead guilty to those charges and fight the others. Sonny would be incarcerated and awaiting a trial for the other charges. That would give them at least another two weeks, if not more. Sonny wanted to speak with Dave before he could make a decision. Eric said he would try and get in touch with him after he left and asked if Sonny wanted him there when they spoke. Sonny needed to get to the bottom of everything and he could only do it alone. Eric said fine, he trusted Sonny. Eric reminded him they only had about a week to make this decision, so Sonny really needed to think about it. Eric would start to speak with some of the witnesses and get into how the evidence was obtained. He said he would be back in a couple of days.

"Here I go. Back to my cell, all alone to think about how to best defend myself against really bad crimes that I did not commit."

Dave was the key. Sonny had to know what he knew. He needed to speak with him sooner rather than later. Sonny needed time to process what he had to say to him. Two days went by before something finally happened.

Sonny was pulled out of his cell and sent to his favorite room. He waited for about fifteen minutes, then Dave walked in.

He had a big smile on his face, and he said, "Sonny, how's it hanging? Wanna talk now, huh?"

Sonny said, "Let's cut the pleasantries and let's talk.

Dave said, "What's the hurry? You aren't going anywhere."

Sonny said fine, let's just talk. Dave said Sonny was being a "very bad boy" and all of the people he screwed over were coming out against him, even his wife. Dave wanted to know why Sonny wanted to speak with him. Sonny said he wanted to speak with him, man to man, and nothing said in the room could be held against either of them.

Dave said, "Now that's the kind of talk that gets me excited. I'm good with that. I have all the evidence."

Sonny wanted to figure out who was setting him up and why.

Dave said no one was setting him up because the evidence came from different sources. People were betraying him, not lying. Sonny said there was no way so many people could betray him, especially his wife. Dave said when Maggie went to the hospital, her name was flagged because Dave entered it into the system. He was hoping she would pop up somewhere so they could speak. They did a video call when she was in the hospital. She denied Sonny beat her, until Dave showed her the video he had of Sonny having "sex" in the van, the night Sonny assaulted him. Once she saw that, she stopped denying Sonny beat her and just remained silent. Dave gave her his number and asked her to call him once she changed her mind. She called him and they met. She explained the plan Sonny had to traffic the girls into the CNU and how Sonny forced her to go along with the plan.

"That's how you got here."

Sonny didn't believe him. It didn't make sense. Maggie knew the whole plan. She knew they were in the clear. She wouldn't lie like that. How the fuck did he get the video? Who took the video and why? The truck would have disabled any cameras nearby.

Sonny asked Dave how he got the video and how it was

taken. The van was mysteriously parked at his station a week ago and they found cameras all inside the back part of the van. Dave started to laugh as he looked at Sonny's face. Dave saw the "feeling of knowing you were betrayed by someone you trusted" come over him. Sonny couldn't believe Johnny would set him up. Why? What did he have to gain? What about the story about his father? Was that not true? But Johnny gave him the phone too. He said it was clean. Why would he set Sonny up? His head was spinning, but he wasn't finished. He needed to know more.

Sonny asked about the prostitution photos. Dave said they were anonymously sent to him. Sonny denied he with a prostitute and someone had to have doctored the photos. Dave said they were legitimate photos and they were from a few days ago. They were taken inside a home and it started with a massage.

"Double D? No fucking way! I didn't even know he took pictures. Why would he create evidence he didn't want Sara to see? No way. I don't believe it. No way they all set me up. No fucking way," is all that went through Sonny's mind.

Dave saw how Sonny was falling apart. He wanted to let Sonny know the charges for tampering with the video were being worked on as they spoke, so more charges were coming. Dave was in an all-out laugh.

"Look at you know. Not so tough. Not so sure of yourself. Who got played now? And by the way, thanks for helping me get that promotion."

Dave signaled for the door to open and he left.

There's was no way Eric could uncover everything in less than a week. They needed more time. Even if Sonny got off on the other charges because of the extra time to prepare, how long would he have to serve for the charges he plead guilty to? Sonny felt he could always apply for an appeal. How long would that take? Sonny believed he needed to fight everything to minimize his sentence. These were all questions for Eric. He needed to ask him. For now, all Sonny could do was wait. If he wasn't in there, he could be out there helping to clear his name. But he wasn't and he had to accept that.

It was a couple of more days until Sonny met with Eric again. He asked Sonny if he met with Dave and what did he learn. Sonny said they needed more time, because either Dave was lying and he was being set up, or he was betrayed by everyone close to him. Either way would require more time to look into. Eric agreed. He asked Sonny if he wanted to go forward with his plan to buy them more time. There were a few things Sonny needed some clarification on before moving forward with that plan. Sonny asked about a potential sentence for the treason and computer charges. Eric said he wouldn't be sentenced until everything was settled. Sonny wanted to know what he thought he would get if they were able to fight off the other charges. Eric said the underlying theme in the justice system of the UST was everyone makes mistakes and they can still become good people. Unless Sonny killed someone, there was always wiggle room for sentencing. Considering his long record of government service, the sympathy of the court for falsely being charged with the other crimes, and Sonny did those things to get his family back together, Eric felt Sonny could get a minimum of two to five years. If Sonny was found guilty of the other crimes, he was looking at fifteen years plus. Sonny asked if he could appeal the plea if he was found innocent on the other charges. Eric said he could always appeal, but that process might take longer than the two to five years he could be serving. The decision Sonny had to make was clear. He needed to avoid being charged with the kidnapping, prostitution and trafficking charges. He needed more time. He had to go with Eric's plan.

Eric asked Sonny if he was sure he wanted to do this. Once he submitted the request, there was no way to go back on it. Sonny said there was no choice to make. They needed time to clear the other charges. Eric went back to his office to draft the letter and would submit it tomorrow morning. Eric would see Sonny in the afternoon, once he heard back from the court.

Numerous thoughts went through Sonny's head.

"How did I get here? Really, how did this happen? Everything was going great. We had a lot of fun down the stretch. We had problems, but we solved them as a group and took some time to celebrate our victories. Maggie was played. I can't believe she said I beat her. There's no way. But would she give me up like that based on some video and pictures? Then lie about the girls to get me more time? No way. I don't believe it. No way. She would have confronted me. I know her. There's no way. No fucking way. We always had each other's back. No matter what.

Double D? Giving up some photos, knowing I could turn him in for giving me a sample of the virus? No way. He's my boy. Ride or die. We've been through so much shit together. We're godparents to each other's kids. Vacations together. No way. No fucking way."

As for Johnny, Sonny believed he could have set him up. The only thing was why. What was his motive? He seemed so believable. So trustworthy. Why? It wasn't money. It had to be personal. But what? He always had the means to bury Sonny if he wanted to. Johnny could have had him killed. Why go through all of this? To rub it in Sonny's face because Maggie got across and he didn't? He still didn't know why.

Again, Sonny didn't sleep at all. Way too many things rushing through his head. Did he have to accept that he was betrayed? Should he continue to deny it? Or was he set up? If so, by who? Why? He still didn't know how Maggie was doing. Was she safe? Was she thinking about Sonny? What did his boys think? What had been their reaction to all of this? Sonny felt he couldn't take this much longer. He was never a hurry up and wait person.

It was daylight now, so Sonny figured part of his fate was already sealed. In a few hours, he would know how his short term future would play out. He hoped Eric had some good information for him.

It was time. Sonny was taken away from his cell and met with Eric. Eric submitted the deal in person to the prosecutor. As a good will gesture, he let Eric look a little more into the evidence before officially allowing him to do so. Eric said for the treason and computer charges, they had video and audio from the cameras of the handlers at the HUB when Sonny was there with his "niece". They also found a computer virus and knew it was planted when Stargirl was on the computer. They also had the video evidence Sonny tampered with. There was no disputing what they had, so it looked good that Sonny made the deal. As for the other evidence, the dump of the phone showed Sonny was in contact with the guy in the CNU for getting him the girls. They also had the video statement made by Maggie, confirming his plan to sell the girls when he got to the CNU. They had the video from the van, which tacked on the prostitution and assault of an officer charges. The photos with the other prostitute just solidified Sonny's behavior. Eric said Maggie was given a deal to make the statement. She was granted admission to the CNU in exchange for her testimony.

Sonny began playing everything over in his head.

"Does that make sense? Did she figure that would be the

only way she could be with the boys? Did she just cut me off and take care of herself? No way. That's not her. I need to see her. I need for her to say it to my face. I just don't believe that."

Eric said Sonny would be taken to court tomorrow to swear to the deal. He would then find out where he would be held until the rest of the charges were dealt with, and they could get a feel for how the judge felt. Sonny asked Eric if he could see the video of Maggie's statement. Eric couldn't make that happen until next week, when he was given all of the evidence. Eric would get a suit for Sonny to wear in court from his house. Eric asked which suit he should take. Sonny wanted his favorite dark blue suit, with a white shirt, which was on its own in Maggie's closet, and a bunch of red and blue ties. Sonny would figure out which one he liked. Eric said to clean up good first thing in the morning, and he would be brought to court at 8:30 a.m. Eric would be waiting for Sonny at the courthouse.

Another long night. Sonny couldn't eat, couldn't sleep. Out of all of the things he was facing, the only thing he kept thinking about was Maggie. Sonny needed to see the statement. He needed to speak with her. He needed clarity. Sonny knew she didn't do it. He felt it in his bones. All night long, he played it over and over in his head. There was no way she betrayed him. It wasn't in her. She was a rock. Sonny could always count on her. He would never believe it.

The next morning, Sonny was taken to the showers, given breakfast and brought to court. He was the only prisoner on the bus, so he knew he was getting the full attention of the court. They drove into the building and Sonny was let out in a garage. They walked into a secure area, just like the old days with the US Marshals office in SDNY. Sonny was immediately greeted by Eric. He took Sonny into a room, where he had his suit waiting for him. Eric said he wanted to let Sonny know something before he went into the court room. This case was a major embarrassment for the UST and there had been zero press on it. They wanted to adjudicate this as quickly as possible, without any attention drawn to it. This could only help the case. As Sonny got dressed, Eric said there was no need to go over procedure or to tell him how to act, because Sonny had been through this numerous times. Eric added that they lucked out with the judge. He was very lenient with the law and with sentencing. They wished each other luck and went into the courtroom.

After all of the formalities, the judge got down to business. He mentioned all of the charges against Sonny and asked if he understood them. He continued with reading off the charges Sonny was making a guilty plea on. The judge asked Sonny to sign deal if he agreed to it. Sonny signed the deal and the judge began to speak about all of the other charges and that Sonny was a disgrace to the UST. He stopped short of calling him a degenerate because the other charges were pending. The judge ordered Sonny to be held in Puerto Rico until a trial date was set regarding the other charges. The judge asked Sonny if he had any questions and he said no. The next court date for the attorneys was in three days. The judge wanted to take care of the remaining charges swiftly and accurately.

Sonny met with Eric again before he was taken away. As he took off his suit, Eric said the judge had to make a strong statement about the charges. He couldn't get a read on him, but not to worry. As soon as Eric finished with the judge at the next appearance, he would officially be given all of the evidence and they would be able to attack it. Eric wished Sonny well and said he would still be kept away from the other inmates. He promised to get Sonny out of this mess with the least amount of time. He said he was all in.

Sonny was taken back to the detention center and put back into his cell. He was now a convicted felon. Wow! Words he never thought he would say. Now the UST didn't want him and the CNU would never take him. What did Sonny have left? Was it worth the fight? Should he just get it over with a take a deal for the whole thing? No way. He had to clear his name. He needed his boys to know he did some illegal things to get back with them, but he never did all of the other things to embarrass them. Sonny was never with a prostitute. He didn't have sex with Luna. He didn't plan to sell the girls off into the sex trade. He was still the same honest man who instilled all of the good into them as young men. Sonny had to clear his name.

As the sun was going down, Sonny was pulled from his cell. He asked what was going on and they said he was being transferred to Puerto Rico. Sonny was taken to another cell, near the airport. He was told he would spend the night here and would leave on a flight in the morning, 6 a.m. The food was the same, but the bed felt a little softer. He actually got a few hours' sleep. But it was never enough. Sonny woke up as the sunlight was hitting his eyes.

He was quickly taken out of the cell and brought on the plane. It was a small jet and about a dozen more inmates were on board.

A guard threw a breakfast sandwich at Sonny and said "Good morning. I hope you enjoy the flight."

Either Sonny was hungry, or it was a decent sandwich. He was probably hungry. He couldn't believe they would give them anything that remotely tasted good. It was a smooth flight and it went by quickly. They were wheels down in Puerto Rico at 11 a.m. They said the temperature outside was 85 degrees and sunny. Sonny could only imagine how comfortable the cell was going to be in that heat. Oh, joy.

It was about a forty-five minute bus ride to the prison. It was an old school looking prison. Bars, barbed wires and brick. It looked like it was a giant oven. They were taken off of the bus and brought inside. It was air conditioned inside. Let's see how far inside it went. They were strip searched, which included all areas where something could be hidden. Sonny knew it was coming, but he was still embarrassed.

One of the guards yelled out, "We have a special guest arriving today," then called out Sonny's name and asked him to step forward.

All of the guards cheered and kicked Sonny as they went passed him. The last guard grabbed him by the neck and took him away. As they got deeper in to the prison, the temperature and humidity rose. The guard said since Sonny was special, he had his own house. He opened a cell and threw Sonny in. Definitely a few steps down from his first cell. Sonny knew there was lots of corruption around there, so he needed to be on his toes, and be prepared for anything.

Sonny was kept up all night by the guards.

They kept walking by the cell, banging on the bars and saying things like "So you like little girls" or "Traitor."

By the time the sun came up, two guards went to Sonny's cell and opened the door. One of them went in and introduced himself.

He said, "Hi, I'm Willie and this is my prison. Nothing happens around here without my blessing. If you get taken care of in a good way, it's because I let it happen. If you get taken care of in a bad way, it's because I let it happen. Get it?"

Sonny said yes. Willie clubbed him in his leg and said he

was to address him as sir.

Sonny said, "Sorry, sir. It won't happen again."

Willie laughed and said, "Look here. We have a quick learner."

Sonny said he didn't want any problems and would play ball when he had to. Willie said Sonny had to be initiated before he could be considered "one of them."

Sonny asked what the initiation was, and he pointed out of the window and said, "Tomorrow morning, I will let you loose out there with the rest of my guys, and I let you back inside at noon. Whatever happened in between isn't my business. When you come back in, you have my protection."

He said to eat up and get rest today, because Sonny would need it tomorrow.

"I'm fucking doomed. I guess this is how it all ends," is all that Sonny could think

There was no way any of them would take it easy on him, knowing what he did for a living. Sonny felt he would have to go by the saying, "Find the biggest guy and kick his ass." That was his only hope to gain a little respect. It could mean the difference between life and death.

"What the fuck!"

It couldn't be the end. Sonny had to clear his name. He needed the boys to know he wasn't a creep. And there it was again, creeping back into his brain. Maggie. "No way. No fucking way. Not her."

He needed to focus. He needed to be mentally ready for tomorrow. There was nothing in the cell he could use to make a weapon. He needed to see what they gave him with his meals.

Lunch and dinner came and went. Nothing they gave Sonny could be used as a weapon. They verified he returned anything he could use. It was only Sonny. His old ass and brain. It had to be enough. But could he survive for hours? Could he run and hide? He needed sympathy. He needed a reputation. He needed help. He needed sleep. He needed to get out of there. He needed his family. That was his focus. His family. Sonny knew he wouldn't get any sleep, so he just prayed. He wasn't a religious person, but Maggie was. He used her strength and belief in God and prayed all night. He prayed for God to take care of his family. He asked for His forgiveness, but said he wouldn't hold it against Him if He couldn't do it. Sonny also asked for a way out and promised to love and take care of his family if He helped him.

The sun started to come up. If it wasn't for his current situation and location, Sonny would have enjoyed it. He had a view of the ocean and saw the sun come up. At least he knew he was on the east coast. He listened for the guards to come. He wondered when they would get him. Sonny guessed it would be after breakfast, to give everyone a chance to wake up. He was right. They brought him something to eat. As soon as he was done, they came and collected the garbage. Sonny waited another hour before someone came to get him. It wasn't Willie. Sonny believed he was set up somewhere to watch him in the yard. He probably got off on this stuff. The guard brought Sonny down toward the area where he came in. He gave Sonny a bag which contained his outside clothes. He said to put them on.

"What the fuck was going on? Did this make me an easy target? Get the guy in the street clothes," is what ran through Sonny's mind.

Sonny believed the guys in the yard could easily identify someone in street clothes. What bastards.

Sonny finished getting dressed and was brought toward a window with a guard standing behind it.

He gave Sonny a pen and paper and said, "Sign this and you're good to go."

Sonny thought, "What the fuck is this guy up to? Am I signing away my body? My money? Does this clear the prison in case of an accident or if I get killed?"

Sonny started to read it and the words were really small.

He asked the guard what it was for, and he repeated himself "Sign this and you're good to go."

What the fuck did Sonny have left to lose? Fuck it. He signed it and slammed it down on the table.

The guard said, "Watch yourself before I throw you back in your cell."

The guard took Sonny around the other guards, out toward the yard. He opened the door and guided Sonny past the inmates, who were all screaming at him. He passed Willie, who just smiled and tipped his hat. The guard continued walking Sonny toward the gate. He signaled for the guard to open the gate and he let Sonny out of the prison.

"What the fuck just happened? I'll tell you one thing. I'm not going back to ask the guard," rang in Sonny's head.

Sonny kept going, waiting for someone to call him back or fire a shot in his direction. He kept walking. He never looked back. He must have gone a mile before he stopped and looked around. He was a little familiar with Puerto Rico. Sonny visited it frequently when he was younger, but he never ventured out of the hotel zones much. The only times he did were mostly for arrests or search warrants. He did not know where he was. From the rising of the sun, he knew he was on the east coast, but where? As he walked farther west, away from the prison, he realized he was walking parallel to the north coast. He walked onto the beach and looked around, trying to figure out where he was. He saw a small island to the east and a bigger piece of land to the west. Sonny was walking for miles, and still was in the wilderness. He had to be on Vieques. Half of the island was rough and raw. The small island to the east was Culebra. Which meant Puerto Rico was to his west.

Now that he knew where he was, Sonny needed to find a way off of the island to get to Puerto Rico. He didn't have any money, so he had to call someone. But first, he needed to find a phone. Sonny must have walked another 4 or 5 miles along the beach, heading west. He finally saw what looked like to be a town. He saw people in the distance. As he got closer, the people walked back inland. He finally came up to some houses. They weren't close to the standard of house in the northeast, but they were houses. He knocked on a few doors and no one answered. He continued to walk down the streets, and he didn't see anyone. It was as if the people of the town were all shuttered in because of a stranger in the street. Sonny didn't want to alarm anyone, so he continued on. He knew he was close to the ferry, so he figured he would just wait until he got there to figure something out. It was probably around 1 p.m. now, and the sun was hot. He needed a drink. Sonny saw a garden hose on the side of one of the houses he passed, so he took a quick drink and got out of there before anyone saw him.

As he walked along the beach, he saw the ferry depart the island. The area was a lot more populated. The dock must be around the next turn, about a mile away. There it was, the dock for the ferry. Sonny went up to the ticket booth and saw it cost $20 for a one-way ticket to Puerto Rico. It might as well have been $20,000 because he didn't have that either. Sonny didn't see anyone asking for change, so begging was out of the question. No one was entertaining anyone, so that was a no. He walked around the plaza, trying to think of a way to get some money.

Suddenly, a guy went up to him and said, "You need money for the boat, right senor?"

Sonny said, "Yes, I do. How did you know?"

He said if a Caucasian man didn't go right up to the booth and buy a ticket, that meant he had no money and was probably released from prison. Sonny looked around and he didn't see any Caucasians. He felt that around there, a guy like him was just a white ex-con. Sonny asked him what he could do to get on the ferry. He pointed Sonny in the direction of the ferry. The man said before Sonny got there, he should look to his right and he would see dozens of men sitting around. They were waiting for a job to pay for the ferry. Before the next ferry came, a man would come and pick a bunch of them to work a job for the night to pay for the ferry. Sonny asked how they got picked. The man didn't know, but he believed it depended on how much work was available for the night.

Sonny thanked the man and went to hang out with the night laborers. None of them spoke English, and Sonny wasn't confident enough to engage them with his Spanish. He saw none of the men were eating or drinking, which made sense because they had no money. They were in the shade, but it was still hot and humid.

Sonny went to get up and at least soak himself in the ocean to cool off, and one of the guys grabbed his arm and said, "Quédate aquí," which meant to stay here.

Sonny didn't know why until he saw a man come toward them with bottled water. He handed each of them a bottle and spoke in Spanish. From what Sonny understood, he said he had a lot of work and needed many men. All of them would get work and get on the ferry. He looked at Sonny and went over and spoke in English. He said his name was Raul and it looked like Sonny had a rough day. He asked Sonny what his story was. Sonny said he was released from prison and needed to get to Puerto Rico to contact his family. Raul had heard that sad story many times before. He asked Sonny how he got to the ferry. When Sonny said walked, Raul informed him he was very lucky that he made it, and that many people disappeared making that trip. He had work for Sonny on a yacht. Raul would get him cleaned up and dressed once they got to the other side. Sonny thanked him and promised he would repay him once he got back on his feet. Raul said it wasn't necessary. The work that Sonny would do for him was more than enough.

The next ferry came in an hour. It was probably around 4 p.m. now. The ride was about thirty minutes to Puerto Rico. The water was clear and beautiful. The ocean breeze felt refreshing. About halfway through the ride, Raul handed out sandwiches to the guys he was hiring. He asked Sonny what he was going to do on the island. Sonny said he had to reach out to a few people and figure out where he was going. An ex-con of the UST didn't have many choices. The mainland of the UST didn't want him. The CNU didn't want him. Raul said Sonny could stay on the northeast side of the island and find honest work, or he could venture to the southwest side and take his chances. Sonny explained he wasn't planning on staying. Raul said once Sonny made peace with the fact that he wasn't going back, he should go to the southwest side of the island and see how long and hard it would be to get back. There were ways, but not many people made it. It took years to earn passage and most of the time, they were denied going because they became valuable workers. The sooner Sonny found a job and settled in on the northeast side, the better. Sonny thanked him for his advice and said he would prove him wrong.

Raul smiled and said, "Keep dreaming gringo."

They arrived in Puerto Rico and waited last to disembark. Raul kept all of them together. Raul asked Sonny to stay by his side. They walked off of the ferry and Raul led them onto a bus. There were about thirteen people that were working that night. They drove less than five minutes to a small airport. Raul directed Sonny to stay on the bus and he took the rest of the guys into a hanger. About fifteen minutes later, Raul got back on the bus and drove off. Sonny asked what the guys were going to do at the airport.

He said, "Never mid them. I got you a good job tonight. You will pay off your debt to me and make extra money on tips."

They stopped about five minutes later, and Raul brought Sonny into a store. He spoke to the owner and asked him to get Sonny dressed. He got Sonny a black pair of pants, a white shirt and a pair of shoes. Sonny asked him how he was going to pay for it and Raul said he would get paid well for Sonny's work tonight, so it was included. There was a shower in the back of the store that Sonny could use before he got dressed.

The shower was awesome. It was like a shower in a five-star resort. Lots of pressure, good soap and shampoo. Sonny didn't want to get out. He finally finished his shower and dried off. He heard a knock at the door, and it was another guy who came in and did his hair. He trimmed a little off of the top and blew it dry. It looked good. Sonny got dressed and met up with Raul by the bus. Sonny thanked the owner and the guy who did his hair. He got on the bus, and Raul explained the job to Sonny. Raul said Sonny would be working for a billionaire on a huge yacht. He was having a party and needed people to serve food and drinks, and clean up when it was done. The yacht would stay docked for the whole party. Once the party was over, Sonny was free to go and do whatever he wanted. He said not to leave early or Sonny would pay for it dearly. Sonny smiled and said he wouldn't be a problem. Raul knew that and that's why Sonny got the good job. They pulled up to Puerto Del Rey Marina. What a beautiful scene. Lots of huge boats. Lots of people having a good time. They got out of the bus and walked over to the yacht. It was called Freedom. How ironic. It was huge. Only a billionaire could afford this thing. Raul said to walk on to the yacht and tell the captain that "Raul sent me." Then tell him your name and follow his orders.

"Simple enough?"

Sonny said, "Yes, I got it. Thank you for your help. I don't know how I would have gotten off the island without it."

Raul smiled and said, "That's what I do. It's my gift. I should change my name to Mr. Roarke."

Sonny laughed, shook his hand and boarded Freedom. He walked up the ramp and met with the captain.

Sonny said "Raul sent me."

The captain asked what his name was.

"Sonny Rizzo."

The captain directed him to the top of the yacht.

He said, "Just head upstairs and someone will help you out."

Sonny went up the stairs and was greeted with a huge roar. He looked around and it was Maggie, the boys, Johnny, everyone.

"What the fuck? Am I dreaming? Is this a nightmare?"

They all rushed Sonny and squeezed the air out of him. There wasn't a dry eye anywhere. Sonny could hardly stand up, so someone grabbed a chair and put it behind him. Sonny looked at Maggie and she couldn't stop crying. He asked her what was going on and how they all got there, and why did they abandon him, and how did he get out of jail, and... he had so many questions. And Sonny was still angry. Eric approached Sonny and said he was best suited to tell him what happened.

He said once Sonny started getting Double D and Johnny involved with getting him over to the CNU, Johnny reached out to Mike and started to come up with a plan to quickly get him over. Mike said something had to be extremely urgent and dangerous for him to rush someone through as an informant. He said, even then, he wouldn't be able to get them both through. The first time Johnny met Maggie, they exchanged numbers. Johnny called Maggie and said he needed Double Ds help with a plan to get them over to the CNU, but she couldn't tell Sonny what was going on. Maggie said she wouldn't as long as the plan sounded good and she thought it would work. Johnny and Double D came up with a plan to have a fake virus pop up in the UST, and for Sonny to smuggle it over to the CNU. The CNU would take Sonny over once they were ready to confront the UST with the evidence. But they needed a way to get Maggie over too.

They devised a plan to make Sonny look like a sleaze and an abuser. Johnny and Mike coordinated to set up the meets. Johnny wired up the van and had Luna seduce Sonny into having fake sex. The wild card was the ranger. Everyone hoped nothing would happen, but when it did, they had to rearrange the plan. Johnny gave Sonny the phone, which was used to call a low life in the CNU. Double D provided photos from the massage party. Then Sonny had to tamper with evidence to cover up the incident with the ranger. The ranger had Maggie give a video statement, where she told him Sonny devised a plan to escape to the CNU by selling young girls into the CNU, and Sonny forced her to help. Becky provided a video statement saying she witnessed

Sonny verbally abuse Maggie. There was plenty of evidence stacked up against Sonny. Now enter Joe Russo. Joe had a young genius, Stargirl, who could get into any system. Her only problem was it was too time consuming to get into the network one server at a time. She needed access at the HUB level to make things work quickly. Joe set them up with a meet and it all went to hell. They didn't anticipate any issues, but no one knew about what Ronnie did. Joe knew Stargirl needed hours to get into the main server of the Council and gain administrative privileges, so he had her copy just the server's directory titles, not the data. She pretended to get into the server and showed Sonny the directory titles. Sonny deleted the directories she created and left.

Joe had to come up with a reason to get Sonny to bring her to his HUB and set the virus. The shootout was the perfect cover. Although, Joe was upset with what happened, he didn't want to let Maggie and Sonny down. He knew what happened was out of their control and Becky really liked Maggie. So Joe guilted Sonny into having Stargirl gain access to the computer at the HUB. Once there, she set her virus and left. The next day, she gained access to the whole system.

Maggie made a deal to move over to the CNU, in exchange for her cooperation to get Sonny detained, and ultimately incarcerated. Since Mike was going to be on the bridge, he would be the one who escorted Maggie to the CNU. Dave would get Sonny, and Maggie was free to stay in the CNU.

Maggie had to remain silent. She couldn't change her story, go to the press, or petition to get Sonny out. The boys couldn't be told the truth either. The plan had to play out for it to work. Johnny and Double D had to remain silent as well. Sonny had to do the rest on his own for it to work. They all decided it was best Sonny didn't know the plan, so his emotions would be real and raw.

Once Sonny spoke with Dave and was brought to the detention center, the plan continued. Johnny hired Eric to be Sonny's attorney. Eric knew the whole story before Sonny told it to him. He made sure Sonny stayed on the right path of the plan. He helped steer Sonny into making the decision to plea to some of the charges. Eric knew Sonny would be sent to Puerto Rico, where the rest of the plan could play out. Once Sonny was transferred to Puerto Rico, Joe had Stargirl go into the Council's server and erase all of the evidence in the case. She planted 2 viruses at the HUB. One that was easily found, and one that wasn't. Now that she had full access, it was simply done with the striking of a few keys. No more videos, photos, statements, nothing. It was all gone. The only hope the prosecution had was to take additional statements and try and get additional copies of evidence.

The van was the original evidence, so the only copy was erased. The photos that were anonymously sent in and were untraceable. Maggie could not be reached to make another statement. Becky refused to give another statement. She said it hurt her too much. The creep who was going to buy the girls in the CNU couldn't be found. Even the handlers who saw Sonny bring in Stargirl refused to make any statements. They said if the videos were erased, they couldn't remember what happened. They took the Blue Code of Silence.

With nothing left, the prosecutor had the case dismissed with prejudice and sealed forever. No one could ever dig it up or refer to it. The only thing the prosecutor was able to do was keep Sonny out of the mainland. He said since the evidence mysteriously disappeared, and he knew Sonny was involved, but couldn't prove it, he released him on the condition Sonny never returned to the mainland of the UST. That was what Sonny signed at the prison before he was released.

Eric was telling the story while they were a good distance from everyone else. Sonny could still see Maggie crying and being consoled by the boys. Sonny was still overwhelmed with all of this information. He understood it, but it was too much, too quickly. He just went through hell and now everything was going to be fine. Sonny asked Eric to get him a drink. He signaled for someone to get Sonny a drink and asked if he was OK. Sonny said he understood how Maggie got out and understood how all of the charges were dropped. He didn't understand how he was getting in to the CNU.

Once Mike gave the virus in and they began to look at it, they would have seen it was a fraud and Sonny would be stuck. Eric called Mike over to handle that question. Mike said he held onto the virus and only submitted the paperwork. He said he would submit the virus tomorrow and let it be known that Sonny facilitated the deal to get the sample of the virus. It would take weeks before they found out it was a fraud. At that time, Sonny would have already been in the CNU. It will look like Sonny was lied to about the virus, to set up a sting on possible traitors in the UST. The CNU knew they couldn't send Sonny back to the UST, they knew Sonny tried to help the CNU by getting the sample of the virus, and his family was already there in good standing. They would never kick Sonny out.

Just like that, Sonny's name was cleared, all of his charges were dropped, and he was going to become a citizen of the CNU. Maggie ran toward Sonny and he opened his arms and hugged her.

He said, "I knew you wouldn't betray me. I knew it. I always had faith in you."

They cried together and the boys joined in. Sonny looked at Andrew and he was in crutches. His ankle swelled up a little more after he tweaked it and that was that. His team lost without him, in seven games. Gavin was a pitcher, so Sonny guessed it was easy for him to get away. They brought their wives and kids over. They got so big. They knew Maggie and Sonny from the video calls, but didn't remember meeting them in person. Sonny asked Gavin how they got the yacht and he said Johnny helped secure it. Then Sonny realized something else. How did they know Sonny would get on this yacht at this time? What if he didn't get on the ferry and meet Raul? What if he didn't get the job? How did it happen?

Johnny came over and gave Sonny a huge hug. He asked Johnny how he pulled it all off. Johnny said yesterday, Eric let him know Sonny was going to be released today. His family was already on standby to travel. Johnny made the call and got the whole family to fly down to Puerto Rico and get on the yacht. He called his buddy Raul and told him to look out for Sonny, and the rest was history.

"His buddy Raul? Is there a place where he doesn't know anyone?"

Sonny looked around for Double D and Johnny said he couldn't get away, and if he did, it wouldn't look good. Johnny agreed to be the middle man between Sonny and Double D and said Double D wanted to plan a vacation together. Johnny wanted to be included as well. How could Sonny ever deny Johnny from anything? He turned out to be the guy who took on the brunt of the work. Albeit, it was a little unorthodox, but he got it all done.

As Sonny sat there, with his family and dear friends, he began to realize how lucky he was. Although he now had to live in a place where his values didn't exist, he was with his family.

For the short term, he was lucky Willie didn't get him down into the yard. For the long haul, he was surrounded by people who loved him and who would go through great lengths to make sure he was happy. You couldn't say that about too many people. Especially in today's world. In their divided nation, with their divided freedom.

Printed in the USA
CPSIA information can be obtained
at www.ICGtesting.com
LVHW070806270624
783942LV00019B/134